3/13

# Abide with Me

# Sabin Willett

Simon & Schuster Paperbacks
New York London Toronto Sydney New Delhi

Simon & Schuster Paperbacks
A Division of Simon & Schuster, Inc.
1230 Avenue of the Americas
New York, NY 10020

This book is a work of fiction. Names, characters, places, and incidents
either are products of the author's imagination or are used fictitiously. Any
resemblance to actual events or locales or persons, living or dead,
is entirely coincidental.

First Simon & Schuster trade paperback edition March 2013

SIMON & SCHUSTER PAPERBACKS and colophon
are registered trademarks of Simon & Schuster, Inc.

For information about special discounts for bulk purchases,
please contact Simon & Schuster Special Sales at 1-866-506-1949
or business@simonandschuster.com.

The Simon & Schuster Speakers Bureau can bring authors
to your live event. For more information or to book an event
contact the Simon & Schuster Speakers Bureau at 1-866-248-3049
or visit our website at www.simonspeakers.com.

Design by Esther Paradelo

Manufactured in the United States of America

10  9  8  7  6  5  4  3  2  1

Library of Congress Cataloging-in-Publication Data
  Willett, Sabin.
  Abide with me / Sabin Willett.—1st Simon & Schuster
trade paperback ed.
    p.   cm.
    I. Title.
  PS3573.I4454C66    2013
  813'.54—dc23          2012003716

ISBN 978-1-4516-6702-8
ISBN 978-1-4516-6703-5 (ebook)

*for Matty, faa*

*Constantly I dream of it—Nostos—*
*That day when I see home again.*
*And if some god has marked me out*
*For ruin, so be it. Hard my heart—it will endure,*
*As it endured the war across the sea.*
*Let the trial come.*

*The Odyssey,* V, 219–24

# PROLOGUE

"*T*ell me about her—your Penelope," the captain said.

The eyes bore in on him, luminous, locking him in focus. There was never anything offhand about the way the captain looked at a man.

"Don't follow you, sir."

The captain stood up and paced to a corner of the little brick-and-mortar. When he spoke again, his voice had the detached quality it took on when he read poetry, as though he were speaking to someone no one could see.

"*The Odyssey* is a story about a soldier. A mariner, a storyteller, a tactician, a lover of women, a man of wits, a survivor. He went to war for ten years and for another ten tried to get home, where his wife, Penelope, waited in a great house, besieged by an army of suitors. She outwitted them, held them at bay with stories and excuses, waiting for his return."

Outside, a moaning wind blew from the west, rattling the plywood door in its frame, scrabbling to get in. On the table the lantern hissed and sputtered, making only a pale circle, leaving the room in shadow.

"You think you have a Penelope back home, Private?"

He did not know how to answer. *Waited in a great house*, the captain had said. A part of him wanted to tell the captain everything, to lay on the table what he had carried for so long. But the answer was complicated, and he was afraid it would only make him look foolish.

The captain continued. "Those men? They believe Penelope is waiting for them. Every guy drifting off in his bunk right now is thinking about her. We all do it. The mind wanders, and we think we remember the way she looked at us once, when she wanted us . . . Did she give you that?"

Unconsciously, he'd been fingering the chain. He looked toward the captain and nodded.

"She's even around your own neck. Every soldier carries Penelope with him."

He asked: "You, too, sir?"

Years later he would remember the captain's answer, but he could never summon the expression on his face. Lupine eyes beyond the dim glow of the lantern, and a voice in the shadow— that is what came back to him.

"Penelope," the captain said, "is a story. You want to survive Afghanistan, don't confuse it with a story. You've got to stay focused. You've got to be all in for this world. Remember this: Penelope doesn't exist."

# PART ONE
## *The Soldier*

# ONE

July 10, 2009

*A*fter midnight, the kids in Hoosick Bridge and Williams-town were on their cell phones.

"Were you there?"

"That cemetery—you know the old one down Route Seven at Indian Massacre Road? Off to the right? Anyway Maggie *saw* it. Her and Blake and Robbie and Annie B. and them were down there to go drinking and walked in and saw the body. Dumped on the grass in front of the headstones."

"A soldier in his uniform. Annie screamed and ran out of there pretty fast."

"A soldier? Who?"

The day began chilly and damp, and in the predawn blackness the fog massed like smoke against the windows at Toni's Lunch. A set of headlights poked feebly through, and the first of the pickup trucks came into the lot, its tires crunching over the gravel. Toni set Mel's coffee on the counter and put the corn muffin on the grill. He came in and took his usual stool and sipped on the coffee awhile to wake up. She was in the kitchen getting things ready for the morning, clattering pans and spatulas and chatting with him through the cutout where she put the orders up.

"That's a helluva fog out there," Mel said. "Couldn't see one side of Route Seven from the other. Cold, too."

"After all the heat this summer, I'll take it, Mel."

He took another sip. "Funny business last night on the police monitor."

"What?"

"About that body down in Lanesborough."

"I didn't hear," said Toni, coming to the cutout.

Toni's Lunch was a squat, flat-roofed brick building, the lower courses blackened with time. It stood near the tracks and the river, on the west side of Route 7. The name notwithstanding, Toni paid rent each month mainly by selling breakfasts.

The fog lightened to a dark wool as the regulars began to arrive, workmen, construction guys, contractors, retired men who'd reached the age where sleep after 5:00 a.m. was impossible. They climbed down from their trucks to take their usual counter or booth seats and have their usual eggs and sausages and home fries and coffee.

Toni was bringing breakfast to Pete Mallincrodt, telling him Mel's news about the body down at the cemetery on the way to Lanesborough.

"Lots of bodies in the cemetery, Toni."

"Smart guy," she scolded. "A *new* body. A soldier dumped there."

"I heard it, too," someone said. "Kids seen it, they were all talking about it last night."

Ernest Gillfoyle looked up from his breakfast. "Dead soldier? Down Lanesborough way?"

"That's what Mel told me."

"Well, the body come to life, then," he said.

The breakfast chatter fell quiet. "Because I seen him just ten minutes ago. Walking up Route Seven. Damn near killed him myself as I come along in all this fog."

* * * *

He liked to be walking before the sun was up. He liked to be seeing not seen, hearing not heard—and this meant being awake while others slept. Occasional headlights loomed suddenly in the early morning darkness, and he remembered obscure shapes outside the line—green figures in the NVG, and the captain, catlike, slipping over a rock into the dark.

It was still chilly. Wan light penetrated the fog from the restaurant windows across the road. The old guys in baseball caps were sitting with their coffee—they looked like ghosts through the mist. It seemed like nothing had changed in Toni's, nothing at all. The same guys who had been eating in there the morning he took the bus to Basic were still eating the same eggs off the same plates.

Coffee would have tasted good, but he didn't stop. His business wasn't with them.

The morning warmed. Wisps of blue began to peek from the top of the sky, and in Hoosick Bridge the wool was whitening. The fog would lift. At about 8:30 Jane Herrick turned the aging Mercedes wagon off of North Hoosick Road into the post office lot. She'd come to collect any last RSVPs from the mailbox—she hadn't quite accustomed herself to the idea of responses on the Internet.

Lucy was in midconversation with Francine McGregor, the town clerk, as Jane walked in. ". . . strangest thing as I was driving up—oh, *hey*, Jane," Lucy said, using the soft tone some of them had for her now. On her face was that sad, sorry look that now passed for friendship—from the ones who still talked to her.

"Good morning." Slim, erect Jane Herrick walked with a subtle lean now, favoring the hip bothered by arthritis, but unbowed nevertheless, her voice still just slightly too loud—not overpowering, but with that hint of command, despite all that had happened. Her hair had gone white during the winter of '04–'05, but she was still a handsome woman. She had never been arrogant, never condescending, but she had been a Morse and was a Herrick, and even now a patrician reserve was steadfast in her. For the most part she was alone at the Heights now—the girls were rarely home—but in that house, it had always been the women who were strongest.

"... when I drove up this morning," Lucy continued, "there was this *soldier* . . . "

"Yes?" asked Francine.

"... walking along Route Seven toward town."

"Where?"

Jane's fingers had stopped working the mailbox key.

"Coming out of Williamstown."

"Just one by himself?"

"In his uniform, and with a big pack on his back, marching along the northbound lane, wearing that, you know, that what do they call that uniform?"

"Camouflage?"

"That camouflage uniform like you see them in."

"Strange to find just one soldier out by himself, walking," Francine said. "You see the Guard go by sometimes, a dozen of them in trucks."

The post office door opened, and quickly closed again.

"Did you recognize him?"

"Hardly got a look. But he'll get to town soon enough—he was headed this way. Jane, you don't suppose . . . Jane?"

But Jane Herrick didn't hear. She had already left the post office, and at that moment was sitting in the driver's seat of the Mercedes, her knuckles white against the steering wheel.

Step, step, step. With a little water to stay hydrated, he could walk forever. The captain said only a selfish man, only a small man wouldn't hydrate. A man was at his peak only when hydrated, and if he wasn't at his peak, it would cost the squad.

Why had he left the bus at Pittsfield and begun walking again? You'd think he'd walked enough for a lifetime. Maybe it was the watchfulness of the passengers across that narrow aisle, looking like they wanted to ask him things but were afraid to. Maybe it was the ones behind him. He liked people where he could see them. All those eyes close upon him brought him back to patrols down to the village in Komal, the way the Afghans would stare, and if you looked back and caught their eyes, they would smile in a false way. He remembered the village elder, Ramitullah, wearing the same smile the day he was in the headman's house, where he and the captain argued over tea about snipers and wells, and all the while, as the *mutarjim* rendered the Pashto, the old Afghan wore that false smile.

Walking alone was better. The pack did not trouble him. He was used to monstrous packs weighted with weapons, ammunition, water, MREs, entrenching tools. He had humped an entire M240 up Sura Ghar. He'd carried packs up staggering goat trails in the stinging, airless cold that made a man suck for breath, packs so strapped with ammunition that if a guy stumbled and fell to his back he just lay like a bug with its legs whirling, lay there sucking on that nothingness, until someone pulled him to his feet again. He'd carried them up and down those mountains until his lungs expanded, or some other magical thing happened—he was never sure what it was that changed after that first six months—that let him at last get air, and spring from stone to stone as light-footed as the enemy themselves.

He was all hard edges, all lean muscle and bone. His thighs were roped, his calves and arms corded, hardened, his elbows and cheekbones and knees sharp, his back a machine. He could carry a pack for eighteen hours a day, with just a catnap for an hour here or there, and even then be wakeful enough to reach for the knife at the sound of a car door. He walked with that inclined posture he'd always had from the age of eight. It looked like he was in a hurry, leaning toward his destination.

Sergeant Brown said, "Murphy, you walk like you trying to beat your own self there."

Pockets of thick cotton still blanketed the low places. On Route 7 there were more cars and trucks now. He didn't like sudden noises behind him, but these he recognized well enough—just civilian vehicles on a road. There were no explosives weighing down the rear suspensions.

The green peaks of the Taconic Hills were jutting clear from their white skirts. Each landmark along the road, each shop, fence, house, each farmer's field presented itself for his inspection. He listened to the metronomic beat of his boots on sand and gravel, and remembered.

*Boots crunching on sand and gravel.* Crunch, crunch, crunch, and turn. Crunch went the footsteps outside, punctuating shrieks of wind, keeping time to it. And inside Second Squad's sandbagged hooch at Firebase Montana, one of the guys was asking, "The fuck's he doing out there?"

They lay on their plywood bunks calculating the minutes until their next watch, listening to the wind whip and moan and beg and scream and whisper and then fall silent, hearing in the brief lulls the captain's boots pacing the gravel, and now and again a snatch of his words over the wind.

"You know what he doin. Give a little education, in case Haji listening."

His first night up there. The small hooch was hammered together like a kid's fort from two-by-fours and plywood and buried, cave-like, in sandbags. It would be his home for twenty-one months. It was crammed with bunks, thick with the smell and sprawl of men, crowded with Kevlars and ammo belts and IBAs hanging from nails, and boots jammed between the bunks. And socks—everywhere socks hung from lines. A diesel heater warmed the little den, cooking the stink of sweat and bad feet and cigarette smoke, and now and then with the waft of MREs: of cold turkey Tetrazzini or Swiss steak. He lay on his stomach and listened.

Someone asked, "What he readin tonight, Sarnt Brown?"

The squad quieted down to hear it. And the disembodied voice came in and out, with the wind.

*"... this batter'd Caravanserai*
*Whose Portals are alternate Night and Day ..."*

A howl of wind cut it off, and someone said, "He doin Omar again."

"Battered caravan be this hooch and no doubt." It was the big private stretched out in the upper bunk across from him. He was a kid from Mississippi, doughy and soft and large, with a grin that never left him, not when eating, complaining, shitting, under attack from Taliban RPGs, not ever. His name was Billy Hall Jr. Grinning Billy Hall Jr. was a stone killer with the .50 cal. He was stretched out on his back, his hands folded behind his head, staring at the rafter twelve inches above, grinning. "This here the number one poetry base in the US military. I Googled it and there's an official top-secret report the Pentagon done at taxpayer expense. Northern liberals decided we gon rhyme the sonsabitches into surrender."

"Omar Khayyám, he call this one," Sarnt Brown was explaining. "Montoya—give me the glories of this world!"

Montoya had an iPod with twenty thousand songs, and he could rap or sing the lyrics of all of them. Montoya was a walking library of lyrics. "They stick to my brain, like Velcro, you know?" he once explained. He piped up from a bunk near the back:

*"Some for the Glories of This World; and some*
*Sigh for the Prophet's Paradise to come."*

The hooch sang out in unison now, loudly enough for the captain to hear outside.

*"Ah, take the Cash, and let the Credit go*
*Nor heed the rumble of a distant Drum!"*

"Welcome to our world, cherry," said Billy Hall Jr., rolling to his side and grinning at him. "On a side of a fucking Afghan cliff, with mortars raining down your ass from all over this valley, the Army put a poetry school. You get your poetry school in Basic?"

He answered: "Mechanic school."

"Well, we could give you a truck to work on, except you'd have to carry it up here."

"Nothing here but wind and Haji ghosts," someone added.

Billy Hall Jr. rolled back onto his back, grinning that big, sly grin from his biscuit-from-the-oven face, with a cigarette hanging out of one corner. "And a fifty cal."

"Jamming when you most need it—maybe he can fix that," someone said.

"And fucking goats."

Someone asked, "Get your goat school, dude?" And then they were laughing, and the talk fell to which one of them would first have carnal knowledge of a goat, or of his sister, or of a goat's sister.

Later that night, someone was asking, "Prophet's Paradise—whatsat mean anyway, Sarnt? Is that, like, Bagram? Or this shithole?"

"Firebase Burnshitter!" someone said.

"Y'all crackers go to *school* instead of poppin your sisters with Billy Hall up in them barefoot counties, you might read better," said Master Sergeant Theodore Brown. "You might know what it mean."

"Shit, Sarnt, *your* sister busy most nights . . ." said Billy Hall Jr. Laughter.

"Sarnt a eddikated man," Billy Hall Jr. went on, "so eddikated he ended up here!"

"It mean, enjoy what you can, when you can," Brown said. "It mean, take the cash. Spend the cash. The future all bullshit."

Montoya sang out: "Take me away from the hood, like a state penitentiary / Take me away from the hood in the casket or a Bentley . . ."

"Shut the fuck up, Montoya!"

"Fuck alla y'all inbreeds," Brown said. "I like old Omar."

Listening to this, stirring it now and again from his upper

bunk with a crack about this one's sister or that one's stink, grinning Billy Hall Jr. was regarding the cherry, whose face had betrayed him.

"'Smatter?"

Roy Murphy shook his head.

"Ain't no secrets in Firebase Montana. Up here, you jack, three other guys get off."

And so carefully, quietly, Roy Murphy asked whether the CO of a US Army Airborne unit in the dead center of Taliban country, as a standard kind of thing, liked to wander around in the dark with a headlamp, reading poetry.

"To be fair, you ain't exactly got a poetry *reader* for a CO," said Billy Hall Jr. "You got a *poet*."

Montoya said, "Poet of death, dawg. Poet of life and death."

*Sizzlecrack! The knees like Emma's marionette. Report! All fall down.*

He stopped on the roadside, shivered by the memory. And then a sun shaft popped through the fog and reminded him that when you hear it, you're alive, and he started again. Crunch, crunch, along the highway. When those memories got hold of him, he might walk straight out on the pavement and into the grille of an eighteen-wheeler and see nothing but Billy Hall Jr.'s sunburned face, grinning the way to his seventy virgins.

She knew. She knew it was him. She parked in the drive and hurried up the porch steps, because she knew. She tried to calm herself with false hopes. Maybe it's not him, it could be anyone in a uniform. But in the pit of her stomach she knew who it must be and where he must be heading. She paced to the kitchen and then back to the parlor and she steadied her shaking hand against the mantel over the fireplace. He was coming *here*. On this of all days! To ruin everything, after these years! In how long—two hours? Three? Dear God. And then, later today *they* would all be arriving—all be here at the Heights!

It had taken all Jane Herrick's strength to endure the looks she received in town. Some were expressions of solace, but others were the lowered eyes of resentment. Sometimes she could almost feel them judging her. Only the Heights had kept her in Hoosick Bridge at all, and the irrational idea that she, as the last of the Morses, was its steward, that she must somehow rescue the house from the shame into which it had fallen. She could still dream that one of the girls would settle here, restore family to the Heights, bring it back to what it had been. Thoughts like these roused her from bed each morning. The bad time was in the past now, for she had come to life again with the prospect of a celebration, the first in years, the next in a line that stretched back through generations. The proper place for this celebration was the Heights. It had seen a dozen milestones like this.

Emma had asked, "Mom, are you sure?" and Jane had answered, "We need to get back on the horse"—Jane, who'd never ridden a horse in her life.

And now he was coming straight up Route 7. She felt the same tremor she'd known so many years ago, when Emma ran with the boy during the summer before the eighth grade.

Jane returned to the kitchen and tried to sit at the table but could not be still. Rising, she went to the leaded-glass windows by the front doors and looked down Washington Street. Outside it was a quiet summer morning. The street was empty, save for the Tillys' car driving slowly down the hill. She returned to the kitchen, grabbed her coat, and went back outside to the car, for she simply couldn't be home alone when he came. She had to go somewhere where she could calm herself and think. As she stood by the Mercedes in the morning sun, she thought, Why am I wearing my coat? It's warm today. She took the coat off, opened the door, and tossed the coat in the backseat, then drove off, thinking, Why must everything be so confused?

But about the one central thing she was not confused. He was coming. She'd always known that he would come back for Emma.

* * * *

The two-lane highway looked much the same as it had that summer he'd left. They'd put a wind turbine up on the ridge—that was new—and the Mexican restaurant outside of Williamstown had a new name, but the antiques store, the golf course, the cornfields, the Store at Five Corners, none of them had changed. It was not far now. He was just a town away, just over the state line from where he had left her five years before.

He wore his shades now against the glare of the July morning, but he liked the feel of the heat on his shoulders. Here July's warmth was pleasant—nothing like the killing, searing heat of the Afghan summer. He was remembering Billy Hall Jr., who liked to make presentations. "Yo, Murphy, in consequence whereof you being at the single most ridiculous installation on the entire face of the planet Earth, a grateful nation is proud to honor you with the Medal of Stupidity." Hall was always issuing decrees from the Pentagon or the White House, sprinkling them liberally with *wherefores* and *thereofs*. His lips tried to form the words the way Billy Hall Jr. used to do, up at Firebase Burnshitter. He was humming, "diddydum, diddydum." He was remembering anapaests, and poetry school as winter came on in the Korengal.

It was freezing at night and wisps of snow hung in the air. The snowcaps on the surrounding White Mountains grew larger, creeping down the mountain by night, every morning occupying more territory.

The men had gathered in the ammo brick-and-mortar, and the captain was saying, "Four men on this op. We're going tonight, and we're going light. The enemy's been getting a little cocky in his approaches. Intel says he wants to give us one last send-off before bugging out to Pakistan for winter, and will be back Tuesday. This particular op might get a little interesting, so it's volunteers only."

The men laughed. They knew what that meant.

"My volunteers are Brown, Montoya"—he looked up—"Murphy."

"Who the fourth, sir?"

"Dickinson," said the captain.

"Sounds exhilaratin, sir," said Montoya, and the men laughed again.

Later that day Roy Murphy was alone in the dark of Second Squad's hooch, swearing to himself, pulling his gear together, ramming it violently into the pack. The door opened and Billy Hall Jr. came in.

"'Smatter, man?"

"Nothin."

They were alone in the hooch. Hall asked, "Then why you packin that thing like you want to hurt it?"

"It's *nothing*." Roy Murphy whirled on him, and through clenched teeth he said, "Hall, I'm not scared of any mission, you understand?"

"Whoa, dawg!"

"But I'm not stupid, neither."

"Well, that's debatable," said Hall, "but I'll go with you on it. What's not being stupid got to do with your attitude, man?"

"I'm supposed to go out there with fucking *Shakespeare*?"

Billy Hall Jr. nodded then, getting it at last. But strangely, the grin seemed to grow and grow on his face, like he was savoring the best joke he'd heard in months. His jaw worked as though chewing cud, and he grinned away, until at last, Murphy demanded, "The fuck's your problem, Hall?"

He was grinning ear to ear by that time. "Cherry!"

"*What?*"

"Cap'n ain't sane, that's sure enough, but he got it."

"He got *what*?"

"The mojo. I'll tell you something. If that motherfucker out there with *you*, then the odds are better that we'll buy it back here. That's a fact. Cap'n got the mojo." He winked at him, and shambled out of the hooch with "Believe I'll go on outside now, and take the air, leave you to abuse government property on your own."

To the men in Army Airborne, *light* was a euphemism. Each

man on the op carried more than one hundred pounds of ammunition, water, weapons, entrenching tools, and MREs. Captain
Dickinson was no different. Four kilometers down the mountainside they found the two positions he wanted. By dawn they'd
scratched two fighting holes in the rock and moved enough stones
to lie behind, with the captain and Murphy in one, and Brown and
Montoya in the second, a hundred meters farther downslope and
to the east.

"Cap'n, why we setting up down the hill? We get 'em before
they come up?"

"No," said the captain. "Not before."

"I don't understand."

"The enemy gets excited. He shoots off all his firecrackers,
and then gets sloppy leaving the parade. So we'll lie quiet as he
goes up toward Firebase Montana, and visit with him after the
parade, on the way down."

Brown smiled. "You gon read him a poem, sir?"

"We'll give him a few anapaests."

"Anawhat, sir?"

"Anapaests. Just like it sounds, Sergeant. *Diddydum—anapaest.*
Tomorrow you're the poet. You give him some diddydum."

"Roger that, sir."

Dawn was coming up in the east, over Pakistan. Captain
Dickinson said, "Hit your MREs, and then get some rack. We'll
do four-hour watches. Murphy, you're first watch on this post."
And then the captain was out, sleeping soundly on that cold Afghan slate as though it were a king bed in a four-star hotel, and he
a mogul who'd just signed a deal.

All day they lay in position, as the stones warmed in the sun;
and then all night, as they cooled to freezing. They belly-crawled
away to shit or piss, scraping a place in the rocky ground. The
enemy didn't come. All day the next day they repeated this. And
into the night. Still he didn't come, and they ran out of MREs and
water.

In their separate cutout, Montoya and Brown were grumbling

about the intel that had sent them there. "We been bullshat again," Brown whispered.

"Till dawn," said the captain. "If he stays away another night, we'll head back."

But the enemy did not stay away another night.

Just after 0300 Brown caught movement in the NVG clipped on his Kevlar, 200 meters downhill and to the south, rising to come abreast of his position at about 150 meters.

"Sarnt," the captain was whispering in his headpiece. He'd caught it, too.

"Got eyes on 'em," Brown whispered back. Now all of the op team were awake, watching. One, two, six men moved slowly up the mountainside. Six became ten. Strapped from their shoulders were AKs and RPGs, and two labored in the rear, one with a large tube, the other with an object they couldn't make out.

Murphy's pulse was jumping, his skin prickly. He'd been in firefights, he'd responded to IEDs. But he'd never lay in wait for a full-on ambush.

A whisper from the captain—"That look like an RPG launcher to you, Murphy?"

"Too big, sir."

"That's what I'm thinking. I'll be goddamned."

"What, sir?"

Staring over the rock, he whispered *"Damn!"* in a kind of admiration.

"Sir?"

"It's a *mortar*—and it's *ours*. Haji got his hands on one of our two fifty-twos. That first one has the launcher, the other one the baseplate. Where in the Christ . . . ?"

They watched them come slowly up the spur.

"They're humping *our* mortar up to shell Montana. That's just . . ."

"Sir?"

"That's *disrespectful*," the captain said.

The captain watched for a minute longer, until they'd slipped out of view up the hillside. The mortar bearers had lagged a bit off the pace. He rolled to his back and drew the knife from its leg sheath.

Roy Murphy was watching, wondering what that was for. "Sir?"

"If we fire, they'll fall back, probably with the mortar." He glanced up again. Collapsing the stock, he clipped the M4 to his vest. "And I want my mortar back." Then the captain slipped over the rock and was gone.

Jesus Christ! Where'd he gone? What the hell was he going to do? Roy Murphy waited five minutes. Waited another forever until it was eight minutes. Ten. He scoured the mountainside with the NVG. *Do I—follow him? Call Sarnt Brown? Just lie here?* The NVG brought everything up greenish and spooky. He heard nothing.

He decided to call. "Sarnt Brown, Captain's gone after 'em."

"He's *what*?"

Fourteen minutes. Fifteen.

In the eighteenth minute the shape reappeared. Murphy picked him up again in the NVG, moving swiftly over the rugged mountainside with a tube on his shoulder like a length of pipe.

He collapsed in the cutout. The M252 tube lay next to Roy Murphy. "Had to leave the baseplate," he said. "Heavy bastard." A moment later the captain was whispering on the radio. "He's on the east ridge, about a click from your line. In thirty seconds he'll miss his mortar launcher. So I've revised the plan. At oh four-thirty commence shelling." He read out a map coordinate. "Do not overshoot, gentlemen."

"He'll miss his mortar, sir?" The question crackled back in the headsets.

"Brief you later. Commence at oh four-thirty. Out."

In that darkness, the captain's face seemed to give off its own light.

"Look alive—they'll come right back to us," he said, like he could barely wait. Like it would be a party and they would all get to hide behind the couches and yell, "Surprise!"

Oh, he was alive then. Never more alive than that dark morning. The way it came on with noise and rush, the captain's choreography at the center of the explosions, the bursts, the fire. The adrenaline rocket that sweet ambush sent through every vein. They did come back, they came back pell-mell down the slope; lit up by shelling from above, they swarmed to the trap and were ambushed from below. The enemy never came close enough to get off a clean shot at anything. Eight fell in the first wave. It was a hell of dark and noise and fire burst, but the hell was somehow contained. It took forever; it was over in seconds, and as dawn came up, the enemy was hiding behind a rock outcrop at two hundred meters, only a few of them left, their way down the mountain blocked by Brown and Montoya's position.

"What have you got, what have you got?" demanded the captain.

"Just them behind those yellow rocks, at eleven o'clock."

"How many?"

"Four, I think, sir. Maybe three."

As the sun rose, it became a stalemate. All through the morning they were exchanging fire, with Dickinson and Murphy on the flank, and Brown below, until the sun was high.

"Any way to get a position to the north, get a shot on them?"

The headset crackled. "Negative, sir, we're both pinned—no way to move."

"Roger, hold your position," the captain said. "Time to finish this." Then to Murphy: "Private, keep them engaged. Get a burst off every twenty seconds or so. Start with a few bursts now."

He sighted through the scope and let off a burst, and then another. *Diddydum.*

The answering fusillade sent stone chips flying. When he turned back to where the captain had been lying, he'd gone again.

Again—crazy! Hall was right—he *was* crazy. An hour passed. But Roy Murphy had a job now, and he focused on that, keeping up the bursts. Focus, squeeze, wait. Lie back. Turn, focus, squeeze, wait. He thought maybe he got one of them, or his weapon anyway, the way the AK flew back. He was on the headset:

"Sarnt Brown—I get one? Can you see?"

"Can't tell, Murphy."

He kept up the bursts. And then he and Brown received a short message from the captain. "Engage in constant fire, sixty seconds from mark. Keep your fire down the mountain, please." A pause, and then, "Mark."

In the ensuing melee they did not hear the captain's short bursts, which came from uphill and to the rear. Neither did the four Afghans.

In Second Squad's hooch, he would tell the story, and tell it again the next night, and the next. The story of Diddydum.

"Captain took their mortar from 'em? Just *took* it?" is how the questioning began.

"He left," said Roy Murphy. "It was quiet. Then he come back with it."

"He come back with it!" men repeated.

"When he went for the mortar team, you didn't hear his M-Four or nothing?"

"He took a Ka-Bar."

"The fuckers have a mortar, and he took a *knife*! Murphy, you the grunt, dude. You lettin a officer do that shit on his own?"

"Had to clean my weapon, you know."

Appreciative laughter, then. The cherry got off a good one. The captain was a stickler for clean weapons.

It went on, the curiosity of those warriors. "Musta done one of them with the pistol," Montoya said.

But there had been no sound.

Someone said, "That wasn't enough, he had to go and take out four Hajis in that uphill nest later in the day—alone?"

"Well, we distracted 'em some."

The laughter again. We distracted 'em!

Billy Hall Jr. was loving the new material. He issued a new order. "Attention, y'all. Pentagon regrets to inform you of some bad news. The Taliban gone and been disrespectful."

Laughter.

"The aforesaid Taliban been extremely disrespectful, so we gon have to go and visit with them."

Howls. Hoots. Cries of "Disrespectful!"

"So this here the mission. Sarnt Brown, go on out there and fetch me back a mortar. Pursuant to which CENTCOM has issued you the manners manual, case Haji's impolite. Specialist Montoya, you go get Osama bin Laden—bring his ass back, too, and if he don't say please and thank you, you gon give him a severe reprimand!"

Riotous laughter then, which cascaded into a maul, as men rolled from the bunks and headlocked each other, crashing into the hooch's walls. They pounded each other's heads, laughing so hard there were tears in their eyes. It was a Firebase Montana party; mauling and laughter, and bourbon smuggled up from the forward operating base at Bagram, and then there were insults fired at each other, and at the pussies in the FOBs who would never know a moment like that, at the respective pussies in the Navy, the Marine Corps, and the Air Force, and then at the pussies who played for various football teams, and then the usual broadside at sisters and mothers. There had never been an operation so flawless. Not a man injured. Not a man even footsore. The enemy that had so often wrung harm from them humiliated. The riot spilled out to the captain's quarters, and they begged him to come among them.

"Cap'n, read us one. Go on, sir, read us one!"

"Respect! Show respect to the captain, or he gon take your weapon!"

More laughter. "Read us some anapaests!"

They were like children to him, in a way. The captain was smiling when he came into the hooch, but his eyes still blazed with that wild light that Roy Murphy had seen, and that Brown, the longest-serving of them, feared. His eyes burned with it that night. The younger men loved it, but it made Brown and the lieutenant nervous—it was just this side of insane.

"Gentlemen, congratulations! A successful op! We inflicted heavy casualties and took none."

A whoop from the men.

"We gave the enemy something to think about, and tonight we are feeling good!"

"He gonna have to mind his manners!" someone said.

Still with that light in his eyes, the captain now fell to speaking softly, so that the men in the back of the hooch strained to hear. "When you're feeling good is a dangerous time in Afghanistan. You—Murphy!"

"Sir."

"You study history in school?"

"Not too much, sir."

"And why was that?"

"Busy making bail for his momma, sir," said Billy Hall Jr., and the hooch exploded in mirth again. But they calmed down quickly, seeing the way the captain had Murphy fixed in those crazy eyes.

"Why was that, Murphy?" he repeated.

Reddening a little, Roy Murphy shrugged. "Teacher didn't think too much of me."

"You need his permission to read history?"

"No, sir. Guess I didn't see the point, sir."

"The point, Murphy, is not to be condemned to repeat it!" Now the wild eye passed over the whole hooch, and they were all avoiding it. "How many of you know what happened twenty clicks from this firebase in January 1842?"

Silence.

"Aw, that's history. We don't see the point of knowing any history!"

No one spoke.

"The British had come four years before. And they were feeling very good when they marched out of Peshawar to the Khyber in 1838. Singing bar songs as they came through the pass. They were feeling even better when Kabul fell a few months later. An easy victory, and life was good! And then, not so good. In 1841, up in Kabul, British HQ was torched. Incendiaries. Improvised devices. Sound familiar?"

No one answered. On he went. "November. What was going on in November 1841? Anyone?"

Silence.

"What might have been going on for a month or so that fall?"

One of the men ventured, "Ramadan?"

"Right, Nadal. Ramadan. Same as it ever was in Afghanistan. Ramadan—when a Muslim gets in touch with God. When he gets inspired to cast out the infidel. But we don't need to study history after all, cause we'd rather relive it, am I right, Private Murphy?"

Roy Murphy stood silently near his bunk, taking it, and the other men were wondering, Did that really happen, like he said, with the British, all that time ago? It must be true if the captain said it. *History.*

"Back to our friends the Brits, who had their HQ torched by the Afghans and all of a sudden weren't feeling so swell during Ramadan 1841. They felt even worse in January 1842, when their Afghan allies bugged out on them. Gentlemen—is the ANA any different today? The British were chased out of town and into this country where you are right now—two valleys over, where the great-great-grandfathers of these same Pashtuns came down from the hills and cut them to pieces. All but one of sixteen thousand troops that set out four years before. All but one gone. One! A slaughter at Jagdalak Pass, and only one guy made it out to tell the story."

The hooch was silent now.

"So never feel too good when you're in Afghanistan. When you're feeling good the Afghan will greet you, and smile at you, and welcome you to his home, but he will never forget that you are the invader. He's seen you before. Nothing much has changed here except the flags on the shoulder patches."

Silence, for another moment, until someone said, "Poem, sir!"

"You want a poem?"

A whoop. Cries of "Yes, sir!"

"Wilfred Owen, then."

No book for this one: the captain knew it by heart. As Roy Murphy would in years to come, from studying the volume that one day would ride in his pack. It ends this way:

> *My friend, you would not tell with such high zest*
> *To children ardent for some desperate glory,*
> *The old Lie; Dulce et Decorum est*
> *Pro patria mori.*

"Good night, gentlemen. Get some sleep. Murphy, you did pretty well today. But read some history, son. It wouldn't kill you."

Oh, he remembered all of it as though the images were tattooed on him, as though the earbuds were in his ears and it was playing on an iPod. He could hear the words, he could feel that diddydum coursing through him like white light bursting every vein. Only once was he ever as alive as in the Korengal, only once, and just the memory of that quickened the pace a little. Step, step, step.

And then—there it was in view. Standing just where he remembered. He squinted to see the bullet holes he and Emerson put in it, but they were gone—somebody must have replaced the sign. His mind's eye conjured up Billy Hall Jr.'s flabby silhouette, backlit by the rays of sun coming over the eastern mountains. He could picture him standing to the sandbagged .50 cal, with a cigarette dangling, could hear his twang: "Murphy, I b'lieve we's about to en-gage."

"Welcome to Vermont, the Green Mountain State," the sign said.

The Howell Professor of History emeritus came last to breakfast that morning.

White-haired, blue-eyed Professor Roger Emmanuel, lately retired from the college down in Williamstown, was a figure often seen and heard in town. He sang in the choir at St. John's Episcopal Church and always got the comic lead in the annual G & S production. An audible sigh, and a bit of laughter, too, would greet the arrival of the Byronesque figure to the microphone at town meeting, for they knew that he would say something funny, and something else they didn't understand, and that he *would* go on. At the college he'd been one of those lightning rod figures. Deans resented Professor Emmanuel as a showboat, the faculty groused ("What has he published in the last fifteen years?"), while those shallow hedonists who crave nothing but entertainment—undergraduates—swarmed his lectures.

In the best academic tradition, the professor was also a gossip. For years the college supplied him with a rich lode of trivial intrigues, but after his retirement he mined Hoosick Bridge for new ore. He was always stirring gossip along, on street corners and in Toni's Lunch. He cataloged the events of the week over coffee cups, and then offered the line from Gibbon's *Decline and Fall* that made sense of them.

The professor was often seen in the summer on his bicycle, and frequently, too, in the winter on his brisk walks, striding out for an hour or more from the little house on Woodford Road, four blocks from the center of town, where he lived alone. Dale the carpenter built a small library as an addition to accommodate his books—a job, he said, that took twice as long as it should have done, because the professor was always interrupting him to talk. "To be honest with you," Dale said, "I never knew what all he was talking about."

Everywhere he toted his manuscript, in a brown cardboard box carried in a green canvas sack. It was said by some to be a biography of Ethan Allen, by others a broader history of the Green Mountain Boys. He'd been working on it since he retired. Toni got a peek now and again, as he would scribble away on the pages over late breakfast at the lunch counter.

"I don't know what it is," she once told Francine, "except it's thick, and has a million footnotes."

The professor took a stool at the counter, set down the battered Kinko's box, ordered coffee and an English muffin, and asked, "Toni, my dear girl, is it me, or does the town feel oddly *electric* this morning?"

"He stopped in Stewart's—the soldier. I was down there to get gas. He come in, picks up a roast beef sandwich and a water from the fridge."

"What'd he say?"

"Nothing, really."

"Well, what'd *you* say?"

"*Nothing.* That was the thing of it—nobody said nothing! He drops his pack outside, he come in, six, eight of us all just standing there in Stewart's paying for our gas or coffee or whatnot, you know? Staring. Monica, behind the counter staring. He goes and gets his sandwich and gets a water, brings it up to her."

"That's it?"

"No. She rings him up, and he pulls this envelope from his pocket. Near enough a white brick, the thing. Opens it up and pulls out of there a hundred-dollar bill."

"Really?"

"Seen it myself. Fat envelope full of hundreds. He pulled one out and give it to her and put the envelope back. He took off his sunglasses. He had a look in his eyes that . . ."

"What?"

"You didn't want to interrupt him—you know? Like if you said something, you'd be interrupting him. He had somewheres he was going and you didn't want to be in the way. You looked at him and you knew, he's been over there. In all that mess, he's been there. You could just tell.

"While he's at the counter, Monica—her hands start shaking, she's trying to make the change and shaking. Nobody's talking at all. Monica hands him the change, and he puts the bills in that envelope, puts his sunglasses back on, and off he goes. Just like that, bang, the door shuts behind him. Nobody said nothing except Burt Fredoni was in there, he calls out, 'Welcome home, son,' as he was leaving, but the soldier, he never said nothing, I don't know if he heard him at all."

"I'll be damned."

"I seen him when I drove out a few minutes later, walking up toward town, the sandwich in one hand, the water in the other."

"Well—who was he then?"

"That's the god-damnedest thing. That's what we all in Stewart's were asking each other soon as he left. Who? He was familiar to me. Skin all leathery and dark, black hair, what he had of it. Medium height, not tall, but a strong look about him. His eyes set close. Big hands on him, too. He was familiar. I'm sure I recognize him—everybody was saying that! Except, nobody could say who he was."

All those people in Stewart's stared at him like a freak had turned up in Hoosick Bridge, like he had two heads. Same thing as on the bus. Did any of them even know there's a war on? He felt his skin prickle under those looks. He just wanted to get out of there.

By the register there was a display rack of candy, bags of Swedish Fish and Dots and chocolates and such. On top was a placard with Bugs Bunny on it. As he left and quick-stepped north along Route 7, that picture of Bugs reminded him of Elmer Fudd, and he remembered the evening they all went to the movies, and the Warthogs lit Elmer up.

"He ain't never hit no one yet," Montoya was explaining to him up at Firebase Montana. "Elmer a nervous motherfucker. He know he got to shoot and move quick, before we find him. He shoot so quick he never hits nothing. We get him one a these days, for sure."

Not long after that, one evening after chow, another sniper shot cracked off the mountainside below the firebase, and Billy Hall Jr. raked the opposite ridgeline with the .50 cal. The captain had had it with Elmer's random shots. He called for a strike, and on this night they were in luck, because the Warthogs happened to be in range, and so his call was granted by the command. Instant excitement gripped the firebase, for this was a 3-D movie—you waited a whole month at Montana for this kind of show. This was like going to the stadium-seating theater at the AMC, only better. A minute later, Nadal said, "I got 'em!" A whoop went up as the men spotted the two dots in the sky, and then they crowded the sandbags to watch the dots take shape as A-10s and dive toward the ridge.

The hogs shattered it with an astonishing hell of fire and explosion, and the men shouted and whistled, but the whooping soon died down and the men were quiet. "Jesus," somebody said.

"They musta done Elmer with all that," said Sarnt Brown, softly.

He never hit nothing, but he was a pain in the ass, and so maybe this was his day. Nobody would survive that, the squad was thinking, as the A-10s pulled out in formation and climbed toward the setting sun.

Some of them were feeling a little weird about Elmer. They'd gotten to know him in a strange kind of way. They'd been living with Elmer for so long that each man in the squad had hung a face and a personality on him. The faces were more hapless and bungling than dangerous. And to be just *crushed* like that. Burned to ashes.

"I wonder what old Elmer look like," someone asked, as though he were still alive.

"Like a lump of fuckin coal, dawg."

"I wonder if I ever seen him down the village. If he's a old dude or a kid. Yo, Nadal, you think he's a kid?"

"If he is, he's a dead kid."

"I think he's a old sumbitch, one a them pencil-leg mother-fuckers watch us when we come on patrol, smile at us in town, then scamper up the hill on his little pencils, with his AK flapping, and he can't shoot it straight. Can't hardly see, probably."

"Bet he was a kid," one of them said. "Fourteen years old, and ever time he fired his carbine it kicked him into a hole."

Someone added, "Don't matter now."

The Warthogs were dots in a distant sky. It was eerily quiet, like when people walk away from a church after a funeral. Roy Murphy had watched this with them, his hand straying involuntarily to finger an object he wore around his neck and beneath his T-shirt. He said nothing.

Billy Hall Jr. stood up behind the sandbags and broke the silence by yelling across the valley, "Yo Elmer! *Dude!* You still there?"

His voice echoed faintly off the mountains. Then silence.

"Use your *sight*, you heathen asshole! This here Billy Hall Jr. H-A-L-L, and he want to lay some virgins right *now!*"

But the men didn't laugh at this. They laughed at death a lot, but not at this. Sergeant Brown snapped, "Hall, zip that shit!"

You could joke about death, laugh about it, but you didn't tempt it. Even wearing your IBA. Even with your Kevlar on, standing to the .50. Even from fucking Elmer, who had been crushed to coal dust and was dead as hell. You didn't tempt it.

"The Afghan theater is in the round," the captain always said.

# TWO

*B*y midmorning Hoosick Bridge was buzzing with the news of the soldier's return. He'd been seen along Route 7. He was in Stewart's. Somebody must be back from Iraq (or Afghanistan—one of them). Who? Why was he walking? Why was there no one to meet him? Malcolm Esdaile later claimed that he pulled up alongside him and offered him a ride, and that the soldier shook his head—didn't say a word, just shook his head and kept walking. Malcolm did not recognize him. At first he was not recognized generally, not with his hair short like that and his skin brown as a berry and behind those sunglasses.

Diane Nardelli described the unsettling tableau of that same young soldier standing at the top of Washington Street, at the corner of Spring, just across from the Heights—coolly examining the house. That was a little later in the morning. Not at attention exactly, but like it was a post or something. It was a little creepy, she said. She was driving south on Spring, and just before turning left at the corner onto Washington she saw him there across the street. That's when they put it together. As Francine reminded Diane, Emma Herrick went with the youngest Murphy boy, Roy, that summer after high school, and then Roy went off to the service and basically was never heard from again. "You know, he never called his mother *once*, not even once, never wrote a letter or sent an e-mail or anything. Never came home on leave. Just gone like he fell off the face of the earth. Except she knew he was alive because when a soldier is killed they always come and find the mother in person and tell her. And so she knew he was alive and yet he never wrote her a note or sent her an e-mail one single time, her that raised those boys up in the Park on her own. Now Eliza, everybody knows she's had those problems. But she was still the only mother he had. Not to hear anything at all—that was the most awful thing for her. Worse than if he was killed."

Diane said, "To be honest with you, I didn't recognize him, but now that you say that, it must have been him." For a soldier, all of a sudden, on that day of all days—that very day—to be standing at the top of Washington Street in Hoosick Bridge, alone, like he was on watch, like he was on guard or something, just looking at the Heights and not moving or anything—"Well," she said to Francine, "it give me a chill, and I didn't exactly get a good look at him, but you're right, who else could it be?"

Years later, this would be remembered. How the soldier had come to the top of the hill, and there stopped and stood at attention, across from the Heights. With time, many more would claim to have seen him there, staring at the house, motionless, watching without expression. Like a sentinel, they said.

After three commercial blocks, Washington Street curves to the left and begins its lazy climb to the junction with Spring Street. It acquires a flanking lawn, about thirty feet wide, bordered by a parallel gravel road that sets off the town's matriarchal Victorians. They stand to their stations, like ladies in waiting attending the dowager queen at the top of the hill.

In the summer when the maples are in leaf, there comes a particular spot on Washington Street where the tower first juts above the canopy. The soldier knew this point and had been waiting to reach it. He stopped there, and looked up the hill, as he had done as a boy, as he had done as a young man. The slates of the roof rose above the trees just as he remembered, and the sun glanced sharply across the east-facing windows in the tower.

He carried on up the street until it came into full view, the gaudy, three-story Victorian mansion that he remembered. At Christmastime when Eliza Murphy had forgotten to get a tree up at the trailer, he used to ride his bike down Route 7, and across Forest to Washington, and then up to this point, the cold wind cutting through him. He'd come to this spot, and look up at the great tree that presided in the bay window at the Heights, visible all down the avenue toward the town, its tiny white lights shimmering through a gauze curtain, and wonder what it was like to be in that house, with that tree, and that family.

Except for a twelve-year span after college, Jane Morse Herrick had lived at the Heights for all of her fifty-eight years. She had gone away to the city, but in time, like generations of Morses before her, she had come back. She brought with her a handsome young man named Tom Herrick and married him at St. John's, and afterward, the reception was held at the Heights, in a huge marquee erected in the backyard. The couple moved into the house, and Tom took up with Burt Fredoni's little accounting practice. Three girls would arrive: Emma, named for Jane's grandmother Emma Morse, who had presided over the Heights for almost fifty years; Anne; and Charlotte, who was always known as Charlie.

Tom Herrick received the blessing peculiar to a father of daughters. The only man in a family of women is always the object of plans, surprises, and most of all, study. His needs and wants are examined, cataloged, celebrated, predicted. He becomes a sort of pet, and his faults and failings are sources of humor and even pride. Like all such men, he was closely observed. The failure of that observation was one of the ironies of the bad time, five years before.

The tower was Emma's haunt, as it had been her mother's before. It was home to her American Girl dolls, her books, and the marionette playhouse. It was the club room of her friends.

Neither Anne nor Charlie ever cared for it as much. They thought it was too cold and lonely up there. But Emma ran up to the tower whenever storms came, to watch the rain streak the old windows and thrill at lightning strikes over the Taconics. On a clear evening in summer, she'd look out over the lower rooftops east to the Green Mountains, watching a red-tailed hawk float a lazy circle far away.

It was in the tower that she first made love with him.

At the junction at the top of the hill, at the corner of Washington and Spring Streets, the soldier stood in the morning sun. He had come to this spot from the other side of the world, over mountain ranges, across continents and the ocean, covering thousands of miles by plane, bus, and foot, to reach a house in a small town in Vermont. As though she should be exactly where he left her. As though time had stopped at a particular hour on an August morning five years before, and now would resume. As though the hands of the clock should be at rest, and his the job to wind the mainspring. He had come with that sole and unexamined purpose. And now he stopped, unready to advance. For the first time he recognized that his purpose was flawed.

In five years, he had never called, written, or e-mailed her. He had not tried to call her from Fort Drum a week ago, or from New York a day ago, or even from Pittsfield last night. A call would have confronted the present; it would have found the Emma of today— found her long departed, married, hostile, dead, God knows what—and that discovery would have buried forever the Emma of yesterday, whom he had carried with him in Afghanistan. He left the bus in Pittsfield, uneasy among those strangers to be sure, but also with an unconscious falter as he neared Hoosick Bridge and journey's end, where truth awaited him. He would have to surrender the past, and confront the certain impossibility of the present.

The white paint on the porch rails was cracked, and some of the gray deck paint on the porch flooring had peeled away. On the third floor one of the shutters was missing. Some of the lower courses of shingles were curling up on the south wall. He noticed pink petunias in the hanging baskets gone leggy, the flower stems brown and ropy. The grass was freshly mown—in fact the mower was standing next to the side of the house, where it had been left, but no one had trimmed the edges around the beds, and grass had come up between the stones in the walkway.

He saw no one on the porch, or through the windows. No car was in the drive. The house was silent.

He listened. From down the hill came the sound of a lawn mower; more distantly, a radio. A car approached slowly on Spring, passed by the Heights, picked up speed again. He stood watching, hearing, feeling the quiet all round, feeling his heart thump in his chest, remembering how he'd lie awake in Afghanistan remembering this house, trying to beat back his memories of it, because you had to stay focused. He used to say to himself, "When I'm back"—he would remember all of this when he came back. But at night he would picture this house, this porch, that summer. Her.

He crossed the street and trotted up the steps to the porch. And then something strange happened: in his head he heard the captain saying, *What we are is the same.*

He'd always known that the captain was like the Herricks. That was why at first he despised him and then, ashamed, he was intimidated by him, and it may also explain why, in the end, he loved him. It sounded in his head like the chorus of a song, as he reached the very steps of that place where he himself had been so despised, so feared, so briefly loved. The same as the captain, the same as all of them—him. The only thing the captain ever said that wasn't true.

He was coming up the steps, he was remembering other steps.

"Come!"

It was night in the Korengal. Cautiously he entered the officers' hooch, where the captain sat at his little table, with its neat row of books, and its three-ring notebooks, and his laptop, his back to the plywood door. The lieutenant was there, too, at the table with the radio, to the left side. The lantern hissed, and away outside was the low roar of the generator. Lieutenant Callahan asked his business, and he was a little embarrassed.

"Sir, that poem Cap'n told us?"

"'Dulce et Decorum Est,'" said the captain, without turning.

"I was just wondering, could I ask you about that, sir?"

The captain did not answer at first. He tapped a few keys, folded the laptop, and then turned slowly to face the visitor. The light was dim, and the captain's lined face looked serious that night, but his eyes came alive, as they always did, when he started talking.

"Sit down, Murphy."

It felt awkward sitting down in the presence of these officers, in their very home. But he took the chair as ordered—took the Kevlar off his head and set it on the plywood floor, then unfastened the IBA vest and eased it off his chest.

"Wilfred Owen, you said, sir?"

"Yes."

"Was just wondering . . ."

"Yeah?"

". . . who he was."

"A soldier who served in the First World War. I don't guess you studied that, either, Murphy." The captain smiled pleasantly.

"No, sir."

"Well, the good thing about study is, the deployment is lifetime. They called it the 'Great War.'"

"Sir."

"They should have called it the 'Great Stupidity.' Never was more criminal stupidity gathered into one conflict. Generals of criminal ignorance. Stupidity of purpose, stupidity of execution. Five hundred thousand casualties at the Battle of the Marne, in seven days of trench warfare. *Five hundred thousand.* Can you imagine that, Murphy?"

Once outside of Kabul the patrol ahead of Roy Murphy's hit

an IED and lost three men. There were ten casualties overall. The carnage was horrible. Twisted metal and charred flesh and blood were on the road, while garbage and sand blew in the wind, and the screams filled his ears. Just horrible. Twenty seconds after the explosion, he arrived to this staggering, noisy scene of death, this scene of ten casualties.

Five hundred thousand? No, he could not imagine it.

Usually the wind howled outside the hooches at night, but sometimes, and that night, it was still as the glass surface of a pond, as still as expectation itself. On nights like that he'd lie abed, and when he heard things—far-off, faint things—he'd wonder who might be coming for him. Inside the hooches the men would talk softly, lest they fail to hear them, too. They always wanted to hear the thing that was going to get them before it did.

"Sir, that Latin at the end . . ."

"*Dulce et decorum est pro patria mori.* You want the translation." He smiled. "It is sweet and honorable to die for the fatherland."

"And then he wrote it's a lie."

"Yes."

Lieutenant Callahan turned to watch, spellbound. In a fire-base, on a precarious slope in Afghanistan manned by squads of Army Airborne, in the absolute eye of the Taliban storm, a poetry seminar.

"If it is, sir . . ."

"A lie then, a lie now."

Roy Murphy lingered a moment longer, decided to ask the question that was really on his mind. "Then why you, sir? If I can ask."

"I don't follow, Murphy."

"Why are you here?"

"You think I came here believing it's sweet to die for my country?" The captain smiled ironically.

"No, sir, I mean . . . I mean you could of been anywhere. You graduated West Point and you went to Princeton College—"

"University." Captain Dickinson smiled.

"Sorry. And you can recite poetry and you can kill a mortar team with a knife and, sir, I mean, you could do anything you want in the world. Be anywhere you want, doing anything you want in the world."

"And?"

"And you're here."

The captain turned for help with this strange question. But the lieutenant declined with a polite nod. "Like to hear this answer myself, sir," he explained.

Roy Murphy continued. "Most of us, this was . . . kind of the only option. At the time. But you're different, sir."

The captain had a finger to his forehead, with his eyes down, as though studying. Then he lifted them again and frankly examined the young soldier who sat before him. "Murphy, we're not different. Where it counts, I think we're the same, you and me."

No one spoke for a bit, and certainly, Roy Murphy didn't want to be the first to call bullshit on that absurdity.

"How we arrived at this valley may be different, but what we are is the same. Take Princeton. You know what Princeton is, Murphy?"

"No, sir."

"Princeton is a bunch of geniuses who will lecture you on how the world works, and write books and papers on how the world works. Except most of them, it seems like, have never been in the world."

"Sir."

"Now you and me, we are in the world, are we not?"

"Yes, sir."

"And do you know how it works? Do you understand why, and for what purpose we are here, and with what purpose our enemy engages us, and how all of this is going to come out?"

"No, sir."

"Neither do I," said the captain. "So you see, we're not different."

The men listened to the hiss of the lantern, thinking, and then he went on.

"We're in the world, and it makes no sense to us. Princeton is not in the world, and it makes sense to them. But you do know how a SAW works, and how to unjam a fifty-cal, and what movement in the night-vision means, don't you?"

"Yes, sir."

"So do I. That makes us the same."

"Yes, sir."

"All right, Murphy. You're excused."

He'd put his IBA on and snapped the chinstrap of his Kevlar and was at the door when the captain stopped him. "One more thing, Murphy. Every man in the unit is willing to die. Not for a decal on a minivan, or a crowd in the seventh inning God blessing America and ordering another hot dog. Not to beat the Taliban or al Qaeda, and not to 'defend freedom' or any of that other political bullshit, and surely not to rebuild Afghanistan, as if Afghanistan were ever built in the first place.

"But every soldier in this unit *would* take a round—take a hundred rounds—for every other soldier in this unit. I will. You will. Those guys out there, every one of them will. They may frustrate cach other; they may hate each other. But they will. Not too many people in the world like that. But we are like that."

"Sir."

"So you see, we're not different, you and me."

"Sir."

*"Dulce et decorum est pro amicis mori."*

He stood at the door, not knowing what it meant, but knowing what it must mean.

"You have a wife hasn't divorced you yet, Murphy?"

This strange question came straight from the blue, pinning him in the doorway. Roy Murphy did not smile. To the captain it looked like he was pondering the question hard—like the answer was unclear.

"You do, don't you?"

"Well, sir," Roy Murphy said finally, "she didn't exactly marry me yet."

"Best kind of wife," said Captain Dickinson.

There was no "Come!" at the Heights that day. As he reached the doors and lowered his pack, he was taken by surprise, for he had never seen the inscription before. He'd been inside the Heights just once, five years before, but that day they'd hurried in the back door, by the kitchen. All through that summer of '04, whenever he'd come for her, he waited in the drive until she bounded from the house. He'd never before stood at the twin oak doors of the entrance, and so never before seen the inscription set into the lintel above them. The square capitals were small, the black paint faded, but the words perfectly legible.

### COME HOME TO ME

He waited for about a minute, maybe longer, before hoisting his pack and descending the steps. But then a flash of white caught his eye. And as he came around the corner he could see the back, where it was set up. The big truck must have come up from Pittsfield just the day before to erect it there, while Jane Herrick watched from the kitchen. He stood there for a long minute, looking at it. Thinking.

He put his pack down again, and circled around to the other side of the house and walked up the drive to the garage. From there he could see the back side of it. Then he went into the garage.

It took his eyes a moment to accustom themselves to the dark. Inside was a heap, a jumble pushed away from the door as though by a bulldozer, with just room at the front for the lawn mower, the garbage cans, a rake, snow shovels, jerricans. He felt his breath quicken, because he didn't like things in heaps, in piles, he didn't like things jumbled up. It agitated him. He told himself, It's just a garage nobody's cleaned up in a while.

Behind, he saw sawhorses, an outdoor table painted white, but rusting, its umbrella, a little red Toro rototiller with ancient dried mud on its rusty tines. Piles of lawn furniture. A workbench stacked high with cardboard boxes, a spool of wire, long-handled shears, a hammer, a jumble of wrenches. A pile of stuff that no one had touched, powdered with dust. The windows were murky, the frames buried in cobwebs, the light itself thick with suspended dust.

His eyes moved across the mess, and then were caught by something behind a pile. Something yellow. He picked his way through the piles toward it.

It leaned against the garage wall, an old hose coiled over the seat. The tires were deflated, and a rusty chain had fallen off the sprocket and hung limp on the shaft. A thick rime of dust covered the seat. It amazed him that it could have shrunk that way. He stood for a moment, then he turned and picked his way back outside again, left the garage, recovered his pack, and set out. He could walk forever with a pack.

On his face as he headed out to the road was neither sadness, nor disappointment, nor anger, nor joy. His was the expression of a man thinking. Planning.

As he walked north, he drifted again to a different memory: a recent one. He was recalling a black night, dark as pitch, just a few dozen hours after the curtain fell for him in Afghanistan, when the stars were hiding, and Fowler and Billy Hall Jr. had watch, and Roy Murphy lay in his bunk listening to snores, trying to contain the rage.

Lying in that bunk in the darkness, the plan had come to him— the track into the village, the location of the house, the layout inside. He considered the clatter and weight and noise and smell of an M4, and the advertisements it would leave—cartridges, bullets. There were other ways, as the captain had showed him. He thought about the first rule of the squad. They would never leave one of their own out there, they would always come and get him, and that gave him pause, putting them all at risk like that. And then he remembered the captain. Two guys were more noise than one, more talk than one, more risk than one. More memory than one.

When he could lie still no more, Roy Murphy left the hooch. Finding Fowler at North Side Sally, he said, "I'll take watch for you."

"I'm fine wit it, Murphy."

"Can't sleep. I'm wide awake. I'll get it."

"Where's your IBA, dude?"

"Don't worry about it."

"All right, man," said Fowler, "if you want it so bad." He headed off to bed.

Three minutes later Roy Murphy materialized from the darkness and hovered next to Billy Hall Jr. at Main Sally. Hall had not heard him coming.

"Jesus *Christ*, Murphy, don't do that shit!"

"Be cool, Billy."

"Sneaking up on people like that. What you doing out here?"

"I got Fowler's watch for him. Couldn't sleep."

Billy Hall Jr. worked that around his head for a moment, then said, "Well, don't you gotta get your post, then?"

"Yeah—Billy, lemme see that Ka-Bar."

"What for?"

"Slow night. Thought I'd carve some soap."

"Some . . . *soap*?"

"Yeah. Some soap, man."

"Carve some soap. The fuck you talking about, Murphy?" Uneasily, Hall handed it to him.

"Billy, do me a favor, man. Take a few walks around the perimeter tonight. I've got a bad gut. Might have to be in the burnshitter now and then. Just take a look once in a while, make sure nothin's up on North Side. Okay?"

"Murphy," said Billy Hall Jr. uneasily, "could be I misread the manual on this, but I don't believe we *got* soap up here at Firebase Burnshitter, now do we?"

"Bad gut. Remember that." Roy Murphy raised a single finger to his lips and left Hall and disappeared into the darkness. In a minute he was outside the wire and into the night and gone down the mountainside.

That is where the memory stopped. For years after, when so many other memories returned to vex his sleep, this one did not. So many things happened in Afghanistan at random, or unjustly, or stupidly; so many times an event came down like a heat-seeking missile from a clear blue sky, without purpose, as though God were stumbling drunk in Heaven, and firecrackers fell from His pockets. Those other events would become mainstays of memory, they would plague him. But not the memory of that night. The exchange he made was as just to him as it was ruthless. And so the details left and did not return. He felt no remorse.

Marv Hubbard spotted the soldier around lunchtime, along Route 7 where it leaves the town center and begins to climb north toward the Park. But the soldier did not go as far as the Park. He turned in to the drive of Torruella Ford.

Krissy, the receptionist, saw him coming up from the road. Most customers sort of wander into the showroom after poking around in the lot for a while. And no customer ever turns up on foot. But he walked fast up the drive and into the showroom and dropped his pack and said to her, "I need a truck."

Like, *now*.

"We can do that." With the quick eye and false smile of the hungry salesman, Aaron Mutner had seen him, too, marching into the drive. Mutner was at Krissy's reception desk with his hand extended. "I'm Aaron. It's nice to meet you, uh, Mr. . . ." Roy Murphy glanced at him, not filling in the name. He returned the handshake perfunctorily.

"Sir, if I can ask, are you, are you back from . . . ?"

"An F-two-fifty diesel. One owner preferably. Under eighty thousand miles. An oh-five or later. You got one?"

Aaron withdrew his hand. "We can do that, might be

eighty-five or so, but I know the truck, and it's a beauty. And I'd like to just say, sir, that we appreciate, everybody here at Torruella Ford appreciates what—"

"An oh-five or later. With the new grille and suspension. And no rust—"

"—you're doing for America." Aaron Mutner petered out.

The soldier's eyes narrowed, and there was just a flicker at the corner of his mouth. He looked at Mutner. "That who it was for?"

Aaron reddened, didn't know what to say. Other salesmen had now sidled over to Krissy's desk to get a look at the returning vet, still not recognizing him.

"Need to get it registered today," Roy added.

"Well," said Aaron, glancing at his watch. "We can definitely try, but you know, for sure on Mon——"

"Not interested in Monday."

"Okay," said Aaron.

"Get your runner ready to go up to Bennington today."

"I can do that. For sure."

"Don't show me nothing that's been in an accident. And I want good tires."

One of the mechanics had come in from the bays and was watching this. "Roy?" he called out.

Roy Murphy turned and nodded. "Darrell," he said. He turned back to the salesman. "Today."

"Roy, welcome back, man," said Darrell.

And now Aaron Mutner recognized him. This guy was *Roy Murphy*, the scary kid from the Park who used to get in trouble all the time and was sent to Juvie *on account of being in an actual gun-fight*, and then went out with a Herrick girl the summer after high school. People talked about it all over Hoosick Bridge—how he went with Charlie Herrick's older sister—the beautiful one.

Aaron had been a rising sophomore at Taconic Regional then, working that summer at the movie theater in Bennington, and in those days Emma Herrick and Roy Murphy were supernatural beings to him. Murphy's mystique grew with the years, for he had gone off to the wars (to Iraq, Afghanistan, one of them). And then people thought he must have been killed, or had something horrible happen, because no one had ever heard from him again. Roy Murphy, who went out with Charlie Herrick's older sister Emma, and then fell off the face of the earth, now was standing before Aaron Mutner, in Torruella Ford.

And wanting his truck *now*, not Monday.

Aaron wondered, Is it possible that Roy remembers *me*—from high school? That he remembers the night during the summer of '04 when he appeared in the lobby of the AMC Theatre with Emma Herrick (she wearing a brilliant white T-shirt and short-shorts and flip-flops, tanned and with her blond hair in a clip; he in baggy jeans, a blue flannel shirt, his hair cut short—a dark, unsmiling, frightening figure)? Does he remember that the two of them stood across the refreshment counter, the princess and the outlaw, transacting business with him, Aaron Mutner, and that Aaron handed Roy Murphy a popcorn, a medium Diet Coke, and a bottled water? That she smiled and said, "Thank you"—to him, to Aaron Mutner? (Roy Murphy said nothing, of course—left crumpled bills on the glass counter and didn't wait for change.)

Of course he would not remember a moment like that, a trifle. They were celebrities in Hoosick Bridge, and Aaron was then a faceless peasant, a rising sophomore with bad acne, wearing an AMC uniform while handing out snacks to the movie crowd. But the moment was stamped on his memory. Beautiful Emma Herrick, eldest daughter of the first family in town, with the delinquent from the Park, parting the throng in the AMC lobby like it was the Red Sea and they were Moses and his date, and the eye of every ticket taker, candy seller, and moviegoer on them. They moved through the funnel of the velvet ropes, and then turned to the right, away from the horde of kids all shambling left for Cinema 1, the big stadium screen. He even remembered what was playing that night (*Spider-Man 2*), and how he watched Emma Herrick and Roy Murphy go down the corridor the other way, to the right, Roy balancing the popcorn and the soda, and

Emma having slipped her finger over the hem of his pocket.
They moved away from the crowd, toward Cinema 3, the small
screen at the back, to sit apart with the two dozen white heads,
retirees, professors, and oddball liberals who had come to see
*Fahrenheit 9/11*.

But of course Roy Murphy would have forgotten that, if he
ever knew it at all, Aaron thought, as he led him across the lot to
show him the red '05.

The soap was scrawled across the windshield: $18,999. Roy
opened the hood and leaned up over the grille, and with his head
down said it had better have a new alternator belt, which they
could put in while we waited for the runner to come back from
the registry. And Aaron said they could talk about that for sure.
Roy Murphy unclipped the top of the brake fluid reservoir and
then reclipped it. He rubbed powder from the battery points.
"Original?" he asked.

"I can check on that for you, sir." (He thought of saying, "Roy,"
or "Mr. Murphy," but then shrank from that familiarity.)

"Okay, check. And bring me back a hammer."

"A hammer?"

"A hammer." He climbed into the cab as Aaron scurried back
toward the shop.

"Not sure about that battery," Aaron said a moment later, a
little winded. He handed him a hammer. "Didn't see anything in
the paperwork." Now there were faces in the showroom window,
watching. Roy Murphy took the hammer and shimmied under-
neath the truck, while Aaron squatted uneasily in his sports jacket
and tie and tried to direct small talk that way. "Sure is good to
have you out and safe and back home, sure is good," he said.

Ping.

"What you figure to be doing now? I'll bet you'll take a nice
vacation. You've sure earned it. Maybe do some fishing or something. That's what I'd do if I were coming back from, from . . . you
know. And this is a great truck for pretty much, you know, going
wherever a guy might . . ."

Ping, ping, ping—BANG.

"might want to get away to. Where you going to be living, if I can ask?"

Roy Murphy slid back out. "You'll be replacing that muffler, right?"

"Well," said Aaron, "that's definitely something we could talk about."

"And get her registered today?"

"We'll sure do our best on that."

"No doing your best on that about it. You going to do it?"

"Yes, sir. You know, we could take her for a test drive, if you like."

"Don't need a test drive," he said.

He tucked back under the truck. Then he shimmied out again and said he wanted it up on the lift after all. So Aaron drove it into the bay and put it on the lift, but first Roy Murphy himself clipped a power drill to a compressor hose and loosened each of the lug nuts. No one stopped him. They put the truck up for him, and he took off the wheels, one by one, and said it needed new shoes all around, and Aaron said yes, they could sure talk about taking care of that. And then he was inspecting the steering mechanism, he was checking the transmission fluid, he had the car back down and the hose on the tailpipe as Darrell gunned the engine and he ran his hands around the cylinder head and asked Aaron whether they'd had any trouble with the compression. Aaron, looking like the victim of gastric distress, said there was nothing in the paperwork.

Finally, when he was done, Roy said, "I'll take it."

Aaron let out a big breath. "Great. Good! Let's go into my office," and Roy Murphy followed him back into the showroom, but he would not go into Aaron Mutner's "office," which was a desk on the side of the showroom with a little half partition running out from the wall. Roy Murphy remained at the main desk, where Krissy, the receptionist, was sitting, her eyes darting back and forth between him and Aaron Mutner, until the salesman came out and asked, "Why don't we go back and sit down where we can talk?"

Roy Murphy said, "We can talk here."

"Well, financing, what you want to put down, what you'd like us to finance, all the figures and paperwork and those type things. It'll be easier in—"

"It's fine here," said Roy Murphy. "Thirteen for the truck, with new shoes, alternator belt, and muffler. Don't need financing."

And Aaron Mutner looked crestfallen and said he was genuinely sorry, sir, if there was a misunderstanding, but the price was $18,999 like it said on the windshield and they could let him have it for eighteen five, and maybe even a hair under that, but it was a good truck with a powerful six-liter engine and that new grille and front suspension, and you saw yourself the excellent condition of that interior and of the body. Sure he didn't want to talk about financing? They had some good packages, real attractive low-money-down packages. We could sit down at his desk and work through the paperwork, and besides they needed to do the Patriot Act forms.

"Patriot Act forms?"

"Yeah, you know, you need two forms of ID and there's some paperwork on it."

"Forms to prove I'm a patriot?"

"Sir, I don't make the rules, I just—"

"Does someone think I'm not a patriot?"

Aaron said very quietly he was sorry, it was a stupid rule and he was sure they could take care of it somehow.

Roy Murphy said he would have the truck and he would pay thirteen five for it with new brake shoes, alternator belt, and muffler, which they could put in next week. He would pay cash. But they had to have it registered today.

"I just don't know," said Aaron Mutner.

"You know Christopher's, though," the soldier said.

"Christopher's Ford, down in Pittsfield? Sure," he said, uneasily.

"They have an oh-five. Seventy-two thousand miles. It's green. I like green better. If I got to pay all this money and not have my truck today, I'll get the color I like."

Aaron Mutner tried to slide off to the office so that he could commence the little shuttle dance with the invisible manager, in which he would disappear, and then return, having worked over that manager on the customer's behalf to the tune of another hundred dollars off the price. Roy Murphy shook his head. He would not sit down in an office or go into the back. They didn't have time for that. If they were going to haggle with a returning vet, they would have to do it right here where everyone could see and hear. And fast.

The excitement they had felt around the dealership when this young vet apparently fresh from the battlefield came into the showroom had changed to embarrassment when he half took apart the truck, and was now complete discomfort.

Then Roy Murphy pulled out the envelope—that big, fat white brick. He counted out one hundred and forty crisp bills, which he had cashed upon withdrawal of five years' pay from the Army. It took a couple of minutes for him to do this, and they all stood by, watching. He placed the pile of bills on the counter. No one in the dealership had ever seen anything quite like this.

He said, "Fourteen thousand dollars cash, with the new brake shoes and other things I said. The truck sold and registered today, the fixes later. I'll wait for the registration. You'll need to get going."

Roy Murphy went over to the urn and poured coffee into a white Styrofoam cup, and then he sat down on his pack. If being in the Army teaches a man anything, it teaches him how to wait. When it was time to wait, he could wait for the next geological age. Or for the few hours until the runner was back with the plates.

# THREE

*T*he music cast its lure into the summer night, teasing them out of their houses to the porches, out to the lawns, out to the grassy shoulder of Washington Street itself. They looked up the hill, where the music was playing. Many of them had seen the big van up from Pittsfield the day before, and late that afternoon they noticed all the cars. Some walked a little way up the avenue, until they could see better. The few from Hoosick Bridge who had been invited were already there.

The night was humid and moonless, warm and suggestive. Stars winked between the clouds. On Spring Street, the streetlights reflected off a file of cars extending past the bend in the road, cars with exotic license plates; not just Vermont, Massachusetts, Connecticut, and New York, but here and there Colorado, California, Florida, Delaware, Oregon, the District of Columbia, Texas. It was clear, as Jane Herrick had wanted it to be, that people from far away—important people—had come to the Heights. That such people of quality still came to this house.

Nearer to the house were the guests: handsome young men in chinos and madras shirts jogged up the porch steps, here and there one in a khaki suit. Slim-legged women in polo tops and

Bermuda shorts strolled the lawn, tanned and lovely, laughing as they greeted one another. Behind the house, the twin white tent peaks gleamed in the night, and the buzz and burble of loud conversation, of laughter and occasional applause, floated up between the sets of band music.

The idea of a celebration at the Heights had divided the town. Some said that Jane and the girls had been through enough. Let them be. But there were sour neighbors, too, pinch-faced townspeople with long memories, to demand, "Where did the money for that party come from?" More than a few of them called the lawyer Ernest Holt, who made careful notes.

What the professor might have given for an invitation! He had retired to Hoosick Bridge after 2004—too late to have known the family—and could not simply crash the party, of course, but neither could he keep himself entirely away. It was about 9:30 when he left his house for a walk, and went along Woodford Road, catching the music as he made the turn to Washington. It grew louder as he walked up the hill to Spring. He saw the guests on and around the porch and in the yard, and fondly remembered summer parties like this at the college. He walked slowly, glancing occasionally back over his shoulder at the house, until he reached, in the long file of cars, a truck, and felt a sudden shock. For inside he had seen the dark, confusing figure of a young man tossing in the driver's seat, asleep but agitated, rocking. A US Army pack was on the passenger seat beside him.

My goodness, thought the professor, as he hurried away—*he's here!*

Weeks earlier, when news of the engagement party went around Hoosick Bridge, the professor had begun pressing Toni for details. Was Emma Herrick marrying the boy who went off to the service?

"No, no, he's from college. They say he's very nice. I haven't met him myself."

And so they reprised Herrick family history over muffins and cups of coffee, describing the very different ways the girls had responded to the family's misfortune. The youngest daughter, Charlie, had taken flight. She'd been too young fully to have known what it had been like to be the first family in town. That ended just as she came into Taconic Regional, and she took refuge in being Charlie, rather than a Herrick. She became one of those kids who all but live at friends' houses, always there on weekends and half the school nights, too, with clothes hanging in their closets, going off on vacation with other families, the ones who took pity. She was at college now, and though she was only up at the university in Burlington, not so very far away, she was the daughter seen least often at the Heights.

"And the middle one?"

"Anne is a totally different girl," Toni explained. "She tried to be the glue. It made her so sad—she wanted to preserve the past. She thought that if she could only keep everyone happy in the moment, if she could only soothe them enough, so that they wouldn't argue, wouldn't dwell, things might be like they were before. She was a hardworking girl, quiet, made very good grades in school. Not social like Charlie, not outgoing in that way. And without that quality that Emma had. These days, she's the one you see most often up here. Nicest girl you'd ever want to meet, Anne Herrick."

"Quality? What was Emma's *quality*—tell me?" The professor arched his wild eyebrows. It was the oldest daughter he was most interested in—Emma they were all most interested in.

"She's the hardest to explain. Mel, how would you describe her?"

"Emma Herrick? Beautiful girl."

"Personality wise, I mean."

Mel frowned, searching for the phrase. "How would you describe any of them, and what went on? Like her father, maybe. You were kind of in awe of each of them."

Toni nodded. "Tom Herrick was a *handsome* man."

"He had that—what would you say? People wanted to be around him."

Toni smiled. "I know plenty of women who did. Which explains, you know . . ."

"Charismatics?" the professor interrupted.

Mel answered, "That makes it sound creepy, which wasn't the way of it. It was just that a person was attracted to be around them, you know? Emma has that from her father. But she was also just, just determined to put him behind her, after it all happened, that's how a lot of people saw it, anyway. So she went hard after a career. The steel is from Jane's side."

And what about the boy? the professor wanted to know. That summer, Emma Herrick went with a boy from the Park. What was his name?

"Roy," she answered. "Roy Murphy."

"That's the one," Mel said, "the one in that shooting. I never understood that, to be honest with you. But then, none of us saw it coming. Beautiful girl, family like that . . ." Mel closed his eyes and sighed.

"Tell me about the boy Roy Murphy," the professor said.

Toni tried to describe him, tried to describe what happened. "Everyone was shocked they went together, because she hadn't been a wild girl or anything. It wasn't what you expected. I guess there's a little teenage rebellion in every kid. That's what they put it down to."

"But what was he *like*—this Roy?"

And Toni struggled to get that right, for in his way the boy was as enigmatic as Emma had been. "In trouble a lot, reform school, is that what they call it now? Juvenile detention? Something serious that happened up at the Park, anyway, like Mel said. He was quiet, a loner. Lots of people were scared of him and said he was trouble. But I remember Vic DiBello used to say, after Roy was sent away, what a shame it was, that the kid had worked at his company summers, and he was a hard worker, very reliable.

"He went with Emma that one summer, after high school, and then joined the Army and I never heard what happened to him. Anyways, that's all history now, Professor. Emma's going to get married. A nice boy from college."

And that's when Toni said it—as the professor would later teasingly remind her. ("Did I actually *say* that?" "You did—your very words!" "You're making it up!" "My dear Toni, you stood right there at the counter, and said, 'I don't suppose Roy Murphy will be at the engagement party'!")

Three blocks north on Main, sandwiched behind a New York and in front of a Delaware plate, the red F-250 diesel was parked, its windows rolled down to the night.

Half a pizza was cold in a box on the passenger floor. Next to it, three warm bottles and three empties filled a Budweiser six-pack. Roy Murphy was dressed in his fatigue bottoms, a brown T-shirt, and his tan desert boots. His head lay back between the headrest and the door. He'd dropped into a dead sleep.

The pack on the passenger seat held most of what, besides the truck itself, he still owned. Uniforms, civilian clothes, a thermal fleece, a sleeping bag and pad, a first aid kit, a water bottle, a shaving kit, a flashlight, a manual, an envelope with discharge papers, another with the money, foul weather gear, gloves, a knit cap, sneakers, flip-flops, two towels, a mess kit, a white cardboard box containing a red, white, and blue ribbon, from which hung a star. Also in the pack were two books, each with an inscription he knew by heart.

On the title page of *The Collected Poems of Wilfred Owen*, C. Day-Lewis, ed., 1965, the sharp black scrawl read, "For Specialist R. Murphy, Dulce et decorum est pro amicis mori. With respect, I. D. Dickinson, Capt., US Army."

In the second one Roy Murphy had put a bookmark to keep his place. It was laborious going for him, full of tedious accounts of hand-to-hand combat between warriors with difficult names. Each day he read one hundred lines nevertheless, struggling, his lips moving over the unfamiliar words. Sometimes the words swam on the page, until he remembered what the captain had taught him, and slowed himself down.

It was a war story. At the center of the story was a warrior who had been dishonored. They had taken his woman. The book was called *The Iliad*. The first words were "Sing, Muse, the wrath of Achilles."

He knew its inscription by heart, too, and always turned to that first, running his finger across the words the captain, with eerie prescience, had scratched out under the illumination of a lantern on his small table at Firebase Montana. Then he would leaf ahead to the day's hundred lines. The captain had written,

*The greatest soldier in history had a harp in his tent. Remember always Afghanistan. (Read aloud.)*
*—I. D. Dickinson, Capt., US Army.*

*Remember always Afghanistan.* The sounds and sights of Afghanistan were so present with him now that *remember* was a word unequal to that presence: water to its wine. He saw and smelled and heard and tasted Afghanistan every day.

Also resting in Roy Murphy's pack, next to the two books, was his nine-millimeter Beretta M9 pistol, with holster, belt, and two fifteen-round magazines, and the special operations bayonet, in its black nylon sheath, that he'd borrowed one night on watch from Billy Hall Jr.

The soldier's memories were like other companions of the day; awake, he could admit or bar them from his door as he chose. But he could not police his own sleep. Sleep was treacherous. In the guise of a dream, the one memory that he barred came creeping and sidling upon him. It shook him physically so that he rocked in the truck, so that he made vague, involuntary sounds of distress, until he gasped and was awake again.

For a moment the old panic washed over him. The rasp of his breathing filled the cabin. He turned sharply to look behind him but saw nothing except the row of cars in the dark.

*The memory again.*

He told himself what he always told himself. The memory is

history and I know history and because I know history I am not condemned to repeat it. His breathing slowed. He blinked, bringing himself back to where he was. His watch read, "22:39, 10 July." He settled back in the seat to think. As he calmed himself, his focus returned.

Whenever they planned an op at the firebase, there was always, at first, a deep fear, to which no one would confess. You were going out there where seventeen things would go wrong, and it would be the smallest, the most trivial, that would kill you. It would not be a coordinated attack from a dozen Taliban troops—it would be the bleat of a goat. Or an NVG battery would fail or a clip would jam. But as the plan emerged, as it was broken down to its smallest, most mundane parts, a calm would settle in. It was that way when they planned the ambush; that way the night he lay awake in Second Squad's hooch and made his own plan to slip out beyond the wire alone. At first a man always thought, I do not want to do this. No one would want to do this. But with its increments and fine detail, the plan would settle the mind. That which he had feared at first, he could come to embrace.

His breathing settled to normal, and he thought, I should be in uniform. He pulled his T-shirt off and rifled through the pack for a uniform top. His torso was muscled and still combat lean, hard, dangerous. He pulled the shirt over his head, buttoned it deliberately. He tightened the laces in his boots. Dressed, he squinted through the windshield and along the sidewalk. No one was passing by toward the house now, and because the party had not yet crested, no one was leaving. The music cascaded merrily through the night air.

Specialist Roy Murphy, of First Platoon, Battle Company, 240th Airborne, pulled the last thing from the pack and held it in his lap. He touched the cool metal with his fingertips. He took a deep breath, and then another, calming himself. Then he restrapped the pack, opened the truck's door, hopped lightly to the street, and was hurrying with that quick step he'd always had—as though he meant to beat his own self there.

# PART TWO
## *Emma*

# FOUR

May 2004

O n a hot spring night, just after 10:30 p.m.—long after
    Emma and Brian and Maggie and everyone else in the class
had arrived—came the surprise video salute from their very own
class president. Suddenly the face of Emerson Rodriguez, whom
none of them had seen since February, was grinning at them from
a huge screen, and they greeted him with an earsplitting cheer.
They had to replay his message, since the cheers overwhelmed it
the first time through, and when it finished, some of them were
wiping tears away, but laughing, too, for he'd set them free from
the funk—half sadness, half embarrassment—that had dogged
them since the bitter morning when he'd suddenly disappeared,
when their class president was suddenly transformed into a de-
portee. The music fired up again, and the party would rocket to
a new level, fueled by sweat and by the gin and vodka kids were
sneaking in soda bottles through the back door.

Emerson's virtual appearance had lanced the class's gloom.
*This is our prom—we have a right to enjoy it!* When he said, "TacReg
Oh-Fourever!" they yelled, and when he said, "Imma come back, I
be seeing you guys!" they screamed and cheered louder. When he
said, "Don't nobody drink or dance or hook up or nothing, cause

the President watchin' you!" they roared, "Pres-i-dent, Em-er-son!" And when he said, "I love you guys, all right?" every girl was crying, and half the guys, too.

It was just a minute later that they noticed the young man standing alone at the double doors, and a stir ran over them like a wind across water.

"Who *is* that?"

"Wait—that's Roy *Murphy*!"

"Get out."

"Check it out. It's Roy Murphy come back—look at him!"

Look at him indeed. The long, unkempt dark hair—gone. The Papa Roach T-shirt, the baggy jeans, the chain loop from the pocket, the oil-stained boots, the greasy jacket frayed at the cuffs—all gone. His hair was cut short. Not buzz cut, or mul-leted, or gelled, or spiked. Just short, neatly clipped, parted and brushed. He wore a jet-black tuxedo and a gleaming white shirt. Not a gag tux, not a zoot suit with a purple cummerbund or a pink vest rented from Mr. Tux, as some of the guys wore. It was *real*—with the silk stripe on the trousers, the patent leather shoes, and a narrow lapel on the jacket, a small black tie in a subtle bow around a starched collar, and three studs on the stiff shirtfront. He had found it on Craigslist and bought it from a Williams College undergraduate. There was no sense of discomfort about him—you would not have guessed that this was the first and only night in his life that he would wear a tuxedo. He was forbidding, but in a new way. He didn't look like a kid in a costume. He looked like a groom.

He was scanning the room, and people began to wonder, Did he get here in time for the video? Maybe he didn't see it. People were saying, He's been off in Juvie since, when was it, November? Nobody's even seen him in months and months—does he even know what happened to Emerson? *Maybe he's looking for him.*

But Emma knew whom he was looking for. In her belly she felt the same jolt she'd felt five years before at Bungalow Rock.

She could not remember when she'd last spoken to him. The

events of senior year had brought him to mind, reminded her of
Roy Murphy—and of Emerson, and of herself—as they all had
been during that summer after the seventh grade, and how far
off all of that now seemed. In the days since February, she'd often
brought that summer back to mind, remembering *that* Emerson,
*that* Roy Murphy, that self, as though lingering over a box of old
dolls discovered by accident in a cupboard—quaint dolls that are
too small, that seem to have aged too quickly, so that their painted
youth is eerie, and you want to put them away. And through the
final spring of high school, when both boys were gone, Roy had
disappeared from her consciousness, as surely as he had from the
town.

And now he was back.

Kids were asking, "What's he doing here?" And: "He's not
going to graduate—is he?"

Still he stood by the door, searching the room. And every one
of them, including Emma herself, had in mind the word *gun*—the
silvery image of a gun gleaming at night. Because he had used one.
Not hunting, as so many kids had with fathers and uncles—not
just clowning around in pickups with someone's shotgun, shooting at road signs on joyrides. He had fired a pistol, four times in
deadly circumstances, and gone to Juvie for it, and now had materialized from thin air at their prom. That was the first thing they
thought of.

Emma was on the dance floor with her date, Brian Hampton.
(Earlier that evening, tall, earnest, bashful Brian had arrived at the
Heights in the Hampton family Volvo precisely on time, as always,
with a corsage and a camera for photographs. He was welcomed
by Jane Herrick, and as always fell to talking with her excitedly.)
Emma was swiveling, peering around Brian's shoulder to watch.
*How did he get here? Why did he come? Who came with him?*

"Murph!" someone called out.

Darrell Demetrios, a happy-go-lucky stoner wearing a long,
skinny tie, was now with him. Soon a few more kids from the Park
encircled Roy Murphy, commenting on his tux, probably. Roy

Murphy did not appear to say anything to them. Maybe shook a hand. But he was searching the room, searching, until . . .

*Turn away, dance with Brian*, she thought. But there was no turning from him. He was coming by the line of latitude that he always took toward her. It was exactly like the very first time they'd spoken—an exact repeat. Popular, confident Emma, the star of the class, the top student going off to college in the fall, felt again a panic. And then he was right next to them.

Brian was too tall for himself in those days, skinny and self-conscious, with a smooth cheek that flushed quickly. "Hey," he offered.

Roy took no notice of him. "Dance with me?" He didn't mean Brian. It was somewhere between a question and an order.

Her breath was in her throat as she nodded.

Sheepish, a little frightened, Brian choked out, "Sure, Roy—sure." And stepped away. Brian had never spoken to Roy Murphy before. He never would again.

"I remember that color," he told her.

He meant her dress, which was why the remark confused her at first. It was a new dress, lemon yellow, backless, stunning, bought for this occasion at Jane Herrick's insistence, a purchase kept secret from Tom Herrick because of the economies that had come over the house that year. One afternoon the two of them had snuck off to Manchester to buy it. It had never been off the hanger except in front of her mirror. So how could he remember the dress?

"When I met you," he explained.

She struggled for a moment longer, until it came back to her—the yellow bicycle.

"The Trek?"

"I remember things," he said.

He made no move to dance with her. His hands were at his sides. They stood at the center of the dance floor in the darkened, thumping hall. He was content to look at her, to do only that, as though to fix her in his memory. Emma was not yet the stunning woman she would be at twenty-one, but she was becoming that woman. Her eyes were vividly blue, but there was something oddly foreign about them, the suggestion of an almond shape—prone to disappear, when she smiled, behind a puff of cheeks. Her jaw was strong, like her mother's—it thrust her smile forward. Her hair, usually parted on the side and clipped in little-girl fashion, had been restyled and swept back in a way that said the slim and fetching Herrick girl, the blond and beautiful Emma Herrick had grown up. That night, in the yellow dress, she was a siren.

But she had no command around him that night. When her eyes met his, she felt again that old jolt, and so she looked away. She did not know what to do, or where to look, or what to say—unusual for her—so she fell back to class secretary manner. The class secretary could bestow courtesy on all members of the class, even Roy Murphy. "Roy, I didn't even recognize you! You look so great—in that tux! Did you see Emerson's video?"

"I missed it."

"But you know about . . ."

"Of course I know."

The music pounded off into a new song, and all around them their classmates were dancing, but watching. Still the pair only stood, their hands at their sides, his eyes locked on her, and Emma smiling but avoiding his eyes. Around them, at the fringes, everyone watched. Or whispered, "Dude, it's Roy Murphy—with . . . *Emma!*" It looked to them like a confrontation. Like some important exchange was happening here, now, at prom, between these two people.

"The tux, and your hair! I didn't recognize you at all with your hair cut like that!" Chatter was her usual defense against the unknown, but chatter was impotent against his intent stare.

Brian hovered at the closest edge of the room, watching.

Roy Murphy leaned in to be heard. "I think the Army'll cut it more."

"The *Army?*"

Then she was following him across the floor to the far corner.

Following dutifully and thinking, I followed him from Pine Cobble School in the fifth grade. I went down to the Hoosic in the seventh grade hoping he might be there. Why on my prom night am I still following him?

As they walked to the far end of the room, she turned, shrugged helplessly at Brian. He shrugged back. She followed Roy Murphy to the corner anyway. She was a little frightened, a little embarrassed, but something else altogether was happening, a switch was flipping. A key was turning and tumblers were falling. Emma Herrick, in that moment, had entered a detached present, an unmapped frontier, a wild place. It was a territory without law or consequence. Anything might be possible in such a place.

"What are they *talking* about?" Maggie Byrne demanded of Alicia Flannery, as both looked on. Maggie had known Emma since kindergarten. She had a dark and sinking feeling, watching that corner.

Now and then Brian would start to move in, approaching, hovering, falling back from the invisible but impermeable bubble that surrounded them. At one point she turned his way and mouthed, "A *minute*, Brian." She was inconsiderate to her own date—Emma Herrick, who was never inconsiderate to anyone except her parents. They were in that corner, the two of them, for the longest time.

And then they were gone.

She lay in the front bedroom on the third floor at One Spring Street, the dormered room with the faded wallpaper print gravid with lilac blooms, and the old white writing desk in the bay window, too small for use, now given over to perfumes, lotions, framed photographs of friends and sisters. The desk had been her mother's, and before that her grandmother's, and before that even Jane didn't know, and now it was Emma's. A wind had come up, and in the bay the gauze curtains danced and billowed like ghosts. As she dozed off, a voice in her mind was asking, What if someone saw?

And another voice chided, So what if they did?

She drifted in and out. On a child's bed she tossed, no longer a child. In the frontier of sleep, her old country fell behind her and her destination lay up ahead, a landing not yet visible. And the strange boy was there. They were kids; she followed him down paths through a dark wood, recklessly. They flew through a corridor of billowing white gauze; they flew by her father, whose face was blank, and her mother, who shouted something she could not hear. And then they were not children; he had grown, and only his eyes were like a child's, and he was asking her a question that she could not hear. In her wild dreams, a voice was speaking. Was it his voice, was it hers?

Yes, it said. Absolutely yes, of course yes, absolutely now, yes now, not later, not maybe, not soon, not a minute to waste—*now*.

"Em?"

A moment to take bearings as she woke again. It was dark outside. From the end of her bed, in her old, familiar bedroom with its too-small little-girl desk and too-small bed, Maggie's earnest face swam into view. And behind her, Anne. It was her old life again.

Softly, "Hi, Mags. Anne."

"Ohmy*God* Emma! What *happened* last night?" Maggie blurted.

The curtains hung limply now. Through the open window, she could hear night sounds coming up from below: Charlie's voice floating from the porch, the clink-clink of metal tags as someone walked a dog past the house.

She sat up on the bed. "Did you and Seth have a good time?"

"It was fine. Emma, don't change the subject."

"I'm thirsty."

"I'll get you some water," Anne said. She hurried downstairs, and in a minute returned with a glass. "You didn't answer one message!" Maggie was saying.

Anne came up to the pillow and handed her the glass. "There's sand all over your pillow, Em," she said.

"We went to the beach. Do you think he's handsome?"

"I think he's *psycho*," Maggie cut in.

"What beach?" Anne asked, gently.

"I'm not actually sure."

"Lake Dunmore?"

"No, the ocean. Connecticut, I think. Maybe it was Rhode Island."

Maggie leapt in again. "The ocean? That's like four hours . . . ?"

"It was late. Or early. Watch Hill. Is that Rhode Island?"

"Or five hours even. How did you . . . ?"

"His motorcycle. God, my butt hurts." Emma laughed softly.

"His *motorcycle*?"

She smiled, remembering how, as they raced south, she'd clung to his chest, yet thrown back her head, amazed at the brilliance of the stars above them.

Anne sat on the end of the bed, picking at the embroidery on the old cotton bedspread. Maggie stood behind her, regarding Emma in the manner of a concerned physician. "Did he have the gun?"

She laughed out loud. "No he did not have the gun!"

"Emma, he was in Juvie—he tried to kill somebody! He's a stoner psycho dropout from the Park!"

"He's not a stoner, Mags, he's an old friend. And he didn't try to kill anybody." She said the last without conviction, because in truth she had no idea.

"He's an *old friend*?"

Questions tumbled from Maggie in a jumble of horror and curiosity and envy. Was it really just the two of them? What was his motorcycle like? Was it cold? Where did they sleep? And what did she mean, "old friend"—*when* was she friends with Roy Murphy from the Park? Anne listened quietly, with a half smile, for she remembered that summer.

"This is the craziest thing you ever did in your entire life and I'm not even kidding! He's a total Park thug with an IQ of—"

"Maggie, no! Don't be such a snob. It was natural to be with him."

"Oh, Em, stop. You're going to bring him down to Yale to meet your new roommates in September? That will be natural? You totally humiliated Brian," she added.

Emma knew it; she'd known it while she was doing it. She stole a guilty glance at Anne, who frowned, looking intently at the bedcover. Emma liked Brian, but it *was* sad, but Brian was inevitably part of the past now.

Maggie's cross-examination continued: "Your mom said you didn't get back until dinnertime?"

"Mom was so freaked out," Anne said. "She was calling Mrs. Byrne, Mrs. Galloway, Brian was here, and . . ."

"Brian was *over* here? Oh, God." Emma lay back. "Maybe he should go out with *Mom*, he'd be happier. I couldn't really call. We slept on the beach, until the police came."

"Police?"

"Then we moved up the beach and slept some more. And then, I don't know, was it lunchtime? We were starving. He still had on his tux shirt, and I was in my dress. God, that dress is *totally* ruined." She laughed, looking over toward the yellow heap in the closet.

Maggie paced the room, but Anne still sat at the end of the bedside, in an attitude somewhere between wonder and devotion.

"We went to a sandwich place," Emma said. "In a tux and a gown, and me with sand in my hair." She smiled, remembering how people stared.

"And then?"

"And then he brought me home. He was . . ."

"What?"

In class secretary voice, she said, "He was a gentleman."

"Oh, *stop*."

Emma drifted away again, far from the conversation, summoning back to mind what had happened, wanting to linger over every single thing he'd said and done. They sat on the beach, and as the night cooled she leaned into him. She recalled the pale luminescence of the surf, the soft, regular sound of it coming in against the sand. The smell of salt. The hard feel of his shoulder. How he put the tux jacket around her shoulders but did not reach his arm around her.

"Emma, will you do like you said?" he asked. "Move to New York City?"

"You remember that?"

"With your *doorman*?" They both laughed.

"I remember things," he explained.

How soft-spoken he is, she thought.

"I don't know. We'll see after college, I guess. It's so weird you came tonight."

"Weird?"

"Wonderful, I mean." Her face was against his arm, and she wrapped her hands around his elbow. He was looking out at the water, listening to the waves come in. He said quietly, matter-of-factly, "You're the most beautiful girl I ever saw."

She mumbled some trite, flattered thing that you say to deflect a compliment, and changed the subject. "Roy, was it . . . ?"

"What?"

"When they sent you away . . ."

"Juvie?"

"Yeah. Was it . . . *awful*?"

He was quiet for a moment, and then he said, "It was the second best thing that happened to me so far."

He explained that, while it was a kind of jail, with rules, and locked doors and high fences, and guards, and a lot of busywork, there was a predictability to it. "Everything's a privilege. You put a foot wrong, they take the privilege away. Then you do a thing right, they give it back. A lot of kids acting tough, but you know they're scared. The thing is, life is clear there. I can go this way, or that way. Right or left—no middle. I can end up like these kids, or not like these kids. I got clear choices, you know? I never felt like I had clear choices before."

The way he'd said "so far"—the best thing that had happened to him *so far*. No, *wait*—"The *second* best thing?"

"It *was* the best thing," he said, "until tonight."

So she was tongue-tied again. And stunned not just by what he'd said to her, but that he already had that kind of perspective. It made her feel small. What was the best thing, or the second best thing that had happened to her *so far*? By comparison a trifle, whatever it was.

She changed the subject again. "But why the *Army*?"

"I didn't exactly get into Yale the last four years. They take anybody in the Army, though."

"You're not just *anybody*."

He turned to her, and put his hands on her shoulders. She felt the size and power of those hands. For the first time in her life, it was thrilling to be helpless. In the darkness, the whites of his eyes were all she could clearly make out of his face. Her breath quickened, for she thought that he might at last kiss her. More than anything she wanted him to kiss her then. But he didn't.

"I know I'm not," he said. "But they don't."

He let go of her and turned back again toward the water, gathering his knees. "And really, you don't, either."

They sat together on the beach until the police came, and then they walked back to the road, and when the two cops left, they returned to the beach and walked for a while, until they found a dune they could lie down behind and out of sight. Before they fell asleep, he said, "Emerson should've been here tonight," meaning not just at the prom, but that he should have been right there with them on the beach, the way it used to be at the river in the summer after the seventh grade.

When she drifted back from her reverie, Maggie had stopped pacing and now stood by her bedside, fixing her with the stern eye of a lifeguard blowing a shrill whistle and pointing until her charge swims back inside the ropes, back to shore from danger.

"Emma," she said, "be *serious*. This was your *prom*."

At seventeen, Maggie Byrne was already a dues-paying member of the conscience of the little community. She knew, if her old friend Emma had momentarily forgotten, that the first family in town had certain obligations. Memories were being created. Proms and prom dates—not to mention your oldest best friend since kindergarten—are not to be trifled with in this self-centered way. *This was your prom*—you only get one.

Anne said nothing. Emma looked over toward her younger sister. Did Anne judge her, too? She was still perched on the end of the bed, fussing with the stitching on the bedcover.

To be fair, Maggie had a point. He *was* a boy from the Park, he *did* on a cold November night with deliberate intent fire four rounds from a Glock 9 mm in close proximity to two different human beings, *one of whom was his own mother*. The police *did* come and arrest him, and he went to Juvie for it.

# FIVE

The Park was the sprawling trailer park on the west side of town, across Route 7. Rows of single-wide trailers and a scattering of double-wides sat up on cinder blocks, sometimes with three or four cars out front, on blocks or bald tires. There were Kawasaki and Suzuki dirt bikes covered in clay soil, and shinier street bikes polished by the young men sitting in front of decrepit trailers. Bicycles lay rusting in the weeds. In the heat of the summer, toddlers with droopy diapers and blackened feet wandered in and out of the patches of weed, and kids went along the dirt tracks of the Park, and sat on the stoops; their sharp ears were tuned to the distant throb of engines—of motorbikes and cars that sometimes brought fathers and brothers for a visit.

Tom Herrick never set foot in the Park in his life. Nor did Jane. Even Emma during that one summer after graduation was never so at ease in the Park that her senses didn't quicken a little when he'd pull off the highway and enter. But Roy Murphy had spent his whole life there.

Leo Murphy had been a rough character: loud, a brawler. Years later, some still remembered him in town, and no one regretted his leaving it, least of all Eliza Murphy, who lived with him and those babies in that small trailer in the years before he left. It was said by some that he'd gone to New York, by others to Florida, by others that he'd gone to prison, and by still others that he had abandoned this family for a new one. The details were unclear. And maybe Eliza was *still* Leo Murphy's wife, although Leo had not been seen in town for many years. Roy Murphy was the last of the three boys living up there.

The precise circumstances of his arrival at the Park so many years before were disputed. Most said he was the last of Eliza Murphy's children, of course. But some, like Francine McGregor, maintained that he was not Eliza's at all, that Leo brought him there as an infant, from somewhere else—that Leo handed a dark and silent infant to her as though he were a bag of groceries: "Here, take this!" Some said she'd been badly beaten for protesting that she already had two unruly toddlers and hardly any money to raise them and no help from him, and she'd be goddamned if she was going to raise a brat from some tramp he'd screwed somewhere, one of his women.

Francine was adamant on this point. "He was Leo's but not hers," she said. "Leo always had that same way about him the boy does—like he'd burst through a wall to get what he wanted. The difference was, Leo scares you with noise, and the boy scares you with quiet."

But this story was disputed by others, who said that Eliza had three kids by Leo, and Roy was the last one. In any event, he lived there and she was referred to as his mother. It was natural to think of her that way. There were comments about the looks of him, but then again, kids don't always look like their parents. Sometimes they come out a little darker. Particularly the Irish: a carrot top like Leo Murphy may have a dark kid—it happens all the time. She was Eliza, and he was Roy; they were both Murphys of some stripe, both members of a family that had gone wrong, and he lived in her trailer and so people naturally assumed.

The oldest boy, Sean, had left (to New Hampshire, people

said), and by 2004 the second, Mike, was more out of the trailer than in. It was mainly just Eliza and Roy living there. She had a boyfriend, Joe Pettibone, who drove a white Toyota pickup with rust at the fenders that needed a muffler and still had only one side mirror from the time, years before, that Roy had vandalized the other one. It was a truck you could hear coming half a mile away. Joe would be gone for a long time and then return to the trailer for a week or so. He worked construction off and on, sometimes doing drywalling, sometimes working with a well contractor. He had had a few brushes with the police and was said to deal drugs.

It was never good between Joe and Roy. Joe Pettibone didn't like the way the boy looked at him, didn't like his silences, and that feeling of being studied by this brooding boy whenever he was trying to relax.

"Don't you got somewhere to be?" he'd once demanded, when Roy was in the sixth grade.

"Don't you?" Roy answered.

In truth, when Joe was around, Roy Murphy liked to be somewhere else. He didn't want to look at either one of them. At night Eliza and Joe would go to the bedroom and leave him alone with the television and the couch. Or if they stayed out in the living room, he'd cross the Park and sleep at Emerson's trailer, where everything except Emerson's room was neat and tidy, and Mrs. Rodriguez might have chiles rellenos cooking or something good to eat. Joe's visits generally ended with a yelling match and sometimes more. There were police up there from time to time, and Eliza Murphy would be seen around town wearing sunglasses, not large enough to cover everything, and sometimes a week would go by when she'd called in sick to the Rite Aid and no one had seen her at all.

Before he left school altogether, Roy Murphy began getting in trouble up at the Park. More than once he was seen in the county building, sitting on the wooden bench outside juvenile court with a piece of paper folded in his hands. Eliza Murphy was sometimes there with him, when she could get off shift. No one ever saw them speaking, and sometimes he sat there alone. In time, the probation office put a sticker on a new file for him. Next to Sean's. And Leo's, which had not been opened in many years. A newer and thinner folder, but with his own name.

It happened two nights after Halloween, just after an early snow-fall, during what nominally was Roy Murphy's senior year in high school. "Nominally" because his attendance was sporadic to begin with, and of course, this incident ended it. At school the next morning they were saying that he had been arrested up at the Park and this time it was serious. *There was a gun.* He had shot a guy in his own trailer. Or outside his trailer, some people said. Or shot *at* a guy. Cops had been up there and they had taken him away, and in every corner of school people were talking about it.

"Did he . . . did he *kill* him?"

"No, he missed him or something, I heard he missed him."

"Why—what happened?"

"I don't know, it was some kind of fight."

"Who was it?"

"This guy Joe Pettibone, a dealer. It was a drug thing, they say, him and Roy Murphy, a drug thing that went wrong."

"Murphy was dealing? Dude, Murphy doesn't even get high!"

"What do you think, man? Up in the Park, what do you think goes on?"

It was a couch night. Mike Murphy was twenty-two that year, and for weeks at a time when he was broke or a girlfriend had thrown him out, he'd come back to his mom's trailer. He in turn would put Roy out of the second bedroom to the living room, where Roy would sleep on the couch. Roy was wearing a sweatshirt and jeans and a pair of wool socks, because it got cold in there at night.

If Roy had been in the second bedroom—if Mike hadn't come home and taken it over—the whole thing probably never would have happened.

They burst into the trailer late and loudly drunk, stumbling against things, against the kitchen counter and even the couch Roy lay on, although he was pretty sure they didn't see him there. Joe's down jacket sailed toward a kitchen chair but missed, and hit the linoleum with a muffled thunk. They stumbled to the back of the double-wide and the door opened and closed and then he heard the bed groan as they hit it, and their laughter.

Roy lay silently on the couch, knowing what was about to happen. She kept one of his pipes in the little end table by the bed. He would fill it and light it and offer it to her. Tomorrow, she would lie near comatose until noon. She would miss work. Joe Pettibone would spend a couple of days on this couch, watching television, until the fridge was cleaned out. Then he'd go.

And then Roy's mind's ear replayed that curious sound, from a few seconds ago, that had not quite fit the circumstance. Thunk. The coat had made the wrong sound when Joe tossed it.

From outside the trailer, on the corner, a streetlight shone through the little window in the kitchenette. Roy looked over at the coat lying on the kitchen floor, and in the faint light saw the handle gleaming dark and suggestive from its open pocket.

From the other direction, the direction of Eliza's room, he smelled it, and heard Joe's murmur, egging her on.

He slipped off the sofa and crouched on the kitchen floor and reached into the pocket. In his hand it was black and sleek and cold and wonderfully heavy. He had used a shotgun before and a hunting rifle. He and Emerson had sometimes gone out in a pickup shooting at signs and mailboxes at night. He had personally filled the sign at the state line with holes roughly making out a *T,* while Emerson had made a mess of the *R.* But he had never before held a pistol.

He fingered the trigger and sighted down the short barrel at the stove. He disengaged the catch and slid out the clip. Through the pinholes the brass backs of the bullets shone in the half-light. The magazine clicked when he slid it back in. He flipped the toggle on the side of the stock.

In the bedroom Joe laughed, a hacking sound, like a crow might make.

The sound was a kind of ignition for him. All those years Roy Murphy had listened, helpless, to that complacent cawing, hated it, and been powerless against it. He looked down at the gun in his hand. And then Joe laughed again.

Later he couldn't remember how it happened, exactly, that he had walked deliberately to the back of the trailer and opened the bedroom door. They were both naked to the waist, and her ribbed chest cage, her arms blotchy and blue, and her wasted breasts all showed ghastly in the overhead light. Lizard-like, Joe hunched over her, curled over that pipe, his skinny back white as a perch belly.

As the door opened, she screamed and pulled at the quilt to cover herself.

Roy Murphy stood in the doorway with the gun in his right hand and said, "You get away from her. You get out of here right now." He did not feel calm, but his voice came out level and so calm that he surprised himself.

"Jesus *Christ*, man, what are you doing? Gimme that thing for Christ's—!"

As Joe rose up from the bed, Roy pulled the trigger. He pointed the pistol away from them and shot a hole through the wall of the trailer, and the kick of the pistol threw his arm back. The explosion in that small bedroom made his ears ring.

"Jesus Christ, Jesus fucking *Christ!*"

Eliza screamed, and Joe fell back to the bed with his arms over his head. The crack pipe clattered to the floor, and the ejected cartridge rolled to the wall. In the narrow hall behind Roy, the door to the other room flew open, and Mike stood at the threshold, his mouth agape.

"Get back in that room," Roy Murphy said.

Mike retreated and slammed shut the door.

"I'm going to the kitchen." Roy was staring at Joe. His voice was preternaturally quiet. "Then you come out of here. You come out of here quick or I will shoot you. Take the pipe and the crack with you and don't never come back."

He backed out of the bedroom and away down the little corridor and stood in the kitchen. He tossed the coat on the couch and stood where Joe wouldn't be able to get at him as he came through the living room. With the gun in two hands, he pointed down the hall toward the back of the trailer, where Joe would come. And in a few seconds Joe came down that corridor fast, trying to button a shirt and cursing as he grabbed his coat.

"Gimme my gun, you little asshole!"

Roy shot again. He aimed near Joe's feet and put a second hole in the trailer, this time in the floor, and for a second Joe stood frozen with his eyes gone wide. But only a second.

By this time there was a commotion outside the trailer, shouts and lights, and in the bedroom Eliza was screaming.

Roy said, "Not going to tell you again."

Joe bolted for the door, saying, "You're both fucking freaks, both of you!" The door slammed against the trailer and hung open there in the cold, and Roy heard the truck door open and slam shut and the engine kick on.

The parting remark set him off. He had put up with too much, for too long, from this lizard Joe, and so he went out after him, slipping on the frozen ground as he leapt down in his sock feet from the little wooden landing outside the trailer. Strangely, the thought in his head was I only had a bat last time, and still you brought that truck back here, and now you will see I am serious.

An audience was gathering. People from all over the Park were rushing over to the sounds of the shooting, but not too close—hovering away from the trailer, under the streetlight on the little dirt track that wound around and through the Park. It was frozen and patterned with a scant snow. Flashlights bounced in the dark, and a woman screamed when Roy Murphy with a gun in his hand burst out of the doorway in his socks.

The truck had backed away from the trailer, but Joe fishtailed when he slammed it into drive and floored the gas pedal. Roy stopped and aimed with two hands and fired at the truck twice. The first shot was wide, and the second hit the right taillight, which exploded in a gratifying way.

Still, he shouldn't have done that.

The lawyers and even Judge Grossman might have worked around the incident in the trailer somehow, they might have called it self-defense or child abuse or something, and of course Joe could be (and later was) prosecuted for violation of his probation, possession of an unlicensed firearm, and possession of a Schedule II controlled substance. (Roy himself was going to have to testify—a little vaguely about Eliza's role—before Joe pleaded out.) But shooting at the truck as Joe was trying to get away, with all those bystanders who might have been hit or conceivably even killed, not to mention Joe himself, that was too much for the system to absorb quietly.

Hoosick Bridge PD found Roy sitting alone on the wooden step in the cold, without his shoes on. The gun lay on the step below him. His mother was still in the bedroom, too traumatized by the shooting to move from the bed. When they tried to question Roy, he would say nothing except, "I'm tired of him coming around here with all his shit." Energized by the sudden notoriety, however, Mike held forth about the manifold sins of Joe, and how he and his brother had repelled the drug dealer.

It was Roy Murphy's gun, it was Joe Pettibone's gun, there were two guns. It was a drug deal, it was not a drug deal. Joe had beaten Roy's mother, it had nothing to do with Roy's mother. The stories at Taconic Regional and around town varied. But everyone agreed that this time it would mean Juvie. A kid like that, who'd shot a gun at someone up at the Park, you couldn't have him around school, around town. *He'd almost killed someone*—everyone in town was talking about it.

At the Heights, Jane Herrick put together that this wasn't just any hoodlum. She called her husband at the office, insisted on interrupting him from a client meeting. "Tom, my goodness, you know that shooting two nights ago up at the Park? It was that same boy that Emma was running with that summer before the eighth grade! When she used to go down to the Hoosic on her bike? She used to go down there every morning it seemed like and meet that Mexican boy—Emerson?"

"Yes."

"And his friend, the other boy—remember? That's the boy she was interested in. Remember I had to take her away to Maine that summer?"

"Yes."

"That's the boy—Roy Murphy—it's the same boy who tried to kill someone two nights ago at the Park—the same boy!"

Life was precarious. You could bring your children up right, live in the right part of a town like Hoosick Bridge, with the right sorts of neighbors—you could protect them and still they might brush this close to a young hoodlum from the Park. She did not know precisely what had happened between her daughter and that dark, brooding boy during the summer before the eighth grade, but a mother senses when something is happening. She had sensed it then; she had worried and paced the porch, and then she'd had to take Emma off to Dominique's place in Maine, and down to Patty's at Candlewood. Her instinct had screamed, *Separate them!* Thank heaven that was in the past, she thought, thank heaven, four years later, Emma was so far removed from all of that.

As for Roy Murphy, the boy from the Park, said to be the last of the Murphy brothers, the system had tried. But this was not his first brush with the law. There had been that malicious damage to property, and an assault, and a second assault. Roy Murphy was not unknown to Hoosick Bridge PD; he had been to court and been warned before, by a juvenile judge who felt his whole courtroom darkened by the look in the boy's eye. And so it was official, he was trash, and you have to take the trash out, lest trash rot what it touches. The judge sentenced him to eighteen months in Juvie. They suspended all but six.

In a few days he was gone.

# SIX

*W*hen people in Hoosick Bridge said, "After February," they didn't mean the month, they meant the second of the two events that bookended that remarkable winter: the first being the shooting up at the Park, and the second, in the new year, what came to be known by the name of the month. So that later, people would say, "February—now that just wasn't right. They were only trying to make a living. It's not the easiest work in the world either." It happened on a clear, bitterly cold morning just after milking up at the McAllister and Steinhart farms. They came in vans—so many vans!—and rounded them up like the Holsteins they tended, and took them off those farms and put them on a bus and bused them to a detention center in New York, and within days they were gone from there, too—disappeared.

And not just at the two farms. As a loathsome DHS bureaucrat would memorably boast to the local TV news, it was a "coordinated operation."

At Taconic Regional later that morning, Maggie Byrne, sitting outside the principal's office, heard him yelling into a phone, "Are you kidding me? You have got to be kidding me!" But they weren't kidding him.

For that was the year that Emerson Rodriguez's ebullience had officially slain the high school. He was the kid who bridged every impossible social chasm: Emerson Rodriguez, '04, whose first toddling memory was of his mother's trailer at the Park, whose very name she had substituted for his birth name— Emilio—as a naïve expression of faith in her new land, because "Emerson sounded more American." Emerson had on a lark run, and not merely been elected but by near acclamation anointed class president at Taconic Regional. Short, peppy, irrepressible, darling of classmates, faculty, town, he was the kid for whom the principal's office had made special calls to be sure a place and a scholarship was reserved at the university up in Burlington.

Until February. For the coordinated operation picked up not merely the mothers and fathers—mainly mothers—working the milking parlors for Steinhart and McAllister, not merely Mrs. Rodriguez, who'd been up at Mason Steinhart's for twelve years. A cruiser and two DHS vehicles were up at the Park, too, before dawn, with two agents rapping on her trailer as the neighbors peered through windows. He might have been president of the class, but before his earliest memory, Emerson, too, had committed the sin of foreign birth. And so he'd vanished into a van on a frigid morning in February, leaving nothing behind him but a few spooky voice-mail messages. "Don't worry about Em, bro," he said on one of them, "TacReg Oh-Fourever!"

On that first morning at school, girls cried openly in the halls, and boys punched lockers. And for a month the school and the town seethed about it. Pastor John had rarely been so emotional in any sermon. The *Journal and Tradesman* ran Emma's op-ed on its front page under the headline WHAT KIND OF COUNTRY IS THIS?

They wrote to Vermont's congressman, they wrote the senators, they wrote the president, the senior class staged a little march on Washington Street one Wednesday morning and cars honked in support. The story was on the local television for a little while. There was an affecting piece about McAllister; with his sons gone and with that arthritis, he couldn't milk the herd himself and had to sell it because he couldn't find Vermonters to milk them. But after a while the press ran out of angles. The story wasn't a story anymore. The slow, quiet acknowledgment of helplessness came then. By the time of the prom, the Class of '04 had learned an important truth. In the end you cannot fight the government, and so it is better not to try. It had learned the irony governments understand—that as time passes injustice becomes more tolerable, not less.

That was the same winter that Jane Herrick found the letter, in a pile of papers Tom left by the side of the blue armchair in the parlor. He'd fallen asleep in the chair. When he nodded awake he took himself off to bed, but just as he was lying down he recalled the letter and hurried back downstairs, because he knew she always tidied up the parlor before she came to bed.

It was three pages, single-spaced. The official letterhead caught her eye, and the words "Ms. Barbara Pisani" in the first paragraph. But she heard his tread on the stairs and had to set the pile back down. Barb Pisani, she wondered, her pulse quickening, could that still be going on?

Long after its brief appearance and disappearance that night, Jane would think about the letter. Many times that spring and summer she was desperate to ask, "What was that about Barb Pisani? A three-page letter? Don't I deserve to know?" But the tension in the house was soon too sharp. It was impossible to raise anything with Tom Herrick after May, because after May there was nothing except the Murphy boy.

The Murphy boy was why none of them saw it coming. When in October they revisited what had happened, they looked back on signs written in neon, but no one had read them, for the early part of that year was simply too preoccupied—first by February, and then, after that dreadful prom, by Emma and the Murphy boy. Because by Memorial Day, Roy Murphy was not simply back in town, riding a motorcycle brazenly around

Hoosick Bridge. He was riding it to the Heights itself, as though he'd been sent on a mission to Jane's very house. He was standing astride that motorcycle on Jane Herrick's driveway, waiting for Emma to fly down the stairs and burst from the front doors. And he was not waiting long.

# SEVEN

*O*n the Fourth of July, 2004, Emma brought Roy Murphy to the tower.

The house was full of the special quiet of a summer afternoon. The creak of a floorboard bounded into far corners, colliding with the horsehair plaster walls, echoing into distant rooms. The Herricks were gone to the Morse gathering Aunt Patty held each Fourth on Candlewood Lake. Emma had longed for this day, schemed about it, arranged suddenly to have her shift called for work so that she had to bow out of the family trip, planned it down to the last detail; down to the picnic in a box stored in the cupboard by the south window; down to the blanket brought up from the closet and folded on the couch.

She climbed the staircase a step ahead of him. How *exciting* was his mere presence, as they ascended to this feminine retreat. His heavier tread on the stair, his breathing behind her, his smell, his masculine bulk were alien here. Most keenly with each step she felt the surge of betrayal's onset—that she herself would lay open to this strange and interstitial boy a sanctum special to her family, long the redoubt of its women and girls, certainly never visited by a lover. That surge electrified her.

What was she doing? Not Maggie, not her mother alone had asked the question, all through June, since the prom. She asked it of herself even on the stair. Sometimes she wondered whether the seduction of this adventure lay in its effect on everyone else—the astonishment and dismay this dealt to friends and family who had always put Emma in the adult-pleaser box. Did she love Roy? He was darkly powerful, almost primitive to her. It was not attraction so much as compulsion. He spoke little, but his comments were pointed, and his questions penetrating. He never read anything; he didn't own a book or a computer, but she had convinced herself that his mind was keen. There was no artifice or convention to him—no uncertainty, no self-involvement. What he wanted, he wanted; and to his want, her response was elemental.

And Emma also thought, It doesn't matter anyway. She was on a short leave from her life, with her past behind her and her future not begun. She was about to go away, and he was about to go away. They were in a border territory, a place without consequence. So she thought.

She never shared these thoughts with him, or anyone. And she tried to deflect Maggie by saying simply that it was "natural" to be around him. That was the word on her lips that summer. It was a natural attraction. It was easy. That was the thing—they meshed so easily. There was no need of talk. But already, during the briefest separations that summer, matters of a day only, the waves of restlessness came, an unquiet that grew with the length of his absence, and subsided when he was near. He had become a kind of addiction for her.

They reached the landing and the final steps. In the tower room, the afternoon sun slanted through the window on the west wall. The sun was altogether brighter than she had planned for. Her skin tingled in a new way. She took him by the hand and pulled him into the room. When the door had shut behind them, they fell into a long kiss. They maneuvered slowly across the floor, she tiptoeing toward the couch.

"Wait," she said. "I want the window open. I want the air." He had already pulled her T-shirt over her head and was tugging at her bra.

She had wanted this since the night, earlier that summer, that he took her to the McRearys' empty vacation house, up Carpenter Hill Road, and they swam by starlight. She had planned it, scripted it. In meticulous detail she had imagined every gesture and turn as though choreographing a dance. He would undress her slowly, exquisitely slowly; they would stand naked in a dusky half-light, the air bringing the skin alive. She would caress him; then he her; clouds of desire would boil up, as clouds do on a summer afternoon, unhurried, building over long minutes, at last purpling the sky as the storm burst. She had imagined a soft hand on shoulder, cool skin on skin, a look of love in the eyes. Him strong but gentle, herself supple, sinuous, coiled, and undulating. For weeks, just imagining these things brought her almost to climax.

She had planned a dance, but it was not to be a dance.

The storm burst instantly, before weather built and threatened, before clouds gathered, before there was time to run together for shelter and delight in the rain. Before the blanket was spread, before any step of her plan could even start she was gasping in the sheer strength of him, the viselike power of his arms, the press of his jaw on hers, the grinding force of his pelvis into her own. The light was harsh, not soft, the heat oppressive. Skin was not soft but hard with muscle and bone. Loud and sharply ludicrous was the shuddering of the couch (the couch had not contributed to the sound track of her plans), and she was still saying, "Wait, Roy, wait," wanting him, but not in this way. There was no undulating dance.

In this unscripted grappling, a darker persona took possession of her. An impulse more powerful than reason gripped her as it had never done before.

He loomed above her then like a wild animal, dark and heaving, his face shadowed from the harsh sun. Sweat dripped from his forehead to her shoulder, her face, her mouth. In a tangle of muscle and half-shed clothing and acrid sweat he climaxed in her repeatedly, and at that moment she would have squeezed the life from him.

He lay there panting and, at length, drifting. She grew more wakeful; in the afternoon quiet the world of plans and schedules and calendars and hierarchies returned. Her mind went to calculations—to the thirty-seven days before he left for basic training. To the fifty-two before she was due at Yale. To the three and a quarter hours it would take her parents to drive home from Candlewood. To whether the diaphragm had worked—which seemed impossible after that hurricane.

And, despite things having gone not at all according to her plan, to planning how, and where, and exactly when they would make love again.

In the picnic basket she had packed sandwiches, blueberries, potato chips, carrots. But he took nothing except water, and gulped thirstily at the bottle, sucking it dry. Then he rose and began to explore the room, his hands moving across the spines standing in rows on the dark walnut shelves that her great-great-grandfather Morse had installed more than a century before.

"All these books," he asked. "You read these?" He pulled one out. "Withering . . ." He stared at the cover in his hand.

"*Wu*thering Heights."

"Wuthering? What's '*wu*thering'?"

"I think it means 'windy.'"

"Why don't they say windy?" He reshelved the book, and turned then to a picture frame that hung on the wall by the door. Behind the glass was a small, circular object, about an inch across, tarnished green, set into a matte of blue-black velvet.

"What's this?"

He lifted the frame from the wall and held it in the light from the window. The framed object, dark and discolored, was smashed and dented in the middle. Along the rim he made out stars, and the word *Vermont*.

"Family legend," Emma said. "That button was on Ezra Morse's coat when he went off to the Civil War. He was in a terrible battle, Fredericksburg, I think. The button deflected a bullet and saved his life. For the rest of his life he carried it in his pocket, as a lucky charm."

Roy Murphy hung the frame back on the wall and turned then to the marionette playhouse on the shelf. The impossible dark triangle of his muscled back was turned toward her. His back was to Emma a wondrous thing.

He removed the wooden playhouse from the shelf and set it down on the floor, and then unhooked a red puppet, dressed in painted kneesocks, a bright smile painted on its face.

"My dad," she explained, "he made it. The playhouse. He sent away for the marionettes."

He struggled to contemplate such a thing—a father who built a playhouse, or sent away for marionettes. Who existed at all.

The room was still too warm; the afternoon air coming in from the windows was hot. They crouched in their underwear by the little wooden stage that Tom Herrick had built for her seventh birthday, and Emma made old Geppetto dance. Roy watched the dancing puppet, fascinated by the tiny strings, and how she could manipulate now a leg, now an arm.

"All fall down!" she said. Geppetto crashed to the stage floor, and his elbows and knees flew out comically. But suddenly the puppet was not funny. It lay splayed on the stage, its legs unnaturally akimbo in cruel destruction.

"That's just what we used to do, when we, you know, made puppet shows," she explained, rushing. "We used to put on shows for each other on rainy days. The puppets would get into arguments. And we'd try to make different voices for them. 'Geppetto, what have you done to my nose?' It always ended with the puppets collapsing after a fight. It would take hours to untangle the strings."

Quietly he said, "I'll be coming back, Emma."

She picked up Geppetto and turned away from him, and began to separate the strings, avoiding his eyes.

"You want me to come back, don't you?"

"Soldiers die in Iraq every day, Roy."

"What?"

"Every single day you read about it. They're riding along and they go over some bomb in the road. Don't tell me you're coming back, like it's up to you! You're going there, and that's all anyone can say."

"There or somewhere, wherever they send me. But I'm coming back," he repeated.

She dropped the puppet, returned to the couch, and began to dress. "You don't understand," she said.

"What don't I understand?"

"Anything. You don't understand anything! Iraq, Afghanistan, us, this!"

"All right. Explain us to me. Explain this to me."

She bit her lip, thinking, Maggie said he was violent, he was dangerous, he was in Juvie, he was a psycho, but he never even yells. It's always me who yells. She looked at him and said, "No bullshit, right? That's what you always say?"

"No bullshit," he agreed.

She took a deep breath. "You're the Park, I'm the town. Except for one summer after the seventh grade. In a few weeks, you'll have one future, I'll have another future, and those two worlds are like, like Jupiter and Saturn. You're going over—somewhere—to get shot at, for what reason I do not even know, you do not even know. And I'm going to Yale." She added, "For what reason I do not really know either."

She stood and held her arms wide. "So our worlds are . . . here. Okay?"

She spread her arms wide. Her golden hair was backlit by the sun blasting into the south window. He could see the fine golden down on the silhouette of her arms and her slim brown legs. Her mouth was full and angry, and her eyes flashed pale blue, and he thought he'd never seen anything so beautiful. God never had permitted him such a glimpse even for a second. The gentle mound of her rose beneath her panties. The robin's-egg T-shirt was pulled tight across her breasts. He could want her so badly, want to tear cotton from her and plunge into her, and a moment later need her at a distance, held back from being spoiled by his touch. He thought of the dark places he had known, small rooms in trailers, secondhand couches he had slept on with only a dirty sheet for cover, rooms with yellowed newspapers stuffed in the windows to stop the draft. He thought of places where people stooped beneath a low ceiling, where in the night someone would burst in loud and stinking, where the talk was coarse, where the tables were littered with Doritos bags and beer cans, where you never saw even a single book or a shelf to hold one, where carpets were stained and faces were drawn, where outside, the weeds grew up beyond the steps and at night ugly shouts and grunts and heaves and cries and curses filled the air. Where lizards peddled oblivion in little pipes. That he should have come from that world and now see a thing so beautiful as the way she stood there angry and crying and golden: this image would be precious to him for years.

So he was only half listening to the words.

She said, "The only world we both have is this little hour in this room. Let's not kid ourselves, Roy! This is us. All right?"

She dropped her arms and turned away from him because she was crying. She felt guilty because she knew that all of this was so because she had contrived it so. She had cast him for a role and decreed an intermezzo, which ends as a matter of its own definition.

Except that she was crying not just for guilt as she repacked the picnic basket. That afternoon she could not reconcile her belly with her head, the animal yearning with the trained distance of class and circumstance. She cried because she thought that for her he could never exist outside this contrivance, cried because she knew that the dark hunger she had felt a few minutes before would give way to calculation. Cried because there were only minutes left.

She hunted for her cell phone to check the time.

"Roy, you've got to *go*," she said. "Otherwise the fireworks will be *here*."

He pulled his shirt on. "Okay. Alls I said, Emma, is that I'll come back."

They knew, somehow. The looks on their faces, the cold silence, the implausibility of a work shift at a day camp on the Fourth of July said that Jane and Tom Herrick knew. And then, the next morning, that word crossed her father's lips. Emma turned on her heel and ran out the front door into a rainstorm and was gone, holed up at Maggie's for three days straight, returning at last in stony silence. Jane Herrick found herself in a shouting match with Tom that ended with her slapping him, and him stomping out into the rain as well. They had both fled the Heights to the rain.

That he could call his own daughter such a thing. That it should have come to this, in the Heights, her family's house that had seen so many generations. That Emma's own father should have called her a tramp in this house.

That summer, the Heights was stirring. Silences and harsh words and door slams proceeded to shouting matches, and sometimes even to screaming matches with Emma—it was unlike anything that family had known before. The tension emanated in waves from the very plaster walls, the oak treads on the staircases. Anne and Charlie crept quietly from their rooms, tiptoeing so as not to trigger the house's emanations. They would quit the Heights for a friend's house: as that summer wore on, they were always calling at suppertime to say they'd be staying somewhere. The house itself was out of joint, and its tension would crack like a rifle shot at their sister's mere word, or their father's, or their mother's. It seemed to Jane that Emma had provoked them beyond all reason.

What kind of self-destructive impulse was behind this? What sort of statement was this for a bright and beautiful girl to make on the doorstep of Yale? Out until late in the night, out all night sometimes; drinking no doubt, riding on the back of the motorcycle of a common criminal. And at night she'd be up there at the Park with the Murphy boy and the rest of those people. Where he had tried to kill a man in that wilderness of shootings, and drug dealers, and every kind of depravity.

"Did you pick him out of a police lineup, just to spite us?" (Surely, Jane thought, it *was* just to spite us. She could conceive of no other attraction.) What did we do to her? she wondered. "Emma, please! *Please*. Why? What are you trying to prove?"

"I'm not trying to *prove* anything, Mom."

"He went to jail!"

"He was in juvenile detention for protecting his mother. I would think you'd have some sympathy." But Emma's counter-arguments were percussive—the rat-a-tat of footsteps running down stairs and bursting from the doors. And when Tom Herrick came to bed at all that summer, Jane could feel his wakefulness like an electric current running through the sheets and pillowcases. Some nights he would never come up at all, sitting alone in the parlor, waiting for Emma's return, seething for hours, leaping from that darkness as she tried to pad barefoot into the hall. Upstairs, when she heard the shouting, Jane would squint at the clock: 3:00 a.m. 4:00 a.m. 5:00 a.m. She grew haggard from loss of sleep. And from the loss of something else—that he would not be her partner in this. And so she tossed with it in the darkness, too.

One humid afternoon late in July, while a summer thunderstorm boiled up in the west and passersby in Hoosick Bridge were hurrying for cars and cover, Jane caught sight of Maggie Byrne through the window at Garibaldi's Coffee Shop and ducked inside. Grasping her arm, she said, "Maggie, you've got to do something! Talk to Emma, Maggie—talk to her! You're her oldest friend!"

"I've tried, Mrs. Herrick. I can't do anything," Maggie said. "No one can."

That night, as the storm lashed the Heights, Jane Herrick

climbed the stairs and in the tower shut the door behind her, thinking, College must end it: all of this surely must pass when Emma goes off to college. It was an insight not unlike Emma's own.

Rain streamed against the windows. The old marionette playhouse lay out on the floor. Tom had built it in the garage years ago, and taught his daughters how to manage the crossed sticks and make the puppet dance. Someone must have pulled it out recently. It was off the shelf, and Geppetto hung from his hook with his strings tangled. She picked him off the hook and sat with him on the couch. It settled her to straighten out the strings. Then she, too, made him dance clumsily across the stage as in older times, his elbows and knees flying akimbo.

This must pass, she thought. A month and she'll be off to college and the Murphy boy will be in the Army and . . .

Outside the dark rain slammed the tower in waves, and thunder cracked the sky. Geppetto clattered to the stage, a jumble of limbs. Cruelly Jane Herrick finished her own thought. ". . . and go off to Iraq and never come back."

During that summer of 2004, hawks and doves split Hoosick Bridge in equal measure and with equal passion. That Roy Murphy from the Park was going off to the war proved to doves its illegitimacy—that they were reduced to fighting it with such trash. To hawks, it showed that the country didn't properly support the effort. You had to shake your head, and people were careful not to give voice to what they were thinking. Although no one would say it—too many good men already had paid the ultimate price in the Vermont National Guard, too many good families were already nursing a wounded father, or left without a son—the news brought a sneaking relief. The war now served the same useful purpose as Hoosick Bridge's transfer station. You could dump unwanted things there, and they would be transferred to someplace else. Someplace vague and uncertain—some distant place. The war like the transfer station was the place for refuse and castoffs.

No one said this out loud, even if some thought it, but hadn't the community tried with Roy Murphy? Hadn't he had two, three, five chances? Hadn't he even tried to take up with the Herrick girl, as though by pulling her down he might pull himself up and out of the Park? It wasn't as though the town hadn't tried. They'd done their best. So let the Army have him, if they were that desperate. Good riddance.

On the eleventh of August, Emma rose early and took a small package of white tissue, tied with a red ribbon, from where she'd hidden it, at the back of the middle drawer in the white desk. She crept quietly down the staircases from the third floor. The keys to the Mercedes wagon hung from the hook outside the kitchen.

She drove the car up to the Park, where she had dropped him off barely four hours before. It was a cool morning, and there were traces of mist in the low places as she drove north on Route 7. At the Park, all was still. The wheels crunched on the dirt and gravel road and then came to a stop outside the trailer, just as the door was opening. He came out alone. Neither Eliza nor Mike was with him, or visible at the small window. He tossed the duffel bag and day pack in the back and got in the car, and she drove him to the bus depot in Bennington.

Lying between them on the console, she realized too late, was a shiny blue envelope, with a heading in white letters: "The Freshman Experience at Yale."

He glanced at it, then back at the road. "Emma, I don't have a speech or nothing," he said, quietly.

"I don't either."

They drove on in silence. When they reached the depot, the bus hadn't yet arrived. "Don't get out and wait," he said. "Let's just do this."

He reached and pulled her to him. They kissed, and then her arms went around him and she hugged him fiercely.

"Will you have an e-mail address?"

"I never did before."

She gripped his shoulders for a long time, until she could feel his restlessness, but this was so that he would not see her eyes, and guess that a part of her was relieved. At the last she composed herself and pulled back, holding his face in her two hands.

"I'll go," he said.

"Wait, I have something." She reached down to the door pocket and handed him the package. She smiled at his surprise. As he tore the paper away, she explained, "I took it to the jeweler's, and he put it on a chain, so maybe . . . maybe you could wear it. If you want."

He held up the chain in his left hand.

"It's always been good luck in my family," she said.

"It's a loan?"

"It's a *gift*," she said.

He dipped his head and put the chain over it, and then tucked the button below the neck of his T-shirt. Then he kissed her again and was out the car door. He took the duffel bag and day pack from the back and shut the hatch.

Through the passenger window, he leaned back into the car and said, "Emma—it's a loan. I'll bring it back."

Just as swiftly he was gone, swinging the duffel over his shoulder. He did not look back at her as he hurried into the bus station. Not even once. It's like he's running, she thought, that way of walking that he has.

She backed the car from the spot and pulled out to the road. *You put it on, but you didn't look back*, she thought. Neither will I.

There was no resolution, but there was at least relief, when at last the morning arrived. Tom had already gone to work, and so it was just the two of them in the car, with Emma driving, and Jane silent in the passenger seat.

They found the dormitory—a massive crenellated pile—in the center of the Old Campus, a castle presiding over the happy, gridlocked chaos of move-in day. Jane leaned helplessly against the car door as a pleasant man from Virginia materialized from somewhere, with his son, and they began to take charge of the cases and boxes. They were unpacked all too quickly and all too cheerfully. When the last of Emma's things had been carried up the stone staircases, mother and daughter stood awkwardly on the sidewalk, recognizing, as one does, that a moment that calls for some sort of special word had arrived too soon, and was about to slip away uncelebrated.

"Well," said Jane, with determined cheeriness. "New beginnings!"

Emma forced a smile and nodded. "New beginnings," she agreed.

"I wish this summer hadn't been so awful," Jane said. "He really does want the best for you—we both do, Emma."

"I wish, too," she said. But she would not speak of her father today. His selfish withdrawal over the past months made her too angry. She had not forgiven his strange and erratic behavior. What had Roy Murphy ever done to him? And for that matter, what had she done to her father? Always before she had been his favorite. He should have known her. He should have known (somehow) that it had only been her intermezzo.

She stood a moment longer on the sidewalk, amid the armchairs and mini-fridges and boxes, the smiles and sunshine. It felt like the scene in the old films where the steward is calling "All aboard!" and the passengers had better hurry up the gangway. They had better say their good-byes and get aboard. As though the massive pile behind her were about to embark.

They embraced stiffly. Jane Herrick had always been the patrician queen at the Heights, but when Emma pulled away, her mother seemed somehow diminished, and she felt a momentary sadness for her. But it passed quickly. She turned her back on Chapel Street and felt a new breeze bellying her sail. A voyage was about to begin. It was precisely as she had planned it would be. The past was over; the future began today.

The intermezzo had been navigated. It had been a wild and dangerous territory—it had frightened and electrified her. But Emma was the captain of her life, not Jane, not Tom, not Roy

Murphy. She was the captain even of its reckless sojourn in the frontier. And now the voyage she had planned—her real life, as she thought of it—was scheduled to begin. The no-man's-land had fallen astern, and Roy Murphy with it.

So thinking, she went in to find her new roommates.

# EIGHT
## July 10, 2009

*A*s he quick-stepped up the street toward the Heights, the music grew louder, assaulting him now. His heart pounded the way it used to do in Firebase Montana, when an op was about to start.

Better move fast, better get this done and get out of there quick, or I'll never do this at all, he thought.

He reached the yard. The party crowd around the house came into view, their faces turning his way as he hurried in, registering the surprise of people confronting something alien, a strange arrival in costume. He felt a tightening in the pit of his stomach. He did not want to be here, to do this, but he couldn't just ignore what had happened, just go along as though it hadn't happened at all. He had to tie it off.

The first person he recognized was Jane Herrick, standing guard at one end of the marquee, where the flaps were rolled up. Had her hair been white when he left town five years before? But the expression was the same. As though she had been waiting for him, with that same haughty look she'd always had when he used to come around that summer of '04, only now not so proud, not so much the queen. She stared at him like he was some rabid animal loose on the street. Looking as though she would call the police to report his mere existence.

He pretended not to notice her and moved quickly inside the tent.

The crowd was large—a few hundred at least. A dance floor was laid out on the grass at the far end of the tent, and dancers whirled on it. There were round tables with white tablecloths, a buffet of food at one end, and a bar, and the band was at the back, playing loud, working up to a crescendo.

Once before he had met her on a dance floor.

She stood to one side of the parquet, in among a little circle of guests, with their cocktail glasses in their hands, all but one in their crisp and ironed clean cotton, their madras, their linen glowing in the light. It staggered him a little—that after these long years she could have returned from that mythic fortress she'd held in his mind to this backyard. And so he stopped.

He did not recognize any of those people—did not know that they included Emma's fiancé, George Forrester, the Forresters, her roommates from Yale, and that the animated girl in the circle who at that moment was loudly telling a story was George's younger sister, Isabella.

Isabella Forrester was petite, very slight, with dramatic features beneath a mass of hair that for that particular evening had been dyed crimson—one of those small women whose faces seem just slightly too big for their bodies. Izzy was not beautiful, but she was magnetic, minx-like, and she was all bold suggestion. She wore a loose tank of white silk, which hung low, revealing the top half of a butterfly tattoo over the right breast. She wore skintight pants and leather boots.

Izzy had been determined since birth to confound. Since being thrown out of prep school, she had carried on a bohemian battle against what she regarded as the dull conventions of the family. At first the news of her older brother's engagement was a source of amusement. George would fulfill his dull destiny by marrying a woman who could only be as dull as he, a scrubbed blonde, *of course*, another anodyne edition of people-like-us. In this she found an opportunity for self-gratification, for it was easy to lampoon all of them. But later she was encouraged to learn of the dark history that surrounded the Herrick family. That had piqued her interest. Her parents had sharply implored her *please* to show some restraint at the party, some respect for Mrs. Herrick at least, who had been through a lot, and to show her new sister some respect, too. Please could she just be restrained for once?

My new sister, Izzy thought—*as if!*

The Forresters' urgent requests had of course precisely the opposite effect. Izzy had been flirting all night, with groomsmen, with friends, with some of the older, married men, turning over in her mind which one she might tease to distraction. Until the moment Roy Murphy arrived, Izzy had spent the evening stealing the show.

But Roy Murphy did not notice her. He did not know who she was and never saw her at all that night that he could later remember. His eyes were fixed on the woman in the pale green linen skirt and white blouse, an image that for him was the only color in a black-and-white scene. Her hair shone, brushed to a sheen. Her smile filled her cheeks, puffing them out and up against her eyes. She was as beautiful as his most precious memory, but it was as though he was looking at her from behind glass, where she moved in a world different than the one he remembered. Like she'd said. In his dreams her arms and legs had been downy, but now they looked smooth.

She saw him across the tent, and her eyes went wide, and her lips formed the syllable of his name, as a question.

He waited, his hands at his sides, as she extricated herself from the group and crossed toward him, with a guy in tow. He was fair-haired, slim, wearing chinos and a golf shirt and round glasses with wire rims, half a step behind her.

"Roy!" It was her voice again, after years of never hearing it; her voice, but yet her class secretary voice. Her party host voice—the one she always used on dance floors.

"You're back! Roy!"

He saw the flash from her finger as the stone caught the light. "I said I'd be back."

She reached to embrace him—chastely—and he accepted the embrace, not returning it, except with the faintest brush of his hands on her lower back, fingertips just touching the blouse, as though careful of a shock. But not careful enough, because they both felt it. He started, his nostrils inflecting as they caught the unfamiliar scent of a new perfume she wore that night, one that jarred with his memory.

Scores of others now sidled toward them, catching sight of Emma's embrace with this young man in uniform. They moved carefully, casting quick looks at one another, to see if someone else knew who this was. They began to form a semicircle behind Emma, by the east end of the marquee. Roy stood facing them all, his back to the night.

"You look different than I remembered," he said.

"When did you get back?"

But he had turned to George. "What's your name?"

"Oh, I'm so sorry! Roy, this is my fiancé, George Forrester. And his sister, Isabella."

"Izzy," she corrected.

"George, everybody, this is an old friend from . . . school, Roy Murphy, who was in the service. Roy served in . . . it was . . . was it Iraq? Or Afghanistan, Roy?" She turned to explain to George, or maybe to the watching world: "Roy never wrote—to any of us!"

She was rushing. Anne put her hand gently on Emma's arm.

"Are you out now, Roy? Are you done? Or on leave? Anyway, it's wonderful you could come to our engagement party!"

George extended his hand. "George Forrester," he said. "Hi."

Roy took the hand slowly, as though examining it before shaking it. Then released George's hand and dropped his own to his side.

The band had stopped playing a minute before. Someone had told it to stop, maybe, or maybe it was just one of their breaks. The noise in the tent had abated, and conversations were falling away, as when a sail falls slack in the instant that a ship is becalmed.

"The Afghan conflict seems like it's getting worse and worse," George offered awkwardly.

"*God*, George!" said Izzy, now charged with excitement over this surprise development, this young soldier back from seeing and doing God knows what in what she dismissed, when she thought of them at all, as Bush's oil wars. He looked dark and un-polished and hard, and somehow knew *Suzy Q* of all people, and clearly must have had some kind of *thing* with her. It was written on his face. And hers, which before this moment had been irri-tatingly serene all evening, despite Izzy's best efforts to provoke a reaction. Here was this soldier like a ghost come to haunt the garden party and sow among these people far more consternation than any tank top or tattoo of Izzy's would ever do.

But Roy Murphy saw neither of them. "Engagement," he said, "we used that word for something else. Emma, this will make you happy?"

"This? Oh—yes!" she answered, embarrassed. Repeated it louder then, to convince everyone she meant it. "Yes, very happy!"

"Your parents, it will make them happy?"

At this point, conversation stopped. It grew quiet, and the quiet soon became horrible, all through the tent and the yard. Even Izzy bit her lip.

Emma's smile collapsed, and she looked away. The blood had left her face. Anne gripped her arm more tightly.

"Honey," said George.

But she waved him away. "You didn't hear."

"Honey, I . . ."

She was thinking, You never wrote a single e-mail to *anyone* back home. You just left, and were gone—*gone* gone—and so you didn't hear.

George tried again to intercede. "Roy . . . um, let me talk to you for a minute. Hon, let me talk to him. Roy . . ."

"He's dead," she said. "My father."

George reached to her, trying to put his arm around her shoulder, but Emma stepped to the side.

"I didn't know that," said Roy Murphy.

"No. You were gone."

The crowd behind her had fallen silent, and Roy Murphy felt his face reddening with embarrassment, for he didn't know what to say. These laconic, educated partygoers watching him, smooth and comfortable, would know exactly what to say. Their whole lives were training for what to *say*.

Only once could Roy Murphy recall seeing Emma's father. The memory was distant now, hazy, although at the time it had shaken him, made him nervous and angry. It was after supper, one evening during that summer of 2004, still light out, the July evening young, when he had pulled into the drive at the Heights, and stood there straddling the motorcycle, the balls of his feet on the gravel, waiting for her, full of excitement and anticipation. And suddenly he felt that shiver of consciousness that he was being watched, that he had been watched from the moment of his arrival, that a man stood silent like a statue on the porch. He looked at Roy blankly, a pale figure bearing some resemblance to Emma, but without her color, without her glorious smile—a blank version of her face. He was a figure of her blood, but bloodless. Roy hadn't known what to say then, either—he pulled off his helmet and nodded, but Herrick never said a word to him or even acknowledged the nod. He just stared. It lasted only a few seconds, for Emma came bounding out the front door, down the porch steps, and ran over to the bike. She took the spare helmet from the back, leapt on, and shouted, "Bye!" at her father, and they were off. Later that night, he'd asked her why her father hated him so much. She deflected his question with a hurried remark, something about him "acting strange" that summer, but of course Roy Murphy knew it was more than that. It was what he was. They both knew.

Tom Herrick would fade from view, as just another hostile adult in a hostile town full of them. Roy did not see him again, and Emma, who spoke constantly about her sisters, her mother, his mother, his brothers, rarely mentioned her father.

It was still hushed in the tent. The throng were waiting for the young soldier to say something, waiting to judge him somehow. He felt like a specimen laid out before them, someone they would drily analyze later. His eyes went from Emma to the fiancé, George, across the silent crowd of faces ringing the couple, and he wondered, should he ask *how* he had died? When? These people all knew what to ask, what words to use, but he never had known. And so he took a breath and went on with what he'd come to say in the first place.

When it was over, and he had gone, Emma was drying her eyes with one hand and in the other clutching the chain, and trying to resume her party smile. Nearby Izzy stood intently, for once speechless herself.

"Who *was* that?" Izzy asked.

She was a wreck for the rest of the night. Later in the dark, up in the gloomy bedroom on the third floor, as George gamely made love to her, she lay beneath him with eyes wide, wanting what she dared not want. All through her sleepless journey to the dawn, Emma would replay how the day had brought her to the moment that Roy Murphy spoke, and what he'd said.

The text messages from friends in town had started coming in at about three. She'd guessed that the soldier must be him, and for the rest of the day wondered what would happen, whether he might turn up. But there had been so many preparations, and she and George were late getting up from New York, so she hadn't had time to do more than think, It's been so long, he never even e-mailed, I'm sure he's not interested. If he comes I will deal with it then. She hadn't forewarned George—it would have been too much to start getting into all that on the very afternoon of their engagement party.

She lay awake in the darkness reliving that tableau, how he stood, alone, at the opening of the tent, erect and foreign in his uniform, how the party guests retreated from him at first, and then circled back, watching. She remembered what they all felt with this living reminder thrust upon them. That the country was at war, but not *they* exactly. Young men were killed every day, but not *their* young men, not the young men at this party. Dying was for other people in this war of convenience. Theirs was the class of making policy, his the class of being killed by it or, worse, of somehow surviving it and then coming back home and walking around in plain view as a living and embarrassing reminder.

How small a party guest had felt then, recalling some college seminar in which he'd made a smug argument, conned from a blog or a textbook, about "evolving war paradigms," or "geopolitics." *Geopolitics* was a fancy word for a small state whose senators and congressman said no to wars in Asia and then sent a greater percentage of its men and boys, and of its women, too, to die there than any other. And now, they found, geopolitics was not just something you could outsource, someone you could hire and export to a distant place no one could find on a map. Geopolitics would come home, to the tent in your backyard. To your engagement party.

She pondered the strange question he'd asked George about cash and credit. As she rewound and replayed the words in her head, the revelation came to her so abruptly that she sat up in bed.

It was the most he had ever said to her.

"Emma, I couldn't send you an e-mail or nothing. I mean I could of, most guys did that all the time. But like you said that day about the two worlds. There's that world and this world. You can't be in that world and send an e-mail to, you know, *Yale*. I can't anyway. Some guys, they'd be always thinking about e-mail. Soon as we rotated off the firebase, their e-mail with only one thing on their minds—whether their girl or their wife was still theirs. They're out in Afghanistan and their girl is back in this world and is she still theirs? That's what's grinding them down. That's what they got to find out. And what are they going to find out? Nothing good. Either it's happened, she's in that other world and isn't their girl anymore, or it hasn't happened *yet*. So the guy can have it to worry about until the next e-mail.

"Guys always looked worse after reading e-mails. I figured, I'm coming back. I'll deal with it when I'm back.

"And something else, Emma. Some of those guys are dead now. Or alive and wishing they hadn't made it, which is worse. They had bad luck, you could say, but maybe they weren't paying attention. You're in Afghanistan, you have to be all there, you know? You got to pay all the attention you have. One little kid in a market with a look on his face that isn't right, one little flash of light on the hill across the valley, you won't never see it if you don't pay attention. A guy has some of his attention on whether a girl in some other world is still his girl, and bad things happen in the world he's in.

"I didn't say I'd send fucking letters. I said I'd come back. And I come back to the house this morning. I seen the tent. Tents like this in the summer—I'm not stupid, I know what that's for. So the future was like you said, Emma, the two worlds. Like you told me that day in the tower."

She remembered how speechless they all were. It was at this point that Roy Murphy turned to face George—George, always so facile and easygoing, George who could talk to anyone. George was speechless, too, as Roy Murphy held his eye and said, "You're that other world." And she remembered George's discomfiture, and how in her mind she shrank from George in that moment, how she felt not sympathy for him but something like resentment.

"You ever been in the tower?" Roy asked. "Nice up there, but time goes by quick. You got to take the cash, and let the credit go."

Still no one else would speak. Roy turned back to her.

"Emma, I come tonight to tell you one thing so you don't have no doubt about it. If this is what you want, this world you're in now, I come to say, go on then, it's not mine. But remember you put yourself in that world. That wasn't me. And my decision hasn't changed. I'm here now. To do what I said."

He lowered his head and withdrew the chain from around his neck.

"Here." He handed her the chain. "Brought him home."

The button rested on her palm, and the chain fell upon it.

"He never got hit."

"It's yours, Roy, it's yours! It was a gift!" She extended her arm toward him, the button and chain in her hand.

"No, Emma, I guess I was right." He had moved to the entrance of the marquee, and as he looked back that last time, she seemed to have receded into that comfortable circle of pastel shirts and linen dresses and Bermuda shorts, summery and bright in the lights of the tent, of slim, smooth limbs and unscathed faces, tanned arms, hands holding cocktail glasses, a protective company intently observing an interesting intrusion, and ready to close ranks around their own, when the intruder had gone.

"It was always just a loan."

She called to him. But she was calling to his back, she was calling to the darkness. For he was already gone, quick-stepping into the night.

For a long time Izzy lay awake, too, in a bed at the Taconic Motel across town, which the younger guests had taken over, and to which they repaired, when the party wound down, to drink by the little pool. Earlier, feigning more drunkenness than she actually felt, she had hooked a finger in the madras shirt of one of her brother's friends and led him to her room. He'd been looking at her earlier. She figured him for twenty-five or so.

In the room she was ferocious. There were no preliminaries. She pushed him to the bed, slipped off her silk camisole, straddled him and pinned his arms before he could so much as speak. He tried to kiss her, but she pulled back from his kiss with a teasing half smile. Her mass of hair falling in his face, she began to move over him. He lay back and let himself be coaxed. Izzy moved slowly at first, as he began to breathe heavily, and then more rapidly, grinding herself on just the spot until he thrashed and groaned. She picked up speed, teasing him into high frenzy.

"Wait," he said, "Izzy . . ."

But it was too late.

She looked down at the stain, and then up at his eyes. "Poor baby," she said. "Better go night night."

She swung her leg back over him and sat on the edge of the bed, as he lay there panting. She unlaced and removed her boots, glancing at him contemptuously. And then she decided that one last provocation was in order, and so she stood and shimmied out of her pants and then dropped her panties.

He reached toward her. "I could . . ." he started to say.

She pushed his hand away. "I'm jailbait," she said. "Time for you to go."

When the door closed behind him, she thought, These people—they are all so *pathetic*.

But not everyone tonight had been pathetic. That soldier was not pathetic at all. Izzy lay in bed thinking about him. Here in this sad little hick town, with its sad row of Victorian houses pretending they were somewhere important, and that crazy Herrick mansion, something had gone on between Suzy Q and the soldier. *That* was delicious. All that stuff about a tower, cash and credit, guys being killed because they were lovelorn on e-mails, two worlds—what was all *that* about? Lying naked beneath the sheet in her motel bed, scornful and at the same time content with her easy conquest, Izzy smiled at the night's revelations. There was far more to be mined from this wedding than she could have dreamed before. It was full of promise.

In the soldier Izzy had recognized something. He was hard, *scary* hard, maybe dangerous. You could not trifle with him the way she just had done with whatever his name was. But in that hardness was reality. That soldier did not fit with any of them, least of all with Emma. And he had been with her, that was clear. His darkness fascinated Izzy.

My new sister, she thought—she has a secret!

As Izzy lay in the motel bed, she remembered that they said his name was Roy Murphy, and that he had come back here, to Hoosick Bridge, the town where he grew up.

# NINE
## Summer 2009

The red Ford truck was seen all around town. It was over to New York and down to Massachusetts. As he drove by, people said, "That's Roy Murphy, back from Afghanistan," for they knew now that it *was* Afghanistan, not Iraq, where he had served—that much of the story had circulated.

In a few days the truck was towing a used landscaper's trailer, and soon after that a box on the trailer held a weed whacker, rakes, shovels, tarps, fuel cans, tools. For a few weeks he towed a used riding lawn mower. This was a brief but acute embarrassment. A landscaper with a home owner's riding mower is like an airborne unit on patrol with 22s. He needed to find a used Scag.

In the early days he had no grand plan. He would get a truck, work as a landscaper, cut someone's grass, and then someone else's. The growth was organic, and as the little business gained traction, he nurtured it and guarded it like a precious thing, turned each waking hour to it, protected it against a world that, he knew, would try to take it from him. He had only the vaguest sense that this mission would serve a larger purpose, for in the earliest days he was focused solely on the short horizon he could see. The next job and the next job and the next, on how he would get business before the summer was out and then how he would tide the winter over with snowplowing and where he would map his—as he thought of it—spring campaign. For the captain had taught him that, if you just sat in your firebase, then it was only a matter of time before they hit you. If you wanted to hit them, you had to go out after them. You had to leave the wire. Only by doing that could you take the advantage.

In Overton he rented a small barn with an attic room. He installed a woodstove in the garage downstairs and ran the stove-pipe up through the attic. The garage was more for keeping tools under cover than for covering himself, and he was obsessive about tools, about oiling blades and greasing machinery, about keeping things sharp. He had stones and a grinding wheel, and he could spend hours at night, alone in that garage, honing blades until they shone like fire. The attic was scarcely habitable. Hot in the summer, dirty, it had a small bathroom and shower, and a tiny kitchenette with two burners and no stove, walls without insulation. When winter came on, it would be drafty, and condensation would ice up the insides of the windows.

It was the best place he'd lived in years.

He took the Ford up to Bennington and had it detailed. They painted "Murphy's Landscaping" on the door in black letters, with a phone number. He was seen in Overton, and in Williamstown and North Adams, and up in Bennington, and over in New York as far as Greenwich. But no one saw Roy Murphy in the Park, not even once.

Many in town would later say that he came back to Hoosick Bridge on a destructive mission and that from the moment of his return every step was bent on conceiving and executing that mission with remorseless determination. The story would be told with a mix of fear and envy. Discoursing in Toni's Lunch, Professor Emmanuel described Roy Murphy's return in more cosmic terms. Murphy was the soldier come home, to find that during his years of sacrifice, years spent across the seas, other men, who made no sacrifice—calculating, acquisitive men—had usurped his place.

"Don't you see?" he asked Toni, late one morning in the diner. "It's his *nostos*."

"His what?"

"The warrior's return, after a perilous journey. It is a special kind of homecoming, a special pull to a singular place in the world, that only the wanderer can fully know. It is powerful and irrational, some say dangerous."

"A special pull to Hoosick Bridge, Professor? If you say so." Toni refilled his coffee.

The fact that upon his return Roy had gone straight to the Heights set off in Professor Emmanuel a flood of questions. So that thereafter he was always asking Toni whether the soldier Roy Murphy had been into the diner that morning, what his news was, pumping her for more information about the past, the old Herrick love affair, and the distant past—What was that, again, not the high school part, the junior high school part? What happened then?

For most in town, the idea that Roy Murphy had returned on some kind of mission (whether born of love, or vengeance, or both) was hindsight: people later averring they had noticed or even said things at the time when, in truth, they had not. Certainly *he* had not. And he would do anything—he would drop dead trees, he would mow lawns, he would mulch beds. He would pull up outside a house in Hoosick Bridge or Williamstown or Bennington and knock on the door and say, "I'm Roy Murphy, I'm just back from the service in Afghanistan, trying to get a business going. If there's any work I can do for you, I'll give you a fair price." Or "Noticed you have a pool out back. Be happy to close that up for you this year, and if you have any other yard work, let me know."

What could they do but give the vet the job?

About two weeks after he returned, his cell phone chirped with an unknown number.

"Murphy's Landscaping," he answered.

"Roy Murphy?"

"Yes."

"This is Nick Torruella calling."

"From . . . the dealership?"

"Yeah, that's me. How're you doing, Roy, can I call you Roy?"

"Doing fine, Mr. Torruella."

"Call me Nick. I wanted to call you about the truck, see how it's working out for you. Is it working out all right?"

"So far, so good."

"Great, great, glad to hear it. The other reason I'm calling, Roy, is I just wanted to extend you my personal thanks for your service to this country. God knows we could use a few more young men like you."

This surprised Roy a little. As a boy, he had seen the Torruella Ford ads on television, the strutting bantam with the white pompadour flashing a grin, always with flags and balloons. That's what he remembered from the television, flags and balloons, and the little man jabbing his finger and saying, "We will not be beat!" He thought he knew what Torruella meant, but the way he said it—we could *use* a few more young men—sort of sounded like Torruella thought that the country was him, and that he was running low. So he didn't say anything, which forced Torruella to go on.

"And so if there's anything I can do, anything at all, I want you to call me, okay?"

"You need any yard work?"

Torruella laughed, a booming laugh. "That's pretty good, son! Real good, I appreciate that! I think my people have it covered, but we'll sure keep it in mind. Now, Roy, mainly why I was calling was to see whether I could get you up to a dinner we're having, Bennington County Republicans Harvest Dinner on September seventeenth, maybe come and speak about your experiences. Nothing very formal, just talk. Nice dinner, good guys. We'd be very proud to have you."

"A speech?"

"Not a speech in so many words, just talk, you know, nothing too formal or anything. There's thirty or forty of us get together for these dinners, try and keep up a little spirit to support the troops. Might be more than that, if people knew you were coming."

Roy thought for a moment. "I'm not much of a talker, Mr. Torruella. Unless you want to talk yard work. You take care now."

The next day Roy made a rare visit to the public library. He knew they had computers there, and a librarian helped him get online. He found a lot more than the dealership. A Google search turned up ski resorts, a housing development in Pittsfield, two assisted living facilities, and a lot of Republican party fund-raising. Also one unflattering attack in a left-wing Berkshire weekly about Torruella's cheerleading for the Iraq war. (The article noted his extended stay in Canada in the late 1960s.)

Roy scrolled down through the stories. He read slowly, but easily now. A dark smile came to his face. All day he thought about it. When he drifted off that night, he was still thinking about Nick Torruella.


"Mr. Torruella? Roy Murphy calling. You said to call if I needed anything, sir."

"Roy! Glad you called. Go ahead, son."

"It's that landscaping business I mentioned. I'm setting up, but it's already kind of late in the season. I'm doing the best I can getting it going. Being I just got out of the service, I don't have credit, and the business could use a loan."

There was a pause. "How much do you need?"

"Seventy-two hundred. For a Scag mower. It's a commercial—"

Torruella said, "You come up to the dealership this afternoon, I'll have the check for you."

"Thanks, sir. I sure do appreciate it."

Roy trotted down the steps from the attic to the garage. It was dark and cool down there. On his way to the door he stopped and ran his hand across the yellow deck of the mower sitting up on his trailer. It was a sixty-one-inch deck on a zero-turn machine, a fantastic piece of used equipment, a commercial-grade riding mower—a Scag Cheetah, in fact. He'd just bought it for cash.

"Much obliged, sir," he said later that day, as he put a card down on the desk. "And if you need any work up here, your other businesses and what have you, call me any time."

The next Monday, Roy had a job at Pine Meadows, Torruella's assisted living facility. That was his first real score. The big one came later in August. He'd driven to the ski area, which in the summer was a golf and summer-camp "recreation center." He drove slowly through the condominium development, and over to the lodges, and he got out a few times to examine the lawns, the plantings around the condos. Then he pulled up and parked in front of the summer manager's office.

The manager would long remember the day that the hard man with the military haircut came into his office and said: "I can save you three thousand dollars a month, starting today. Cut your grass neater, too."

The manager was so taken aback that for a moment he didn't even ask for Roy's name. "We've got a landscaper," he said.

"I know."

"We've been with him a long time."

"Paying for the privilege, too. Show you something?" Roy Murphy took the manager out to the great lawn that spread before the lodge. He crouched. "See that little curve to the stripe?"

"Yeah, what is that?"

"The outside blade on the deck isn't sharp. One blade's sharp, one's dull. DiBello's not taking them off each night and sharpening them."

The manager could see it. "You know him?" he asked.

Roy nodded. "Got to keep your blades sharp. Want to save three thousand dollars this month? Tell you what I'll do. I brought my mower up here. I'll cut this lawn now, you come out and see what you think in fifteen minutes."

"He was like, so intense," the manager explained later. "When I saw the cut, well, it was quite a difference. And you know, three thousand dollars!"

He did not know that Roy Murphy was in no position, that

morning, to service a job of that size; he had the Scag, but he had no dump truck, no credit with the greenhouses, no ready source of plantings, no stores of mulch and gravel and crushed stone, no employees, no references, and no phone other than his cell phone.

Soon enough, Murphy's Landscaping would have all that, and more.

Most mornings Roy rose at 4:30 and read his hundred lines of *The Iliad*. Out loud, as the captain had instructed. It was slow going, but he was determined to finish. When there was a job, he was out the door and on the road by 5:00. He'd get a coffee at Dunkin' Donuts sometimes, and sometimes he'd pull into Toni's Lunch.

One morning he was in Toni's and Pete Mallincrodt introduced himself and asked how his new business was going.

"Tough time of year to start, sir. Tough to get the new customers you need."

From the kitchen Toni called out. "Pete, you gotta be careful of this guy, he's a businessman!"

Roy asked whether he had a lawn, beds, anything that he needed help with. A few minutes later, when Toni came by to refill the coffees, Mallincrodt had yielded. Roy was saying, "Well, thank you, very much, sir, I appreciate it. I'll get up there Sunday morning, about eight, that all right?"

"*Sunday?* Business can't be that slow if you're working Sunday mornings!"

"Told you, Pete," said Toni.

A ghost of a polite smile. "I kinda started behind," he said. "Got a ways to go."

He had a ways to go, but he did not yet know *where* he was going. A plan swirled, gathering around him without yet taking shape. He felt its presence, but did not know its object or even his own place in it. In those early months he served it with a maniacal determination to build his little business. That drive pulled him from his bed; it drove him through the morning and the afternoon and into the night. There were hot, lonely nights in late summer, when he was living job to job, the business flapping little wings but not yet off the ground. When the last phone call was done and he'd sharpened the blades and greased the hubs of the Scag and cleaned and reracked his set of tools, and the last note was made in the book in his peculiar scrawl—letters half in block capitals, half in lowercase, the spelling atrocious—he'd climb up to the attic room, sit down in front of a fan, and drink a beer and eat cold Chinese food from Hunan, or cold pizza from Hoosick Pizza, and then, when done eating, drink down another beer. He had two chairs up there and a bed and a television, but he couldn't stand the television, the yak-yak of it. Laugh tracks angered him—situation comedies about New York people who never did anything but stand around in apartments and make jokes. Guys were still in Afghanistan, and it wasn't just that these people, and the people watching them, didn't care; it seemed that they didn't even know. Half awake and half asleep, he'd sit and think of his brothers back at Montana. He considered sending them e-mail, but the idea only frustrated him more. What would that do? What good would e-mails do them?

Sometimes the memories were of her. Had she married the guy with the wire-rim glasses yet? He often detoured by the Heights, as though it might give him a clue, but rarely saw anyone there. Once he caught a glimpse of Jane Herrick. But since he'd turned his back and walked out of that tent into the night, he'd had no contact. He began to forget how Emma had looked that night. The picture of her in his mind was from years before.

Meanwhile he was getting calls from guys who'd heard he was back in town, heard he might be able to use a crew. The first one didn't last a day. He hired a second, and the second was soon gone. The third one stuck. The kid worked hard and was never late in the morning, because Murphy scared the shit out of him.

"Mandel," he'd said, "I'll pay you more than DiBello will, but if you ever call in sick on a Monday, I will come to your house and find you at six in the morning and if you are not sick already then you will be before I leave. You want to work hard and make money, I'll take you. You want to fuck around, I'm going to consider that you lied to me."

"Roy—shit, I want to work, man!"

"You want to work, we'll get on fine. People who lie to me, I get crazy with them."

And when he looked at Mandel that way, and talked about getting crazy, the kid shook visibly. "Okay, okay!"

"I'll start you out two dollars above DiBello. Then we'll see. If you're not worth it, you'll be done here. You'll be crawling back to him. You still want to try? Those other guys weren't worth shit."

Mandel took the job, and he stuck. The calls kept coming, and soon Roy Murphy had a crew of four. At night the phone was now ringing with new jobs, new customers who'd heard about him from a friend or neighbor. Ringing with guys returning his calls about parts, about equipment. One night Nick Torruella called again. He said he wanted to put up a stone wall up at his place in Shaftsbury, did Roy Murphy have a crew that could handle that?

"Sure," he said. "I can be up there Tuesday morning."

He'd never done a wall in his life.

"And also, about the speech," Torruella said.

"Maybe we can talk about that when I get the wall done," he said.

Torruella repeated that he should call him Nick, assured him that he had nothing to worry about, all he had to do was talk, it wasn't really a speech as such, it was just telling people about what he'd seen fighting radical Islamists, and the party would be real proud to hear from him.

"Radical Islamists?"

"Yeah. The Taliban, al Qaeda . . ."

"Wasn't much time to stop and talk religion, sir. Anyway, I'll see you Tuesday. Thanks for the business, I appreciate it."

Roy was up for several nights laboring through a book he'd found at the library on how to prep and build a drystone wall, and he'd spent a few mornings behind the garage, practicing with stone and string guidelines. Up in Shaftsbury, he and Joe Rouleau, his newest hire, turned themselves inside out to get the job done in three days. When it was built, Roy Murphy handed the businessman a bill so small as to shame him, and would not take a tip but would be real happy to talk about expanding the contract on Pine Meadows.

They stood on the patio, surveying the work. Torruella said, "Son, you got the business. I'll have my people replace the current contractor next week and you'll be in."

"Well, I appreciate that, sir."

"You are just one helluva worker, Murphy. You're a credit to the service, and a credit to your country. Now, what should we schedule for a dinner, what would work for you?"

"Been thinking about that, sir. It's just not for me. But thanks for the business."

Torruella flashed darkly, but just for a moment. There was an awkward silence, for he didn't like being used. On the other hand, it was a funny way to be taken—he had a beautiful new patio wall for half of what it should have cost him. Torruella's pique gave way to recognition, and respect. Roy Murphy was kin, somehow: he was a businessman who would get where he wanted to get, by whatever means. With such men, Torruella knew, one could be an ally or an enemy—but never a friend. There were only two ways of it.

He studied him for a moment and then, having made his choice, said, "All right, I understand. But you listen to me, son. If you *ever* need something, you ever need *anything*, you better come straight to me. Or I will be royally pissed off. You need anything, you come to me, you understand? No questions asked."

"Well," said Roy Murphy, "I'll sure keep that in mind."

This young man is good for business, Toni was thinking. He was at Toni's Lunch about half the mornings, sometimes so early that he even beat Mel in. And now a few of his crew were coming in, too—young kids bleary and half asleep, pounding sugared crullers and coffee.

"I hear you're doing great with your new landscaping company!" she said one morning.

"It's just job to job," he answered.

"Listen, with me, it's order to order. Same thing."

Toni was one of those people you had to talk to. You could come into the diner sullen, silent, and angry at the world, and she didn't care, she'd talk to you in a sunny way. She got into your head without prying, somehow.

"And anyways, Roy, I hear it's job to a lot of jobs."

"Where'd you hear that?"

"I've got my sources."

"Well, I got my expenses," he said.

She was interested in this young man. Everybody in town was talking about him now, remembering that he was the kid who'd had a love affair with Emma Herrick all those years ago, before the bad time. But Emma, naturally, had gone off, and was going to marry that college boy—what was his name again? In Connecticut or somewhere, supposed to get married in the spring.

"Well, you're going great, everybody says so. They say you don't do anything but work, though."

"What else would I do?"

"For fun? Lots of things."

He shook his head.

"Young guy like you must have a girl. How come you never bring a girl in here?"

"Ask your sources."

"I have."

She brought him coffee. He let her fuss with him in this way, for some reason. No one else was permitted to.

"Put a little love in your life, young man, that's what I say." She grinned.

"In love with my job."

"Job can't keep a man warm at night."

"Unless he works nights." And he smiled back—just a little.

"And a young guy will burn out if he doesn't give himself a break now and then."

"He will?"

For some reason, she was particularly mischievous that morning. "Come on, all those years in the service, now you're a free man, why don't you have a girl?"

"Give me your application, I'll have my people look into it," he said.

She cackled merrily all the way back to the kitchen, then returned to the cutout and said, "You need some girl doesn't know better. I like my men broken in a little." And then laughed merrily again.

At about two in the afternoon a green Toyota dragging its muffler turned in to the ski area drive and pulled up and parked. The door opened with a painful metal groan, and he stepped out.

The one they always called my brother, Roy Murphy thought.

Michael looked thinner than Roy remembered. He stooped some; he'd lost bravado. His face looked paler, although his hair was still that flaming red. Mike looked around for a moment before catching sight of Roy over by his truck. He tossed his cigarette to the ground, waved, and made his way across the grass.

"Roy, how you doin', man!"

"Mike."

Mike hugged him awkwardly, his body scrawny against the thick block of muscle that was Roy Murphy.

"You're back in one piece! You're cut, man! Little brother the war hero and shit!"

"What's up, Mike?"

"What's *up*? You're up, man, you're back! Heard you were back and figured you'd call or whatever? Like come by or something, bro—you know? Smoke?"

Mike offered him one from his pack. His teeth were going bad, and his smile was like all those smiles Roy Murphy remembered from the Park. Smiles with an agenda. It was better not to smile.

"I quit," Roy said.

"You used to smoke all the time, man!"

"Smoke almost killed me," he said.

Mike lit one. "Heard you had, like, this new business and a guy said you were up here at the ski area." He looked around. "Nice. Anyways, just thought I'd come and say, you know, hey. Like get together or something, get a drink, you know, chasing pussy, like the old times."

"There were no old times."

Roy had a way of speaking that was cold but without rancor. It took Mike aback, and he tried at first to laugh it off. "Well, whatever, man, I don't want to hold you up or nothing, I know you're busy. Just came up to say hey. I figured we'd get together sometime is all, you know? That's all."

That smell on his breath, at two in the afternoon.

He went on: "Everybody in town's like, fucking Roy Murphy come back from the war, man, got this business, he's gonna kick DiBello's ass, you know?"

Mike was fidgety. He kept waiting for a response, and not getting one. He'd speak, then wait, then speak some more. At the stone wall across by the lodge, Mandel had stopped weed whacking. He was pretending to fuss with the spool.

Mike said, "And, little bro, I was wondering, you know, if you could use another crew or whatever?"

Roy Murphy's face betrayed no emotion. "I could," he answered. "I'm short-staffed."

"Shit, that's great! Man, thank you, that would be really cool, you know, because at the moment I've been a little, you know, a little short myself and whatever and—"

Roy cut him off. "Who'd you have in mind, Mike?"

Again he asked the question without obvious rancor. Yet sometimes a few words from Roy Murphy could drop the temperature, as though a front had just come through and you needed to put on a coat. Mike stood there dumbstruck, humiliated, his head low-ered against that fresh cold. He looked up for a smile, something, looked for a hint that maybe they could laugh this off, too. That his brother was playing with him. He shifted his weight, working up something to say.

Roy Murphy was motionless, staring at him. He was good at waiting. "Who'd you have in mind?" he repeated, more slowly.

"You know, fuck you, man. You come back and you don't even call or nothing? You don't even go up and see Mom?"

Mike had started to back away, to shrink from the one who had always been called his brother, but who had humiliated and frightened him now. "You don't even want to help your brother or nothing? Who'd I have in mind? Who'd I fucking have in mind?"

He turned and hurried back to his sad little car. He climbed in and slammed the door, and he backed the car out of its park-ing space, and then slammed it into drive. The muffler kicked up sparks until the car turned the corner and was out of view. Roy Murphy watched calmly, listened until the sound of the engine had faded away. Then he looked over at Mandel.

"Trouble with that string?"

"No no no, boss, I was just, you know . . . fixing it . . ." Mandel fired up the weed whacker and went back to work.

Roy Murphy walked across to the parking space. He ground out the cigarette on the blacktop with his heel. Then he picked up the butt and carried it back to his truck, and tossed it in his trash bag.

*My brothers are at Firebase Montana.*

# TEN

*U*p at the Heights, pasted in a black leather scrapbook still shelved in the parlor, was a particular photograph of students on the afterdeck of the SS *France*, bound for Southampton, England, in September 1971. Girls with straight hair parted in the middle smiled; long-haired boys in loud ties and garish jackets and ties askew affected cool disdain. To one side squatted a boy in an oxford shirt and a perfectly knotted bow tie. He was confident, astonishingly handsome, his smile a broad one. He was with the group but apart from it. There might be a sudden intake of breath when a visitor, leafing through this scrapbook, came upon the page. The eye was drawn to the boy—drawn then as it would be later—the face easily recognizable as Tom Herrick's.

And as very like Emma's, too.

Jane Morse Herrick had been called a handsome woman. She was tall; her demeanor was intelligent, if a little severe. She grew up with an erect and graceful carriage, which all of her girls, Emma and Anne and Charlie, would inherit. But she was not beautiful in the way her eldest daughter was. People often said that, with that beauty and that mind, Emma was bound to do well, she would go far, they would all be proud of her. People would say that she was *talented*, she had a *great future*, she was *impressive*. In later years, they did not recall that they had used the very words to describe her father. They would not link father and daughter in their minds except to admire how she had risen above him.

But that came later; in Hoosick Bridge they had thought well of Tom Herrick for many years. He was admired for his easygoing nature, for his volunteerism, for his family, and most of all for what he'd done with Burt Fredoni's little accountancy and life insurance firm, which had grown into Fredoni & Herrick. Descending from his porch at just before seven each morning, Tom would walk downhill along Washington to Maple; turning right and then left on Addison, he would cut the sweeping corner made by Washington as it enters town, and in three more blocks arrive at Fredoni & Herrick, which stood near the center of the town's small commercial district, at the corner of Addison and Washington. The light was always on in there early in the morning—"Tom's studyin' up," people said. And on God knows what all—Iceland bonds, swaps, puts and calls, a fund that didn't do a thing but buy foreign money, and then trade that money for other foreign money for a killing. He'd worked on Wall Street before coming up here. He'd learned all their ways, their tricks, their angles. Then he'd married Jane Morse and they'd taken her family place at the Heights. He'd grown the business on little bits of savings of three or five or eight thousand dollars from the lawyers and the doctors and the dentists and the Realtors, from the dairy farmers and the shopkeepers. The little firm did so well that people who had savings or a retirement account in a mutual fund in New York or Boston would pull it out and put it with Tom.

He had a way of explaining that comforted clients, made exotic things (completely impenetrable in those monthly statements that everyone just threw away) sound simple. He called his investment strategy "ridge running." Don't wait for the top to sell and don't buy at the bottom, he liked to say. You had to not be greedy. When the market was going crazy, you couldn't go crazy with it.

And when markets were down, you had to look harder for value. Some company was always doing well. You just had to find it.

"But the money managers at Fidelity know that, too, and they're down. How do you beat them?" Burt asked him once.

"I worked in the city with those guys for five years, remember? They're greedy. They're always too long one side or too short the other."

And Burt nodded. Tom used phrases like "too long one side" that Burt didn't fully understand. The important thing was, the business was doing well.

Tom said, "The problem with being Fidelity is that you have so much money, you have to spread it around the market, which means your performance will not differ from the market's. Not substantially. But if you're small, you can ignore the market, and look for the companies that are prospering. There are always some."

"Well, we're small enough, I guess." Burt laughed.

But not as small as they had been before Tom turned things around in the early years of the decade. They were growing fast. Those were good and heady times. Tom made finance so reassuring. You could make money, each year, steadily, maybe a little less in a lean year, but with care, there was always progress. People believed in Tom Herrick right up until the October evening when they heard the news.

And so, too, it was easier to see in the daughter what they wanted to see—a beautiful young woman with a dancer's grace, with fair hair and those oddly shaped yet electrifying eyes, with her own bright future—easier to see that and ignore anything more complex within her.

As to the matter of Emma and the boy from the Park during the summer of '04, they liked to refer to it in town as a "brief flirtation." But it was more than a flirtation, more than a fling; it was a kind of addiction. For ten weeks the lovers could not be out of each other's sight and touch. They were everywhere together. The hunger for each other shouted from their every look and gesture—this was common knowledge in Hoosick Bridge. That the boy had been a particular hoodlum named Roy Murphy who was in trouble with the law, that he later left town for the service and was never heard from again—this was puzzling, but known.

In Hoosick Bridge they all knew, most assuredly they knew that it was past. It was a fact, but a historical fact. In time, Emma herself could come to embrace that convenient fiction, and think she had confined Roy Murphy to the metes and bounds of a finite and historical summer. She dropped him off at the bus station at 6:45 on the morning of August 11, 2004, and he left for basic training, and her intermezzo ended. She could deceive herself that her force of will overcame the summer heat of 2004. Force of will was an aspect of the Morse character—exerting control was what Morses did.

Years later, in those solitudes that survive even marriage—in bed in the darkness, in the shower with the frosted-glass door shut and steamed—sometimes it would hit her in waves. *In the summer of my eighteenth year a power came over me whose like I never felt before or since.* She would remember how mist clouded vision itself. How she was propelled toward him with a force that could not be explained by all the physicists of Yale. The sight of him, the scent of him, the feel of his hand, the hungry look of him, the embrace of his arms set off a sensation that she loved and craved and that in the deepest part of her she feared, because it was the only ungovernable thing in her life. The power made playthings of them. It was the urgent and insatiable force of *now*. During that summer it commanded that they find a place *now*—a bed, a chair, a countertop, a car, a garage, a closet, a barn floor of rough planks, anyplace, so long as it was *now*—where they might make love. Quickly and furiously, clothed or unclothed. That force threw them together like fighters in the ring who can go nowhere but to each other's embrace; they were like exhausted and sweat-soaked fighters who clutch each other even as the referee pulls and tugs to separate them. His efforts are in vain against the force that draws the pair together, even in exhaustion. That force was activated by mere presence. It never left until he did.

But then it had departed—she was sure of it. He was gone and the heat subsided. Matriculation engaged, for two weeks, Emma's penchant for plans, projects—her genetic destiny for convention. In those few days, she congratulated herself that she had navigated her intermezzo. All summer she had feared that she would miss him—but after he left Hoosick Bridge, she did not. He was gone and the heat of that summer was gone, and that was proof enough that she had mastered what had happened. She had not searched herself with mature scrutiny. For there was a kind of ember glowing within her that she did not recognize, or refused to.

But all was overwhelmed by the October shock. That those two shocks—the force of that brief love affair and the civic earthquake of October—should have come in the same year, one hard upon the last, seemed unaccountable—or accountable, as some in town thought, as the work of the Heights itself. It was then that Roy Murphy's spirit made its farewell—paying its respects, as it were—on a single night, before vanishing from her consciousness for years. That next morning, you would have thought the ember was buried under a mountain of ash.

Emma came home that Sunday. The next days were a blur of dark suits and ties and dresses, of umbrellas. It seemed always to be raining. On Wednesday, every pew in the Episcopal church was jammed. (In Hoosick Bridge that morning there were questions, there was anxiety—but only Burt Fredoni and Jane and Emma herself had begun to grasp the depth of what had happened.) Pastor John spoke, and somebody else had a eulogy. No one would rehearse the cruel narrative; they all skirted around it and looked for words of comfort.

Anne had written a remembrance of episodes from childhood, and a friend read it. Some in the pews wondered if Emma would speak, or if she had written something, too. Hadn't she put that wonderful op-ed in the newspaper when Emerson and his mother were deported, not even a year earlier? But Emma was silent. She seemed barely present. When the organ began the hymn, Anne had to nudge her to rise. The choir struck up the first verse, and Anne and Jane followed dutifully, and snatches of lyric began to float into Emma's consciousness.

> *Where is death's sting? Where, grave thy victory?*
> *I triumph still, if Thou abide with me.*

It was a familiar melody, the sort you heard long ago, and that got into your head. Emma had no thought of singing. She listened for the words, catching snatches through the strained vibrato of old ladies in the choir. She watched them. They looked moved; she thought they were trying too hard. *O Thou who changest not, abide with me*, the old ladies sang, and all around Emma the congregation followed, murmuring words of comfort that no one believed. She stared at the coffin and tried to recall a face that already was slipping from her.

Rain splattered on the windshield, and the driver wore a black raincoat, and she thought, He does this for a living. Us and then the next people and the next. At the cemetery more undertakers in raincoats scurried with umbrellas to herd them, heavyset men stepping daintily around the puddles. She did not like to look at the hole in the earth; she stepped away from it and stood in the rain and turned her head aside. And she would not throw things in the hole, whether flowers or dirt; she thought that was barbaric. When it was over they went silently back to the limousines. Her mother walked erect and alone, and she and Anne and Charlie walked a step behind and Anne took Emma's hand. A man had his arm up like a tour guide in an airport.

The Heights was crammed with people; they stood elbow to elbow. Hands were on her, arms embracing her. People in dark clothes filled the parlor and the dining room and the kitchen. Outside the weather continued cold and raw, and the damp, oppressive gray had worked inside the Heights, too, so that Emma shivered now and again and held her arms around her chest in a vain effort to warm herself. She smelled damp wool, heard the murmur of low conversation. There was Maggie, with mascara messed by tears, hugging her, and behind Maggie, doleful, tormented Brian. Brian's parents. The Gilsons. The Byrnes. The Fredonis. An inconsolable sound echoed from an upper room: of Charlie sobbing violently. Anne sat on the end of the couch, stricken.

Jane Herrick stood in the corner of the parlor, by the French doors, embracing and being embraced. She was pale and drawn, but erect, dry eyed, and it seemed, as Emma watched, that she was more consoling than consoled. She greeted them as they shuffled in, sometimes a little loudly, it seemed to Emma. Maybe she needed to show that her pride was undiminished. Jane Herrick had not wept that anyone could see. She was anchored there—uncertain of the future, but unbowed.

"Such a shock," people whispered. "It's too much. It hasn't registered yet."

Emma went out to the porch, still shivering. She stood at the east corner and watched the rain dripping from the gutters, and she thought, The gutters are full of leaves, no one has cleaned the gutters this year. She looked down Washington toward the dark and silent town where Fredoni & Herrick had for days been a scene of morbid fascination, and would soon be under siege.

When the people had gone, the house echoed with the ticking of the clock on the mantel. It was said that Ezra Morse had purchased it and brought it back with him from a trip to Europe, decreeing that its tick-tock should always be heard in the Heights. Its face bore Latin numerals in a black Gothic script, and in faded lettering, "Barraud & Lunds, Cornhill, London." The clock had seen every wedding, every birth, had measured out the days, the nights, the departures and returns, the risings and the settings, the arrivals and departures of all the Morses. Even on that morning, Jane Herrick had wound the mantel clock, as the faithful steward of the Heights did every day. The Heights had observed such shocks as this before, and kept its time nevertheless.

But no one could eat. They sat, and Jane held Charlie's hand, and then Anne held Charlie's hand, and then Anne took her sister up to bed, where they slept together in their clothes.

At last Emma rose. She stood by the window. "God, it's started up harder now—the rain," she said. "It's so *cold*. I'm going up."

She crossed the room and kissed her mother. "Love you," she whispered. "You should go to bed."

Woodenly, Jane answered with a question. "Where should I go, Emma?"

Emma felt stupid and embarrassed. Her mother drew strength from the house, she was a strong woman, but the bed—there were limits.

"I'll make you up the one in the guest room."

Upstairs in the linen closet Emma found the linens—such old sheets, she thought, almost threadbare—how many months or years have they lay folded on these old pine shelves? She made the bed in the guest room. She checked the thermostat, but it bore false witness, she thought, for it was not so warm as the thermostat said. She turned it up further and waited for the knocking and groaning to start in the pipes.

When her mother had gone to bed, Emma went up to the third floor. In the small bed in her bedroom she lay wide awake for a long time, listening to the storm, until at last she rose and in her nightgown walked barefoot along the dormered corridor. Inside all was quiet now, except for distant rumblings in the pipes, and the faraway percussion of the mantel clock. The floorboards were cold against her feet as she climbed the last short staircase.

The storm was raging when she entered the tower. Blasts of wind so rattled the old windowpanes that at first she thought one of them might break. Rain pounded the slates, waves of it lashing the western windows. She took the blanket from the back of the old sofa and wrapped herself in it.

The stage he'd built for them when she was seven years old was on the shelf. She set it down on the couch where she had lain beneath Roy Murphy that first time, three months and a lifetime ago—where she had felt his heart pound against her chest and tasted hot sweat dripping from his forehead to her mouth. She pulled the blanket more closely around her shoulders, and sat in the darkness, hugging her knees tight and listening to the rain.

Her father was a man who would do anything for you. All afternoon in the garage he would build a playhouse or repair a bicycle, but with only a distant generosity, removed from companionship. He would do things for you but was most comfortable doing them alone, away from others. He didn't go to functions—he accompanied Jane Herrick to functions. Emma remembered the day that, as a girl of four or five, she'd visited his office. There were two big computer screens at his desk, side by side, with bars and colors and numbers moving on them, and it made her think of piloting some wonderful aircraft. "My daddy flies a spaceship," she had said, and all the grown-ups had laughed. It became one of those amusing anecdotes people told, how mild-mannered Tom Herrick went down to his sleepy little office in town each morning to fly his spaceship.

Except that the story was true, and the rocket crashed to earth.

And there was this dark fact. The source of his coldness and remove had not been Roy Murphy at all, but something more desperate. The day before, she had found her mother on the porch, watching Mr. Fredoni back his Lexus from the drive. "It's the most terrible news," Jane had said.

In that room so electric with memory, Emma sat on the couch, wrapped in the blanket and listening to the rain, and then she heard the faint tread of bare feet on the stairs. Anne appeared at the door.

"Hi."

"You okay?"

"I couldn't sleep. I was . . . remembering. . . ."

"Me, too." Emma shifted the stage to the floor and when Anne sat beside her on the sofa, hugged her sister. Emma could feel Anne's back trembling. There on the sofa they curled together beneath the blanket, and at length Anne's head fell to Emma's lap.

"How's Charlie?"

"All week, she's been saying she hates it here, she can't stand it here anymore," Anne answered. "In this house."

"Should we go down to her?"

"I think she's sleeping now. She was when I left."

"God," Emma said, "starting high school with . . . with all of *this*. And *you*, Anne." But she had not told Anne what all of this was, how her mother's hands were shaking on the porch yesterday afternoon as they watched grim-faced Mr. Fredoni drive off—how Jane had said, "It's . . . it's not there, Emma! The state's attorney and the, the federal one, too, what do they call him? They're calling and . . . oh, my God!"

*The money was gone.* Gone—lost? Or gone . . . She didn't yet want to fill in the blank, not even in her mind. Emma knew that her sisters were not ready for this.

"I'm the only one who gets a pass, gets to go away," Emma mused.

"Em, nobody gets a pass," Anne said and began to cry. They sat without speaking, listening to the rain on the roof. The storm had grown fierce, but after a day of such chill and relentless damp, it suddenly felt cozily conspiratorial to cry together up there beneath their blanket, with wind and rain attacking the tower, but not reaching them. The sisters had had no such confidences since . . . since before Roy Murphy had come back to town.

Emma asked, "Remember my yellow bike that Dad bought for me?"

"I was *so* jealous," Anne said, still sniffing.

"And Mom got all freaky about it? 'You are not to ride that bike on Route Seven!'"

The memory brought a smile. Anne stopped crying, too. "I think she really meant, *across* Route Seven."

"Exactly. Dad didn't get it at all, but she did."

Anne prodded. "Well?"

Above them, the rain pounded down as Emma answered. "The weird thing is, you might say it was Dad who introduced us."

\* \* \* \*

For her tenth birthday, Tom Herrick gave Emma a brand-new electric yellow Trek mountain bike. It looked outsize when she climbed on it for the first time. Her feet strained for the pedal at the bottom of the revolution, and Tom had to lower the seat right to the frame. But her eyes had gone wide, for the bike unlocked something in her. At six and seven, Emma had been one to play in the tower room, where the American Girl dolls had their elaborate homes, and the puppets and marionettes their little stage with the painted balsa wood curtains in the corners. At nine, excursions to the neighbors or to town soccer were parentally controlled. The electric yellow racehorse changed that. She made one circuit of the driveway before she was off, riding it down Washington toward the town. Each day that summer she pressed farther and farther from home—careening around the neighborhoods, going farther down distant streets. The bike was the first freedom that she'd ever known.

In years to come there would be other bikes before at length there was no bike at all, but the yellow Trek was the One Bike. In the fall, it was Emma's pride to ride it to school. She would not accept a lift in any but the filthiest weather. And before the snow had gone, she had the bike back out of the garage. She had to take it to school.

It was the Trek that introduced her to a dark, scowling boy from the Park, in the Pine Cobble school yard, one day in April, after school got out for the afternoon. He was a boy who sat in the back of the class, who barely spoke when Mrs. Steiner called on him, and sometimes for days at a time was not there at all. Already in the fifth grade the barrier that divides the Park from the town was rising, walling one set of kids off from another.

Emma was unlocking the Trek. She looked up, and he was standing there.

"Hi," she said, a little frightened.

"That's a cool bike."

"Thanks."

"Wanna go down the Hoosic? I know a good jump."

He sat astride an old Sting-Ray, a strange-looking thing without gears, with rust along the rims and chain. His hair was black, and his face framed by dirt, as though he'd taken a splash of water only to the oval around his nose. And before she could answer, he turned and pedaled away. Maybe she followed him because she was too frightened not to. She rode from school down to River Street and across the river on West Ford Road, where it becomes a dirt road and meanders with the stream along toward Pruitt's Farm. From the road he dove into the trail that ran along the riverbank, bouncing over tree roots.

They came to the jump.

When she went back to find it years later, the path was still there, more littered than she remembered, and the bike jump, too. It wasn't much to look at. But on the April day that she first followed Roy Murphy, it seemed a mountain cliff to her. And so many months went by before she worked up the courage to try it herself, and take her first fall, and try it again, and land. The path led steadily downward until it reached a point in the trail where an ancient flood had eroded the bank. There the path dipped sharply and then rose to a lip. Beyond, the path fell away again to the river.

That afternoon he flew off the seat, the bike cartwheeling down the hill. Then he lay at the bottom.

"You okay?" she called out.

"Course," he said weakly. He sat up. "You try!"

"You should wear a helmet," she said.

The next morning, before school, Roy Murphy came across the school yard in that way he had—would always have—that was not running but was more than walking, too direct, too blunt, leaning forward, as if he would burst through any barrier. Emma was holding Maggie's arm. Maggie, too, was frozen, and for once stopped talking.

Then he was standing in front of her. She could not meet his eye, but felt it.

"Emma—try that jump again?"

"I better not."

He said nothing, but turned and walked quickly away. Maggie Byrne waited until he was out of earshot and then pronounced him a jerk.

Her mere name: you might mark her doom from the moment Roy Murphy said it. Still a child rattling out a juvenile invitation in the rough cadence of the Park, yet more softly pronouncing that word. A person might mistake it for kindness, the way he said her name. Of such kindnesses dangerous consequences are born.

"You were so quiet, I thought you were asleep," Anne said.

The percussion on the rooftop was still steady, a hard rain, but a regular one. The wind had subsided. Emma shifted and sighed. "Just thinking was all."

"About Dad?"

"No. I was, I . . ."

Anne said, "Roy."

Emma did not answer. Anne stroked her hair and asked, quietly, "How did you meet him in the first place? You never told me."

Emma spoke softly, too. "Forever ago. Maybe I always knew him. That's what it felt like."

"But were you always . . . ?"

"No. It was in seventh grade that . . . that something happened." In that darkness Anne could not see her sister smiling, as she remembered a spring day near the end of the school year, in the lunch room at middle school, when a strange new wind was felt, from an unexpected quarter.

Twelve-year-old Emma Herrick was going to cause a stir for reasons she could not name. She had a new attitude in the seventh grade. At home her anger would flash at Jane Herrick like a sudden lightning storm. She would slam doors. As Anne's eyes went wide, she would taunt her parents with loud music or reckless profanity.

Sometimes she was "grounded," a sentence of house arrest that afforded many opportunities for scornful martyrdom, and for brief but heroic escapes.

That day in school, Emma walked past her friends' usual table in the cafeteria. They called to her and she did not answer. She carried her tray to the end of the room and affected to search distractedly for a place to sit down—and by chance to find a spot that happened to be across the table from Emerson Rodriguez, who by sheer accident was sitting next to Roy Murphy.

"Hey," she said offhandedly, just happening to notice them before focusing carefully on opening the milk carton. She could almost feel them all at the other end of the cafeteria, whispering, *She's sitting with Park kids—Emma!*

Emerson was grinning from ear to ear. "*Emma!* Sup, girl!" Turning toward Roy Murphy, he said, "Dude, this my girlfriend Emma Herrick. We goin out."

Emerson was the envoy who crossed freely between the worlds. Class clown status was his passport from the Park, where he lived with his mother, to the town. Caramel-skinned, pudgy, with a straight-brimmed baseball cap perching at an angle on a nest of hair that had almost enough curl to elevate his full height, with cap, to five foot two.

She scolded, "Emerson, we are *not!*" (She just happened to sit there because there was an empty place to sit, that's all.)

"Emma, lemme tell you some advice. Don't have nothing to do with that Roy Murphy, he ain't nothing but trouble. Stick with me, I be your daddy. If he give you any trouble you let me know and I gonna mess him up." Then to Roy, "Don't make me mess you up again."

Roy Murphy ate his lunch in silence. There was no sign that he'd even heard Emerson, who bobbed in the seat at his side, worrying at him the way a puppy crouches and leaps at the ear of a grown dog, and the dog doesn't react. "I told you, Murph, she likes me. All the girls, they got to come to Emerson like moths to the light, dude, like horses to the water! She no different."

Then he spoke. "He just called you a horse. Or a bug maybe. You ever do that jump, Emma?"

Her name again. Something jangled inside her. She had not heard his voice in a long time—it seemed like he never spoke in school—and yet it was as though they'd never left off the conversation.

"I *tried* it."

At twelve, Emma had almost reached her full height. She was taller than most boys—taller than he was—sapling slender and still boyish herself. Her face was changing, but her body had not yet begun its metamorphosis: she was not one of the early bloomers whom the boys lust after in middle school. One part of her had reached its full development, and thereafter through puberty and her young adulthood would scarcely change: the instantaneous smile that could send her cheeks up against her eyes; a smile so broad it made her appear to squint. In the Park, smiles were not like this. Smiles were sour or ironic or manipulative; they had always a freight. Roy Murphy had learned to read smiles and mistrust them, but her smile astonished even him.

"Ride *bikes*?" Emerson scoffed. "Murph, you loser. Emma, you don't need no bike! You and me, you know, go to my crib in the city for the weekend in my X-five."

"You have your license already, Emerson?"

His grin exposed the gap between his front teeth. "Shit, you think I need that? Cops know not to mess with Emerson! I don't need no license!"

"Just a car seat," said Roy Murphy.

Anne listened raptly in the darkened tower as Emma told the story of that lunch-room exchange so long ago.

"What made you sit with him?"

"Something just came on me. And that weekend I got the Trek out again. The tires were all flat, I was trying to fit the pump on. You needed a special thingy on the valve, so I had to find it in the garage, and I was going to fix the brakes—the brakes on that bike were a pain, they either didn't stick or they totally stuck all the time—you know? Only Dad knew how to fix them. Anyway, I was in the driveway getting nowhere with all this and Dad comes out, and he goes, 'Hauling out the old bike, huh?' In a very *Dad* voice."

"Hello, young lady!" Anne mimicked fondly.

"Exactly."

Anne sighed. "He had no clue sometimes."

"None. I was being shitty, like I was that whole year." Now Emma was the mimic—of her own middle school, irritated self: "I'm *just* going for a ride!"

Anne rubbed her sister's arm. "You *could be* kind of . . . dramatic sometimes. What did he say? Did your claws scare him off?"

"He just went on speaking in 'Dad.'" Again she mimicked: "'This kind of brakes, Em, they're fussy. Let me get the thingabob keys. Let me show you. Let me take care of that. Let me adjust the seat, too. Let me do it *myself*.'"

"And you smiled sweetly and . . ."

"And went hormone psycho." And again Emma mimicked her earlier self. "'You *don't* need to make a big deal out of it! I'm *just* going for a bike ride! Just riding *around*, not going anywhere in particular—*God!* Why do you have to make such a *big deal* about it!' I was such a shit to him for two straight years. Why weren't *you* ever a shit, Anne?"

"I *was*—but nobody noticed."

"On account of me."

The question lingered for a moment longer, before Anne gave it voice. "So were you? Just riding around, I mean?"

Emma hugged her sister tightly and closed her eyes, remembering the feel of the warm rock on her back, through long summer afternoons from years before.

"Just riding around. And maybe possibly happening by accident to ride down somewhere along toward the general direction of the river, where the boys were."

\* \* \* \*

A massive willow stood on the north bank of the Hoosic, throwing its green-gold hair over the huge boulder that kids called Bungalow Rock. From the downstream side of the rock, you could jump into a pool. Upstream, the rock sloped down to water level. This is where they learned to fish. Roy Murphy found—or stole—a spinning rod and some rusty fishhooks up at the Park somewhere, and he and Emerson rode their bikes down from the Park to the river. All summer they would ride to the river and clamber around the willow and out to the rock.

They fished with worms, catching perch, mainly, and once in a while a trout. Sometimes when Emma Herrick had allowance or babysitting money, they would ride their bikes to Stewart's and she would buy them all sodas or ice cream cones. Once when it rained they dashed off on their bikes into Pruitt's hay barn and hung out in the loft all afternoon, listening to the rain crash against the tin roof. If it was hot they would go jumping off the bridge at West Ford Road. She and Emerson would hop the barrier and jump from the road surface, but Roy Murphy would climb atop the steel superstructure, then knife into the air as though hurled from a cannon, arching his back like a wild animal. He would plunge into the one deep hole beneath that bridge. Then they would return to Bungalow Rock and lay there for hours, watching white ships scud across the blue of the summer sky, the sun dappling in and out through strings of willow leaves.

Emma was the first to catch a fish, the first day they ever learned how to do it. It was that first Saturday, when she'd ridden the Trek down to the Hoosic, and sure enough found Roy digging for worms while Emerson lounged against the willow.

"Emma!"

"Hey, Emerson. Where's your car?"

"In the shop. Getting a tune-up."

Roy Murphy had scooped a few worms into a plastic cup. He held one up to Emerson and said, "Put him on."

"Dude, you serious? That's disgusting!"

He turned to her. "You want to?"

She did not. "Yeah?" she said tentatively.

She pushed the squirming worm onto the hook and got worm guts on her fingers and forced herself to look unperturbed. One end of the worm was still thrashing around.

"Mmm, mmm, he look good," said Emerson.

"Gotta do him twice," Roy said, "or he'll drop off."

He took the hook from her and poked it through the worm again, and then they clambered out to the big rock past where the willow branch jutted over the stream. Roy stood with the rod. He had seen some fishermen down there sometimes, and he tried to mimic them, waving the rod back and forth, and then casting the line the way they did. But the line wouldn't come out of the reel. He waved it back and forth over his head until the bobber was caught in the willow.

"Dude, it's broke," said Emerson, helpfully. He scampered off the rock and climbed up the willow to get the bobber.

Upstream, a fly fisherman had been watching them. He began to wade in their direction, while Emerson was up in the tree. An adult approaching was never a good thing. "Shit, man," said Emerson, "let's go."

But Roy Murphy had figured it differently. He didn't move.

The fisherman came slowly downstream toward them. "You guys have a little problem?" he called out.

The man reached the end of the rock and climbed out, his waders dripping big puddles of water. He was a sight, with his rod, his waders, and fishing vest with its little ruff, and its many pockets, and pair of tweezers hanging from a string off a plastic fob, and his net clipped on his back. His rod was much longer, and the reel looked thinner than theirs. "Ever fished before?" he asked, genially.

"Lots of times," said Emerson, from the branch. "Salmon fishing, tuna fishing, whale fishing, alla them."

The man smiled. "Bird fishing?"

"My friend's just learning," Emerson said.

"Well, there's a couple of tricks to it," the man said. "You've got a spinning rod there, so you don't cast it like a fly rod. See this little metal piece? This is the gate. The line won't come out unless you flip it back this way." He showed them. Then he showed them how to hold the line with a finger and release the line just as you gave the rod a flick, to send the bobber and the worm away into the river, and then reset the gate by winding the crank on the reel. He reached into one of the pouches in his vest and pulled out a little metal box. Inside were some hooks and a spare bobber.

"In case you lose this one," he said, handing them to Roy. "You guys got your fishing licenses, right?"

"Course we do," Emerson scoffed.

The man laughed, and he clambered down and waded back upstream.

"You do?" Emma whispered.

"Course," said Emerson. "In my car."

Roy began tossing the line upstream into the eddy, where the bobber sat, flipping the gate and then letting it fly out and then setting the gate again by half a windup on the reel. Emerson again provided the commentary. "Ain't no fish there, dude! Put it up over there, over in that pool."

Roy fished for a while without catching anything. "Them fish laughing at you," said Emerson. "You got to give it to the man."

Roy handed the rod to Emerson. He cast it out a few times but then lost interest.

"Let's go jumping off the bridge," he said.

"Want to catch one first," said Roy.

He fished some more without any luck and then handed the rod to Emma. She tossed the line into the river and reeled it back. She tried reeling fast and then tried reeling slow and then reeling first fast, then slow. After a few more tosses into the tea-colored water, her mind wandered. She was splashing the water at the edge of the rock with her toes, not paying attention to the bobber. Suddenly the bobber disappeared and the rod bowed violently and started thrashing around in her hands. She cried, "What?"

Roy yelled, "You got one! Reel it in, Emma, reel it in!"

"Dude, it's a shark!" Emerson said.

She struggled to turn the reel and hold the rod at the same time. When she got the line reeled in halfway, she saw the fish's silvery shimmer as it darted back and forth under the water.

"Keep reeling him in, I'll get him," said Roy.

The fish was close to the rock and Roy plunged in from the bank, making a terrific splash, clambering around and grabbing the line. He pulled the flopping creature onto the rock.

"Shit, he big!" said Emerson. "Look at him!"

She had caught a fat brook trout, a beautifully spotted, pink-bellied fish, about ten inches long. The fish flopped on the rock and slipped out of Roy's hands. He got hold of him again and Emerson was trying to hold him, too, and then he flopped loose and was bouncing in the air.

"Hold him!" said Emerson, laughing. Roy got hold of him finally and tried to whack his head against the rock, but the fish slithered out and was flopping around again.

"What are you doing?" she cried.

"Trying to kill him!" Roy said.

"I don't want to kill him!"

"Got to kill him if we're going to eat him!"

"I don't *want* to eat him!"

She whirled the rod and jerked the line up again, and the trout went sailing back into the water.

"What'd you do that for?"

"I don't want to kill him," she repeated.

The rod was bowed again as the fish took off across the eddy.

"Well, all right," Roy said, "I won't. But you gotta reel him in again so's I can unhook him."

"She got some *attitude*, that girl," said Emerson.

It was a night without hours, a night that suspended the laws of physics. Dawn would be placed on hold, and the night would last precisely as long as it needed to. In the darkness, Anne whispered: "Earth to Emma."

"Sorry, I was just thinking about it—Bungalow Rock."

"That was where . . . ?"

"That was where it really started, you could say. The prom was more like . . . like, he's back, it's *him* again, my old friend that I was embarrassed about all through high school and don't have to be anymore. But that summer I used to hold his hand on Bungalow Rock. Sneak kisses."

"I remember," Anne said. "You'd go off on your bike, and Mom would pace up and down the porch, up and down, up and down. I'd watch her. I was little miss hide-in-the-closet. What was that book—it's up here somewhere?"

"*Harriet the Spy?*"

"Yes. Anne the Spy, watching everyone else. Anyway, Mom knew something was going on. She always knew things like that— *then*." Anne caught herself, changed course. "Em—today, did Mom seem . . . different at all?"

"*Today?*"

"I know, I know—*duh!* But I mean, she wasn't quite, I don't know, plugged in. Afterwards, at the reception."

"Loud."

"Yes."

"We're all distracted."

"I guess."

They were silent for a bit. Emma was still thinking about the summer after seventh grade. "I used to come home for dinner, and Mom would be like, 'Where do you go all day?' Of course she found out. That's why we had all those trips at the end of the summer. Boston for shopping, the Clark, that trip to Mystic—remember those submarines?"

"Yes."

"*Submarines.* She was pretty intent on separating us. Mystic, Aunt Patty's—she took me to Maine. I always wondered how she found out."

"Mrs. Byrne. I was spying on them that day, too."

Emma sighed. "April—of course! She's *such* a . . ."

"They were on the porch having iced tea," Anne explained, "and I was in the yard, around the corner, eavesdropping—I've spent half my life eavesdropping on the *interesting* people."

"Oh, stop."

"It's true. Anyway Mrs. Byrne goes, you know how she talks, 'Was that *Emma* I saw down at the river Thursday?' And Mom's like, 'At the river?' Trying not to let on that it's a big deal. Like she's mildly interested, you know? Trying not to be *too* interested. 'When, April?' And Mrs. Byrne goes, you know, Thursday or something, whatever it was, and then she adds, 'With some . . . *friends?*'—you know, saying 'friends,' like that?"

"*That*'s our April!"

They were silent for a while, and Anne asked, "Soooo . . ."

"Yessss. . . ."

"What *were* you up to, Em?"

She paused before answering, listening to the now steady, reassuring thrum of the rain on the roof. At last she said, *"Fishing!"* And then, for the first time in a week, Emma laughed.

If it were sunny, after fishing awhile the three of them would lie on the rock. Roy and Emerson might have cigarettes and a lighter that Roy had stolen from his mother.

"You want one?" he'd ask.

"You shouldn't smoke," she'd say.

One day she asked him where he would go when he was grown up.

"He ain't goin nowhere, dude," said Emerson.

"Well, I am," she said.

"Where?"

"I'm going away to college and then I will live in New York City in a large apartment with many bedrooms. And a view of Central Park and a doorman."

"Whatsat? Dude at the door?" Emerson asked.

"Moron," said Roy Murphy.

"A dude that stand at the door and open it for you all day?"

Emerson struggled with this astonishing notion. "That's like—his job? 'Mizz Emma, lemme open the door for you.' And you be like, 'No, Doorman, I'm not ready to go outside yet.' 'Oh, dude, I will close it then. Lemme know when you ready. You ready? Okay, *now* I open the door for you. Miss Emma, when you comin home?' 'Doorman, Imma come home in three hours.' 'Okay, I be ready to open it again. What a busy day for me, allatime opening and closing this door!'"

"*Idiot*," Roy Murphy said.

When she'd stopped giggling, she explained that the doorman would be *down*stairs and her apartment *up*stairs.

"Well, all right," Emerson said. "Imma live in Washington, DC."

"Why?"

He grinned. "Cause Imma be president. Imma get doormen with guns."

"A Mexican moron can't be president," Roy Murphy said.

"I ain't no Mexican moron."

"If you're born there, you're Mexican. And a moron, too, for being born there."

"What you know about it, Roy Murphy? You never been outta Hoosick Bridge! Gimme a cigarette."

"I'm out."

"You got any more of those Starbursts?"

Roy gave him the last piece. They were quiet for a minute, and then Roy asked, "You really going to New York City?"

"Yes."

He smiled darkly. "I'll take *your* house then."

"Me, too," said Emerson. "Emma's house *nice*. I *like* that house!"

"He'll be the doorman," Roy said.

"Mom would *love* that," said Emma.

"She can live there, too, if she wants. She can, like, do the laundry. Not your father, though."

"Why not?"

"He don't like scum from the Park."

Roy Murphy looked straight at her as he said it. She didn't know how to deny it or what to say, but was thinking, *She doesn't, either.*

"Scum from the Park!" Emerson started rapping. "Such a sight—Scum at the Heights! What the world coming to! Hood-lums in the kitchen, too! Down at the water, hangin wit your daughter—oh, man, you really didn't oughta!"

They snickered at Emerson, but their eyes were on each other. "What are you gonna do, Roy—really?"

He thought about it, then said, "Get a motorcycle. Then I'll be out of Vermont, anyways. Ride around the country. Then go on a plane around the world."

"Why?" she asked.

"Why would you go to New York City with all those people?"

The temperature had climbed above ninety degrees, and the cicadas were humming. They were hot and bored with fishing, and so they swam in the river. Later they lay on the rock again, making wet shapes that dried quickly in the sun. The heat of the rock and the warmth of the day baked into them. He lay next to her, and she stirred, inside, at his closeness. And then she felt it. He'd put his hand on hers, and that was the first time she felt the jolt, like touching an electric socket by accident. She would never forget that feeling.

Then, for Emma was at heart incautious, she wove her fingers through his.

Maybe she had drifted off, and then drifted back, for after a long while she realized that Anne's body was shaking, and she knew that, in the darkness, she was crying again.

"Oh, *Anne.*" She sat up and put her arms around her sister, rocked her gently. And then it was silent no longer. The words came through Anne's sobs.

"Why did he have to *do* that?"

"It's all right," Emma whispered.

"What did we do to him to make him do that? Why couldn't he just have *talked* to us?"

"I don't think there was anything talking would do," Emma said.

"But *why?*"

"It's all right."

"Was the business so bad, that he would do that? Wouldn't it get better? We loved him, didn't we, Em?"

Emma said nothing. It was too early, too early.

"He was a good man. *You* believe he was a good man, don't you? Wasn't he?"

"Yes," she lied. "Yes, he just wasn't . . . strong enough."

"But just . . . He didn't have to do *that*. Whatever had happened in the stupid business!" Anne was sobbing now. "It would have been all right. We could have made it all right!"

Emma pulled away from her and leaned back against the arm of the couch. "Anne—do you feel like you knew him?"

"Of course I knew him. He was Dad." She sniffed.

"Really knew him?"

And after that Anne was silent. Emma came back and held her close again and whispered, "It's all right," stroking Anne's hair. "It's all right." She held her that way and thought, What an odd thing that, at the worst time in the world, people say, "It's all right."

Anne spoke no more that night. She cried softly for a while longer and at last dropped off. But Emma's mind was racing. After Anne had fallen asleep, Emma slipped off the couch and went to the window. The rain had eased. It was more of a mist now, and she stood at the window, looking down toward the town, where scattered lights shone in the darkness—down where her father had built that cancerous business. Down there, for reasons unexplained, he had hazarded his life, and theirs. She listened to her sister's settled breathing. Below the window was the slate roof of the third floor, and below that the porch roof, where she used to sit with Anne on summer nights, and where they'd conspired in a particular episode of literal eavesdropping one warm night that summer after the seventh grade.

The front doors opened, and Jane and Tom came out to the porch. In the summer they'd go out there after dinner, she with a glass of wine, he with a beer or sometimes a gin and tonic.

Distinctly the girls heard their father say: "Well, I don't know, there's a lot of stories, but nobody knows for sure where he came from."

Jane's voice was quieter—Emma could not make out the words—but its tone was more insistent, challenging, while her father, as was his way, tried to soothe, responding, explaining, making things gentle. The way he always did, so that after he had talked a thing through, that thing that before didn't make sense at all now made sense. It was his special gift.

Emma was embarrassed that Anne was hearing this. Anne sat motionless on the roof, her hands around her knees, listening intently.

"Nobody knows where Leo got him. Barb says he brought the infant home one night, handed him to her, said, You have to watch him. In those days before Leo left, she was afraid; she did what he said. That's the way Barb explained it to me."

More from Jane, muffled, impossible to make out.

"He had a sister out in California, I think. Or maybe a girl-friend," he was saying. Her mother said something, and he an-swered, "Jane, it's not the boy's fault if the mother's overwhelmed."

Jane spoke again, more sharply than before. The girls strained to hear, discerning the name Leo distinctly, several more times.

Roy Murphy had never mentioned a father, a Leo, who had "left." He didn't talk much about home at all. All he'd say was that he lived up at the Park with Mike, and sometimes, when he was home, the oldest boy, Sean. Once she had asked Roy, did he live with his mom and dad? He had said he didn't have a dad, and when she asked, then, whether it was just his mom and his brothers, he had been vague. "I guess," he had said.

Down on the porch, her father said, "Burt says it was the sister's boy. Sister, girlfriend, you hear both things."

Jane murmured, and Tom answered, "Jane, I don't know any more than you about where he went. Trouble with the law in New York is one story. Some people think he had another family somewhere in Florida. But look, they're just kids. I wouldn't get too worked up over it. They don't have to go up to the Park."

Outside the Heights it was still and dark, utterly silent. Down the hill, the streetlights shone on a lonely, glistening Washington Street. In the tower Anne's breathing was regular, nasal, childlike. But still Emma's mind raced. In this place, on this night after her father's funeral, try as she might to invite Tom Herrick, it was Roy Murphy who had returned to the tower. She had not seen him since August. He'd never called her. At the end she'd asked whether he would have an e-mail address, half dreading its receipt, but he'd never e-mailed her either. Was he still somewhere in the US in training? Had he been sent overseas? She didn't know. That was how she had wanted it, as freshman year of college began. He had not been back to trouble her mind.

Until tonight, of all nights: tonight, when she ought to honor her father, and her mind would not comply. Stubbornly it went to freshman year in high school—the day Roy Murphy appeared suddenly in the hallway outside the cafeteria, accosting her bluntly, as was his way, in that sea of bodies ebbing and flowing around them just at the end of lunch period—in that watchful throng of witnesses. The girls in school were talking after that. "Emma was with Roy Murphy. Outside the cafeteria. Sara *saw* them. He asked her out."

"Roy Murphy asked Emma *out*? What did she *say*?"

She had not wanted to say yes. By then, eighth-grade summer was already a part of history. She vaguely knew of troubles about Roy Murphy. Widely bruited in the school were his visits to juvenile court with Eliza Murphy, who sat silently on the bench outside the small courtroom, wearing dark glasses and trembling, until it was over. Roy Murphy was filling out and acquiring an air of juvenile menace. He was a bit below average height, but thick across the shoulders. His hair grew long, and his prominent brow ridge and early beard gave his face a harsh aspect. The face dark with dirt in boyhood grew dark and unkempt with growth. The wrestling coach tried to get him to come out, but he wouldn't. Sometimes he wasn't in school at all, for days, for a week at a time. His friends were the stoners and future bikers from the Park—and Emerson, who was everybody's friend.

Emma had been too startled to think of a response. By that time the electricity was more frightening than compelling. There were the kids from town and the kids from the Park, and she was one and he was the other. The wall was up: complete, illuminated, manned with armed guards, for Emma had grown to the same social awareness that her mother had. Her family were leading people in this small town, and she was a leading girl in the school. Even in this small town, there were expectations.

So it was a startle reflex as much as an answer when she said, "Okay."

And then he turned and walked away, disappeared back into the hallway crowd as suddenly as he had emerged. He hadn't even explained when or how, exactly, they would "go out."

"You said *what?*" Maggie Byrne demanded of her later that afternoon.

For a few days she reached each hallway corner at school in dread of finding him coming around it. She could not hear a telephone ring without fearing that it was him. She imagined him coming to her house, or some other horrendous mortification. But he didn't call. He didn't come. Not the next day, or the day after. The "going out" simply never happened. It occurred to her many months later that what he'd wanted was not to go out at all. He'd just wanted to know the answer to the question whether she would.

From the east there came at last a faint lightening in the sky, and as that long night was coming to its end, still she remembered.

That Roy Murphy worked up at DiBello's Landscaping, summers, and then, it seemed, all the time.

That sometimes he did come to Taconic Regional. People would notice him in the hall or in a classroom and say, "Check it out, Roy Murphy's here today."

That old Phillips, the history teacher, would ask, "Do you have your assignment, Mr. Murphy?" and Roy would shake his head. Not smart-mouthed, not fidgeting, or claiming he'd lost it. He just said, "No, I don't."

That he didn't slouch or hack with the other boys in the back of the room, but sat and watched old Phillips, darkly concentrating, until one day, exasperated, the history teacher shifted his thick glasses and asked why Roy Murphy bothered to come to class at all, and as the class fell silent, Roy answered, "It's interesting."

That there was muffled laughter at this, because people thought Roy Murphy was mocking Phillips.

That he never broke eye contact, and some people could not be sure whether old Phillips was being mocked at all.

And she remembered that last summer—how she had loved him, all over town, everywhere there was a spare or stolen moment or an empty room. How all during that summer she'd wait for him, wait and wait for tedious hours, brushing her hair, clipping it in a knot, unclipping it, brushing it again, putting it in a ponytail, taking out the band, brushing it again, listening for the sound of that motorcycle coming for her.

That she could pick out its unique tone half a mile away, far down Washington Street—that, hearing it, she would fly down the staircases and burst onto the porch, to find him in the drive, in his scuffed jacket, jeans, boots, whatever the weather, straddling the bike in silence, the engine burbling.

That they rode it together, everywhere, up and down the state, in New York and Massachusetts, everywhere.

That they spent long hours on summer nights trying to pick constellations out of the sky, looking up from fields or porches or dirt roads off at the hilltops, peering with a small flashlight at the little guidebook she'd found, then switching it off and looking up again.

That he had an uncanny eye for patterns—could pick from the bright, impenetrable spangle of the summer sky a shape she could not see.

That he seemed to know places, places she'd gone by a thousand times without noticing—how one night he'd invited her to a concert with a wry smile, she thinking he meant a rock band, when it was really just to listen to the frogs in McRearys' Pond before swimming in their pool.

That here, in this place, on the couch where Anne now slept, she had loved him.

That he'd hurried into the bus depot, without looking back.

She sighed, coming back to where she was, to the dawn, cutting it off. She had controlled all of that. She had ended it. She had confined it to its proper intermezzo and had come home tonight to remember her father, not Roy Murphy. That is what I have done, she told herself.

In that night of Emma's grief for Thomas Herrick, her thoughts did not stay with her father, and she never slept at all.

She stood at the window. As the cold tide of dawn began to wash up the streets of Hoosick Bridge, Roy Murphy slipped away from her at last. The choristers had sung,

*Heav'n's morning breaks, and earth's vain shadows flee,*

and he was a vain shadow fleeing from daylight, hurrying away just as he hurried from the car the last time she saw him. She fancied she could hear a soprano warbling the hymn's dying lyric.

*In life, in death, O Lord, abide with me.*

But no one abides, she thought—I have only myself. She turned from the window. Anne breathed peacefully on the couch. "It's all right," she had said in the night, as Anne cried, and at last slept.

It would be, somehow. She would make it so. She turned back to the window, and looked down toward the town. A fierce loyalty rose within her: morning had brought a turning, brought the hard, practical labor of tending the wounded, of regrouping to survive the enigmatic father who'd given them life, of engaging the hereditary instinct of her mother's side to persevere. Above all, Morses persevered.

Well, I will abide then, she thought.

In the cool light of that dawn, Emma began the toil of protecting them: Anne, Charlie, Jane. Of shoveling out hills of ash left by her father. Hard work—and long. For years, there would be no leisure to think of the ember buried beneath.

# ELEVEN

The adviser from Yale drove up to Hoosick Bridge a few days later. They sat together at the kitchen table and drank tea. The woman spoke in soothing tones and said Emma should take a leave of absence, of course she would. You owe it to your grief, she said. The woman spoke of grief as though it were a person.

And Emma was not to worry, she said. "The university understands. If it should be necessary, arrangements can be made, for Yale is loyal to its family."

The woman spoke in these euphemisms, and it was a while before Emma realized that she was referring to tuition. And so they already knew, not just that her father had died—they knew everything.

*Arrangements*, the woman had said. Well then, yes, we will make them.

When the adviser returned to New Haven, she told her colleagues in confidence that she had been a little frightened by Emma Herrick, who did not appear to accept grief, and seemed distracted by something else. The woman had degrees in psychology. She held that grief could not simply be ignored. She was worried about Emma, although she had at least succeeded in convincing her to take a leave of absence. But in candor she was not sure that the girl would ever be back.

In this the adviser was quite mistaken.

When at last the town left them alone at the Heights, Jane and Emma confronted the event. Anne and Charlie had gone back to school, they busied themselves quickly, but Emma and her mother could not shy from it. As women do when there is but one male in a family, they had long studied him. Jane had misread him, and Emma had missed it completely, and so now they insisted on reviewing the evidence, on knowing.

He had been to the True Value that Saturday morning. He had driven the green Acura sedan there and made one purchase. No doubt Sheila rang it up cheerfully, as she would any such item bought in a hardware store on a Saturday morning. (Emma wondered, did she say, "Have a nice day," when he left? And did he answer, "You, too?" That is what Sheila at True Value always says, "Have a nice day." Thoughtless of his family in this moment, flat faced, dull of affect as he had become, her father out of habit would have answered any acquaintance politely.) Tom Herrick had driven from the hardware store to town—to the office at the corner of Addison and Washington, where he parked the car in front of Fredoni & Herrick. He unlocked the office door and went inside. (Emma wondered, Did anyone see him just then? Did someone call out from the street to greet him, and did he wish them a good morning, standing at the door, holding his own death in his left hand?)

Tom Herrick had kept a secret, had abandoned sense and rationality for a secret, had nursed that secret privately, had brooded over it until it hatched and then consumed him, ravaging all life from within until the shell that was left of him simply crumbled away. When such things happen, the police afterward piece together the events, craving a narrative. The smallest points in the narrative are noted, as though a narrative would explain, as though it would help someone understand.

It must have been quiet in the office, as he typed the instructions on the computer and then printed them off and sealed them in an envelope with the note to Jane. He wrote bold letters on the envelope and placed it on the front desk, where it would be seen on entry. Then he went back to the lavatory at the rear of Fredoni & Herrick.

To get at the drop ceiling without a ladder, he had to climb up on the sink. Removing the panel had dislodged dust, which later the police observed on the floor, in his hair, on the shoulders of his fleece jacket. He'd passed one end of the half-inch nylon cord he'd purchased at the True Value over the cold-water pipe that ran through the drop ceiling. He had wrapped the end around and around the pipe, shortening the remainder to the right length before he secured it with a bowline knot.

He did these things alone in the lavatory, on a Saturday morning in October, while three quarters of a mile away his wife turned the flour-spotted, brown-stained pages of the *Joy of Cooking* to the recipes for pies. Outside, on the sidewalk on Washington Street, weekend shoppers passed the front door of Fredoni & Herrick while he made these preparations. This Emma was unable to forgive.

There was one small detail that Jane had not shared. The police, of course, checked his phone and noted that a call had come in from Jane and been unanswered. The police knew—as one knows with precision all the least relevant things—that it was 9:33 when she called, hoping to ask that he pick up a quarter pound of lard at Price Chopper for the pie. But *where was he* when this happened? Still in his car, glancing down at a phone lying in the console, did he see and ignore the name of his wife flashing on the cell phone? Or was he already in the lavatory, passing the cord over the pipe, when the phone interrupted him—did he slip at all, perched awkwardly on that porcelain sink as one hand fumbled with the clamshell phone? It was only a small sink, and he must have wavered, steadying himself against the wall, poised on that slippery platform in a pair of brown tasseled loafers, as he passed the nylon cord up and over the pipe suspended from the floor joist above. Was that when the phone rang? Did he pause, look at it— did his thumb stray to the green button to answer?

They wondered as well why, on this day, he brought his cell phone with him at all, whether it was a kind of lifeline, as he left his home and drove down the hill that fatal morning, a last means of being summoned back from the brink. And if it was a lifeline, why had he let it slip?

None of this was known.

What flicker had passed across his face when he saw her name, if he saw her name, Jane wanted to know most of all. His face had been a blank canvas for so many months. Was there any expression in that moment? Did the letters on that little screen— JANE—shake his resolve, or steady it? These are the questions that the electronic age poses but does not answer. She felt he owed her that answer.

For he left a note, but no explanation. The note was full of administrative details like where the will was located, and what lawyer she should call (apparently he had not thought through the obvious fact that in the end there would be no estate to administer). The letter closed with a curt apology, but no explanation— for any of it—no explanation for what had gone before, none for this.

He did not sign the note. The page bore no ink. He typed at the bottom, "Thomas Herrick," and below his name, the date, as though composing his epitaph, making his last mark on history a light one, with the formal distance of Thomas, and without the human touch of ink to paper. The note was, at least, honest: he did not write that he loved Jane. In his depression he was no longer capable of any emotion. For his children, there was no note at all. This Anne and Charlie instantly forgave. But not Jane, and not Emma.

He died in darkness, alone, with a smell of ammonia in his nostrils. The cleaners had been in the lavatory the day before. Surely it was awkward, if not ludicrous, for a grown man, a tall, handsome man still, to be perched on that sink in tasseled loafers. It would not have been easy to extend his right leg to one side to flip the light switch off. Had he done so? That might have explained why his wallet was later found in the bowl of the sink. He might have removed it from his pants pocket, for a last look at the photographs—of Jane, of Emma, of Anne, of Charlotte—and then dropped the wallet to the porcelain (where it would be found and cataloged in the police report), and extended a leg to flip the switch. Or had he turned off the light *first*, and clambered up atop that sink in the total darkness of that windowless room? (In which case, why had he dropped the wallet?) They both wondered what expression came across his face at that moment. If he hesitated even then.

The answers were unknown, as he was unknown. Tom Herrick's body was not found until Saturday afternoon, after Burt Fredoni, out for his Saturday errands, saw the car parked in front and dropped in to the office to say hello. (Jane would thereafter refuse to enter that office or touch his car again. Burt had to drive the car to the dealership, where it was sold.) The coroner said only that at some time between nine and ten-thirty on a Saturday morning late in October, he climbed up on that perch, in the back washroom, and then stepped off. Into nothingness. Whom they thought they knew but did not know, stepping into that beyond they could not know at all.

The envelope instructed in capital letters that the reader should contact the police, that in no event should Burt, or Jane—if she were the one who had come after him and read these words—go into the bathroom.

During the previous summer Tom Herrick had recognized what was within his daughter and feared it. That fear and self-loathing for his own impotence to face things going wrong—at Fredoni & Herrick, in his daughter's life—were the last real emotions he had felt. The business was then in its doomed spiral. He had fallen into a personal vortex of avoidance that could end in only one way. And then fear and hatred and every other emotion gave way to the flat line of his depression. There was this irony: Tom Herrick accomplished in death what he could not in life. His suicide obliterated, for a time, everything else for Emma. And though the adviser from Yale was wrong to predict Emma would not return, she was right to notice that something other than grief was distracting her.

Emma thought that her father had died a coward, and this she could not forgive. She could be harsh in her judgments, and in lieu of grief, Tom Herrick's death filled Emma with overwhelming purpose. When she returned to Yale in the spring, some of them wondered how she could have come back so soon, how she could attend class at all, and do the problem sets and argue with the section leader about economics, how she could concentrate. They did not understand that the shock of her father's failure had set her to the path that she thought he had shamed. She would study and earn good grades and marry a conventional boy and in a few years take a job in a Wall Street firm. She would prevail in his industry, and by doing these things she would revise *him*. One day she would have children whom she would never abandon. She would do the right way what he had done criminally. And so that spring at Yale she was already rushing, already feeling that she had wasted too much time. She had to be set on that path now. The shock and then the overwhelming purpose that came over Emma obliterated Roy Murphy from active memory. It heaped a mountain of ash atop that ember.

But the ember was patient. It abided Yale. It abided even the great blessing of George Forrester's arrival into Emma's life.

# TWELVE

*H*is love would not be like Roy Murphy's—if you could even recognize "love" in that chemical urgency—it did not launch him like a ballistic missile, to confront her on that path and ask, simply, *"Now?"* George was always careful. He circled, he researched, he worked up his gumption and found an acquaintance to introduce them and then he asked her whether she wanted to get coffee or something sometime.

She said, "Sure."

That was her first word to George: "Sure." She had no objection. There had been other boys at Yale, though none she had taken seriously. Even after they began getting together, it took her a while to develop curiosity about him, for she was still preoccupied by purpose. He was a law student, and a little more grounded than the undergraduate men she'd met. Pleasant, soft-spoken, he was genial, and not unattractive. He was witty and good company without the self-involvement of her younger classmates. He was intelligent but not an egghead (he did not seem to fit very well at the law school, actually). His father worked in a consulting firm in Boston, and the family was prosperous. He took her to the house on Nantucket. Most of all it was clear that he loved her.

One Sunday morning in March of her senior year, she decided that they would marry. It had been a nerve-racking year for people finishing college. Markets had collapsed in the fall, and financial jobs were exceedingly rare, but with her drive and grades, she had managed to find an analyst position with a firm whose specialty was buying companies in bankruptcy. He was about to finish law school, and start his clerkship.

They were talking about the fall, about getting an apartment somewhere in New York City after he graduated. They had spoken about what neighborhoods they might be able to afford on his clerk's salary, about why, even in a recession, New York real estate brokers could claim their stratospheric fees. He had a one-room apartment in New Haven, where they were eating the croissants and drinking the coffee she'd brought from Au Bon Pain and gently competing over the *Times* crossword. He had a couch and an old brown steamer trunk they used as a table. The newspaper and the breakfast were on the trunk. He sprawled on the couch, while she sat the floor leaning against it, with her back to him, and the crossword in her lap.

"Down-to-earth person," she said, "With a question mark. Starts with *c*. Seven letters."

He was sipping coffee, reading from his laptop, on which he had opened up Craigslist. "Studio near Prospect Park. Cozy, charming . . ."

"Hoosick Bridge and Yale—all my life I've lived somewhere *old*."

"What else do you have?" he asked.

"The second-to-last letter might be *s*. C four blanks *s* blank."

"Coal miners or something. Colliers—is that what they call them? They go down to earth."

"No," she said, "they go down *in* the earth. It doesn't fit anyway. Besides, it's a pun."

"Sensational studio, block from IRT," he read.

"Does it really say 'sensational'? I wonder what that means."

"It means it has a window. Something -ist, maybe? *C*——ist?"

But she was already filling in the answer with her blue felt pen.

When doing the crossword he always used pencil, and she a pen. "Chutist," she said.

"What?"

"Chutist. A parachutist goes down to earth. George, we should get married." She was now filling in answers rapidly, because *chutist* had opened up three across clues. "It *is noser*," she said.

"Really?"

"Yup. One twenty-one, across, *hound*."

"No, Emma, get *married* really!"

"Really," she answered.

"You know that's what I want. You know that, right?"

She put down the crossword; he put down the laptop; she climbed on the couch and kissed him sweetly and then curled in his lap. Her smile overwhelmed him. That smile always overwhelmed everyone.

"Today?" he asked.

"Silly. We'll pick a date."

"But it's official—call-the-family official?"

"Yes," she said. "Let's call them."

So there was no kneeling, no candlelit dinner, there were no roses. For many months there was no ring. That morning he hugged her on the couch, struggling to contain himself. George Forrester was a young man who'd always held himself in reserve, skilled at adapting to the world. He was not one to impose himself upon it—not one of the loud and confident students in law school classes sparring with the professors. You would not have supposed that he could be with a beauty like Emma. He was a man unsuited to notice, and you could not walk a city block with Emma without the feeling that everyone was watching. He had not come to terms with the idea that she could be his.

He called his parents. Then Emma telephoned Jane and cannoned her at the moon. From that minute Jane came to life again. She saw that the wedding would breathe life into that dying house that all were abandoning. It would erase the shame. From that minute, Jane thought, There must be a party.

Emma's consciousness in those days had moved far from Roy Murphy. She would remember a conventional retelling of the story as a part of her childhood history. There was a fling with a troubled boy from town. He had gone off to war, and had never been heard from thereafter, had never called or e-mailed her even once. As she told herself, as she told Anne, she had grown to love George Forrester, and it was going to work.

A close observer of phrases, Anne noticed the frequent ones: "grown to love" and "going to work," descriptive of a journey but not an arrival. Anne wondered, Who got engaged anymore in college? But ever since Daddy died, she's been in a hurry, she's been full of will. And George is the nicest boy—I mean, *man.*

In those days Roy Murphy was rarely more to Emma than a brief chapter of history. But sometimes more. Sometimes after she made love with George and he had dropped off, Roy Murphy was more. Small details would plague her then—memory of the muscled triangle of his back, the feel of his cheekbone, the size of his hands, the crush of his embrace, the strength of purpose in his concentration, that night on the beach in Rhode Island. Sometimes she would lie awake, remembering the insistence of his hunger, remembering her own racking urgency that summer to be touched, held, penetrated. In the dark she sometimes was overcome by the most disturbing memory of all—that remembered sensation of being shivered from vagina to fingertip. It was frightening to recall the frenzy she'd felt. She was glad it was behind her, that she had found refuge in something gentler, something more predictable.

She escaped physical memory by turning her mind to the practical questions of what on earth had become of him. Whether he was still in the Army, whether he was still over there in that endless war, whether he was dead, whether he'd lost four limbs and was propped up in a wheelchair somewhere in one of those horribly understaffed rehab hospitals reported in the press. Whether he had come back and there was another girl. Whether he was married. This was the hardest scene to picture: not emotionally, but visually. She could imagine him dead or a quadriplegic or trudging through some dusty, godforsaken village in Iraq. Her mind just could not place Roy Murphy at a kitchen counter, across from a girl balancing a baby on the hip.

But these moments of recall were infrequent during that period of her life. Anne was right—for Emma, it was a time of will, of purpose being formed and pursued. It was the time when she would commence in earnest the project of revising Tom Herrick, and no one was better suited than George to help her. The past had been buried by the ash of her father's death, by Emma's subsequent purpose, by George Forrester.

It was buried, but not extinct. Deep within Emma Herrick, unnoticed, the ember glowed patiently. It only wanted a little oxygen.

# PART THREE
## *The Poet of Life and Death*

# THIRTEEN

*A*fghanistan was wind and heat and frigid cold, and in Kabul and Bagram, Afghanistan was bureaucracy, acres of it. They had their ranks and files, their hierarchies of diplomats, spooks, generals, the press; of politicians (American, Afghan, NATO, God-knows-who); even of contractors, whose bosses seemed to rank most of the brass. But the firebase was different, remote from those teeming places. It was an outpost guarding nothing, a middle finger erected in the remote Korengal Valley, manned by three squads of Army Airborne. Solitary, slapdashed with plywood and camo netting and C wire, it clung to an open spur overlooking the valley, shadowed by mountain peaks across, behind, and down the valley. Firebase Montana knew no politician or contractor. From one sally to the other, it was the small but sovereign domain of the poet of life and death. The officers' small brick-and-mortar, the sandbagged squad hooches, the Hescos (wire cages the men filled with rocks to create walls), the .50-cal emplacement and each string of camo netting—all were his. The captain saw all, he commanded all, he simplified all. He was at every man's shoulder, in every man's face, always with those eyes and that slightly off-kilter smile—whether dressing a man down or picking him up, whether taking fire or waiting for it, whether tapping out something on his laptop or hauling a crap barrel with the newest private. During long days and weeks of waiting, his eyes flashed excitement. And when the shit flew, they flashed calm.

Most of them up there were scarcely more than boys. They emblazoned their arms and chests and backs with the tattoos of warriors; most smoked the same foul cigarettes, laced their language the same way, and tried to outmacho each other, but every one of them feared the day of his death. The captain spoke differently and looked differently. In that group of soldiers he might have been regarded as out of place, were it not for the wild light in those eyes, the insane enthusiasm he had for battle, the deliberate manner of his stride, with his head up, when shit was exploding around him, so that the only corporal sign that rounds were flying was the light they kindled in him.

He was in his early thirties—mature years in the Korengal. Lean, vulpine, he had a long face, a cleft chin, green eyes, a way of blankly locking eyes that made a soldier feel younger than his years, that made him want to look away. Emerging unscathed from a firefight, he liked to quote Churchill. "There is nothing so exhilarating as to be shot at without result." The men had only a vague idea about who Churchill was, exactly. Once Billy Hall Jr. answered, "Well, sir, too much exhilaration ain't conducive to good health, you-know-what-ah-mean?"

"But just enough is better than sex, Private Hall," the captain retorted, his eyes blazing.

And someone said, "Aw, give him something he can relate to, sir."

The captain was happiest after the shouting and noise of combat, and the men shared that jangling exultation, and began to feel the addictive draw of battle. They were afraid of it, afraid to death, but it sucked them in, because each firefight survived was a high they wanted again. There was just nothing like that feeling. When things had settled, they'd say,

"Lima, you exhilarated?"

"Got me a full ration of exhilaration today, dude."

Or:

"Gonna exhilarate me some Hajis today, Cap'n!"

Or their favorite:

"Yo, Hall, was it good for you?"

"Oh yeah, baby, real good. Was it good for you, too?"

They said these things, and they laughed, and for a few minutes the fear would be in the background.

The captain could walk forever; could carry what the strongest of them could carry, and knew things they could only guess at. Once Sergeant Brown challenged him in push-ups. Brown was cut like a weight lifter, and spent half of his down hours in the weight room at Bagram, but nobody learned how many push-ups the captain could do, because Brown had to drop out at 186. The anticipation of things energized the captain, and when the men sensed that energy, its intensity frightened them. A sighting of a pickup truck on an access road, movement in the village, radio traffic suggesting an imminent attack, the onset of a patrol, all those things lit the captain's eyes. Their devotion to him was part reverence and part fear, because you could admire him, you could both fear and be lifted by his enthusiasm, but you could not come too close to it.

From any of the surrounding ridges and peaks the firebase might take what the manual called "plunging fire." Sandbags, timber, even brick-and-mortars were little use against plunging fire. The sniper shots were fired from so far away that the first thing a guy heard was the sizzlecrack of the round breaking air beside his head. *FFFthwwtttt!* If he heard anything at all, a man heard that before the report from across the valley.

On the bright side, hearing sizzlecrack meant a man was still alive.

The men called the sniper Elmer Fudd because he couldn't hit anything. "He ever learn to point the sumbitch, we'd all of us be poppin virgins by now," Billy Hall Jr. said.

There were no showers at Firebase Montana, no running water, and the reek of the place was powerful—confected of human shit and diesel fuel and MREs, of sweat that dried in white lines in their crusty socks and brown T-shirts. The smell of the cold food got into clothes and beneath fingernails, and in the plywood of the hooches, too, where it mixed with the smell of fuel, and never aired out. The diesel would get on uniforms. At night, these smells permeated the hooch, colored by gas and sour male sweat. Roy Murphy had his own special pungency. His uniform in particular was a sink trap for all the foul smells of the place.

"By authority duly vested in me by CENTCOM, the Certificate of Afghan Stink is duly conferred on Private Roy Murphy," Billy Hall Jr. said one night, and they all laughed.

The wind was some mitigation. But even the wind never smelled clean to Roy Murphy, not like the icy-clean air he remembered from clear, cold January days in Vermont, or the moist wind, heavy with fragrance, of summer. The wind through the Korengal was gritty, and the sand had an unclean feel, a suggestion of ash and excrement. On a clear day at the firebase, the men sometimes would catch the pleasant smell of woodsmoke from the valley, but that happened rarely, only when the day was calm and a gentle breeze—unusual for that place—drifted west. Mainly, a heavy miasma of diesel, shit, and human sweat hung about the camp.

But Roy Murphy had a memory for smells, and an ability to banish the bad ones, including his own, with a catalog from home: the sweet manure smell of Steinhart's fields in April, of second-cut hay in barns in August, of June rain on hot pavement down in Hoosick Bridge, of cold beer in a glass, of bark mulch on the fingers, of vanilla ice cream. Sometimes he called to mind the calming scent of a clean workshop, of oil on the grinding wheel. Or of the floor polish from that day he climbed the stairs at the Heights, and the leather bindings on the old books in the tower. Closing his eyes, he could summon them all to mind, to cover over the smells of the firebase.

The smells that lived most powerfully in him were of Emma: the soap scent of her skin, the aroma of lotions, of her favorite shampoo, whose name he never learned but whose lemony tang he could not forget. At night, lying on his bunk, he would imagine himself resting his nose across her soft shoulder, and bathe himself again in that imagined fragrance, in that place, in that time.

"He ain't like nobody else I ever know," Fowler was saying, one night in the hooch.

They all recognized Roy Murphy as different, and that made them curious. He was highly regarded for reliability in a firefight. A good soldier is deliberate when the world becomes chaotic; he slows down things that are going too fast. And they had seen that Murphy had the focus for that. Once when the .50 jammed in a firefight, he methodically broke down the entire weapon, piece by piece, while rounds whistled by. He stripped the components, wiped them down, unjammed the ammunition feed, reassembled everything. Guys were yelling, rounds were screaming by, chips flying off the Hesco stones, and Roy Murphy might have been in a laboratory. How he did it without burning his hands off or getting killed no one could tell, but he never hurried. He had that intense but deliberate focus.

He never talked of family, never of a father or a mother or a brother or a sister. He never talked about a woman. He carried no photographs. It seemed sometimes that he went days without talking at all. When one of them demanded, "Murphy, you got a girl?" he didn't turn away bashfully, didn't flush. He just didn't answer.

The night Fowler got talking was Second Squad's first night back to the firebase after a rotation to Bagram for MWR—the Army's acronym for "morale, welfare, and recreation." The squad had returned by the Chinook, and Roy Murphy drew watch that night. As the rest of the squad lay in the hooch, Fowler said, "Me and Murphy was bunked together down there. The guy never once got on dot mil, not once."

"How you know, DeSean?"

"When we rotate, I got to keep contact with my ladies, nome sayin? So I'm like, 'Murphy, come on down to Tillman, we get online . . .'"

Billy Hall Jr. cut in. "Your ladies keeping contact with each *other*, dude. They all together and be like, 'Ooh, baby, uh-huh, yeah, yeah, baby. Don't stop, baby, don't stop . . . Wait, baby . . . *Stop!* We got us a e-mail from DeSean!'"

The hooch exploded in laughter then, but it didn't perturb Fowler at all. "The ladies got to do the best they can till Daddy get home. But check it out: I'm like, 'Murphy, come on to Tillman, we get us a burger, get us a beer, get on line for computer time.' Murphy, he say, 'I don't do that.' And I'm like, 'Do what?' 'Computer,' he say. 'I don't do computer.' I'm like, 'Don't you want to say hello to nobody?' And he all, 'When I'm back, man. I say hello when I'm back.' Y'all know what I'm talkin bout—I get to Tillman, half a y'all waiting on line, too. You ain't never seen him down there that whole time. Any y'all ever seen him on that line? All the rest of us waiting on computer time like it was a hot dinner. Not *him*."

Sergeant Brown cut in then. "Well, maybe he know the computer ain't gonna do you no good. Maybe Murphy's right. You get online, and your woman tell you the faucet broke. You know, the faucet broke and I missed the car payment, and Junior having trouble with his 'rithmetic and we got all kinda problems back home. You be readin this and thinkin, Damn, woman, we ain't even got no sink or faucet up here to *break*. You think, She ain't got no idea."

Someone said, "Ain't none of 'em back home got no idea."

"Maybe better to wait, like Murphy say," Brown said.

They considered it. Each had felt something like this frustration before.

Quietly now, Billy Hall Jr. said, "I don't think he got . . . I don't think he got nobody to e-mail. Back home I mean."

They didn't say much, chewing that over. As bad as it was out here, everyone else had at least one somebody back home, somebody to send e-mail or once in a while a care package. Waiting for his time on a computer accounted for half the waking hours of a soldier rotating off a firebase: checking and sending e-mails, waiting for a sat phone to call home.

"Maybe he's just private, you know? Likes to keep it quiet," one of them said.

"Yo, I was *wit* him," Fowler answered. "He ain't kep nothing quiet, man, he kep it *silent*. He never call no one, never check no e-mail, *nuthin*—nome sayin?"

The RPG attack that earned Private Roy Murphy a medal and a promotion to E-5 came at 0330 on November 6, 2008. A grenade hit just behind Second Squad's hooch while most of the squad were in a dead sleep. He was stone at one second and in the next alive to a deafening explosion, fire and choking smoke and screams. The grenade exploded against a Hesco behind the hooch, and immediately the diesel stove and the walls went up and guys on the south wall who had caught shrapnel from the stove were screaming.

"Get out get out get out!" someone was yelling, but it sounded faint because his ears were ringing with the explosion. A jumble of bodies grabbing M4s—they always grabbed their M4s, they would do it in their sleep—and making for the door, bumping and slipping, dragging screaming guys off of bunks and carrying them out the door into the bitter cold and a chaos of shouting and AK rounds. The captain was out there, his mouth forming words, forming names, but Roy Murphy could not hear, and as he looked around he realized that the new guy, Tatel, was not with them. The hooch was roaring up like dry tinder, and it would be over in a second.

And then he was back in the hooch. The walls were in flame now, and the structure was near collapse. It was burning from the inside, like an oven: still sandbagged and Hescoed outside, but with the flame roaring up the plywood and two-by-fours and the black, stinking diesel smoke boiling up within. It seemed like the fire sucked oxygen out of his very lungs and thrust smoke as thick as wool down his throat. He could neither see or breathe. Tatel's was the rear upper bunk on the right, and with his right hand Roy felt his way back three bunks and then reached up and got hold of an inert leg. The smoke stabbed his eyes even with his lids shut as he felt his way forward. He began to panic. He pulled Tatel roughly until he tumbled down onto his back, and Roy Murphy, now panicked and desperate for air, pushed his way out of the disintegrating hooch, dislocating Tatel's shoulder against a bunk post in the process. A flaming board came loose and down on top of them—and at this point Tatel was Roy Murphy's shield. He screamed horribly. He would be in a burn unit for a month.

Then they were outside gasping and coughing in the cold and someone was carrying Tatel behind the Hesco. Roy Murphy lay there sucking at the air and slowly opening his eyes to it. Someone brought him water and he drank it and it was then that he saw the muzzle flash a hundred meters down the slope. Impossibly close.

What happened next probably took place only because he'd been pulled from such a dead sleep that he hadn't fully awakened, and because he couldn't hear. And because he was angry. If anyone was ordering him to do something, or not to do something, he couldn't hear it, and likely it wouldn't have mattered anyway, because the anger consumed him. He didn't really wake up or get his hearing back until it was all over, but acted as though raging in a dream, for the wire had always exerted a powerful force on him before—he had never before thought of going outside the wire without a full team. Even then, even on patrols down to the town where Afghans served tea, he was restive and mistrustful outside the wire.

The same thing, more or less, was happening to Lima. They were both not so much thinking as reacting to the same observation, which was that the enemy position could not see North Side Sally. Roy Murphy picked himself up from that cold ground, and suddenly he was through the sally port and outside the wire, and Lima was on his right. They would surely have been killed had not Billy Hall Jr. started the .50 just then, from the firebase behind them, distracting and engaging the enemy position as Murphy and Lima plunged toward it from the flank.

Neither Murphy nor Lima had his IBA or his Kevlar. They

were banshees on the mountain, two guys coming from the flank
at an enemy position with nothing but M4s and the full-throated
yells of wild animals.

About three months later, the command brought the pair of
them down to Bagram to promote each to specialist and pin each
with a Silver Star. But this is not what he remembered. Years later,
living in a small apartment over a garage in Overton, it was not the
attack or the medal ceremony that would rip him from sleep and
have him down the attic stairs and in his garage gasping before
he knew where he was. And it was not the memory of the RPG
explosion or the running down the mountainside into the enemy
nest that terrified him, but rather the hot, stinging blackness of the
smoke in that hooch. The thing he most remembered later was the
smoke.

When Roy Murphy was a boy at Pine Cobble School, and they
tried to teach him to read, words would swim on a printed page.
The teachers seemed to enjoy humiliating him publicly, demanding that he make sense of the swimming words and letters
out loud, in front of everybody. He could hear the titters as he
struggled. The words and letters still swam years later, when he
labored to make sense of manuals and then abandoned them and
just studied the engine parts themselves and how they fit together.
It was always that way before the captain sat him down late one
afternoon in his quarters at Firebase Montana and asked, "You
don't read, do you, Murphy?"

He felt like a bug trapped on a slide under a microscope and
the captain's eyes were up in a lens above him, big as the sun. He
had to shake his head, no, he didn't.

"Words, letters jump around on you, come at you reversed,
out of order?"

*How did he know that?* Yes—yes, that was it exactly. He nodded.

"Follow me, son." The captain led him outside to the C wire.
It was twilight, and across the valley the opposite ridge was gray-
ing rapidly in that fading light.

"See that, Murphy, out there? Just to the right of the summit of Aman Gul, you come down into a draw?"

"Sir."

"And come up from the draw to that dark rock? See that?"

"That's not a rock, sir, it's a shadow."

"No, it's a rock, Murphy. Just to the right of the draw?"

"Down from the spruces? It's a shadow, sir."

"I'm telling you it's a rock, Murphy. Are you telling me that isn't a rock?"

"Yessir. It's a shadow. You can see where the sun is coming from, sir."

The captain smiled. "It *is* a shadow, Murphy. On that ridge, some of it is trees, some rocks, some just shadows falling, and it just swims for most people. It's just a mess. They can't read that ridgeline. Not without practice. But you've had practice. So you can read it."

They watched for a minute. The shadow grew, as the ridge became indistinct, fuzzy. Then the captain led Roy Murphy back into the hooch and he ordered him to field-strip his weapon.

"Sir?"

"Go on. On the table."

Roy Murphy's M4 was reduced to a pile of component parts thirty seconds later.

"That," the captain said, "is just a mess to most people. Assemble your weapon, soldier."

Less than a minute later, it was an M4 again.

"Most people, they can't read that mess at all. You couldn't read it at first. But you practiced and now you read it fast. First time you ever reassembled your weapon, Murphy, you do it slow or fast?"

"Slow, sir."

"That's right. You practice by starting *slow*." The eyes burned into him as he said it.

They were alone in the hooch. The captain handed him a book. He said, "Don't read, Murphy, *practice*. Practice on this in the burnshitter. You take a crap, you practice. First time, one sentence and stop. That's it, no more. One sentence, you hear me? Second time, two sentences. Third time, three. You're not reading, you're practicing. You keep practicing until you lose count of the sentences. Got me?"

He held the book uneasily. "Sir."

"They'll swim on you, they'll try to jump around on you, but here's the thing—they can't jump as much when you slow them down. So practice slow. You hit a word you don't know, skip over it. Don't worry about it. You'll get the sense from the other words."

"Sir."

"Murphy, we'll keep this between you and me. You come and see me in a while, we'll see how things are going. Come and see me when no one's around. You got some words you can't figure, you just ask me. Quietly."

"Thank you, sir."

When he left the hooch, he didn't think it would work. He'd been scared of words all his life. But deployment was long, and there was a lot of downtime. Before he knew how or why, he was halfway through the captain's *History of Afghanistan*.

He didn't have that book anymore now, it had gone to the lieutenant. He meant to buy a copy for himself when he got his place. He was going to get a place someday. It would have a shelf full of books, like the captain had, a whole room full of them, like Emma had in the tower.

On a hot June morning, in the dusty shade of a Hesco, Montoya was hunched over his iPod, pushing through menus of songs, trying to find one he hadn't listened to a hundred times before. Roy Murphy slouched alongside, fiddling absently with an object on a chain, turning it over in his fingers. The light glinted off of it, and Montoya, noticing it, removed his earbuds.

"Dude, what you got there?"

Roy handed him the chain, and Montoya held it in his palm. "What is this?"

"A button. From a Union soldier's coat in the Civil War."

"It's all smashed, how you know it's a button?"

"Confederate round hit it. It saved the guy's life. The middle's flattened out, but look there on the top edge."

"Vermont," Montoya read.

"And the stars around the rim. See that? Civil War coat button."

They sat beside each other in the dust. It was hot and still, the sun baking down on the top of the Hesco, and the heat across the Korengal Valley distorted the air, so that the rocks and spruces on the mountain shimmered in the distance.

"Vermont button in Afghanistan," Montoya said. "This war's fucked *up*, man." He turned it over, held it to the light. "I never been to Vermont. Whatsat like, anyway? Snow all the time and shit?"

Roy smiled, thinking of June—a rare smile from him. "In June the hills are green. Right about now the farmers'll be looking for four dry days to get in the first cut, and the landscapers will all be slammed with work. You'd get a hot day like today in June, but then the thunderstorms boil up in the afternoon, and after the rain, in the late afternoon, that earth smell comes."

"Earth smell."

"Yeah."

And Montoya could swear he saw him pull a deep breath in through his nostrils just then. He had put his iPod down, and he held the button now in his lap, turning it over slowly. An object that once saved a soldier's life was a holy thing. There are no false idols in firebases; every soldier who had ever heard sizzlecrack would pray to one.

"Was he Army?"

Roy Murphy nodded.

"Hooah," Montoya said. "What's that, below where it says 'Vermont'?"

"Antlers. It had a deer head in the middle. The Vermont Sixth had them on their insignia. The deer got flattened out by the bullet, though."

"Dude, when this over, you take me deer hunting in Vermont, all right? But not when it's cold. I don't like the cold."

"Ain't deer season when it's warm."

Montoya held up the chain. "You wear this?"

"All the time."

The light glinted from the dark surface of the button. "Wouldn't be much good against an AK round."

Roy Murphy narrowed his eyes and with an oddly serious tone answered, "It makes them miss."

Montoya squinted at him. He couldn't tell whether Murphy was playing with him.

"That night the hooch got hit and me and Lima went out there?" Roy continued, softly. "I didn't get a scratch. Didn't have my IBA or Kevlar on or nothing. Except this."

Montoya examined the button again, reverently, then handed it back. "Civil War button. Where'd you *get* it, man?"

"It was . . . in the family," said Roy Murphy.

"The bowl of night," the captain called it, when he read from the poem—and through those long nights at that lonely firebase, it seemed to Roy Murphy that he was inside that bowl, the jewels overhead, before, behind, at the horizons: not looking down so much as surrounding him. On a cool, still night he sat outside, leaning back, studying the stars. The sounds of horseplay, of murmurs, of curses and laughter floated out from the hooch, and then floated gently away. For the night sky was the same as home, the only thing in Afghanistan that was, and as he watched the stars he could be transported from this place, and back to that one, back to the first summer he'd ever really noticed stars, when Emma used to bring a little guidebook, and on clear nights they would try to pick them out, staring upward, and she'd ask him, "How is *that* a goat?"

It began when he invited her to a concert. "Yes, Roy—yes!" she'd said. "Who? In Bennington? Tanglewood? What time? What should I wear?" And so on. He'd only smiled, leading her on. Later she tugged at his waist, yelling to be heard over the noise of his motorbike. "Wait . . . What are we . . . ? Carpenter Hill Road . . . What *concert* . . . Where are we *going*, Roy?"

He remembered reaching the crest and the unmarked dirt road that led west to the ridge. At the end it opened to a gravel drive. Beyond stood a white house with two brick chimneys, one at each end, all painted white.

"Isn't this McRearys'?"

He studied the house from the end of the drive. The shades in the windows were drawn, and all was dark. There was no car. The McRearys were older, money people from New York who came in the summers, their kids long gone. He worked up there for Di-Bello, and half the summer they would cut the grass and trim the boxwood hedges and mulch the beds for nobody at all.

He stopped by the garage, switched off the bike, and pulled it back on the stand. Immediately the quiet set in—but not quiet exactly.

"Band's warming up," he said. "Hear that?"

"Roy . . ."

"Don't worry, McRearys never come till the Fourth. We did the lawn yesterday."

They walked out around and behind the house, to where the lawn swept away to a field, and beyond, a small pond.

The grass was freshly mown. She carried her sandals, and bits of grass stuck to her feet as they descended a gentle slope to where two ancient maples stood. He pulled a beach towel and a paper sack from a knapsack and spread the towel on the grass beneath one of the maples. She rooted through the sack for a sandwich.

"So, Emma—like the music?" he asked.

She laughed, and then they settled in and looked out over the lawn to the field beyond. The band was in full swing now, the blats and croaks and moans and driving, staccato shrieks of the frogs rising from the pond, gaining in strength as the sun fell to the peaks of the Taconics across the valley. The red-winged blackbirds were gurgling and whistling, too. Two glistening blackbirds with bright red epaulets and yellow chevrons practiced aerobatics over the dusky field, climbing and diving, inches from one another.

"Roy, they're dancing!"

"Don't think so," he said. "Unless they're gay."

Of course they were both males. One sought the other's territory, and the other defended fiercely. What looked like a dance from a distance was war up close. All that summer, he'd been thinking about soldiering, wondering what it would be like, and that night he realized that even here there were wars, fought tenaciously to protect a few square feet of the McRearys' lonely field. The frogs and the blackbirds reduced male experience to its essentials: battles over inches of ground and an insistent, moaning croak for the girl.

The frogs' chorus was working to a crescendo.

"A whole concert, just for us," she said, lying back against him, her head in his lap.

A light breeze was playing ripples and eddies upon the gray-green sea of field grass as the sun sank now to the far hilltops and shadow climbed up from the valley. Her silky hair was between his fingers. Whenever he reached this part of the memory, his thumb always began to circle against his index and middle fingertips, his hand remembering the fineness of her hair. His mind, his eyes, his fingers: all parts of Roy Murphy would remember her.

He told her it really *was* a rock concert, and thousands of fans would come. "Wait," he said, grinning now.

Presently the shadow crept up the field to the lawn, passed them, and made its way on to the house. The first concertgoers appeared then, just at the verge, where the waving grass met the darkening lawn. More came by the minute, and then they were countless, thousands, millions of them blinking on and off in the dark-ness, hovering in the air: fireflies all over the field, blinking to the band.

"They all have their candles," he told her.

But the mosquitoes were coming out, too, and he hurried her to her feet.

"What, you have a *key*?"

"No, better."

Around the side of the house, beneath the southern porch, beyond a boxwood hedge, the surface of the McReary pool glimmered like chrome in the darkness.

He remembered how she stood on the pool deck facing him, cocking her head, her mouth screwed up in amusement, how in a moment his clothes were on a chaise lounge, and he was leaping into the night air. How she laughed when he came up splashing and gasping. He remembered the tiny pile of her clothing on its own chaise lounge, her silhouette so slim in the darkness, her feet small and luminous against the copingstone.

Now, years away from it, he could call that moment exquisitely to mind: the slim, lovely length of her, the arch of her small feet, the gleam of her toes upon the stone, and a moment later the look of her as they circled each other in the water, her head bobbing above the surface, her smile bright, and nothing in her eyes but trust. Alone in that pool, at a remote house, miles from anywhere, naked before the town delinquent, she never that night showed any doubt or hesitation.

They did not want to leave the dark water, even as the stars brightened above them. Laughing, then touching, then parting to look out across the field at the twinkling lights of the concertgoers, and then lying back in the pool, staring up at the stars. They did not want that evening to end. And it had never fully ended for him, not years and half a globe away, for the stars always brought it back. The memory was a narcotic. Recalling each detail would bring him to a kind of trance, and the narrative would freeze there with the dark, lapping water, the bright gleam of her eyes, the taste of her lips still in his mouth, and all around him, the bowl of night.

The door to the burnshitter banged open. Lima and Billy Hall Jr. came scuffling along then, Billy Hall Jr. rattling away with some story or another. He caught sight of Roy Murphy and laughed. "Astronomer's out again. What you see, stargazer, Uranus?"

The memory slipped from him, the shape of her receding into dark water, the cries of the frogs fading. It all gave way again to the low bass beat from the hooch and the murmur of the men and Billy Hall Jr. laughing at his stock joke. Roy got to his feet. But his eyes were upward. The same King Cepheus, the same dippers, the same archer had overlooked red-winged blackbirds locked in graceful struggle, had heard frogs oblivious in desperate song, had watched a boy and a girl circle in the water.

"Everything here's different," Roy Murphy said to them, quietly. "The land, the mountains, the people, the language, the look of things, the trees, even the wind's different, even the dogs are different, everything—everything you hear or smell or see. Except them. Except Capricorn, and Sagittarius, and the dippers. They're just the same. At night, it looks like home." He went off to the hooch, Lima following, and the door closed behind them.

Billy Hall Jr. lingered for a moment in the starlight. "Looks like home?" he asked, of no one in particular. "It's *Afghanistan*, dude."

The old man's knuckles were like sprouts exploded by a frost, large and mottled. Gray-bearded Ramitullah, the village headman, gripped the handle of his cane as he walked. He wore an off-white shalwar kameez, the ends of the kameez ragged and dirty, and on his head, a dun-colored woolen pakol. A long nose like a wall sconce protruded from an even longer face. That face was brown as a chestnut, scored with lines and cracks by years of Korengal wind, and the old man's eyes and mouth behaved like bad neighbors, at odds with each other. The toothy smile was calm and unmoving, like a guard at a sally port on a sleepy morning, but the old man's dark eyes were on patrol, jumpy, on the move, taking in information, never yielding any.

Ramitullah's son led them into the house, and Ramitullah eased himself to sit on the floor of the main room, where an old carpet of faded red and purple was spread. He set the cane down behind him. Except for a wooden hutch in one corner, there was no furniture. He surrounded himself with the son and three other men from the village, and the captain and lieutenant sat on the floor before him. Ramitullah spoke about the well in a monotonous Pashto drone, his left hand extended, the back of the hand gnarled, the palm toward the carpet, the hand rising and falling as he made his points. Occasionally he paused, waiting out the translation of the captain's questions and comments, the face never reacting, always with the same smile. His wallah-wallah, Billy Hall Jr. called it—*Wallah* was the old man's regular invocation of the Almighty, meaning, literally, "by God," and Billy Hall Jr., who had listened to the *mutarjim* faithfully render Ramitullah's punctuation on other visits, would mimic him up in the hooch to get the squad laughing. "Time to get out of my bunk, by God. What will I wear this morning, by God? Smelly socks, by God—by God, the same socks as yesterday!" But Wallah was no joke to Ramitullah, or to the flinty men who sat, cross-legged, to left and right: as far as the squad could tell, there was no joking at all about him. Just the steady and joyless smile, the hand rising and falling as though dribbling a slow and invisible basketball to the beat of the Pashto, the restive eyes measuring, calculating, recording.

When Ramitullah finished about the well, and the promises made and broken and made and broken again by the Americans, the captain spoke. He wanted something done about Elmer Fudd. They waited for the translation to come back, watched Ramitullah's unchanged expression, his blank, impenetrable face. "This is in God's hands. It is not a subject for me, but for God," Ramitullah said, and the other Afghans nodded.

"It's *the* subject. To me and my men, there is no other subject," the captain said.

The captain spoke coldly, and Roy Murphy watched as Ramitullah's half smile did not change. He felt he knew it. He was standing in the doorway to the headman's main room, unarmed— the captain's rule was that they could not be armed inside the man's home. Only the guard posted outdoors could be armed. While the translation came back about the sniper, Ramitullah's glance crossed his, and Roy fixed that glance. It seemed to throw the old man off for a moment, so that he interrupted the translation, muttering something hurriedly. The captain turned and ordered Roy to relieve Montoya, and send him in. Roy Murphy was glad to go outside and get his weapon back.

The patrol climbed back to the firebase late that afternoon, its "goodwill op" complete but, as with everything in Afghanistan, unresolved. On point, with his loping stride and his usual contempt for the manual, the captain barely seemed to breathe hard, even when climbing in that country, tossing back observations as Roy Murphy struggled to keep pace. What had Roy thought about Ramitullah—why did he suppose Ramitullah wanted him out of the room?

"He don't like the look of me, sir."

"Can you blame him?"

Roy Murphy was unsure whether it was a joke. As they climbed higher, the captain began one of his disquisitions, and for twenty minutes discoursed on how Ramitullah's weakness— his poverty, his lack of education—was the source of his power. "We've got billion-dollar budgets, we've got Warthogs and artillery and Black Hawks. We've got troop carriers and training and satellite intel. And what are you going to do with all that stuff against a goatherd, who's maybe got a crate full of old AKs in the grain cellar and a brother-in-law who can get him an RPG? A guy who's in play? With them, with us, with the highest bidder—who knows? Take him out, and ten more like him spring to life."

"Don't think he's with us, sir. Not with that phony smile."

"Blow up a tank and you've blown up a tank," the captain continued. "Take out a poor village headman and you make a martyr. We are opposites, and that's what makes him strong."

It was still hot, late in that afternoon. A killing sun hung like a lamp above the western peaks, and the sweat banked around Roy Murphy's armpits and wet his chest as they climbed. It trickled around the band of his Kevlar and rolled to his nose. The captain went on. "So the Pentagon, from its armchair, says, 'Win his trust.'"

As far as Roy Murphy could see, the captain hardly sweated at all—just a fine bead of it appeared on the forehead when he stopped and turned. The rest of the squad had lagged below them on the slope.

"You're from Vermont, Murphy?"

"Sir."

"Small town?"

"Hoosick Bridge, sir."

He nodded. "Suppose a foreign army, speaking a strange language, sets up a firebase on a hilltop overlooking Hoosick Bridge. Sandbags. A fifty-cal. Every couple of weeks a dozen of them come into town. Kevlared, armored up, safeties off, you with me? Patrol comes into town right by everybody's house, by their kids, their wives, their sisters. By their front doors. They go into the mayor's office, and they say, 'We're here to help you. We're your friends. Tell us about your problems. Help us fight the evil New Hampshire tribes and we'll get you some medicine and fix your well.' You with me, Murphy?"

"Sir."

"How would the mayor of Hoosick Bridge react?"

The squad was just below them now. He could hear the scrabble of boots on the stones, and Billy Hall Jr. talking as the men came up the path.

"Don't know about the mayor, sir, but how I'd react, is thinking how to get rid of them."

"Exactly," said the captain, softly.

The squad reached them then and stopped, sucking air. The captain barked, "Gentlemen, is this a nature walk? Hall, save your chatter for half a click, and hydrate, or your squad will miss its dinner."

His smile restored, the captain turned and was off.

"Shit," said Billy Hall Jr., breathing hard, watching him bound up the hill. Billy's hands were on his hips. They passed the water bottles. "Wouldn't never want to miss the six o'clock sitting," he muttered, still gasping on that weak air, "of cold MRE at the Chateau Burnshitter."

They did his memorial up at the firebase. It seemed fitting that it be there. Sergeant Brown and Chappy from the FOB came up, and the lieutenant led it.

The men assembled, and Lieutenant Callahan came forward and tried to get his bearings. He had written out something, but the wind had picked up and was flapping the paper back on itself. "Shit, this isn't going to be easy," he said. They knew he didn't mean the wind. He cleared his throat a couple of times.

"He was more prepared for this than any of us," he began.

"You all know about his books, his history, the poetry. What you didn't know was that he left instructions on what was to be done in the event of his death, and he left those books to many of you, and the thing of it is—" Here the lieutenant paused again to pull himself together. He was really struggling.

"The thing of it is, the books were already inscribed to you. Like he knew or something." He had to stop again. "Jesus Christ, I loved him," he said.

They distributed the books. For Sergeant Brown, the *Rubáiyát of Omar Khayyám*. For Montoya, Rupert Brooke. For Callahan himself, the *History of Afghanistan*. The lieutenant read out the names and the men came forward and they handed out the books.

Roy Murphy was left two books.

Sergeant Brown delivered a eulogy. He told some funny stories and made them laugh. He told some of the warrior stories again. And he talked like a minister, too. "We are children of God, and we walk upon His Earth for only a brief time, and we will never see his like again, until we meet again in the hereafter."

Brown held his new book of poetry out with his right hand like it was a Bible, and he said to them, "He'll be with us. I'll hear him every time I read old Omar." And then he opened the volume and finished with these lines:

*For some we loved, the loveliest and the best*
*That from his Vintage rolling Time has prest,*
*Have drunk their Cup a Round or two before,*
*And one by one crept silently to rest.*

They stood in formation, ramrod straight, most of them in sunglasses, so that you couldn't see the water coming to the corners of their eyes. They had no bugler to play taps and so had to lower the flag in silence. At half staff it still snapped in that Afghan wind. Each man in turn knelt by the shrine: the M4 planted upside down in the dirt, the boots, the captain's Kevlar on top. Each man in turn removed his sunglasses and fingered the dog tags.

Only one of them was dry eyed. He had done his weeping, and would not shed another tear until the night of his own death.

# FOURTEEN
June 2009

*A*t Bagram Air Base, Brigadier General Andrew Kearse moved ponderously, shifting his bulk on creaky joints. He was grave to the earnest young diplomats from State who came and went in Kabul, sardonic with the officers in Bagram. A Diogenes working combat's backstage, where warfare and politics clamor in the wings, he searched for amusement. For those whose humor ran dark, as his did, the players in Afghanistan furnished a rich source of material. The Americans and their Afghan faction were then busy with the fiction that the country was free and independent, that purpled thumbs had purchased an actual government rather than a cabal of thieves, that the Americans were allies rather than an occupying force, and that the war was accomplishing something. This was a precarious show, and offstage the actors and their squabbles multiplied. Kearse moved from one to the next. The only thing that mattered, really, was which one made it to the footlights.

"So what's this latest bed-wetting from the embassy?" he asked.

Two colonels had already arrived for the meeting. They made three in the general's small conference room. Each had the TOP SECRET/NOFORN memo printed off from the classified printer.

"Village elder and his son murdered in their beds, sir," Colonel Cooper answered, taking the lead. It was Cooper's case. "Civilians. Afghans are saying it was our guys."

"Where?"

"Komal. In the Korengal Valley."

*The Korengal Valley*—already famous in the Pentagon as the valley of death.

His glasses perched at the end of his nose, General Kearse read. At length he asked no one in particular, "How the fuck many Ramitullahs do they have in this country anyway—how do you keep them straight?"

He held the report at arm's length, as if to keep it as far away as possible. "The father blah blah, a son in the same house, blah blah. According to unnamed Afghan sources."

"Yessir."

"The unnamed Afghan source—old reliable. Sometime after midnight and before oh four-thirty." He looked up. "What else do we know?"

"Nothing."

"The wife finds them?"

"Before the first prayer, sir."

"She was unharmed?"

"Yes. Hysterical but physically unharmed."

"What did she see?"

"The victims. And before that, nothing, she slept through it."

"They got the knife?"

"Negative, sir."

"Well, what have they got for evidence?"

"An Afghan in the town says he saw one guy leaving. In camo and a mask."

"An Afghan in the town," General Kearse repeated. "Who has no name. Or one fucking name, like the rest of them. Colonel, does *one* guy on patrol sound like us to you?"

"No, sir."

"Is that firebase—Montana, is it—"

"Montana, sir."

"Is it in the habit of sending out one-man patrols at two a.m.?"

"No, sir."

He tossed the report to the table. "Colonel, if this was a model, we'd send her home to eat some pasta, you know? We'd tell her she was too thin. I suppose our solo ninja killer burned a Koran while he was down there."

"No report of that, sir. But . . ."

"But what?"

The colonel frowned. "It's not really Taliban style either, sir. They would claim responsibility, and send anonymous letters to everyone else in the village laying out the elder's crimes against Allah—collaboration with us or what have you—and threatening the others."

"Burglary, then."

"Nothing taken, sir."

"An honor killing. He screwed someone's daughter."

"He's the village elder."

"Well, so am I." The general smiled at the joke, for it was not clear which way the point cut. "Was this Ramitullah collaborating?"

"He was playing both sides like they all do, sir. We put in a new well last year. He'd meet us down there, but the firebase command believed he was aiding the insurgents, feeding them information about our movements."

"This still sounds like a criminal revenge killing to me, and the usual bullshit."

General Kearse turned back to the report and brooded on it for a moment, until one of the colonels said, "There is a little . . ."

"What, Colonel? Spit it out."

". . . context, sir."

"Context. Were you planning on sharing this context at some point, gentlemen?"

Colonel Cooper said, "There were parts we thought maybe we'd tell you about, before putting it in the e-mail."

"Okay, well, that makes sense. All right."

"The CO on-site at the firebase was KIA on seven June. Sniper shot at about oh ten hundred hours. The guy was very popular in the two fortieth. Almost legendary with them, a Captain Ian—"

The general interrupted. "Was that the guy took out a mortar team with—"

"A knife. Yessir."

"Dickinson. God-damnedest report I ever read," said General Kearse.

"Anyway, sir, the men were very loyal to him. Sniper gets him, and three nights—or mornings—later this happens."

The general thought about it for a moment. "CO at Montana, chief in the village. Where the shooter is probably sleeping like a baby, or is Ramitullah himself, or the son. That the context, Colonel?"

"Like I said, sir, there's that suggestion."

"An eye for an eye. Pretty good rule, Colonel, I'll bet there's a Koran verse on it." He smiled wickedly. "Never mind, I didn't say that. How far's the village from the firebase?"

"Five clicks, General."

"One of our guys revenged his CO, alone, in the middle of the night, he got two guys with a knife and didn't wake anybody up, and nobody saw him except the ghost with no name. Well, in my opinion, this is exactly the kind of fairy dust the embassy shits the bed over. So get back with the firebase command and . . . get your report machine going. Get that Partington to help you, he's pretty good. But . . . handle it, gentlemen. Handle it with the right . . . approach. All right? Excused." The general shook his head as they left the room. "Poor bastards," he said, although whom he meant by this was not clear.

The uniforms were pressed: not just clean but *pressed*—with creases in the pants. That is what hit Roy Murphy when the Chinook powered down and he and the squad left the flight line. It hit him again in chow hall. Bagram had grown, swollen with contractors, politicians, Afghans, press, NGOs, riffraff of all sorts. And soldiers, Marines, airmen, even sailors, whose uniforms weren't just clean but creased on the pant leg, the jumpsuits so spic-and-span that the airmen looked like they didn't know what dirt was, like it would offend them. Like this wasn't Afghanistan at all.

Rows of prefab huts of blinding white stood at attention in the sun, each with its little air conditioner jutting a salute, each little box inside turned to the coldest setting. Regimental plaques marked the corners of the dusty roads. Between the intermittent roar of takeoff and landing was the easy commerce, the unhurried stroll of an American suburb.

They offered them showers, and the guys would have liked one for sure, it'd been almost a month, but something passed quickly and subtly among them with barely a flicker of an eyelid. Lieutenant Callahan shook his head. And every man was with him. This wasn't an MWR rotation, and they didn't ask for this visit. Their stink and filthy fatigues would remind this bubble town that Afghanistan was not a bustling suburb where guys could chow on three hots a day and have nothing to worry about except Xbox, the weight room, and the latest YouTube. It was not Fort Drum. Remind them that a man died. So they wore their stink in the chow hall line, strung together by it like convicts. They sat together, and an aircrew at the next table moved away. Let them. They were proud of their stink, proud of their torn and filthy uniforms, black with dirt and oil and brown with the blood of the fallen. Let the file clerks move away.

That afternoon the squad was in the colonel's prefab, overwhelming a narrow corridor with their bulk and their number and their reek, while guys in clean uniforms stepped around and past with polite nods and files under their crisp sleeves.

*Files of papers.* Roy Murphy, squatting in that hall, watched them go by. That's what the war is even here in Bagram, files of papers.

All afternoon they waited outside the conference room to be called in, one by one. Callahan was in there and then Lima and

Montoya and the others. The minute hand on the clock at the end of the hall crawled up one side of the hill and staggered down the other. They'd rather have been on watch at Montana than squatting in this hallway—even Roy Murphy, a master of waiting, the last one they would interview.

Most of the squad didn't know what to think about this. The squad was still shaken. They were a little resentful, and a little scared as well to be interviewed by a colonel and a CID investigator—fucking *Navy*, he was, they would later say—who had stacks of files and reports and who apparently were pursuing some kind of political agenda. But Roy Murphy felt no such fear or ambivalence. He was just angry. All afternoon it worked his gut, the outrage of it, the betrayal by the Army he had served for five years. From which he'd never asked for anything until then.

There was a man down. They had a man *down*. Anybody investigating *that*?

Late in the afternoon they got to Billy Hall Jr. There were preliminaries, and a bit of joking around after Hall got into the little conference room with the investigators. Lieutenant Partington liked Hall's easygoing manner at first. "Jesus, what a long day," he said. He had the look of a man who was ready to check a box. "Hall, just a few formalities to wrap up for the report. You were on watch that night, the log says?"

"Yessir," said Hall, cheerily.

"With Fowler."

"Yessir, started out with Fowler, that's right, sir." He smiled pleasantly.

The lieutenant asked, "Started out?"

"Well, sir, one of the other guys replaced him."

"Who was that?"

"Specialist Murphy, sir."

"He replaced him?"

"Yessir. About midnight. He said he couldn't sleep, he come out and offered to take Fowler's watch."

"That common, switching off watch like that?"

Hall shook his head, still smiling. "No, sir, not really too common, I'd say. Mostly guys don't take watch except when it's theirs."

"After Murphy came on, how did you and he divide the watches?"

"I had Main Sally Port, sir, and Murphy had North Side."

"Did you leave the firebase at any point during your watch?"

"No, sir."

"Did anyone?"

"Not that I seen, sir."

"Did Murphy?"

"No, sir, not that I seen, sir."

"Is North Side visible from Main Sally?"

"No, sir."

"When did Murphy come out, best you remember?"

"Around midnight, I think it was, sir."

The colonel cut in. "Hall, it wasn't logged. Help us out with that, son."

"It wasn't?"

"No, it wasn't."

His big face worked into a frown, but slowly, as though forcing dough through a funnel. "Huh. I don't know exactly why that wasn't done, sir. I figured Murphy or Fowler would of logged it. Don't know why they didn't attend to it, sir." His smile returned.

The colonel carried on with the questioning. "Did you see Murphy at all during the watch?"

"No, sir, not till next morning. Oh, wait, no, I did see him once. He come over to my post." Billy Hall Jr. grinned apologetically. "To borrow something."

"What?"

"Sir?"

The colonel's manner was still friendly, but a little edge had crept into his voice, for it was getting late. "What did he come to borrow?"

Billy Hall Jr.'s lip quivered, and his big sunburned face seemed to redden an extra shade. "Tryin to remember, sir. Wait, it come to me. It was water, sir." And then the big grin again.

"Water?"

"Yessir. He needed a water. Best I can recall, sir."

"Best you can recall," Lieutenant Partington repeated. "You said he borrowed it."

"Yessir."

"So he gave it back later—the water?"

"No, sir, I guess I mean, he come over and *took* a water."

"But you said 'borrow'?"

"I, well, I meant *took*, I guess, sir."

The two investigators exchanged a glance.

"What time did this happen?"

"Pretty much when he come on."

"And when did you next see him?"

"About oh six hundred, sir. I seen him after I was relieved, as we was walking back to the hooch."

"Notice anything different, strange about him?"

"No, sir."

"Any wounds, scratches, any tears in the uniform, dirt, anything unusual?"

"Well . . . he was kinda poorly, sir."

"What do you mean, 'poorly'?"

"Had a bad gut, sir. He'd been in the burn—— the, uh, facility most of the night."

The lieutenant repeated this. "He'd been in the burnshitter?"

"Yessir. He told me, he said, 'I'm not feeling too good, Hall. I might have to be in the burnshitter more'n a few times, all right?' And I says, 'All right.' And he says, 'Okay.'" Hall's face brightened. "I guess that's why he needed the water, sir."

"I guess so," said Partington.

The colonel suddenly changed the subject. "Hall, what did you think about Captain Dickinson?"

Hall's grin vanished then, and his voice fell almost to a whisper. "He was a great officer, sir."

"Was Murphy close to him?"

"We all loved Captain Dickinson."

"Murphy especially?"

"Captain kinda took an interest in Murphy. It was sort of a little secret, sir, but captain was teaching him to, you know . . ."

"What?"

"Read. Read better, I mean."

"To read better?"

"Yes, sir."

The officers shared a glance, and the lieutenant carried on. "How did Murphy take it when the captain was killed?"

"Same as all of us, I'd say, sir. We was all cut up. Him the same, except for maybe a little more so, you know, when it happened."

"No, I don't know. Tell me."

Billy Hall Jr. had choked up a little, remembering that day. He spoke softly. "Roy got to him first, sir."

The lieutenant made a note, and the colonel wrapped it up.

"Son, do you know anything about how this happened down the valley?"

"No, sir, I surely don't."

"Send in Murphy, then," he said. "Thank you, Private."

Billy Hall Jr.'s smile returned to him then, and he got up. Just before he left the room, Lieutenant Partington, who was still sitting at the table finishing his notes, spoke without looking up. "Hall, before you go, just one more thing. I'm just making a note here, need to make sure I got the note right for the report."

"Yessir?"

"Murphy volunteered for watch that night?"

"Yessir."

"On a night when he had the shits? He volunteered for someone *else*'s overnight watch? Do I have that right, Private Hall?"

The lieutenant looked up at him, and Hall stammered, "Yes, sir, I guess that's right, sir."

He turned back to his pad of paper. "Wanted to make sure I had that right, Hall. Go get us Murphy, would you?"

* * * *

He had been in that corridor all afternoon, and his knees ached with squatting. They have saved him for last, and on toward dinner, it was his turn. He got up, knocked, and entered. He shut the door behind him and saluted. The lieutenant and the colonel sat at the table, and each flinched anew at the fresh wave of stink he brought into the little room. Roy Murphy pretended not to notice. Overhead was a bright fluorescent light. File folders and papers and a laptop computer were on the table. In the corner of the small room a Mr. Coffee on a file cabinet quietly boiled the life out of a last inch of sludge.

*At Montana, coffee is food. We chew the crystals in the coffee packets.*

The lieutenant offered him a bottle of water, and he took it. A noise, a dull, pervasive roar like the roar of surf muted their voices. Words came through, but faintly and out of any context. *Report. Investigation. Procedures. Just a formality, you understand. Appreciate your help.*

The colonel said that they were all very sorry about what happened.

*You sonofabitch, saying that about an American you never knew, one of us, whose death you aren't investigating, while you're here running errands for the enemy.* But Roy Murphy nodded, his face a blank.

The colonel said, "We understand the stresses of that environment, and everybody is grateful for your service up there. And I want to say, Specialist, I read Captain Dickinson's report and recommendation for your Silver Star, and you have my admiration. You are a soldier's soldier."

He said it like a speech, like he'd rehearsed it. Roy Murphy nodded again. (You nod at a colonel and say, "Thank you, sir," so that he won't know you are thinking, You don't understand shit about the stresses up there, I never saw one colonel up there ever, and if you did understand you wouldn't be sitting in this room, brownnosing the politicians by running your little investigation, with your file folder and laptop, and brownnosing me with the medals stuff. Nobody wears a medal at Montana.)

But he didn't say any of that, and the drumroll went on. *Just a few questions. Shouldn't take long. Get you some coffee?* The two officers kept glancing back and forth and finally were under way with it. What they brought him there for. What they brought them all there for.

"We understand you took Fowler's watch at zero hundred on ten June," the lieutenant began. "I was kind of curious about that." He was a trim officer with glasses and thinning red hair and clean fingernails. He spoke in a faintly southern cadence that called Billy Hall Jr. to mind, although his accent was not nearly as pronounced. Subtle, in the way he said, "kahna: I was kahna curious about that." Roy Murphy sat directly across from him, looking down at his own hands folded in his lap, at the grime beneath his own fingernails, the grime worn into his fingers, his palms, the backs of his hands, his wrists.

"Specialist?"

The silence grew painful for the officers, but not for him. On watch a man got used to silences. At the firebase there were long days without much to say. There would be time enough for talk later, after the enemy hit them, but there was no hurry before that.

"Why did you take Fowler's watch? Can I get an answer, son?"

"Sorry, sir."

"*Sorry*, Specialist? I don't understand."

"I got nothing to say about it, sir." He tried to make it sound flat, unprovocative, but the insubordination was rattling.

"You got nothing to *say* about it?"

"No, sir."

"An E-Five's got nothing to say about it," Lieutenant Partington repeated.

The colonel cut in. "Let's try this again, soldier. We're about to wrap this investigation up after a long day with your squad. We're on the same *team*, here. We got a bullshit report we got to do and I want some cooperation from you. Do you understand?"

"I do understand, sir, but I got nothing to say." His eyes, which fixed the colonel's as he answered, were coldly insubordinate. Those eyes, but not his mouth added, "Punish me. Whatever you want." And then looked back down at his hands.

They put him out of the room for a minute so they could talk. He emerged to find the squad still huddled in that cramped hallway. He looked at them quizzically. "You guys go on to chow hall, get dinner."

"When they kick your ass, Murphy, who's gonna haul it off?" Nadal asked, wearily.

It hit him then—the first rule of the squad, the rule above all other rules, was that you never leave a man behind. Not ever. Not in the Korengal, not here. They were hardwired with this rule. His squad mates wanted to leave—they just didn't know how.

"It's all right," he said. "It's bullshit. Go on—go *eat*, you assholes. I'll catch you later."

"Y'all stop jackin each other off in there, maybe we could," said Billy Hall Jr.

The officers recalled him, and the colonel lectured for a while. Something about the Fifth. If he wanted to take the Fifth it was his right to take the Fifth. He was not under oath, this was just background, but he could. Something else about the UCMJ, the JAGs. It was the Fifth and the JAGs and the UCMJ, all of this coming at him. They could call a JAG, get a JAG involved, but that would not be wise, soldier, that would not be wise at all and would just elevate things. And besides it would be goddamned ridiculous for a genuine hero, a soldier decorated for valor, to be fucking around with lawyers and such.

Roy Murphy did not respond to any of this. The roaring was back in his ears.

The lieutenant tried a few more questions. Did he leave the firebase while on watch? Did he go that morning to the village?

"Sir, I'm sorry, I got nothing to say about it."

The lieutenant raised his voice. He was not shouting, but he was loud. They had decided, evidently, that he would be the bad cop. Roy Murphy reminded himself it was important to keep his face impassive and not lash out with his fist and drop the man, as easy as it would have been to do so.

"This is a problem, Murphy. I mean, this is a serious and un-necessary problem, son! We were about to get this thing wrapped up, and you want me to bring a JAG in here? If you do, this will not go away, this will not be *over.* Do you want it to be over?"

Roy struggled to keep his face blank but felt scorn leaking around the edges. He fought against his lip curling and his brow wrinkling as though his face would blurt out what he was thinking.

The colonel, the good cop, said, "Murphy, I've done a few of these."

He nodded. *I'll bet you have. I'll bet you've done a whole shitload of these.* But he said nothing.

"And Lieutenant Partington is right. We're about to finish this report. We're about to get down the last of the interviews, with no evidence, not a shred at all, that anyone in the platoon's done anything wrong. And you want to go and light your hair on fire, and have us write down that you refused to cooperate and get the JAGs and every other goddamned thing going here, over a shitsack insurgent bastard named Ramitullah or whatever the Christ it is. The rest of your squad said nothing happened. So nothing happened, right?"

At this point they just disgusted him. *His* body barely cold, in a box in a hangar somewhere on that very base, somewhere within half a click of that room, and was anybody investigating *his* death? They've got to have an investigation about Ramitullah? Run a Chinook up to the firebase, haul us all back here for that bastard? That's why you needed the entire squad to stand down from the defense of a base that just saw a man killed?

He said nothing.

"This is not the smartest way to handle this, son."

They had threatened him with the JAGs, but they did not actually get the JAGs. The lieutenant just kept at him. He started up again, but the noise came back in Roy Murphy's ears, and drowned it out. He was in there for a long time; they didn't give up easy. They were thinking they were one goddamned guy away from having this thing buttoned up; they would break him to it if it meant keeping him all night. So they thought for a while. But Roy Murphy was the champion of waiting.

In the end it was the colonel who relented. He sighed, and flatly, he said, "Forget the night of the tenth. Just forget it. I want to ask you a completely different question about this guy Ramitullah."

That's when his resolve cracked just a little. It was not to help the two headquarters brass. It was just that, concerning Ramitullah, whom Roy held accountable with moral certainty, words came of their own accord.

"I met him."

The officers exchanged a quick glance, and then the lieutenant was making notes while the words came. "Captain took Second Squad on patrol down to Komal. We sat in Ramitullah's house with the interpreter, and Captain drank tea with him and they talked."

"And you?"

"We was in with them for a while and then on guard outside the house, me and Lima. But we could hear all of it, in and out, the *mutarjim* and Captain talking and Ramitullah. The pump was broke in the well, that's what he said. Captain said, 'I told you not to run it when the well gets too low, it would burn out.' Ramitullah wanted another well, deeper, with a better pump. Captain said maybe he could do that, but first he'd got to show some leadership and control over insurgents in the valley taking potshots at us. And he said that was nothing to do with him, he didn't know nothing about it."

"What'd you think of him—Ramitullah?"

"That's what Captain asked me, sir."

"Sorry?"

"When we was going back up to the firebase, after. Captain asked me that. What I thought about him."

"And?"

"I seen him smile."

The lieutenant looked confused. "I don't follow," he said.

"I seen that kind of smile before. Phony smiles the same in Afghanistan as everywhere, sir. I knew he was a lying sack a shit, first minute I ever saw it on him."

"Okay."

"I told Captain he probably sold the first pump. And the son was an insurgent, or feeding them info. That's what I said."

"And Captain Dickinson?"

"Agreed with me."

But there was nothing else he would talk about, and at last it wore them out. Partington said, "Murphy, we're done tonight. We may have to get the JAGs in this thing. We gave you every chance, but it is what it is. I got just one more thing I have to raise with you. The incident on seven June . . ."

He was tired and hungry. It was late. He did want to get out of there. Chow hall had closed hours ago, but someone had said there was now a Burger King up at Tillman: he could get something there and then sleep.

"The men say you were close to . . ."

He didn't flinch or respond. His dark eyes were blank, his hands folded neatly in his lap, and he stared at the grime ground into his nails, the backs of his fingers.

"How did you feel when—when it happened?"

Silence as before, but this one angrier.

"I know, I know, it's a stupid question. But it's for the report."

Roy Murphy exhaled slowly. A lot of chopper fuel and stupid questions and a wasted day for a bullshit report. *How did I feel when he bled out in my arms? How did I fucking feel?* He was already too far over the line of insubordination and cautioned himself not to say anything stupid, but could not help almost spitting out words when at length he answered.

"I. Got Nothing. To Say About It. Sir."

"Damn," one of them said. "You are the *slowest* motherfucker, Murphy . . ."

At last he had gotten out of that room into the corridor, and they were still there. Squatting, leaning, slouching, eyes closed, most of them. They were hungry and tired and stinking. And they were there. He bit his lip for a moment to think that the one rule, the rule of the squad—that it applied even to him. Even when he'd gotten them into all this shit, it applied. No one questioned it. No one had said, "Fuck it, I'm hungry." It was the rule. It always applied.

No one else had ever applied such a rule to him before, not Eliza Murphy, who was said to be his mother, not even Emma. Least of all Emma, who wanted him but then left him behind. He could not speak. He could only whisper, "Jesus Christ, you ass-holes," and turn his head.

Grinning, Billy Hall Jr. said, "Murphy so slow, his momma got up from the hospital bed, went and got laid, had another baby afore he ever come out."

"Well," said Lima, "he ain't in cuffs *yet*. God, he stink, though."

"We stuck with him," Montoya agreed.

When he worked at DiBello's as a kid, guys were always asking about his brother Mike. The probation officers up in Bennington would shake their heads and talk about his brothers. And the summer they were together, Emma wanted to know about his brothers this, his brothers that. It was said in Hoosick Bridge that he was the third of the Murphy brothers.

But he didn't know brothers at home. These were his brothers.

"You done, Colonel?"

Late on the night that Second Squad was interviewed, General Kearse was on the phone with Colonel Cooper.

"I'm not sure, sir."

"Not sure?"

A long sigh. The colonel said, "We interviewed them all. Seven guys know nothing. There was no patrol. Nobody was absent. Nobody went past the watch."

"So what's the problem?"

"The eighth guy."

"Tell me."

"It comes down to a couple of things. First, the watch. The Afghans say the killings happened sometime the morning of ten June. The firebase watch at zero hundred is logged as Hall and Fowler. But another guy, Murphy, took Fowler's watch, said he couldn't sleep, he'd take watch. The switch wasn't logged, Lieutenant Callahan didn't even know about it. And while the new guy is on watch, nobody else can see him. Specialist Roy Murphy. Dickinson himself promoted him six months ago. They were kind of close."

"You interviewed him?"

"Yes, sir. He's a . . . Well, I don't know exactly how to do him justice."

"Try."

"Okay. Let's start with, he's a Silver Star."

"A Silver Star?"

"Last fall, the firebase is under attack, and he pulled that guy out of a hooch and then him and his buddy take on a whole platoon of insurgents in their nightshirts."

"I remember the report. What's the second thing?"

"The second thing is, he is one mean-looking, dark, intense sonofabitch. Whole time we talked to him, he is just seething. The anger is boiling out of this guy. A fucking Rambo."

A pause. "Is there a third thing?"

"Yeah. He stinks."

"What do you mean, he stinks?"

"I mean he hadn't showered. None of them had, but he was . . . Damn, sir, he was *powerful*."

"Sounds like exactly what I want at a firebase, Colonel."

"I guess so, sir. Anyway, I can give you Specialist Murphy's full account right now, if you want." The colonel flipped his notepad and read, "Quote, I got nothing to say about it, end quote."

"About what?"

"About anything. Whatever we asked him, he said, 'I got nothing to say about it.' For a couple of hours. Why he took watch

when it wasn't his, what happened on watch, what he saw, who he
saw, did he leave the wire, did anyone leave the wire, did anyone
come back, what happened in the village. 'I ain't got nothing to
say.'"

"Jesus."

Then silence. It was the silence of rebuke, of the matter not
being handled correctly.

"Christ, did you *talk* to him, Colonel?"

"For hours, sir. He was the last one. We were all but done."

"He wouldn't speak at all?"

"Only talked about one thing—he thinks Ramitullah was
feeding info to the Taliban."

"What about the other guy on watch?"

"Hall. He doesn't know anything, doesn't see anything, he's at
the main sally, and nobody went out, surely not Specialist Hall, sir.
Hall's the nicest country boy in the world, General, answers every
question with a 'sir, yes, sir,' smiles sweetly at you and lies through
his ass."

The Chinook took the rest of the squad back to Montana, but
Murphy was ordered to stay behind. They kept him in Bagram for
almost a week. Finally Colonel Cooper had him into his hot little
office, where Roy Murphy stood before the desk. The air conditioner roared ineffectively, and the colonel had to raise his voice a
little to be heard over it.

"I've got a message from the command, Murphy."

"Sir."

"It's time, son."

It had been a long week, stuck waiting in that bubble of a
base. Being separated from his squad violated every instinct of
training. It was Xbox and movies on the AFN and chow hall and
weight rooms, and he hadn't known what to do with himself except pace. Savage heat outside, and cold in most of the little boxes
that contained his pacing days—frigid cold, except for this office,
where the A/C didn't work.

At first he misunderstood, and his relief was visible. "Thank you, sir. Been looking forward to rejoining my unit. How soon, if I can ask, sir?"

The colonel said, "Sit down, son."

He took a moment to digest it. The colonel said, "It's time for you to leave."

"*Leave*, sir?"

"It will be better for everyone. You'll be given an honorable discharge."

"If I quit."

"If you exercise your right not to reenlist."

"If I don't reenlist," he repeated. "And if I do reenlist?"

The colonel frowned. Answering this question with a truthful account of the legal details might have softened the blow he wanted to deliver, but he rightly guessed that the young soldier had not studied the finer points of the Afghanistan Status of Forces Agreement.

"If you do reenlist," he said, "then life gets very complicated, Murphy. The report includes our interview, your refusal to talk, and CID starts up a formal investigation, and subpoenas you, and you either take the Fifth or go to the brig, or both; and maybe get tried for two counts of unprivileged homicide of a nonbelligerent civilian. Which you will beat, if it's a court-martial, because there isn't shit for evidence except a couple of lying soldiers. But the problem here, the real *problem*, is that this happened in sovereign Afghan territory, away from any active battle, and Afghanistan is a sovereign nation. I have that on very good authority from two dozen lawyers who would never ever set foot in the place. And that means that maybe you get tried in an Afghan court. Murphy, in an Afghan court, this won't take up too much of your time. They'll go right to, I don't know, stoning you to death, and your pecker will be cut off by these people and fed to dogs, and your head up on a pike on the goodwill highway.

"Or, like I said, maybe it's just a court-martial, and you beat murder but get a dishonorable discharge."

Roy Murphy nodded. "And if I leave?"

"If you leave quietly, then the paperwork is, you didn't re-up. Your ugly face is no longer hanging around Afghanistan to be noticed by an interpreter, or a water carrier at the firebase, or somebody in that village during the next goodwill op. The report has the other interviews, and they said what they said, and the watch log says Fowler was on watch, and nobody saw anything, and Murphy? Oh yeah, he was another guy in the squad. What happened to him anyway? His tour ended, and he served his country with honor and went home in one piece, who the fuck knows where he is? He's a name on a list in St. Louis somewhere. The report says blah blah this and blah blah that and that an old Afghan shitsack was killed by Christ knows who, and there's no evidence of jack, and it goes into a file, and Ramifuckingtullah is not my problem anymore."

"If I leave."

Colonel Cooper leaned over the desk. "The Army protects its own, son, but there are limits. You were an asshole when we interviewed you. Don't be an asshole twice."

The worst of it was, they didn't let him back up to Montana, not even for a day. They didn't want the interpreters or the porters or anyone seeing him again. He never had a chance to say good-bye to a single one of those guys.

At the firebase, Callahan assigned Billy Hall Jr. to pack Murphy's gear in two duffels to be sent down to Bagram. Callahan stood by his shoulder while Billy Hall packed up the clothes and the shaving kit and the rest of the gear, the sidearm and the two books from Captain Dickinson.

The bayonet lay on Roy's bunk in its sheath. Hall recognized it, and Nadal did, too—he knew the knife was Hall's, but nobody said anything as Hall quietly put it into the duffel.

A week later Roy Murphy was at Ramstein Air Base. And soon enough, stepping off of a Hercules at Fort Drum. A few days after that he was a part of history, he was nobody you'd notice, just another vet back from Iraq, or Afghanistan—one of them. He was in uniform, but by July 2009, people had been seeing guys in uniform for what seemed like forever. He was just another joe waiting in a long ticket line, another head you'd count off silently, separating you and the ticket counter—just another body in the ruck and chaos and hot, humid noise of the Port Authority Bus Terminal in New York City.

# PART FOUR
## *Abide with Me*

# FIFTEEN

## 2011

*T*he seasons rolled, one into the next. Roy Murphy moved the business to a garage on River Street, bought an acre of land, bought another acre, and then buried them under hills of mulch and crushed stone and sand and rows of trees and shrubs and ornamentals with root-balls wrapped in burlap. He added two bays to the garage, and then another six, and began to fill the bays with trucks and trailers, and the shop with tools. The customers came, and came back, and the men left DiBello and came to Murphy's Landscaping for the work.

The Herrick girls were gone from the Heights now. Emma was in New York, Anne in Cambridge, and Charlie was up at UVM. Only Jane was left at the house. Sadness hung about the place like an old dress on an older lady, and sometimes in the gray afternoons only a single light gleamed from an upper floor. All winter, unshoveled snow lay in mottled heaps, blackening with road muck, and when mud season came, the Heights emerged thirsty for paint, shabby, with a brown lawn and dead plantings. The blue of its shingles faded wearily to gray, and the mass of the house looked gaunt and surly in the afternoons.

Before dawn each morning, driving his truck to the shop,

Roy Murphy would turn left in town onto Washington Street, and climb the hill to Spring. He would turn and slowly pass the Heights on the left, craning his neck as he peered at the darkened windows on the upper floors. Farther down Spring, he would loop back toward River Street. Turning the corner at the top of Washington, one morning early in May, he heard the news. The radio cut to a bulletin, and he had to stop the truck. He idled there in the middle of Spring Street for a few minutes, stunned, before he remembered himself and drove on to the shop. All through that day, and all that night, he tried to get near a radio, a television, hungry for accounts of the raid, the escape, the body disposed at sea. He pictured the squad on the night flight into Pakistan, and remembered how alone a man felt when deafened by the roar of engines, wondering whether an RPG was trained on the helicopter at just that moment. The news said that one pilot put down inside a compound, and another pitched into the garden. He'd seen pilots put those birds down in confined spaces, their faces taut as fence wire.

And all day long, he tried to picture the first guy up the stairs—the one who came face-to-face with that tall, stooping figure. He imagined screams of women, cursing, noise in the darkness, the gun bursts—imagined saying those words: *Geronimo, KIA!* What must that have been like? He pictured the squad falling back—Move move move move *move!*—boarding the chopper, the rotors whirring, bags filled with contraband and a body, and the helpless, now redoubled fear that would have gripped them as the engines whined and strained to pull up out of there, waiting for the RPG that never came.

And then the whoops when they were clear. *Geronimo—KIA!*

He remembered Billy Hall Jr. joking, the night after the ambush.

*"Specialist Montoya, you go get Osama bin Laden—bring his ass back, too, and if he don't say please and thank you, you gon give him a severe reprimand!"*

His crews were in the thick of spring cleanups that day, and he drove all over town, from job to job, but on the job sites and in Hoosick Bridge, nothing was different. People would ask, "Did you hear?" After a brief acknowledgment, they'd return to business. At the shop, the customer and vendor calls were the same. "Make sure it's black mulch, not that red stuff. I *hate* the red stuff," one customer said, and he answered, yes, sir, we don't use the red stuff.

Through the day the news reporting descended into spin and conspiracy theories, and who congratulated the president, and who didn't, and how they said it, and what they didn't say. It so frustrated him that he banged the truck radio and shouted at it, "Enough with the politics!" He wanted details. It was in a town, they said, not a mountain hamlet but a real town. How big a town? How big was the compound exactly? How many flights of stairs in the building? How many of the enemy were armed?

And what about the burial? They would say nothing about that, except that it was at sea. He pictured the gray of an empty sea and a blank horizon, the bloodred lip of sun rising from an indistinct east. He imagined a sack slipping into that vastness, and gone. Was it climax, or was it punctuation? He didn't know how to feel. The shadowy figure whom they had never found, never engaged, was now found, engaged, and in the same breathless report vanished, as though he'd never existed.

Nobody was in the street, nobody even honked a car horn. He wondered, Is it over? Have we won? He was still wondering the next day, and the next. But as the days and weeks of that summer passed, the reports from Afghanistan didn't change, and the work in Hoosick Bridge didn't change, and he came to question whether bin Laden had mattered at all. A sack was there, and then it was gone, enveloped by a gray sea, anonymous. That was it.

That summer, Emma's face had begun to fade from his daily consciousness, her picture to grow fuzzy and indistinct as well. He no longer thought so much about her marriage. She still came into his mind by night, but in conscious thought he always said to himself, Put it behind you. Sometimes he would force himself to prowl the bars in Bennington. A few times, he brought a girl home, but it never worked out well. He couldn't share a bed, and would lie awake half the night on the floor, and then weeks or months would go by before he prowled again. He began to think, Maybe when I get my place, I will get a woman, too, and then I will put it all behind me.

That phrase was in his mind more and more. It was the preface of many ideas, which all began, "When I get my place, I will . . ." The business was a success—he could now afford a better place. Bankers and Realtors would cold-call him that summer, but he always hesitated, something holding him back. He liked the feel of money hitting his account and didn't like the feel of it leaving. Putting off a decision to move was easier. And so he sat alone in the shop, late at night, figuring and planning the next job, the next account, watching the balance in the bank account grow, and the summer passed.

It was one afternoon in October when Joe Rouleau stopped him as the crews were coming in. Did that girl find him? The men were pulling blades off of the decks and setting them up in the vises for sharpening. They were lubing up the riding mowers and checking chain oil in the chain saws, and Roy Murphy was inspecting everything, as he did every night.

"What girl?"

"There was a girl called the shop today asking for you. We told her you were out at KeyBank."

"Didn't see anyone."

Rouleau followed Roy across the bay to where one of the mechanics was working on an older Scag.

"Need to replace that belt," Roy said, pointing.

Rouleau said, "Her name was Izzy, said she knew you."

He thought for a moment. "I don't know anybody of that name."

After the crews left that night, Roy remained in the shop with the books. Some of the wholesalers were raising prices, and he'd been looking to replace a few suppliers anyway. He was going through figures, trying to work out if he had room in the back lot to buy larger loads.

At about 8:00 p.m., she called him on his cell phone. She told him he'd met her at her brother's engagement party two summers before—George Forrester, who married Emma Herrick. He tried to recall meeting someone that night, a sister of George's, but he could not. He could barely remember George himself.

"Sorry, I don't really remember," he said. "Anyways, what can I do for you?"

"Umm, buy me dinner? I'm here in Hoosick Bridge. Kinda have no plans. You busy?"

"You're *here*?"

Izzy Forrester was the kind of girl who thrived in crises, who would not strike out on the path ahead until the bridge behind was in flames. She would not find a new school merely because the old one was going badly—she would wait to be expelled, and for that look of fear in her parents' eyes. Addiction to crisis had seen her transferred to many schools, to "educational" stays in Switzerland and in a rehab facility, and so far to two colleges. But with the latest expulsion had come a new flatness in her parents' voices. When she called to report with bored detachment that she needed the debit card refreshed, her father said, simply, "No." No to refreshing the debit card, no to money, no to another rescue, no even to a conversation.

"I'm sorry, Izzy," he said.

She was furious. But the conspiracy was soon in place: her mother, her brother—none of them was going to bail her out this time. For three days, she couch-surfed with an acquaintance who had an apartment in Saratoga, near school. But that welcome wore thin, and so one morning Izzy rose before dawn and went carefully through her host's wallet, searching for a credit card that might not be missed for a few days at least. (The girl's parents had given her so many.) It ought to be worth a tank of gas.

That's when a memory, stored up for just this sort of rainy day, returned. She had heard occasional rumors over the two years since she'd seen him at that party. Energized by the thought of a new adventure, Izzy Forrester drove to Hoosick Bridge to find Roy Murphy.

The Hunan was where he usually got his takeout. Only once had he eaten in its harshly lit dining room, with shiny plastic table-cloths on the tables and little plastic temples for ornament. The room was papered with a dingy red-patterned wallpaper. A sleepy waiter escorted him across the room to where she was seated. She did not look familiar: a slim, small girl with a mass of long brown hair; she was expensively dressed, wearing blue leggings, Hunter boots high on the calf, a formfitting, dark wool coat with a red scarf tightly knotted at the throat. She stood up and offered her hand. Her fingernails were polished blue, he noticed.

"Still don't remember me?"

He glanced up and down. "Sorry."

Izzy swept the thick mane of her hair up and over her fore-head, from which, all evening, it would fall again, and again be swept. She was not pretty, but there was something dramatic about her.

"My hair was red that night. Anyway, I remember you. You made an impression, even if I didn't." She laughed and sat down.

"You were in the tent?"

She laughed again. "*Everybody* was in the tent. As a matter of fact, you were looking right at me."

He was not handsome, she thought—the thick ridge above his eyes was almost simian to her. But he was a match flame she was drawn to touch. The impression he gave was of force not to be trifled with—and she had always been a girl who lived to trifle.

"So why is George's sister here?" he asked.

"Honestly? To see you."

"You came to see me," he repeated, slowly.

"Like I said about the impression."

They ordered dinner. He didn't like her, she was too loud, but there was something about sitting close to her, some electricity in the air that started to work on him.

Dinner came, and while they ate she belittled her dull and conventional brother, and Roy did not mind hearing it. She told him about the wedding ("The reception was so *fucking* boring, all these lawyers and Wall Street people standing around with their cocktails, sneaking looks at their BlackBerries and droning on about whether the market would come back; honestly, it's all they talk about. The whole time I was dying for a little air"). To anyone else she might have unloaded her frustration with her serene "new sister," who was about as interesting as a statue, and acted like all she had to do at the reception was be adored. But instinct told her not to come too close to Emma with him.

"I guess I just don't fit in with all those people, Roy. Or any of that whole, like, New England college thing they're into. You know?"

He said almost nothing as they ate, frowning sometimes, because he didn't like the familiar way she used his name.

"I must have been adopted or something."

He seemed on edge, so she adjusted course, and tried to draw him out about his business. He would say only that it was going okay. Usually Izzy's storytelling, her cool, judgmental cynicism, her funny and easy contempt for the follies of others would captivate listeners. But she had no control of this conversation. She could tell that he read her bullshit instinctively.

"You dropped out of school?" he asked.

"Yeah, it was such a waste, and . . ."

"You have a job?"

"No. It's just happened, you know, with school. I'm . . . looking."

"What at?"

"Excuse me?"

"What are you looking at?"

"You get right to the point, huh? Some of this, some of that, you know?"

"No," he said. "I don't."

She was unused to conversations like this. People didn't usually press her this way. They preferred her easy euphemisms to the tedious truth.

He checked his watch and said he had to go home.

"Come on, it's early—it's only ten! What do you guys do up here for *fun* at night?"

"We go to bed."

"*That's* getting to the point." She laughed. But the joke didn't register right away. It took a moment for him to snap, "For sleep. I get up at four."

"Four," she repeated. "*Really.*"

"Really."

"I've *been* up at four," she mused. "Lots of times. I don't think I ever *got* up at four, though."

"Time to go." He motioned for the check.

Izzy flipped her hair back around for the hundredth time. "So, any recommendations on, you know, a motel or anything? Or do you have a couch?"

"A couch," he repeated.

"Yeah."

"You don't have anywhere to stay, and you want my couch."

Izzy said, "Depends what you want."

He appraised her frankly with what she thought, but could not be certain, was a kind of smile. "I have a couch," he said at last.

Her father had bought the cute little blue BMW for her three years earlier. It was parked on the street outside. She followed his truck to the outskirts of town, down to River Street, and into a lot where he parked next to a darkened brick building with a row of garage bays off to one side. Hills of loam, of mulch, of crushed stone loomed behind the lot. It wasn't any kind of house or apartment, but her confusion was gone in a moment, as she realized this was his shop. He lives above his shop—he really is a workaholic, she thought.

He led her inside and flipped on the light switch in the office, a cluttered room with cheap veneer siding. Next to the door was a metal desk, and to one side a plywood tabletop rested on two file drawer sets, holding a computer. Notes, memos, a calendar were pinned to the veneer. Behind was some furniture, an old couch, three chairs, and a small table covered with plans.

"So this is yours," she said. "Murphy's Landscaping."

The shop lay dimly visible beyond the office, where tool upon tool hung from racks. Beyond, the trucks and mowers were lined up in the bays.

"There's the bathroom," he said, pointing.

"Roy Murphy lives over his shop." She smiled. "That's cool."

"No. This is just where he keeps his couch. I'll see you about quarter to five." And then he was gone.

In time the wolf pack gathered, bankruptcy lawyers nosing and scuffling with each other, but there was little blood left in skeletal Fredoni & Herrick. Poor Burt Fredoni was a pathetic figure in town now, and his wife, Leslie, holding Jane accountable, never spoke to her after 2004. Suits were brought against those lucky enough to have gotten payments before the end, dragging them back to the communal pain. But those were scraps, and there was only one real scent. And so as the decade came to a close, the attention of the legal pack turned up the hill. They began to lope up Washington Street, skulking at the verge of the Heights, appraising it with hungry eyes. They had their papers, their depositions, and the object of their hunger was plain—they meant to make his fraud hers and rip the Heights from her.

The shame of it had plagued her at first: half the town defrauded, and by one whom she had brought among them and whose name she had taken—by his handsome assurances, his graceful lies, his impenetrable designs. But as the years passed it was no longer shame that she felt so much as isolation, that sense of enemies at the verge. Of the legal whys and wherefores, of fraudulent transfers under Section 548 of the Bankruptcy Code and all the heraldry of the lawyers she deigned to understand not a thing. It was said that Attorney Cook (whom Tom Herrick himself had named in his note) was an aggressive fighter and could help her hold them off, and so she hired him. He was skillful, adroit with defenses, appeals, and most of all, delay. For a while, the mortgage she took out helped fund his efforts. Attorney Cook's defense might ultimately have prevailed, but for a single legal slip.

Even then she was already jumping, unsteadily, from one thought to another. They were like stepping-stones in a mental stream, and she would lose her footing, pivoting on a slick thought, and then become confused about which side of the stream she had come from, to which she was bound. If only she had not leapt from one conversation to the next—if only Hal Cook had been given a sentence, a word of warning, he might have cut it off. The lawyer might have parried the trustee's thrust, and history taken a different turn. But a few words spoken on a January morning at a veneer table would be her undoing, as an overweight man with a bad hairpiece pressed keys on his little transcribing machine, pressing them like daggers into Jane Herrick.

It was the professor who, several years later, found the deposition transcripts, made copies in the county court, and then regaled diners in Toni's Lunch with them, explaining how Jane Herrick might lose the Heights to a lawyer's trick. He sat at the counter across from Toni, his eyes alive with discovery as he flipped through the document, thick with notes that he'd written in the margins, circles, arrows, exclamation points.

The professor read out, "Question by Attorney Holt. 'You were generally aware of his business, of the transactions he engaged in?' Cook—that's Jane Herrick's lawyer—he objects. Then some falderal between the lawyers. . . . Falderoo, falderah. . . . Ah, *here*. Answer: 'Aware of the transactions? I didn't know the details of Tom's work.' Question: 'You knew some details, did you not? Your sister Patricia Tolson had an account with Fredoni & Herrick?' She says yes. Holt questions about the sister and Jane says, 'We don't discuss money in my family, Mr. Holt.' Lovely, that!"

Toni chuckled, picturing it.

"But the lawyer keeps pressing her. And then her fellow Cook objects with the 'marital privilege.'"

The professor explained that this was the rule that they can't make you testify about what your spouse says. He hummed merrily as he continued to leaf through. "Then, let me see, yes . . . Right. There's a whole business about a dinner party. Not long before Tom Herrick's death, he went with Jane to dinner at Burt and Leslie Fredoni's house, and the conversation turned to the office secretary, who was abruptly fired the year before Tom Herrick's death, who, in the months before the suicide, had spread nasty rumors about fraud at the company."

"Barb," Toni said. "Barb Pisani."

"This was how Holt got Jane twisted around, years later, at the deposition. Here it is, let me read it:

```
Q: Mrs. Herrick, you said, 'The accounts were the
   accounts'?
A: Yes. Barb could claim the business was a fraud,
   she could go around town saying all of these
   things, but the accounts were the accounts. There
   were account numbers, with stocks or money, and
   they were what they were, and all you had to do
   was look at that to see that Barb's claims were
   false.
Q: Who said that?
A: I think I did.
Q: Because you knew the accounts were the accounts?
A: Yes.
Q: That would show the true state of affairs?
A: Yes.
Q: So you were familiar with the accounts, you knew
   the statements were accurate?
A: Well, I thought they would show that the stocks
   and bonds and so forth were all there.
```

```
Q: So you had knowledge of the accounting?
A: No, no, that's not what I'm saying at all. Hal, you
   explain it, you're the lawyer.
```

"She means Hal Cook, you see," the professor explained, "and you know, Toni, she doesn't seem quite *right*, Jane Herrick's a little disoriented. Cook asks for a break—was he seeing this, too? But Holt senses the kill. 'This is not appropriate,' he says. 'She's the deponent, not you. She must answer the question.' Back and forth the lawyers go, until at last Cook gives in, and she has to testify."

The professor turned the page. "Holt presses her again, and this is the best part. It says, 'Whereupon, the witness left the room at ten forty-two.' The stenographers are so deadpan, it's the most marvelous thing."

"Gosh," Toni said.

"Yes, she ran out of the room! I guess they must have gone and found her, because it goes on. There is this exchange . . . I marked it, let me find it . . . Ah. Here. Listen carefully to this part, Toni."

```
Q: Before the break you said you did not mean, by
   your prior testimony, that you understood the
   accounting. What did you mean, then?
A: I meant that, at the dinner, I said, or someone
   said, I think I said, or asked, wouldn't
   everyone know that Barb's claims were false
   because the accounts were the accounts? And we
   all talked about that.
Q: What did your husband say about the subject?
A: Tom? Well, he asked me if I was going to be with
   him in this.
Q: With him in this?
A: Yes.
Q: In what?
```

A: In this. He just said, 'Are you going to be with me
in this?' It struck me as odd, and I remember him
asking me that.
Q: What did you answer?
A: Of course I was with him. He was my husband, of
course I would be with him. We got into a shouting
match and he went off to bed, and . . .

His eyes were bright with excitement. "Did you get it, Toni,
'off to bed'?"

But Toni's face was a blank.

"*Cook* does, he leaps right in, and says, 'Wait a minute!'"

"I don't understand."

"Jane Herrick has confused two conversations. In her mind
she's not at the dinner party anymore, she's jumped ahead to that
night, at home, when she argues with Tom Herrick, and he goes to
bed!" The professor was giddy with this discovery.

"Okay," Toni said, tentatively.

"That second conversation would not have come out, if her
lawyer, Cook, had known that it was a different conversation. Because of the marital privilege, you see. But she's confused, in her
mind she's at dinner with Burt Fredoni, and then she jumps to a
later conversation. Holt demands, 'You were going to be with him
in this, weren't you, Mrs. Herrick?' And she says, 'I was his wife, of
course I was with him.'"

The professor closed the transcript and shook his head. "On
that little line, the lawyers built the whole case! She admitted she
was part of the fraud, they said. And so she should have to give up
the house. I suppose there's more to it, but it's just amazing, what
that moment of disorientation could do."

"Wouldn't the judge know? Everyone in town knows what's
happening to Jane."

"They had to settle. There was too much risk of losing all
the equity, apparently. Now, my dear, sweet Toni, how about a
nice cup of decaf coffee, and a tuna sandwich on white toast, with

lettuce but no mayonnaise, please, would that be all right?" And he rubbed his hands together like a little boy.

Emma Herrick was an analyst at Consul Fund (so many of the hedge funds had classical names—whether Consul hearkened to Rome's empire or its collapse was unclear), and its offices were in one of the dark-glassed boxes that line the Park Avenue as it runs uptown from Grand Central Terminal. They still called that world the Street, or even Wall Street, even though some had moved out to Greenwich and Norwalk and Saddle River, and others had marched north at least as far as these glass boxes in midtown. The boxes were as busy as termite mounds: hives of traders, investment bankers, financial advisers.

Her cubicle was small. On a rainy day it struggled to accommodate an umbrella. In this small space her aspiration had met the new reality. The adviser who understood markets, who acted decently, who earned a fair profit through honest toil, who had a client rather than a mark, the adviser Tom Herrick was supposed to have been, and she had planned to become, was absent from this world. This world was not raising America's capital to harness an economy of growth—it was raising poker stakes, wagering against random caprice on a global table. Some of Consul's business was speculation in the offshoring of the American economy, buying and selling the bonds of companies with storefronts in Detroit and factories in Yang Feng. But much of it was the same casino gambling that had preceded the 2008 crash. The trading and the hedging and the longing and the shorting were not about raising capital but simply about betting—betting on anything and nothing.

For Emma, this awakening had been a dark one. What is it we're buying? she would wonder. What is it we're *doing*? Trading a bankruptcy loan not on earnings but because a judge sounded impatient in a telephonic hearing? She was still new to this career, and so lacked the confidence to trust her instinct. It was easy to think she was too inexperienced to make judgments. But the fever

of these hives of finance felt dangerous to her, as though the oc-
cupants, like termites, might gorge on their own tree even as it
collapsed around them.

George was learning a separate craft in those days, climbing
the special staircase of his own guild. His talk in the evenings was
of clerkships and US attorneys' offices and this firm and that firm.
A similar jargon crossed her own lips—the names of this fund and
that fund, this deal and that deal.

It had rained hard and cold that morning. The umbrella,
spread in her cubicle, dripped cold pools on the floor while she
raced through the Albion restructuring documents, tried again
to understand the points in the lawyer's e-mail about the bankruptcy in Delaware. The pools but not the documents had shrunk
by lunchtime, and the pools had long dried by the time the day
slipped into darkness. It was late when the call came through. A
vacuum cleaner whined from the other end of the floor. Standing
in her cubicle, she could look over the tops of the other cubicles,
out through the conference room windows, through the glass skin
of the hive. The lights in the hives across the avenue gleamed
brightly, uptown and down, as analysts still searched the computer
screens for an edge, perhaps stress-testing the same Albion deal
that was on Emma's screen.

But that night she had not found the answer to whether to
trade and at what price, and was thinking she'd go home, try it
again with fresh eyes in the morning. It was then that the phone
burbled, and the unfamiliar number appeared with an 802 area
code, and for a moment she thought that something must have
happened to her mother.

"Emma Herrick," she said, sitting down quickly.

The answer came slowly. The caller seemed surprised not
to have gone into voice mail at that hour. His voice was heavy,
clumsy almost. "Thought it was Forrester, now," he said.

At the sound of that voice, the blood rushed to her head
and she struggled to temper her own, to make it matter-of-fact.
"Roy?"

A silence, and then: "Thought I'd . . . say hi."

"Oh—well . . . Hi." *Now what?* She threw a glance over her shoulder, as though someone might be listening. A brace of analysts was still in the office, and she kept her voice low.

He said, "Shouldn't have bothered you, Emma. Sorry, I'll . . ."

"Don't hang up. It's . . . it's good to hear your voice."

She needed a moment then, to wonder why she'd said that, and he needed one to wrestle with her saying she was glad to hear his voice.

"What made you call?" she asked at last.

"I was sitting here . . . I was lying here with a beer in one hand, and a piece of paper in the other, and I kept looking at the paper with the number on it that I Googled three months ago, and I just, just, kept looking at it, and pulling on this beer, until . . ."

She felt her blood pumping harder, felt her pulse in her throat. Maybe this was just the occupational hazard of every woman in her twenties—the old boyfriend whom drink had made maudlin, who tracked you down by phone at night. He's drunk, and now he's called me, and that is all this is. They weren't supposed to do this, once you were married. Should I be disgusted? Should I scold him? Or should I admit that for more than a year, on slow days at work, I've been Google-stalking Murphy's Landscaping myself?

"Until what?" she asked, quietly.

"Until I got drunk enough."

"I . . . I don't know what to say to you, Roy."

"Well, I never knew what to say to you either. So don't say anything. Just remember."

She could hear the drink now. He wasn't slurring words, but the alcohol had unlocked in him a strange volubility.

"Memory is not your friend, Roy," she said, softly. "You know?"

"It's my only friend."

The phone pressed to her ear, Emma rocked forward, listening to him breathe, biting her lip. "It's your companion," she said at last. "There's a difference. Where are you, anyway?"

They talked of small things for a while. He was home, sprawled on his bed in the attic apartment in Overton, with a cell phone cradled to his ear. The beer cans lay crumpled on the floor. They talked about his place, and the business; about her business, about Brooklyn.

Then he asked her. "Emma, I called because . . . in Afghanistan, it was questions like this that guys always wanted to ask, and never could, and it would drive them crazy, you know? And I always said, 'When I'm back.' But then I came back and never asked it either."

"Asked what?"

"Asked, do you love another guy?"

She took a breath, then another one. He listened to that breath, drank it in. "Yes."

"Him alone? Just tell me."

"Roy . . ."

"I want to hear you say it."

"You don't have that right."

"You can't say it."

"Roy, don't . . . don't do this. He's my *husband*. I'm not going to discuss him with an old boyfriend who calls me late at night—*drunk*." The words escaped more harshly than she'd wanted, so she added, as though to soften what she'd said, "Besides, I'm sure you have a girl."

"I do have a girl," he answered. "Every once in a while I have one . . ."

"That's charming, Roy."

"And I . . ."

"Roy, you know what I meant. Why don't you get a real girlfriend? Seriously, a relationship, a real relationship without this . . . this *god*damned baggage."

But he continued as though he hadn't heard. "I don't remember the names is the problem. I try to remember the names in the morning and the name that comes out is Emma, Emma, Emma. It don't seem fair to me—I don't come to your place in New York City and knock on the door. Why do you keep coming around mine?"

"You *have* been drinking, and too much. I never heard you this way before!"

"Thou who did with pitfall and with gin, beset the road I was to wander in."

"*What?*"

"You know a poem called the *Rubáiyát of Omar Khayyám*, Emma?"

"*You* know it?"

"A kid from the Park?" he mocked.

"No, no, Roy, that's not what I mean, I . . . It's just that . . . that . . ." Her voice trailed off. Quietly, she resumed. "I never heard you talk about *poetry* before. I never heard you like tonight at all."

"Old Omar was the captain's favorite. He used to say it all the time. We'd hear him saying it, and Montoya, he'd get us going in the hooch, and we'd sing it. You can almost sing Omar. 'Some for the Glories of This World!' And—'The Moving Finger writes; and, having writ, moves on,' and—'Here with a book of verse beneath the bough!' But that line the captain liked—pitfall and gin. He was always saying that one. He gave the book to Sarnt Brown, but I bought one when I come back."

"He was . . . one of your . . . friends from Afghanistan?"

"Not my friend. He was—"

There he stopped, and the line was quiet. After a while she wasn't sure if he had actually gone away, or was just sloppy drunk. She leaned over in her little modular cubicle, her head a few inches from the computer screen, waiting, not knowing if this captain were alive or dead, and afraid to ask. Then she stood up again and looked out over the top of the cubicle and across toward the glass conference room. Through its windows the lights of

New York City twinkled. A wave of guilt washed over her, to think of what that world had done to his world, and how indifferently.

"Roy—are you there?"

She thought about the fortresses of glass and steel in this city, and cities like it, these hives, how they had flung the boys from the Hoosick Bridges overseas for convenience, and now the boys were washing back, and at Consul Fund, no one even noticed. Among the analysts here, among George's circle of law clerk friends, not one was a veteran. None was lying alone, in a small attic apartment, a prisoner of memory.

He was quiet for so long that it almost surprised her when at last he spoke again, finishing his sentence in a hoarse whisper.

"He was my captain," he said.

Just then, the BlackBerry vibrated loudly, groaning against the desktop: George. Just as she had been long ago on a Fourth of July, Emma was suddenly conscious of the hour. She glanced at the message in the subject line. Leaving soon?

And that snapped her out of it. This phone call, this reverie was dangerous. The pull of Roy Murphy was dangerous. "Roy, I can't . . . I can't have my head in the Albion restructuring and all of a sudden it's you, asking me whether I love George only and reading me the *Rubáiyát of Omar Khayyám*."

"Do you?"

"I'm his wife. I'm not going to talk about him to an old boy-friend."

"Then don't talk. No talk—no talk at all."

"Roy, it's late, I should be heading home, and . . . and besides, you can't have a phone call and nobody talks."

"You just don't hang up," he said. "That's how it works."

"Don't hang up," she repeated. "Okay, but I can't . . ." Meanwhile her thumbs hurried over the little buttons of the BlackBerry, typing out, Yes, leaving soon, xo Em.

Her pulse was racing. Late as it was, drunk as he obviously was, she knew she should hang up, she should go, and yet she could not, not yet. Thirty seconds became a minute, and then lingered to a second minute.

At last he said, "I was seeing you, in my mind I mean, and feeling like you were nearby. That was nice."

Emma said, "Roy, it's . . . it's not so good if . . ."

"I know, I won't bother you anymore . . ."

"If you call me on the cell, or at home," she said. "It would be . . . awkward. And when you aren't drunk, it would be . . . better . . . Good-bye."

She replaced the receiver in its cradle. Hurrying, she switched off the computer and put on her coat and grabbed the umbrella. She went down to find a cab on the avenue. The taxicab television blared all the way to Brooklyn. Usually she would switch it off—the squawking irritated her—but that night she thought maybe it would help drown out the sound of his voice. But the little screen was not insistent enough. Don't call the cell or home, but I didn't say, "Don't call the office"? What was I thinking with that . . . that invitation? she wondered.

When the cab reached her building in Brooklyn, Emma felt weak. Her hand shook as she ran the credit card through the slot in the charge device. She shivered for a moment on the street, collecting herself, recomposing her usual smile before she went inside and climbed the stairs.

The morning brought bright sunshine, and an e-mail from her boss with an urgent instruction—need updated Albion model ASAP.

Consul was going to do a trade. She had a good, head-clearing shower, and coffee, and began to think of all she had to do that day at work, all she had to do with her mother—and of course, with George. She gave her head a shake. She would reshelve Roy Murphy in her mental library and not check that book out anymore.

That's behind me, she thought. It's *behind* me.

Up in Vermont, Roy Murphy was pacing around his shop, checking tools and orders, nursing a headache, scolding himself for being an ass, a simpleton, for letting liquor talk through him.

That's *done*, he thought. Not doing that again.

In the new day they put these pretenses on again, like clothing. She would not acknowledge the insistent voice in that taxi. He would not acknowledge that he'd been lying in the bed in the Overton apartment, like a radio beacon in that remote place, pulsing out a signal that no one could switch off, silently calling to her:

*Come back.*

On a Tuesday morning in mud season, 2012, two men in a booth at Toni's Lunch were talking.

"They're still at this thing, all these years later?" the one asked.

"Took them years to piece together all that Herrick did. First there was the state investigation, the SEC, then the litigation, then all the bankruptcy stuff, and every step of the way, Hal Cook files another appeal. Every time there's an order, he's up to the district court. The circuit a couple of times, too."

"Lot of string."

"Years of it. But it's done now. The trustee's coming after her pretty hard."

"Was she ever deposed?"

He nodded. "I heard there's a few problems with her testimony."

"Too bad," the first one said. "It's a helluva house. That family had the Heights for years, didn't they?"

They sipped their coffee quietly for a bit, and then one of them said, "They could turn it into an inn, maybe."

"For all the tourists coming to Hoosick Bridge on vacation!" And they both laughed.

The pair hadn't noticed the man eating alone in the next booth. He stood up then and walked to the counter, put down five dollars for his coffee and muffin, like he always did, and

Toni wished him a good day. He glanced at them as he walked to the door. It was that soldier who'd come back from the war and started the business everyone was talking about.

Roy Murphy sized them up quickly as he went by. Two men in blazers and ties, gray slacks. Lawyers.

Up at the Heights, drifting Jane Herrick could feel the circle closing on her.

# SIXTEEN

*H*ow did he finance it, even with the success of the landscaping business? That's what they wondered, later, until the story got around, that Roy Murphy had gotten it from, of all the tight fists, the tight fist of Torruella—that he'd gone right up to his house one night, to make the deal in the businessman's living room, under the prim and watchful gaze of Torruella's wife, Tina. And when he pitched him, Torruella smiled a knowing, in-on-the-joke smile and said, "Roy, a businessman knows when he's met another businessman. I'm getting that feeling about you. Am I right?"

"Trying to build one is all, sir. I'm not in your league."

Tina, a china doll of a creature, a brunette with coiffed hair and a pale green argyle sweater tied over her shoulders, came clipping across the hardwood floor with a tray. It held a scotch and soda for Nick and a soda for Roy Murphy, but he didn't take it.

"He came to me, Tina, when was it, back in oh nine? Came to me for a little loan for his commercial mower."

"My goodness," she said. "Has it been that long?"

"So I make him this seventy-two-hundred-dollar loan. Few weeks go by, and I check around, and find out, he'd already *got* a commercial mower a week before he came to me. Paid cash for it.

Didn't need the loan at all. One month later, he pays the loan back in full, with interest. Now, Tina, why'd he do that?"

She smiled politely, if a little nervously, fearing something unpleasant. "I don't know, Nick."

He smiled again. "You tell her, son, why you did that."

"Needed to cover the mower, sir."

Torruella shook his head, still smiling broadly. "No, that's not why. Come on!"

But Roy Murphy was silent. He stared at his hands blankly.

"You want to know why, Tina? He did it because he knew I'm a businessman, too, and I'd be thinking about my seventy-two hundred. I'm concerned about my loan, not really concerned but, let's say, vigilant. We got a returning vet here, starting a new business. Can he pay the loan back? So what am I going to do? Go on, Roy, tell her."

But he remained silent.

"He's a poker player, Tina, he's going to make me tell you. So I'm unsure about my loan, and what I'm going to do is, give him some goddamned work! Give him the chance to make the money to repay the loan! Which I did, give him that big job up at Pine Meadows, before I'd put two and two together. Didn't I, Roy?"

He nodded. "Yes, sir."

"And his work was excellent, so he got more. He's the one built the stone wall in the back two years ago, honey."

"It's a beautiful wall, Mr. Murphy."

Torruella took a drink and smiled. "That's a businessman. He played me to get his chance. And when he got his chance, he took it. I admire that, Murphy. Just stay the hell out of car sales, you know what I mean, son?"

"I think you give me too much credit, sir. But anyways, the business has done okay, it's grown, and I do need another loan. A bigger one, this time."

So many times during that year of 2012 he would stare at the cell phone, or the little folded piece of paper, and then fall into mental arguments with himself. It was behind him, it was done. She'd said he could call her at work, but to what end? She had a husband—she kept saying that, too. The argument would rage back and forth. She'd given him permission to hear her voice. But what was the point of that? And besides, he would think darkly, she could have called me any time she wanted to hear my voice, any time, day or night. She wouldn't have to worry about any wife either. She could have, and she hasn't. And then he'd count back the days, the weeks, the months, growing angrier as he did. Even as he took out that loan, he was thinking that it was done. Even as he met the lawyer and the lawyer explained the loan to him.

The sisters were asking each other, "When did you speak to her last? How was she?"

Increasingly, Jane Herrick phoned to issue demands. Emma must telephone that dreadful Cook. Anne must instruct Francine McGregor to stop looking at her in that way. Jane's sister Patty simply must rescue the Heights—it was her duty to the Morses. (Patty had neither the wherewithal nor the interest, and the bankruptcy trustee was suing her, too, for her nine percent returns. For Patty, loss was all the Heights signified anymore.) One day in May, Jane was seen cutting the lawn in the rain. Soon after, tarpaulins appeared on the porch, and passersby watched Jane painting the posts, the rail, the ornate balusters. She had not scraped or even cleaned them first, and she was not painting the entire trim, but trying to cover over places where the paint had chipped, or cracked. The work was childlike and sloppy. It was all blotches and paint drips.

And then there was the bankruptcy process itself. Jane had demanded that Cook mail her all the court filings—the motions, the objections, the preliminary skirmishes about rules for the auction, the fee applications, everything. She would call him with tirades about these appalling court filings. Why was he standing for this? Particular triggers for her were the fee applications. "One point five hours, to talk on the telephone with you, and a bill for three hundred and seventy-five dollars? Just talking on the telephone, for more than an hour, and nothing is accomplished?" Cook's own bills to Jane brought renewed and even more indignant tirades.

At last it ended, in the spring of 2013, in a bankruptcy sale up in Rutland, which Jane herself stood to interrupt, right in the middle of the auction, until the judge rebuked her and she stormed from the room. Great mystery surrounded the buyer, at first, for no one had ever heard of any 240 Realty Trust. But the price, $1.25 million, set tongues wagging. The brokers who stayed for the end were shaking their heads—even for the Heights, the price was insane.

Schoff's law office in Bennington was on the second floor of Pritchard Block, above the bank. In its small conference room that Friday morning, they crowded around the table, the lawyers in jackets and ties, Roy Murphy in his work boots and flannel work shirt. The lawyers chatted while Roy, silent, thought about losing an entire Friday to this. After the closing and today's payroll, he'd be down to a few thousand dollars in the bank account. The business would need to earn ten thousand a month, just for the debt service on the place.

The bankruptcy trustee, Paul Sanderman, would get half the sale proceeds, and with it at last wind up his bankruptcy case. He sat at one end of the table with his lawyer, Ernie Holt. Schoff was to his left. Schoff's partner had done the mortgage for Torruella. It was a long and difficult document, and Roy didn't follow the details, except for the one that mattered: if he missed a payment, Torruella would screw him sixteen ways. The last to arrive that morning was Hal Cook, who hurried in with a sour expression on his face and announced, with a sigh, that there was a problem.

"She won't leave. We're just going to have to delay this closing, and Ernie, Paul, you guys will have to do what you have to do. I'm trying to get the daughters to work some sense into her."

"Hal, she'll be in contempt!"

"You saw her in court, Paul—it would make her day to be in contempt."

Roy Murphy interrupted. "What's this mean?"

Schoff turned to explain that, under the court order, Jane Herrick had to turn over the house at closing. Roy had done his part by coming with his financing, being ready to close, but Jane Herrick had violated the order. Holt would now have to go back to court to enforce it, and if Jane didn't back down, the judge would direct a sheriff physically to evict her and her belongings.

"How long will that take?"

"Not too long. Three weeks, a month, maybe, and then . . ."

"A *month*? No."

"Roy, I don't know what else we can do."

"We can close," he said. "I'm here, the money's here, the deed's here, her lawyer's here. We're all here. The trustee can give the title, right? Let's get it done."

"Well, he can, yes, but Roy, she's in the house. We can't accept title with her still squatting there."

"Deal with that later," he said.

The lawyer persisted. "You don't want to do this, Roy. At closing half the money goes to her! The estate will be off the hook, and it will be your expense to evict her. It won't be cheap. And in the meantime, if she's up there in your house, and something goes wrong, she'll be saying things, she'll call the police, she'll make accusations, God only knows.

"And there's one more thing, I must tell you. You have the legal right to cancel this transaction—if you want. To get your money back, and cancel this mortgage. It's a lot of money, Roy."

Schoff would long remember the intensity of his client's dark expression, the fierce focus of those eyes, and the shiver he felt then.

"Close," said Roy Murphy.

When the last of the forms was signed, the mortgage was executed, and the deed delivered, Schoff handed the trustee the certified checks. He turned to Roy and presented him with a set of brass keys, each with a little white tag: "Frt"; "Bsm't"; "Grg"; "Ktch."

"Congratulations, he said."

Roy Murphy squeezed them. The keys were remarkably small, and yet he felt something at the moment that a ring of keys was in his palm. Roy Murphy from the Park, Roy Murphy who never graduated high school, Roy Murphy whom she had never called back—he held the ring, and all these educated people around the table did not. His mind drifted, momentarily, as he studied the keys, before he realized that Schoff was still talking to him.

". . . go up there with you. Hal was hoping to talk to you and his client and I thought it might be a good idea if I came up, too, and—"

"No need," said Roy.

"As you like. But be careful with her." And he offered his hand again and wished Roy luck and was frankly glad when he was gone.

From the window, he watched his client exit the building and head down the street toward his truck. He said to Hal Cook, "Tell her it will be for sale again soon enough. That's an insane mortgage."

# SEVENTEEN

The old lady was waiting for him.

He drove up Washington Street slowly, primed for the moment when he would round the bend and the tower would come into view. And then, as the truck reached the crest of the hill, the Heights stood before him. He came to the stop sign at the corner. Across the street, Jane Herrick's ancient Mercedes station wagon was parked in the mouth of the drive, so that there was no room for his truck to enter the driveway. His driveway.

So it's starting, he thought.

Just then he felt her eye. She had been up on the porch, watching for him.

The truck idled at the corner of Washington and Spring. Across the street, the Mercedes blocked his way. Roy Murphy considered it for a moment. Then he drove up and over the sidewalk and around Jane's car and onto the lawn and stopped on the grass by the porch steps. He climbed down from the driver's side and walked to the porch.

She was perched, watchfully, on the edge of a wicker settee that once had been white and now was mottled gray. He had not looked at her closely for a long time—it had been four years since he'd seen her at the engagement party, and he saw her for only a moment that night, as he hurried into the tent. In the intervening years he'd had fleeting glances of her as he drove by the house, and once he'd seen her in town. Her hair was a striking and imperial white, and the clothes she wore that morning were a kind of reproach—she was dressed not formally but in clothing of a quality to announce the gulf between them. She wore navy, fine wool slacks, a silk turtleneck blouse, a pale blue cardigan, two strings of pearls, and formal shoes, polished to a shine. But within that decorum she looked gaunt and birdlike, her fingers long against the arms of the settee, her eyes agates of contempt. There was no disguise about Jane Herrick's hostility—it was as though she had located in him the single cause of all that had gone wrong in life.

"A truck on the lawn, Mr. Murphy," she said. "Did you think you were still in the Park?"

"Someone's in my driveway."

"The lawyer telephoned, but I knew it would be you. He's having an affair with the judge; that's how you got it, Mr. Murphy. You understand that I will call you Mr. Murphy, and you will call me Mrs. Herrick, should it be necessary for us to speak."

"I understand that you are sitting on my porch."

"This house was built by my great-grandfather Ezra Morse, and it was been home to five generations of the family. You thought you could come here from your trailer park, that you could marry into this family, and of course you couldn't. Then you thought you could just take it—you, a landscaper? And now, you can't wait to call your vulture lawyers and get a deputy sheriff to throw me out on the street! Let me see your hands. Are your hands even clean, Mr. Murphy?"

"Mom—*Stop it!*"

In the midst of this angry speech the front doors burst open. Anne Herrick rushed out and, behind her, Emma.

"Mom!" Emma said. "Roy, I'm so sorry, she—"

"Do not apologize," said Jane.

"I *will* apologize, Mom. You are out of line, you have no right to say such things . . ."

"It really *was* you, Roy," Anne said. "Congratulations."

He had not expected the sisters. Bewildered, he left them huddling by their mother, whispering furiously with her, and went to the southwest corner of the porch, where it curved around the dining room. The deck paint was badly chipped and the paint scuffed away in many places. Floorboards replaced half a century before had curled up at the edges. White flakes peeled from the railings, and here and there were blotches on the balusters, streaks of paint, drips on the floor. A guy could spend a lot of time just repairing the porch, he thought.

Sparrows were nesting in the rafters above the ceiling. They began scolding him, in merry counterpoint to Jane Herrick, twittering, "Did you think you could have this house, Roy Murphy, *did you?*"

He finished his circuit and returned to where the women were huddled.

Jane said, "Mr. Murphy, I want you to understand—"

"Please, Mom—"

"Don't shush me, Emma. I'm *not* going to box up the family things! They belong here. So throw me out on the street, all of you, if that's what you want."

"Mom, I don't think drama is going to help the situation . . ."

Jane Herrick seized the armrests on the wicker settee as though daring them to throw her out on the street then and there.

He regarded them in silence for a moment. "I'm going to take a look around my house now," he said.

The front doors were massive, nine feet high at least, their white paint peeling in spots. They opened outward, with a pull chain inside that secured the left-hand door. Before going inside, he stood a moment at the threshold, stilled again by the inscription.

**COME HOME TO ME**

"I know," said Emma, who had come to his side. "Spooky. Ezra Morse put it there when the Heights was built. There's another one inside, in the hall."

They stepped 'across the threshold. Inside the central hall, she turned and pointed to the inscription above the doors, also painted in faded black lettering. It was difficult to read, for the oak paneling had darkened.

## EVER DWELL WITHIN MY HEART

"I guess Ezra meant you can't leave, without taking the Heights with you," she explained.

He nodded, saying nothing.

A staircase rose from the foyer, wrapping around the central hall and carrying up two stories to the third floor. Hanging on the wall in that foyer in a large frame was a street map of Hoosick Bridge, c. 1895—one of those old maps that show individual houses. The Heights appeared alone on the hilltop. To the left of the front door was the room the Herricks called the "parlor." He entered that room first. A marble hearth trimmed with rosettes and worked columns dominated the room. The engineer's report had said that the flue was cracked and unusable without an expensive relining—no fire had burned there in generations. The blue armchair, the couch and Oriental carpets and books on the shelf, the Herrick television were all still there. A clock on the mantel ticked loudly.

At the far end of the parlor was a semicircular bay window. Stained-glass dormers threw bright jewels of ruby and emerald across oak floorboards dark with age. The ceilings and walls were plaster, ornamented at the chandeliers, with crown moldings trimming the ceiling.

Jane had not removed—in truth she had dusted—the silver-framed wedding and graduation photographs on the side table: of Emma's wedding, graduation pictures of Anne and Emma and Charlie. Roy Murphy picked up the photograph of Emma and

George Forrester and studied it closely, searching the expression on her face, and then sensing, as he put the photograph down, that Jane Herrick was again watching him through the window, from the porch.

"I'm so sorry about all this, Roy," Emma said. "I've been trying with her. Maybe I could show you around at least?"

He should have said no. But for the next few minutes, all he could hear was their footsteps and the murmur of her voice, telling him about this room and that room. So many fireplaces, so many heavy oaken doors, their brass hardware brown with age. The closets were deep, their roomy interiors hid shelves and drawers, and every room held a different memory for her.

When the Heights was built, kitchens were the domain of servants. Cramped and dark, the room had ancient countertops of dark butcher block, a deep sink of black soapstone, an old GE electric stove, and an older Kenmore dishwasher. It seemed to have more doors than walls: a door to the basement, a door to the hall, a door outside. Down the back corridor was a steep back staircase up to the second floor.

Glass-fronted oak cupboards ran up to the kitchen ceiling. The shelves were stacked high with crockery, hills of bowls and plates that took him aback. "In my place in Overton I've got four plates," he said.

"Now you've got a hundred and four."

They came to the dining room, whose Empire table Ezra Morse had bought in Europe and had shipped to the Heights during the McKinley administration. Of all the rooms at the Heights, this one most astonished Roy Murphy. That there should be a whole room of this size, devoted to a single, long table like you'd see in the movies, a room it looked like no one ever used. Dust motes hung in the afternoon sunlight slanting through the porch windows. On a gray cloth was spread still more china, and crystal, and silver urns, decanters, and trays.

"The holiday stuff," Emma explained. "She's been polishing silver—for Thanksgiving." Emma shook her head. "She thinks it's

Thanksgiving. That my husband's parents and family and half of Charlie's UVM classmates are coming. This is what I mean about her."

The matter-of-fact way she said "my husband's."

He asked, "Did you used to have dinner here, at this table?"

"Just Christmas and Thanksgiving, sometimes Sunday, and, you know."

"A room just for that?"

"Pretty much."

She could see him trying to picture it. "What's the most people you ever had in here?" he asked.

In that empty chamber, old voices echoed for her. She remembered the room festive, bursting with the faces of the uncles and aunts, lipstick on the women, Easter dresses, the roar of laughing men in the days of her childhood, when there was money. She remembered the room overflowing, the women rushing in and out with tureens and platters, her grandmother in a blue dress presiding. She remembered as a child eating at the kids' table in the kitchen, wishing she could have a seat in the dining room. It was here, she explained, that a toddler had to walk the table at Christmas.

"Walk the table?"

She remembered the morning Charlie staggered from end to end in a little white dress and Buster Brown shoes. "It was a thing—I think the Morses had always done it when a child learned to walk. I don't remember doing it myself, I remember Charlie. Anne says she remembers doing it. She says there were all these scary faces and she felt like the end of the table was moving away from her. It was just a family thing, you know—one of those family traditions."

He nodded, but in truth he had no idea about such things.

They returned to the foyer and climbed the staircase to the second floor. The carpet runner was worn underfoot, and some of the treads creaked. The dark heft of the banister beneath his fingers was impossibly smooth. At the landing the corridors led off to the opposite wings of the house. They moved quietly along them, opening the doors and peering inside, while she explained that this one had been Anne's, that one Charlie's, here was the linen closet, there was the guest room, this other one had the worst wallpaper— isn't it ugly?

"Anne and I used to climb out this window to the porch roof and sit and watch the town on summer nights."

When he tried to open it, the window shuddered in the frame. "Heavy," he said.

"They're all so old."

They returned to the stairs and the room off the center hall. She said, "The master."

It faced Washington Street, and its bay window gave a view down the hill toward the town. The room was still fully furnished, but like a museum, the four-poster bed neatly made, the mahogany and maple of the bureaus polished and bare.

"She doesn't sleep here anymore," Emma said.

The master and its closets were still home to Jane's clothes, and the master bath was still the one she used. Her shoes were lined up against one wall of the bedroom.

He thought, I am the master of the Heights, now.

He stood between a pair of cream-colored armchairs in the bay window, looking down toward the town, sensing Emma behind him, sensing that her eyes were on him, careful not to turn and make eye contact. And it was more than sense—for he smelled her then, smelled that sweet fragrance of her skin, suffusing the quiet room. She felt the tension, too, and slipped out to wait for him in the hall. Downstairs, the doors swung open and shut as Jane and Anne came inside. Their footsteps echoed off toward the kitchen.

Roy and Emma returned to the landing. An oil portrait hung there, of a stout man with bushy whiskers, a dark suit coat, and a silk cravat, who sat by a desk, his hand on a pile of books, his face drawn with a stern expression.

"Ezra Morse," she explained. "We can take it down for you."

"Ezra," he said softly, his eyes on the portrait. "Whose button I . . ."

"Yes."

"He built the house?"

"He built it."

"Then he should stay. Unless you want him."

He was searching the portrait for resemblance to Emma, but could see none. Still, something about it was familiar. Then he recognized the mountain visible through the window behind Morse. "He's in the tower," he said.

"According to family tradition, that was his favorite room. The story is that my great-great-grandmother threw him out of the master bedroom, and for the last ten years of his life he slept in an Army cot up there. People say he used to fire potshots from the windows, and the neighbors were afraid to come by the house. Morses all get a little crazy in the end."

"Why did she throw him out?"

Emma wrinkled her nose. "It's *very* scandalous. My mother and grandmother would always try to change the subject, or say that he was 'unlucky in love' and leave it at that. Because he was Ezra, you know? They wanted to be proud of the great founder of the family."

"And?"

"There was a woman. The love of his life, whom he built this house for, but he couldn't win her heart, you know, that sort of thing. You know how over the front door it says—"

"Come Home to Me," he interjected.

"Yes. She never did."

"Hmmm," said Roy Murphy and almost smiled.

"*Stop.*" But Emma, too, smiled back at him—just for a moment, before carrying on with the story. "The woman he loved was Ceda Garland, his wife's mother."

"His *wife's* . . . Wait, I'm confused."

"Ceda wouldn't have him, for years and years, and later on Ezra married her daughter, Lydia."

"The *daughter*? Isn't that . . . ?"

"Not his *own* daughter. Hers, but not his. He couldn't win the mother, so he married Lydia, who became Lydia Garland Morse, my great-great-grandmother. But he never stopped loving Ceda, and in the end Lydia got tired of being second fiddle to her own mother. *Very* complicated."

"In *your* family."

"Oh, yes, in my family for sure." Emma sighed.

"Why didn't she just leave—the wife? The daughter I mean, Lydia—the second fiddle?"

"Wives didn't do that back then."

The tour carried on up to the narrow, dormered corridor on the third floor, once the haunt of maids, and of Emma herself. It was empty now, the furniture gone, only the gauze curtains hanging in the bay window. Emma stood back as he peered in through the door of her old bedroom. But not back so far that the scent of her did not wash over him again.

She said, "After the prom I lay in there all day. Anne sat on the bed, and Maggie told me how awful you were and demanded every detail. I think she was jealous."

"Your prom dress—what happened to it?"

"Probably in the house somewhere. Mom saves everything, although God knows she'd never remember now where she'd put it. There's a cedar closet down on the second floor, it might be there."

She had put off, as long as possible, the last, short staircase. The air again felt ionized, as though before a storm.

"I'll wait," she said quietly.

He climbed the stairs, and when he reached the door and had his hand on the glass knob, she called out, "I . . . left you something, on the hook. A housewarming gift."

He pushed open the door, looked behind and saw the chain hanging there. He fingered it a moment before calling back, "Don't you want this—for your family?" But it sounded half-hearted.

"I told you *before* it was a gift! Besides, it has always belonged to the master of the Heights."

The room seemed smaller than he remembered. But leather-spined books still filled the dark shelving. That those books would remain had been one of his hopes for the house, and now it was fulfilled. That musty smell, the quiet of the place, the neat order of it was preserved. And the books, most of all, the books. Beneath one window was the couch where they first made love. Here was the spot where they put the puppet theater—there where she stood with her arms spread wide. *I was on the floor, here, and she stood over there.* It was such a small place, to have commanded so large an expanse of his memory, and for so long.

It was hot and close. The window was stuck and moved with difficulty, and the counterweights bounced inside their tracks. He thought, I will have forty sash cords to replace. It was then that he decided the room would be his alone. No one else would come to this place, unless she did again.

But below, he heard her footsteps, as she went away—descending to the ground floor.

They sat in the kitchen. Jane and Anne had gone off to the parlor, and he could hear their voices faintly. He didn't like sitting with her alone or the way she looked at him, and he didn't know what to do with his eyes. His willful eyes were thirsty for her, but he didn't want to betray that. It was impossible to keep his eyes from her. She had commanded his mind for so long. Emma Herrick, who was married, was now sitting at her table, which was now his table and yet not his table and certainly not their table.

They were alone in her kitchen, which was his kitchen, full of a hundred Herrick plates, in his house with her ancestor on his wall. Everything his and hers and nothing theirs. Roy Murphy never had been one for introspection or indecision. He had walked back into this world with nothing more than an envelope of cash and a force of will, had beaten, whipped this world to order, had formed a squad from nothing, driven that squad hard until they feared him and respected him and performed for him, had built from scratch a business that was becoming the envy of the county. Today he had astonished the town. But with his audacious purchase Roy Murphy had for the first time introduced chaos into his own life.

And he was angry that, after all this time, she was beautiful and he wanted her still. All afternoon he had kept himself from looking at her, kept from standing close to her, tried to avoid that scent and then drunk it in. He had tried to be stone to the grace of her movement, the sound of her voice. It confused him, and he did not like confusion. He smoldered with it, and with something else: embarrassment that maybe they had been right, all those people who whispered about this, all those earnest lawyers neighing at him by the hour, they were right. He shouldn't have done this. It was as the lawyers said, he shouldn't have done any of it. He should have stayed away from it.

Emma was saying, "We just need some time, Roy. I know this is not right, I'm sorry. You bought the house, it's your house, but she's just not acting herself and Anne and I need a little time with her. Would you consider—is there any way, for a month, you could, say, rent it to us? I will pay you the rent, I will write you a check right now, so that we can—"

"Put that away," he said.

While speaking she had withdrawn a checkbook from her purse. Quickly she replaced it. "I didn't mean to insult you. I just need your help."

"You never needed my help."

He had not intended to snarl, to show her the darkness inside of him. He did not intend to show her anything. But it had come out nonetheless.

She thought her mother had brought it on. Of course it would anger a man who had just made this purchase to be insulted and assaulted by a woman behaving as her mother had. She thought it was her mother, when on that day Jane Herrick was no more than a curiosity to him.

"You can see what she's like," Emma said. "Her world is part real, part old memories. This morning, you're at the closing, and she's pulling out china for all the relatives. That's what she was talking about. Anne and I are begging her to call the movers, and Mom's saying the Forresters will all want to come for Thanksgiving—you know? Roy, I'm sorry, I really am. Can you give us a month? She's just, she doesn't have anything else."

It was almost four. His crews would be getting back to the shop, and he needed to check in with them before the weekend. The force of her was so physically magnetic that he needed to move himself away. From her, from this vast house, with all these dim spaces that were his but not his—not his and not theirs, from this quiet house loud with memories, provoking him, taunting him on what should have been the day of his triumph. For four years he had begun thoughts with, When I get my place. And now he had his place and there was nothing to finish the sentence with. She had abandoned him and this house, she had made her decision. Why did she have to come back now?

Helplessly, she said, "I don't know what you want us to do."

"Nothing," he snapped.

"I don't understand."

But he was moving quickly, in a hurry to get out of there and back to the shop, where the men would hang the tools in order and leave the trailers neat in the bays as he required they be left, where the men would be oiling and honing and packing up before the weekend, and the talk would be the familiar boisterous talk of men. She followed him out of the kitchen, through the foyer, past the door to the parlor (she cast a quick glance into the parlor and saw Jane, intent in the blue armchair, watching), out the front doors to the porch.

"Roy, wait . . ."

He hurried down the porch steps.

"Please, Roy, what do you want us to do?" she called out again.

He stopped at the truck and turned. "Whatever you want. It's a big house."

"But . . . what does that mean, it's a big house? It's *your* house, what can—?"

"Is it, Emma?"

He got into the truck and slammed the door.

"Wait, Roy, *wait* . . ."

But he was backing over the lawn and onto the road, and then the truck was gone down Washington Street.

Immensely entertained, the sparrows twittered their applause from above the porch.

It was dark. Jane had gone upstairs, leaving Emma and Anne in the kitchen. Entering the house, he caught the fragrance of roast chicken and saffron rice and peas. The women had already eaten, but most of the chicken was in the oven and the rice and peas were piping hot on the stove.

"I fixed you some dinner," Emma said.

"It's all right. Brought my own." Roy carried a brown paper sack from the Hunan.

In the kitchen she shook her head firmly and took the bag away from him without a word. Then he stood watching her slice the roast chicken and spoon rice and peas on the plate. She poured a glass of burgundy and set the plate and the wineglass on the table, and then pulled the chair away from the table for him to sit, and stood holding the chair, like an insistent waitress—like a nurse. *The patient will sit here and eat.* Anne leaned against the sink, watching this.

His habitual scowl had melted away, the air of menace that he sometimes carried about with him evaporated. Like a boy he took the seat obediently. He leaned forward, and the steam and fragrance rose from the plate and wreathed his face. He closed his eyes and forgot himself, and for that moment Emma, watching him, could see that he was happy.

Anne watched, too, but she was watching Emma.

He picked up the crystal wineglass, marveling at its weight. He sipped the wine. Then he ate.

From the moment of his departure that afternoon, Anne had been troubled by something greater than her mother's behavior. Her sister, the Yale-trained economist and hedge fund analyst, who lived in a New York City apartment with a kitchen like a closet and a fridge like a suitcase in that closet, who survived on takeout, had from the moment of Roy's departure that afternoon busied herself with that meal. Rushing out to the market, returning with groceries, studying the cookbook, fussing, basting, peering into the oven, glancing at the clock, pacing the kitchen like a newlywed. Her sister without speaking had put food before this man not her husband, and it had relaxed the tightness in him. He ate hungrily—and almost dutifully—what Emma set before him.

He had left in anger and exchanged harsh words, and now he sat before Emma, and what worried Anne most was the silence, the superfluity of speech between them. For fifteen minutes no one spoke at all. The tines of his fork clinked against the plate; the electric clock hummed over the sink. They did not look at each other directly. Her sister hovered near him, behind him, by his shoulder, watching him. She moved pepper within his reach before he had glanced up with the thought that he would like some pepper. When he finished the plate, noiselessly she took it away and filled it again and set it before him and he ate what she had served. Still no one spoke.

Anne had never seen her sister attend a man this way.

Emma's fingertips hovered behind and around him, sometimes close, but never touching him. It seemed to Anne that there was intimacy in that restraint. And the easy silence was like a conspiracy that Anne did not wish to join. She said, "I'd better check on Mom," and Emma answered quickly, "No, Anne, stay with us, please, have another glass."

It was late. The food was put away and the dishes were washed, and still the three of them sat at the kitchen table. Two wine bottles were empty. Fatigued at last with the day, Emma asked him what he was doing. When he didn't answer, she pressed, "With the house, I mean."

It seemed to Anne that a spell was broken then.

"That's my business, Emma."

"You're young, Roy, single, you work hard and everyone says your company is doing fantastically well. What are you doing spending a fortune on this huge barn of a house?"

"That's my business," he repeated.

The interlude had passed. His expression was darkening.

"I'm not criticizing, Roy. I'm just—"

"I liked this house, when I was a kid I liked it," he said. "I told you that. Would you rather a developer got it?"

"Guys, I could—" Anne started to say.

"Why did you come back up here from New York, Emma? Didn't I buy this house legal, didn't I pay for it?"

"You think this is going to bring us back together? Is that what you think?"

"Don't flatter yourself," he said.

Anne rose. "I'll go."

"Stay!" he roared. "No reason for you to go. Nothing going to happen here."

They're like dogs, Anne realized, the way one barks and it makes the other one bark and soon neither dog knows why the barking started.

"It *is* what you think, Roy. And you're wrong."

"Guys," Anne interrupted. "*Please*. It's been an incredibly hard day for everyone, why do you have to do this?"

They faced each other silently, breathing hard, and then Emma turned away. "You're right, I'm sorry. But Anne, you and I—we can't stay. Overnight, I mean."

"Go then," he snapped. "Nobody stopping you."

"Why do you have to be like that? Life went *on*, Roy."

"Not for me, Emma. Not for a lot of guys. For a lot of guys, life never started."

She faced him again. "Well, I've moved on. That's just the way it is."

"You and everyone else. Take care of your own selves, vets, because we've *moved on*. This war wasn't so easy, we didn't have a parade in six months. It cost all kinds of money. And they keep fighting back and it's embarrassing because you can't tell soldier from civilian, you can't tell, until a rifle shot drops you. Then you can tell. And we keep killing civilians, anyway they look like civilians, and it's embarrassing, so fuck it, we've *moved on*. Well, if you've moved on, Emma, what are you doing in my house?"

Her temper like a living thing responded to his. "That's it, isn't it?" she said. "You bankrupted yourself for revenge! I thought you were bigger than that, Roy Murphy—I thought you were bigger!"

They were on their feet, squared off—the dogs, pulled apart and briefly quiet, now strained at their leashes to get at each other again. For a moment Anne thought one might hit the other. She wasn't sure which would land the first blow, and then she wasn't sure whether one would kiss the other, or what would happen in that standoff, as they panted and stared, neither backing down.

"Emma!" Anne said. "Roy—please!"

Emma turned away from him and leaned against the counter. Quietly, she said, "My mother won't leave, Roy. And we can't stay. So you tell me what the fucking solution is."

"I can stay," Anne offered.

Roy turned. "To protect her?"

"That's not what I mean."

"To protect her from me—that's what you both mean."

"Don't you *dare* talk to Anne that way, Roy Murphy!" Emma whirled again, and it was clear, at that moment, that the power over him was hers.

Anne tried once again to defuse this. "Roy . . . I meant the other way around. When she gets up tomorrow and insults you again."

"Insults me?" He laughed darkly. "I've been insulted plenty.

Look, the two of you, take her or leave her. You don't trust her here with me alone, then take her. She says she doesn't want to go—then leave her. I don't care. It's a big house." And he left the room. They listened to his footsteps recede.

The sisters decided that Anne would stay the night, so that she could be there to cope with her mother in the morning, but first she would drive Emma down to the motel across town.

Before they left, Roy returned to the kitchen and said, "Take this with you."

He was holding the wedding photograph of Emma and George. "Are there more of these in the house?"

"I don't know," Emma said. "In her room, maybe?"

"Go get them then. Get them and take them with you."

"For God's sake, Roy, I'll get them tomorrow. You don't have to look at—"

"Take them now. Don't leave them here," he ordered.

Anne drove her sister across Hoosick Bridge. Three framed photographs sat on Emma's lap. Neither sister spoke much. Emma seemed far away.

"You all right?" Anne asked, as she pulled into the portico.

Emma climbed out of the car and nodded. "Yeah, tired's all. I'll see you tomorrow. I'll call you—come up early. Thanks—for everything." She looked so tired now. Emma's mouth made a kiss, and she was gone.

Driving back to the Heights, Anne had a revelation. It wasn't exactly that they were like dogs. But their moods were linked somehow, without either of them wanting or trying for it to be so. When one was at peace, the other was at peace, and when one was quiet, the other was quiet, and when one was angry, the other was angry. For Anne, that was the most frightening thing of all.

God, it's *already* started! Anne thought, reentering the house and hearing Jane's voice piping down from an upper room. She hurried upstairs to find her mother in her nightgown, in the doorway of the master bedroom.

"He's destroying it, Anne!"

Roy was in the bedroom, his toolbox open on the floor, disassembling the four-poster bed.

"He already dragged the mattress and box spring up to Emma's room!" Jane said.

"Mom, come with me." Anne took her mother by the shoulders and with difficulty led her away from the threshold and down the corridor to the guest room.

"But he's destroying it!"

"He's not destroying it, Mom. He's moving it. The bed's in his house now. You knew this would happen."

"That was my bed. It was . . ." And Jane began to sob.

"You want the bed, take it with you," Roy called out.

The women retreated to the guest room, and Anne sat with her mother on the guest bed, listening to him carry the four-poster's headboard and the rails and the posts away, his boots loud on the stairs. He reassembled the bed in the empty bedroom that once had been Emma Herrick's.

"He's a savage!" Jane whispered.

His footsteps approached again, and he was at Jane's bedroom door, glowering at the two women. "My bedroom is off-limits," he said. "So's the tower. Don't never go there. The rest of it, suit yourself. It's a big house."

They heard his heavy tread back down the hallway and up the stairs.

The events of that long day, afternoon, and night had shaken Roy Murphy, too. Not in many years had he felt so foolish and ill prepared. He stomped angrily up to the bedroom and slammed the door behind him. He lay down on the master bed, still breathing heavily, working his brow with his hand. What would he do with these people, with this angry mother, with Emma—what would he do with this house? I've got to sleep, he thought, I will sleep and I will go to the shop in the morning and it will be clearer then. It will be a Saturday and quiet and the tools will be hanging in order.

Things will be clearer. So he thought, and at length he did drift off.

He had forgotten, perhaps, or been too distracted—but it was the way of the dream to come slinking and sidling upon him, just when he was at his weakest.

A vivid sun burned in a clear sky, and haze flanked the mountains to the north. It was a hot morning in June, three days before the Chinooks would come, three days before the squad's eighteen-day rotation would begin. He was near the end of his fifth year. It would soon be time to re-up.

The heat baked into the ground and the hooches and the bones, and guys in T-shirts hid from the sun like dogs, in the narrow shade of the Hescos. Guys sleepily debated whether when they hit leave they would get a porterhouse or a sirloin, guys debated Hydrox and Oreos, Bud and Miller, redheads and blondes. It was the beginning of another boring, tedious day at Firebase Montana. Another day when nothing would happen. Guys played cards or listened to iPods or slept or counted minutes or hours or pebbles or ants.

Roy Murphy was on watch at Main Sally.

The plywood door to the officers' hooch swung open, and he strode out with a clipboard in his left hand. He had that confident smile. He was in a brown T-shirt. It was too hot for rattle unless you were on watch by the C wire and had to wear it. It was damnably hot, nobody except watch was in the rattle. He came from the hooch across the compound like he'd done ten thousand times before, heading for the .50 emplacement. His head held up. No reason not to.

He strode toward Roy Murphy. Seeing him, Roy saluted and said, "Sir," like he always did.

And then he was returning salute. Coming across the compound toward the C wire. *He was returning my salute, he was giving respect to me in that moment, in that instant.* He was elevating the right forearm. You could see it come up you could see the fingers of the hand align and the elbow coming up. The hand was nowhere where it could protect him because it was a gesture of deference and respect to another.

*To me, Roy Murphy. And maybe he actually said my name the way he used to toss it off, "Murphy," maybe the word "Murphy" was actually even on his lips in that moment. Once he said we were the same, him and me, but it wasn't true.*

That was the moment when it happened.

*He ever learn to point the sumbitch, we'd all of us be poppin virgins by now*, Billy Hall Jr. said.

*Elmer a nervous motherfucker. He know he got to shoot and move quick. We get him one a these days, for sure*, Montoya said.

*They musta done Elmer with all that*, said Sarnt Brown.

The Warthogs blew Elmer to Jesus. We all seen it and cheered it and Billy Hall Jr. taunted him. The Warthogs got him for sure.

But they didn't.

That was the instant. That was when it happened.

*Sizzlecrack!*

Sizzlecrack and he ducked—he flinched and ducked instinctively, you always did, but ducking wouldn't help, it was an involuntary and pointless reaction, you were ducking after the bullet has passed and you were alive only because you heard it pierce the air as it went by the side of your head. The first shot. A surge of adrenaline coursed through him, and he turned to the left, toward the ridge, trying to get muzzleflash on the sonofabitch, and then the second shot came: the shot no one heard until the report followed a second and a lifetime later.

Because there was no sizzlecrack with the second shot. There was no air but rather skull and brain matter to cleave, which makes no sound like that, and turning toward the ridgeline, he saw not the ridgeline but the elbow splayed, the arm crazy in the air and the clipboard slipping and the knees buckling the wrong way and crumpling and folding. Before the word *no* could come from his throat it was already over. It was over long before his larynx could give force and his mouth form a word, before he could even stop turning his head, it was over. All his reactions were too late.

The captain was three paces away, walking toward Roy Murphy with his elbow coming up to show respect. But now he was a jumble of limbs tumbling, and on account of a second shot from Elmer, who couldn't point the sumbitch and never hit nothing yet. *The poet of life and death said he was the same as us but it was not true, he was not the same, he was better than us and we revered him and loved him and would have died for him.* His last act on earth was to begin to salute Roy Murphy from the Park, Roy Murphy, who was at the prom but as everyone knew did not graduate high school, who did six months in Juvie, who could barely read until the captain taught him how to practice, Roy Murphy who was not and never would be good enough for her or for them or those people or for that house but was good enough to be sent seven thousand miles away, where the geniuses who understand how it all works, who wrote all the books and read all the books planted the flag in the mountains of Afghanistan.

He was shouting "No!" and launching himself to protect his captain, but it was too late for that. No, No, No! And he covered him screaming "*No!*" and now he was on the ground cradling him in his arms and feeling the life flow hot and sticky out from the captain into his own lap, the hot life burning him below just as the hot sun burned him from above and he was crying "No, Jesus *no* goddammit *no* you fuckers No God *No!*" And then he hadn't words at all but low animal noises, gurgles, primal things terrifying to the rest of them—feral sounds that came at that moment from the loner Murphy, who never hollered or even raised his voice before, who barely spoke at all, who never showed fear or any kind of emotion that anyone ever saw, except every once in a while a frustration here and there that we all get. Who never talked about being afraid to die or trip an IED, never mentioned a girl or a mother or a sister, never in a single dark moment confessed so much as a headache.

Nadal sprinted for the .50 and the medic ran to them but

it was too late and Roy Murphy would not let go of the captain anyway. They could not pry him from the shoulders to which his arms were clamped like rebar, clamped as though themselves in rigor mortis. And then he was weeping. In his arms he was cradling the captain's face, as the animal moan gurgled from somewhere deep within Roy Murphy, the water streamed down from his face onto the captain's and mixed there with his blood.

At first it was a weeping for everything lost, stripped from a young man who had clambered from the pit to the surface, who would raise himself from that pit and now must surely slip back into it, a weeping from the deepest kind of hopelessness—hopelessness that for an unexpected time in an unexpected place was privileged to see hope itself, to believe in it, and now had it ripped away. But as the tears flowed hot they became the irrigation, the eruption of elemental rage. He wept and cradled he who had been a man but was now a marionette lying crumpled and broken on a mountainside in Afghanistan, a heap, a pile, with all the strings severed.

It happened before the captain could return salute to Roy Murphy, it happened before the smile could leave his face, it happened before his eyelids could shut. But the wild light flew from the captain's eyes and was gone out of them forever.

In the night the women started from sleep. Was that a cry from upstairs? A cat outside? They could not be sure. They lay awake in the darkness, and held each other, and after a few minutes, hearing no more sound, dropped off again.

He awoke gasping, as he always did after the dream. The shadows in that dormered room were strange to him, and he cried out in confusion. He could not immediately place his whereabouts in this unfamiliar place, lying on that bed. He forced himself to slow his breathing, forced himself to remember that the memory was history, and that he knew history and was not condemned to repeat it. It came back to him slowly. This was his house now,

Emma's room was his room. It was only the dream slipping upon him again. His breathing slowed. In the morning he would get to the shop, where all the tools hung in order, and things would be clearer.

What had she said about the old man glowering from the painting? That he'd built the place for some woman he couldn't have, and gone crazy in the end? *He wanted the mother, and got the daughter. And I . . . I've got the mother, and want . . .*

It was the night of his triumph, the night the boy from the Park had taken Emma's very bedroom as new master of the Heights, and never in his life had Roy Murphy felt so alone.

Emma and Anne met on a Sunday morning, at a coffee shop near Emma's apartment in Brooklyn. It was a place where people hunch over tiny café tables discussing intimate matters while, inches away, other couples hunch over equal intimacies—where a woman agonizes with a friend over an abortion and eighteen inches away a total stranger is confessing his affair. Everyone had a very large coffee and a very small phone, and was triple-tasking—confessing, texting, sipping.

This city was so big, and yet people made do with such small spaces, Anne thought. Her sister and brother-in-law had jobs with impressive-sounding names, but it didn't seem that they were making much more money than the daily expenses consumed. "This is my gym," Emma had joked earlier that morning, as they'd climbed the four flights of stairs to the studio she and George had rented.

The coffee shop was noisy with conversation and the clatter of cups and spoons. Anne cast anxious glances to her left and right and asked, "Can't we go somewhere quieter?"

"In New York? And anyway, why?"

"Because I want to *talk* to you."

"About what?"

"Consider this an intervention," Anne said.

They rose and sidled and squeezed their way outside. When

they were on the street, Emma asked, "What do you want me to say?"

At that moment, standing on Pacific Street, Emma had dropped the mask, and looked pale and fragile.

"That you need help," Anne said. "I'm your sister." She smiled, touched her arm, and asked, "After all this time, you still . . . ?"

Emma nodded helplessly. She said, "Anne, I already know what you would say. Every single thing you've ever thought about this, Anne, I've thought. About him, about George, about me, about you, about Mom. About Hoosick Bridge, about that house. About how many people could be hurt. About how much I would regret—" She cut herself off as Anne listened. Quietly, she resumed. "I know all of that. And you're right—all those things are true, Anne, and also this is true: I think about him constantly. I don't ever get past bedtime without thinking of him. I don't even think I like him. But I can't stop thinking about him."

Anne once had called herself, without bitterness, Little Less Emma. By this she meant that although she was pretty, she was less pretty than Emma; though she did well in school, it was always a little less well than Emma; though her career was moving along, she was a little less accomplished. She was Little Less Emma.

But it didn't feel like that now. As they walked to Prospect Park it came gushing out of her older sister—how it had ended, she thought, with his departure to the service, how she had turned that corner and started a new life at Yale, how briefly she'd been happy. How even after Dad died she'd recovered, she'd found happiness toward the end of college. She was happy when she met George junior year. Happy when they agreed to marry senior spring.

It was Anne's way to nod politely and say little, except to ask, "You didn't think of him, then?"

"Not at all then."

But it had come on with the Heights, somehow, with seeing him there at the engagement party, and then again the day he bought the house.

"I could see it," Anne said, "when you made him dinner. But Em, it passed before. Maybe it will pass again."

"That won't help me, now. Because now I know it will always come back. It may fade for a while, but it will always come back. I can't end it—what do I do, Anne?"

"Give it time," she said.

Emma smiled a wan smile. "It loves time. It feeds off of time."

They walked for a while in silence, and when Anne asked her politely about George, she did not want to answer that question. It did not seem right or fair to George to do so.

# EIGHTEEN

The strange goings-on at the Heights that year inspired many conversations around Hoosick Bridge, in aisles and at counters of the shops in town, in the booths of Toni's Lunch, on the greens of the public golf course. It was astonishing that Roy Murphy had somehow bought the Heights; astonishing that Jane Herrick was still living up there in that old house with the young man she despised; astonishing that he was letting her do so. Jane's absence from town helped feed its fascination. She rarely came into the shops, and on those rare visits, people said, she seemed off. She had been seen in Price Chopper, overrouged at noon. On two occasions the Gilsons, next door, passed her walking along Spring Street early in the afternoon, busy in conversation with herself.

It had come to be understood in Hoosick Bridge that something was happening to Jane Herrick, that she wasn't right. When they saw her in the yard as they walked past the Heights, when they tried to greet her, she wouldn't answer, she would turn away from them. Lucy was up there in the mail truck and tried to say hello, and all Jane would answer was "I know what you are thinking, Lucy Moore. You have no business gossiping about my family." And then hurried away from her.

Lucy later said, "I've known her almost forty years—to see her like that now."

As for Roy Murphy, he was barely at the Heights at all. As early as you might go by on Spring Street, the truck would already be gone—off to the shop or a job site. The truck would still be down at the shop late. With that mortgage, people said, he'd have to be.

But he was up there at night. And that was what people tried to imagine: those nights. White haired (and now going dotty?— everyone said so) Jane Herrick and coarse Roy Murphy, child of the Park, who wanted the daughter and by a cruel irony was now housemate to the mother. The two of them up there alone at night, in that vast, empty mansion, tearing each other's eyes out. People said that the family ought to take her away from there. That it wasn't healthy.

"They've tried, but Jane won't leave," Toni said.

On a cold morning, a guy warming himself over a cup of coffee at Toni's Lunch would wonder, "Why doesn't he just throw her out? Why does he put up with it?"

Or a younger patron would ask, of no one in particular, "Why does she hate him so much, when he lets her live there?"

And Toni, a pot of regular in the right hand, and of decaf in the left, would explain how it all went back years. How, as kids in junior high school, Emma and Roy had something going on. And Jane knew it even then. That was years before their affair the summer after high school, before Roy went off to the service. And then, straight after that, Tom killed himself. Jane Herrick used to be all right, she was a bit of a snob, but nice enough to people. But it was all too much for her.

"She came in here once in a while, to have a cup of tea and wheat toast. She'd always sit in the second booth, right over there by the window. She hasn't been in for years."

"Can't be good for either of those people to be up there, living together," someone would say.

There was another aspect to it. Mel put the matter this way: "You know, Murphy's mother is still up there at the Park. He's never once gone to see her. In the years since he come back, not once."

"Didn't he buy her a trailer? She's in a new double-wide now."

"That's what I heard, but why's Emma's mother living in his mansion, and his own mother up at the Park in a trailer? There's plenty of room."

"It *is* weird."

"What's it got, eight bedrooms or something? And his own mother in a trailer drinking all day."

One of them might then say, "Well . . . ," acknowledging the other complication, about whether Eliza Murphy was really his mother or not, upon which there was no agreement in town.

And Toni would sum up. "It's their business, I guess."

But the main question, the one for which everyone would volunteer a hypothesis and no one had the answer, was this: Why did he buy the place?

No one asked him, that much is sure. Roy Murphy wasn't seen very often at Toni's Lunch anymore. Sometimes, very early, he'd come in for breakfast, but Toni knew that the subject of the Heights was off-limits. Even she could not pry into that one. Although it excited her to think about it, for her theory was that this driven young man, who exercised such fierce control over his life, had beneath everything else a romantic purpose! She'd whisper it—but only when he wasn't there.

"It was Emma. The whole reason he bought that house was to get her back," Toni said.

In the town clerk's office, Francine McGregor phrased it differently: "The reason he bought that house? To get back at her."

The landscaping business had stabilized. Boss, as his crews called him, no longer had to worry about covering every payroll. He wasn't out on jobs so much; he had become a manager—negotiating

with vendors; dealing with screwups at client jobs, billing disagree-
ments, accountants; firing guys who didn't measure up, looking for
better ones to replace them. No longer did he have the same anxiety for the next mortgage payment. The relaxation of that tension
seemed to bring a new one, however. The men noticed that he was
more distant with them, quicker to anger.

It was in the tower, rather than the four-poster bed, that he
spent his nights now, for he did not sleep well in Emma's old bedroom. He had put a cot up in the tower, and he liked that better.
Some nights he'd lie awake, bone tired but unable to sleep, hearing
the wind outside, listening to the faraway creaks of the house set-
tling in for the night. A deeper disquiet had come upon him. He
had cleared the reef and set sail—but to where? Now what?

One night, sitting at Ezra Morse's desk, he pulled a file from
the drawer, and as he set it down a scrap of paper slipped out and
fluttered to the faded green leather of the desktop. It was the girl's
note. That morning two years before, it had been on his shop desk,
when he returned at 5:00 a.m., as he told her he would. He had not
been surprised to see her car gone from the lot. She must have left
soon after he did—she was not one to take an insult lightly, and for
all her bohemian affect, there was no chance of her actually sleeping in a shop. But she had left this note on the desk. And though
he hadn't liked her, something about the note's arch attitude had
stayed his hand from throwing it away; something about it drew
from him a hard smile, not of affection but of recognition. The
note read:

> You're an asshole, Roy Murphy—but an interesting
> asshole.
>
> > Later,
> > Izzy
>
> Ps Call me to apologize sometime.

And then a phone number.
He didn't remember that he'd even saved this note, and

hadn't thought about it again until now. Call that mess of a human being? That would be nothing but trouble. Still, he hadn't thrown the note away either.

Beneath the lamplight, the note lay faceup on the desk, with its girlish handwriting, its postscript, and its phone number. He stared until the script faded and it was not so much a scrap of her handwriting as her indistinct form that lay before him on the desk.

*When I get my place, maybe I will get a woman*, he had so often said before.

"This is *so* sick," Izzy whispered, giggling. "Where is she?"

They had been to dinner, and had a few drinks, and come in late. He checked the thermostat as he always did, turned it back down to low, and then climbed the grand front staircase noisily, his boots almost banging the steps. When they reached the landing, he pointed down the corridor to where a light shone beneath a door. "In her room," he said. "You want to leave, you can leave."

"No, it's cool," she said. "Sick, though."

Then Jane called out from behind the door, "I knew it was only a matter of time, Mr. Murphy."

Izzy laughed again as they climbed the second flight of stairs.

Jane heard two sets of footsteps in the upstairs corridor, and then the door to Emma's room closing.

She was loud. She moaned and shrieked and was vocal in a way that made him think it was practiced, a script or something—where did she get this stuff? "Oh, yes, oh yes, Roy, *yes!*" And so on. He thought, *I don't like the familiar way she uses my name.*

But in the morning Roy Murphy made a point of bringing the girl downstairs when he knew Jane Herrick would be in the kitchen. The girl was still half asleep, her eyes half shut, her hair falling in masses about her shoulders. She was wearing one of Roy's flannel shirts, and nothing else.

"Cold in here," she said.

"I think you two know each other," Roy Murphy said to Jane.

Toni's Lunch was the stock exchange of information about the

Heights. A few mornings later they were trading a new issue. Toni listened to them out in the booths, and heard Pete Mallincrodt say, "He's got a girl up there—Murphy. Some girl, too!"

Some of the guys in the shop liked to talk baseball, and none more than lanky Joe Rouleau, who had played third base for TacReg years ago and was a fanatic about the game and in particular about the Boston Red Sox. He could tell you which Red Sox middle reliever had which ERA against lefties, and who ought to play second base this year. He had pet peeves: intentional walks, the hit-and-run play. He was always going on about the hitters taking the 3–0 pitch. "Best pitch of the at bat! The pitch they worked that count to get, and they *take* it. It is the stupidest thing in the major leagues, and it's like religion to them. *Watch* the three-and-oh pitch, boss. A sweet, fat home run pitch most times, and they take it, and Francona sits there spitting his sunflower seeds!" The men would shake their heads and laugh when Joe got himself going.

That same spring, before he'd bought the Heights, on an afternoon in March, Roy Murphy had him in the office. He said the company might sponsor a Little League team if Joe would manage it. Joe's eyes lit up immediately. Manage a team—really? With uniforms and everything? Damn right he would! "But the games, boss, practices . . . it might interfere with work, and—"

"Don't push it, Joe. You can get your crew up a little earlier. And one thing. I don't want it just the rich kids, the ones with batting gloves and parents at every practice."

"Boss?"

"Get some flyers. Get up to the Park and knock on doors. Get some of those kids out for it. Will you do that for me, Joe?"

And so that spring of 2013 it wasn't just Taconic Savings Bank and Ketzel's Insurance and Nardelli's Sunoco that had teams. The league had a new addition: the Murphy's Landscaping Pirates. They wore yellow caps with the big black *P* and black T-shirts with "Murphy's Landscaping" slanting in yellow script across the front. For the one and only year of their existence, the Pirates would finish last in the minor league standings. (Joe proved to be a decent coach, but he had no savvy for the intrigues of Little League team selection. Besides, Boss was insistent about getting Park kids out for the team, and a lot of them hadn't played before.)

Roy Murphy never coached the Pirates, never ran an infield drill or pitched batting practice, but whenever the Pirates needed more bats or balls, or once in a while, if Joe quietly mentioned there was this kid from up the Park who didn't have a decent mitt, there was money. The kids noticed him, though. In the late afternoons, he sometimes got away from the office or the job site to their games, and sat alone at the end of the stand at Kutzer Field, wearing his Pirates cap, and clapping for every hit, every putout. Roy Murphy had never played baseball himself, had never before cared about it. At first he'd thought this was something to be done for business, to advertise the company. He didn't imagine that watching twelve-year-olds on the diamond could interest him, but something about the clink of aluminum bats on those chilly spring evenings drew him. In the minors there was much disorder: games were mainly swings and misses, errors, comically wild overthrows that catapulted infield dribblers into base-clearing disaster. But sometimes each proper thing happened in its right order. The one boy crouched with the bat held high, the other, gangly, reached back and hurled the ball, the pitch arced toward the plate, the aluminum bat head swung through and pinged contact, the ball bounced toward the shortstop, the fielder took a knee, gloving the ball, while the thud thud of the batter's flying footsteps came pell-mell along the base path. There was the set, the throw over, the first baseman's stretch, and now that vivid intersection, with the ball and runner both reaching first base along different vectors, a sneaker lunging for the bag and a ball snapping in the glove. Safe or out, it didn't matter, it was the seeing of each thing in its proper order that he liked.

But what he liked seeing most of all was the coming home. He liked to watch it develop: a hit, a safe harbor at first, guile and hustle and luck and adventure on the voyage round the bases, and then the coming home. The ball heaving in from the dusky out-field too late, bouncing behind, too late to interrupt the whooping of boys, silvery as fish as they leapt, their caps bobbing, their backs arched with joy for a comrade's return. In the stands, he always stood up when they came home, a smile on his face then, and along the bench, as the hollering calmed down, boys would whisper, "That's Mr. Murphy. You know the Heights? That's his house! He was in the war, you know."

No one on the team heard Roy Murphy speak, except for the one time that none of them ever forgot. It came late in the season, in June, when they were swatting mosquitoes and suffering through another loss to Nardelli's Angels, already six runs down and only in the third inning. Peter Rubin, the Pirates' best but temperamental hitter, was called out on strikes on a pitch low and away, and the boy threw his helmet on the way back to the bench. They were all surprised then to see Mr. Murphy hop down from the stand and head out onto the field, striding with alarming speed toward the umpire. They thought he was going to argue the call, and the umpire thought so, too, standing there in the pugnacious posture of umpires everywhere, with his hands on his hips, glaring as Roy strode down the first-base line. But they were all wrong. Bobby Colangelo, who was on deck, heard him say, "Give me a minute with the boy." The ump called time, and Roy walked over to the bench where the Pirates were sitting.

"Peter Rubin," he said. He spoke quietly, but the boy would never forget the look of that dark brow, and that Mr. Murphy knew his name. "You threw your helmet."

With his head low, Peter said, "That pitch was in the dirt almost!"

"Who thinks it was a strike?" Roy Murphy asked. Along the bench, none of the boys moved. No one spoke.

"Who thinks it was a ball?" Slowly, quietly, they all put their hands up.

A few of the parents were listening to this, and the ump, too, had sidled halfway down the first-base line.

"Did the ump call it a strike?"

"Yeah?"

"Then it *was* a strike."

It was quiet, and the tops of Pirate caps ran motionless in a row along the bench. The boys had their gloves between their legs, their eyes down on their sneaker tops. They were afraid of his eye, but listening intently, trying to understand what he meant, because it was a strike if it was over the plate.

"You can spend a lot of years crying about what wasn't over the plate, and nobody will care. You want to be winners, boys?"

He waited, and then a few of them looked up, and began to nod. Sure, they wanted to be winners.

"Then don't cry about what's fair. That's for losers. When the ump calls it a strike, it's a strike. Learn that rule. You'll get more hits that way."

They were all silent.

"I don't want to see any Pirates throwing helmets again," he said. "Joe, let's play baseball."

That evening, the Pirates lost to Nardelli's Angels by eight runs, and when the game was over and twilight was coming on, and Coach Joe had them packing the balls and bats in the duffel bag, they watched Mr. Murphy stride away quickly over the field toward his truck, alone.

He came back for their games until the season was over, off and on, but they never heard him speak again. He would sit alone in the little stand, and they could feel his presence there. Sometimes he'd acknowledge the parents, shaking a hand briefly and stiffly, never one for chat. Some afternoons he was there for the first pitch, sometimes he appeared in the middle innings, sometimes not at all. The kids on the team knew the sound of his hand clap—they could distinguish it from all others. Sometimes, if a kid got a hit, or made the throw from third base, or caught one in the outfield, he'd look over and see him in the stand, clapping for him. And Roy Murphy always stood, and clapped, and smiled, when a boy came home.

\* \* \* \*

The hot days and nights of high summer came. From this, the most active period for the landscaping business, it seemed unlikely that he would ever be absent. He had not missed a day of work since his return: not a Saturday, not a Sunday, not Thanksgiving Day, not Christmas Day. He had taken no vacation. The Friday that he bought the Heights was the closest he had come, but even on that day he had been in the shop at dawn, and returned again for three hours in the late afternoon. And then, suddenly, in the middle of that summer season, Roy Murphy was gone, vanished for five days.

Joe Rouleau had been in the office the day Roy took the call that launched his trip. "Never seen him smile like that before," he said. "Not once."

He left Joe in charge, with a scrawled list (in that crazy, uneven handwriting of his, part capitals, part lowercase) of the jobs that needed doing and which crews he wanted on which job. He'd be back Monday, he had to go get something done, he said. Something down south. He'd be calling in.

He spent a day in airplanes and anodyne airports, twice changing planes until at last the sun was setting and he had disembarked into the heat and humidity of the delta country. As night came on he drove a rental car south until he reached the exit for Gulf Haven, Mississippi, and there he pulled off and followed the directions he had scrawled on a piece of shop paper to the center of town and a place called Mugshots Bar and Grille.

When Billy Hall Jr. got out of the service, a year after Roy, he had gone home. He had long imagined and constructed this return in his mind. He knew there would be no parade, but he wanted at least a party—a celebration where all his friends and family would come to one place and everybody would thank him for what he'd done and have a drink, or maybe two, and they'd crank up George Strait and play pool and they'd air-guitar Billy's favorite songs. In his mind he had worked up a few Pentagon decrees, a few commendations he could hand out. And maybe his girl Yvonne from high school would be there, too. She'd married a guy, but his fantasy return permitted some suspension of disbelief. You never knew, maybe Yvonne would get wind of it and come by. A guy daydreaming in Afghanistan could conjure such things. And at this party everybody would be happy.

There had been no party. After Katrina, his father couldn't find work, or finance repairs on the house, and the bank had long ago taken it. They now lived in a Section 8 apartment in the run-down part of Gulf Haven known as Green Point. Billy Hall Sr. had grown morbidly obese. All day he sat in the green recliner in front of the TV, hooked up to an oxygen bottle, watching Fox News and railing at the Democrats. His mother, grown stouter, too, was working at Pogey's, and complaining bitterly whenever she was home, about how she had to do everything for him now. Yvonne had married a boy from Billy's own high school class, who had come home from Mississippi State to a job at the insurance. She had two kids already—had he heard?

Billy had a little money left over from the service, although he had spent a lot on sprees when on leave from deployments, and a good bunch of the rest on a red Mustang with low miles. He had enough to put down a deposit and a couple of months on an apartment for himself, and that about did it for him. He went to look for work, but nobody was hiring. He'd stand on the lines and send the e-mails and then at 4:00 p.m. he'd go to Mugshots.

It was good to see Roy Murphy looking tanned and strong and striding into the place like he owned it, with his Army pack slung over one shoulder. Billy put down his glass and bear-hugged him and whooped, and guys in the bar stopped talking to watch. The two sat down at the bar and had a drink. Two hours went by in what seemed like only minutes—on what had happened to this one and what had happened to that one and had he heard about Montoya?

Roy Murphy hadn't heard. It was that next spring, nine months after he left. The squad on patrol walked into an ambush and lost Montoya, and another guy, Nelson, who'd come on after Roy's time.

The radio in the bar was playing a country ballad. "He knew every song, I bet he even knew this song," Billy Hall Jr. said. "You know he had some country on that iPod. Wasn't all that hip-hop shit." They sat at the bar, remembering how Montoya's boyish face would rock back and forth in his bunk, wires hanging down from his ears.

"I was going to take him deer hunting in Vermont," said Roy Murphy quietly.

Billy looked a little heavier, but something else was different, and after an hour or so, Roy figured out what it was. Billy Hall Jr. had grinned through every kind of imaginable shit in Afghanistan. He had a natural smile, but he'd come home without it. He looked the same in every respect but one, and that was that he didn't grin anymore, and this made his whole face different.

They ordered food and ate hungrily. And they kept drinking beers and then Billy Hall Jr. set up shots. Roy Murphy didn't drink much, and mainly he went to bars only when prowling for a woman. He was unforgiving about drunkenness with his crews. He would fire anyone for it; he even fired Joe Rouleau for it once, before rehiring him the next day. But early on that night he looked at Billy Hall Jr. and nodded silently as if to say, Yes, *fucking* drunk—and so they sat in the bar listening to the country music, and they told stories and lies to each other and exposed their memories to the barroom. Roy laughed and Billy Hall Jr. sobbed like a baby and then puked in the sink in the ladies' room, and the room whirled for Roy Murphy, too.

They stumbled out to the street at midnight. It was still hot, even this late at night, and a drunken, nonplussed Billy Hall Jr. stood with his jaw slack at the door of the Mustang, patching all his pockets for his keys, because he'd already forgotten that Murphy had taken them.

"Soldier," said Roy Murphy, "in the two fortieth, we march."

By the end of that night they'd walked two and a half miles, out past town along the highway toward Green Point, including half a mile where they made a wrong turn and Billy was too drunk to notice for a while. "I can walk for miles, drunk or sober," said Roy Murphy. "So can you."

But they hadn't walked far, less than half a mile to where the sidewalk ran out and they began to weave along by the roadside, when a police cruiser pulled over and two cops jumped out. Billy started talking rough, swearing, said he'd fuck them both up right then and there, if they wanted to shoot a soldier that fought for their freedom, do it, he didn't fucking care anymore.

"Be cool, Billy," said Roy.

The younger cop was scared and had already drawn his weapon. The older one looked at Billy Hall Jr.'s haircut and held his head a certain way, and Roy nodded at him. "Airborne," he explained, quietly. "Can I talk to you?"

They stepped to one side, and he said, "I'm drunk as shit, we're both drunk as shit, we were in it together. Billy hasn't been back too long. Having a tough time. He's a good guy, but it's tough when you first get out and nobody even knows where the fuck Afghanistan is, you know?"

"You from up north?"

"Vermont," he said.

The cop asked, "Can you get him home?" Roy nodded and said that Billy wouldn't be any trouble with him.

Billy stood beneath a streetlight, shielding his eyes from the blue lights.

The older cop said, "If you want, we'll drive you boys," and Roy answered, "Thanks, but we'd be better walking it off, you know what I mean? I'll get him home."

And the cop wished him good night and he and his partner went back to their vehicle. They got in, and then the older guy got out again and walked back over to Roy Murphy, and he extended his right hand.

"What?"

"Just wanted to say thank you," the cop said. "For what you done."

Roy Murphy shook his hand. "Except for car salesmen, you're the first one ever said it to me," he said.

The cop returned to his patrol car and drove off.

They walked south from town. In that warm night there were strange sounds, different bugs or frogs or something down here, he thought. The moist, hot air tasted different to him; it seemed a very foreign place, and made him think of his home—that he had one now.

Later they made the wrong turn when Billy was walking half asleep and didn't notice for a while. But they doubled back and at last reached the brick, two-story apartment block set among a little stand of pines. For what was left of the night Roy Murphy slept on the floor. Billy Hall Jr. was out cold until the heat woke him up at midday in the little, stifling apartment. The sun was high in the sky, and the room was baking. Roy Murphy had gone back for Billy's car, and for coffee. Later they would get the rental car and return it.

The next afternoon they gassed up Billy's Mustang and as the sun began to set they started the long drive north. They told stories and listened to the radio, driving through the night, sleeping by the roadside during the heat of the day. Early in the drive, in Tennessee, Roy Murphy asked Billy whether that happened a lot, when he'd been drinking.

"What?"

"Get rough, like you would of done with those cops."

"Them two peckerwoods?" Billy Hall Jr. laughed. Maybe it had happened a time or two, he conceded. "Occasionally. It don't mean nothing."

"You got to be smarter. You got to learn what brings it on and watch it."

"Chickenshit'll bring it on," he said. "People in my grille about chickenshit."

"They're gonna be," he said. "Used to bother me—they don't know, they don't care where you been. They don't give a shit. Used to make me angry. Now it doesn't so much. You got to watch for that, Billy."

But Billy Hall Jr. didn't answer.

"That one cop, he was all right," Roy said.

They drove through the nights and slept in the days, and early on the third morning they reached the Albany airport and pulled up next to the red truck with the black lettering on the side that said, "Murphy's Landscaping."

Billy Hall Jr. looked at it and said, "That where I'm gonna work?"

"That's where you're going to work your ass off, soldier," said Roy Murphy.

But it didn't end up that way.

"Judas Priest, Murphy, this your place?"

They had parked in the drive, and Billy Hall Jr. climbed down from the truck. He stood in the front yard with his mouth slack and his head back, looking up at the Heights.

"*This?* This here your place—this whole thing?"

"This is my place."

"You never said you was rich, dawg. I ain't had no idea. Would of treated you better."

"I wasn't. I'm not."

"Fuck me," Billy said, as they walked up the porch steps.

They found Izzy in the parlor, watching television and smoking, a tumbler making a ring on one of Jane's side tables.

"This is Izzy," Roy said. "Izzy, say hello to a great American, Mr. Billy Hall Jr."

"Welcome home, GI Joes." She didn't move her eyes from the television, and took a drag.

He led Billy upstairs, and on the landing Billy said, "Damn, Roy, she's fine." Roy went on to a bedroom on the second floor and said that would be his.

Billy sure appreciated it, he said—he'd get a place of his own real soon and be out of his hair.

Roy cut him off. "You're not in my hair, Billy. This is your place, long as you want it. It's your place."

And after they had come downstairs to the foyer again, they looked up and saw Jane on the landing, her hand on the banister.

"This your mom, Roy?"

Jane turned and disappeared, and her footsteps hurried away in the corridor and a door slammed.

"Guess not."

"It's a long story," said Roy.

Roy took Billy Hall Jr. to the shop Monday morning and put him on Joe Rouleau's crew. After that first day Roy caught Rouleau by his truck and asked, quietly, how it went, and Rouleau answered, "Fine," in a noncommittal way. He answered like that for a few more days, looking away. The third or fourth time Rouleau shrugged and added, "He's new, it'll take a while."

"He's important to me," said Roy Murphy.

"Well shit, boss, *that's* obvious. The guy don't do no work, he just sits on his ass, he must be *important* to you."

"Give him time."

"Boss, don't worry about it. I'll make it right. Don't you worry about nothing."

And Joe tried. He tried every which way, but it didn't work. That didn't matter to Roy Murphy at first. Because Roy could carry a little deadweight on a crew, and a guy like Joe would just shoulder the load. He thought Billy would come around. He'd always carried his weight in Afghanistan, so it stood to reason that, in time, he'd do it here, too. That's what he thought at first.

But soon the Mustang was gone after work, later and later, turning up in the drive at the Heights at one, two in the morning. There weren't too many places to go in Hoosick Bridge after ten—you had to travel to find a bar open until midnight. Then Billy Hall Jr. started showing up for work late, and the men watched carefully, because tardiness was a firing offense for everyone else.

Roy started to pick up on silences in the shop when he came

282    Sabin Willett

by. Pairs of men who had been talking would go silent. Guys would have sullen looks. Why were there special rules for this guy and for no one else? And then came the day when Billy Hall Jr. took his flask to a customer's. Mrs. Dana saw him drinking behind the barn, and Joe had to bring the word back to Roy.

That night he paced in the tower. In the morning, at the shop, when the crews were loading up the trucks, he took Billy into the office.

"You're not going out today," he said.

"Not going out." Billy's big, jowly face had been sullen, and now went flat.

"No."

"What's that supposed to mean?"

"It means you've got a place in my house long as you want it, but you have to look for another job. Starting today."

"Who died and made you fucking general of the Army?"

"Billy, that's the way it is. Drinking on my job, you can't do that even once."

Billy Hall Jr. went out to his car and disappeared until the next morning, when he drove it into the lilac bush in the side yard at the Heights, leaving tire marks in the lawn. He was discovered, asleep on the porch, in the morning.

In the half-light before dawn, Roy Murphy walked slowly around the bush, listening to the snoring up on the porch. The sprawling, leggy encampment of lilac was half a century old at least. He could trim it and it would come back. He could get a crew up there to repair the lawn.

He squatted down, put his finger in the soft earth of the tire rut that had chewed through the grass, recalling how, yesterday in the shop, Billy Hall Jr. had demanded, *What's that supposed to mean?*

It means, Roy Murphy thought ruefully, you're my brother.

Jane looked for ways to provoke Roy Murphy, and he returned the favor. She was no longer driving then, but when Roy was at work she would back the Mercedes to the end of the drive, by the street, where he couldn't fit his truck around it. He would eat off the fine china and leave it in dirty heaps in the sink, or leave an extension ladder on the lawn. He wore Vibram-soled work boots, and when he'd been in mud he would track it up the stairs and around the corridors to get her started. Sometimes, if he had a fuel pump or solenoid to clean or repair, he'd bring it home, and spread out the parts on the kitchen table.

Izzy was in Emma's old room, but Roy Murphy's visits were infrequent. He had moved up to the tower. Sometimes days would go by when he barely saw her, for she was never out of bed when he left in the morning. But the television was always on, and he would see her sprawled before it in the parlor.

"What am I supposed to do up here?" she asked him once, as he stood by the door.

"Get a job," he said.

"You just say that, like, like . . ." She didn't finish the sentence and returned her attention to the television, not looking at him anymore, hoping he might at least sit with her. But he never did.

He brought a boom box up to the tower, but music only made him restless. He preferred the rattle of the wind against the old panes. At first he had planned to replace the windows, but later he realized he would have missed the sound of that wind. Sometimes he would pull one of the old books off the shelf and read himself to sleep. He had taken to buying books about Afghanistan, about the war, anything he could find. He would bring them up to the tower and read them at night.

Sitting at the desk, alone, he said sardonically to himself, "It's me and you up here, Ezra."

In town, people declared that the goings-on at the Heights had veered from the merely peculiar to the ominous, that some kind of lunacy hung over the place. The professor called it a ghost ship, with dark Roy Murphy its mast, and the troubled girl, and the disturbed old woman, and the tipsy soldier all lashed to him and each other. "I don't know about ghost ships," Toni said, "but

for sure it's not healthy." People said the family would have to get
Jane out of there. That chubby southern kid with the drinking
problem, he wouldn't last a Vermont winter. Nor did they think
the girl would stick. She did not fit in Hoosick Bridge—her being
there was a stunt, people said, to alarm her family in Boston. She
had no job; it was said that up at the Heights she slept until noon
and barely dressed when she rose. She sat before the television, in
pajama bottoms and one of his shirts, smoking. Jane would rail at
her, and the girl would just change the channel and turn up the
volume. And then at suppertime she'd go and wash and begin to
watch for his headlights.

Autumn came, and down by the river, in Toni's Lunch one morning, Professor Emmanuel stirred a cup of coffee. The Kinko's box
sat on the counter next to the cup. There was an unusual quiet,
almost a sullenness in the diner that day.

"The air today feels like a storm coming," he said to Toni.
"Doesn't it?"

It was the rough, shattering blitzkrieg, that sudden white invasion
of lights flicked on without warning in a dark room.

"Get up," he said.

When she didn't respond, he pulled the sheets and blanket
roughly from the bed and threw them to the floor. She lay there
alone and small, a birdlike creature in a long T-shirt, her knees to
her chest, reaching vainly for the blanket, groaning.

"Up," he repeated.

Suddenly she sat. "What the *fuck*?"

He took her by the wrist and pulled her to her feet.

"Asshole! Don't *touch* me, what the—"

"You've already slowed down my morning," he said, handing
her clothes. He stood and watched as she dressed.

In the kitchen there was coffee. He had made toast, too, which
was cold by the time they got downstairs. He told her to eat it,

and she refused. And then he stood over her and it frightened her and so she ate a piece.

The sun had not yet risen when he led her outside to the porch. Down the hill there were gray, indistinct shapes, lights in some of the windows of the houses, the streets empty. The squirrels were busy in the gutters above, scurrying around the porch roof with a show of bustle as he set up the stepladder. He spread out a heavy canvas tarpaulin. Watching him, she shivered, forced back a yawn.

He explained how to change the scraper blades when they dulled, how to change the paper on the sander. He showed her the motion, scraping up and down the first post, as chips fluttered to the tarp. "I want this whole porch scraped and sanded," he said. "Posts, balusters, rails. Do the inside first. When you get to the outside, you have to spread the tarps across the bushes. And be real careful, otherwise I'll be picking up paint chips out of these bushes for years. For today, you've got plenty of work on the inside, I think."

"You want me to scrape paint," she said. "At fucking four o'clock in the morning."

"You live here, you don't have a job, so you'll have a job at home. Start at that end," he said, "and work your away along."

She listened to the jingle of keys on his chain, listened to his steps recede. At the truck, he turned and said, "And it's quarter to six, by the way. Half the morning's gone."

After he'd driven off, she looked dumbly at the scraper in her hand, then at the aluminum stepladder. She surveyed the forest of cracked white posts and rails and balusters. Down the hill, his truck disappeared round the bend down Washington Street.

"Asshole," she muttered.

She ran the scraper up and down the first post a few times, at shoulder height, just below the bare patch where he had scraped to demonstrate. Nothing happened. A little bit of gray appeared, dulling over the cracks in the white paint, but the paint seemed otherwise unconcerned. The cracks were the same, and no paint chips came off.

She dropped the scraper on the tarp and went back inside, up the stairs, and to her room, where she undressed and went back to bed.

At five o'clock that afternoon he returned, striding loudly into the parlor. She did not look up from the television at first. He said nothing, stood there darkly watching her, breathing heavily.

"I don't do *paint chips*," she said, her eyes fixed on the set.

"What *do* you do?"

"You want to throw me out, Roy, just go ahead. Okay? What-ever you want."

He crossed the room and again took her by the wrist.

"Hey! Get your *fucking* hands . . . !"

He led her, swearing, back to the porch. There she caught his eye at last and was frightened by it—her legs trembled as though she might sicken physically. It was one part fear of violence and three parts something more compelling—fear of his contempt.

He handed her the scraper and then pulled up the wicker chair.

"Seriously?"

She scraped paint, feebly at first.

"This is not working for me."

He said nothing, and she ran the ineffectual scraper up the post.

"I can't *do* it! You want me to, like, wash dishes or something, I'll wash the dishes. I've never done this before."

"Washing dishes isn't work. Have you *ever* worked?"

"Fuck you."

He rose and came to the post. He demonstrated, then returned the scraper to her, putting his rough hand on her wrist, guiding her over the surface. She felt blood rushing to her face and turned away. He went back to the chair and sat down.

She rubbed the scraper, and at first there was no difference.

Frustrated, she attacked it harder, and now a few paint chips came off, and then a run of chips.

It was dusk. The dinner hour came. He went inside and returned with a bottle of beer and a glass of water.

"Get *me* one at least? Jesus!"

"You don't drink on the job. Except this. Always stay hydrated," he said and handed her the glass of water. He sat, and she scraped paint.

"The *job*. Right. And what do you pay for this job? Oh, I forgot, room and board in Crazyville. You're going to watch me?"

She fell to random profanities. As the sun began to set, he got up to turn on the porch light.

"Can I at least have a radio?"

"Sure," he said. "When you're working."

He went up to the tower and came back down with his boom box and brought it out to the porch.

"One oh three point nine," she said. And she scraped the paint.

"All right?" she asked at last, exasperated, when she thought maybe she had finished the inside of the first run of balusters.

He got up from the settee and inspected.

"No. You need this now." He handed her the sander.

The sander was heavy, and she struggled with it. Some of the paint had come off, and some clung tenaciously to the old oak posts.

"Do I have to get it all off? Some of it won't come off!" It was getting dark now, and she peered in as he showed her that what was loose had to come off and what was embedded could stay.

Izzy scraped paint. And sanded. And scraped paint and sanded. She squatted to get the balusters and climbed the stepladder to get the posts and the gingerbread filigree by the ceiling. She felt tired, and he went to get her more water. When he came back to the porch, he found her sitting on the floor, leaning against the shingled wall.

"A shift is seven and a half hours," he said. "You've been working for about two."

"I haven't eaten." She had paint dust and chips in her hair. He was a prick, she said, and he'd made his point already and it was late. Did they have to do this now? Tonight?

"You get your dinner break at nine-thirty," he said.

"Dinner *break*?"


At about quarter past nine, Beth Gilson was walking her Lab, Pippi, along Spring Street. She heard a radio playing and saw that Roy Murphy had that girl out on the porch, on a stepladder, scraping paint, while he sat in a wicker chair, watching her.


At last he told her she could have her half hour for dinner. She could go in and get something from the fridge. The way he said it to her, as though she were a convict, or a child—it was the last straw of the night.

"You are a twisted fucking asshole, and I don't have to take another minute of this." She dropped the sander and marched past him to the porch steps, and then around the house to where her car was parked by the garage. She backed it around the truck and raced loudly down Washington Street. Roy Murphy stood on the porch and watched.

She reached town and pulled to the side of the now-empty street, next to the old Fredoni & Herrick building. Crying, Izzy rifled angrily again through the glove compartment, hunted again below the seats, as she had done a dozen times before. But she unearthed no coins, just as she had unearthed none before. The fuel gauge still registered empty. She had no money in her purse, no credit cards that worked anymore. The cell phone worked, but her mother wouldn't pick up. She even thought for a moment about calling her brother instead. But she could not quite do that.

Maybe she had enough gas to get to Bennington and find a bar, and see if she could make something happen. But that was too high risk, even for her. The warning light had been on for a while now.

And so she cried, in her car, for half an hour. Cried with the humiliation, cried because she had nowhere to go, cried because she hated the cold, miserable sonofabitch, and cried for another reason that she still had too much pride to admit—that she wanted his approval. She could cry for only so long before, defeated, she had to drive slowly back up the hill to the Heights.

On the porch, she found the tarp folded in the corner. The power sander, with cord coiled neatly around it, sat on top, with the paint scraper next to it. At least he was not waiting outside. She went inside and hurried upstairs to her room. Still dressed, she collapsed on the bed, body, clothes, paint chips, blanket, and all, and was asleep instantly.

In her confusion it seemed that only minutes had gone by, although in fact it was past five when the light came on, and Roy Murphy stood in the doorway again. This time she rose obediently and followed him down the stairs. She was famished, and ate breakfast hungrily, and then followed him outside.

"I have to do seven hours?" she asked, quietly.

"A shift is seven and a half."

And so it was that Izzy Forrester came to scrape and sand and at last to paint the porch at the Heights. She would do a few hours in the morning, and then break, and then a few more, and then break. Sometimes Billy dropped by during the day and stretched his fleshy length along a wicker chair, telling jokes about Bossman Murphy, topping up her water glass with vodka, and awarding her commendations "for posts duly scraped and the meritorious sanding of rails." He made her laugh. The hours passed more quickly then, although she could see him stealing glances at his watch, and he always left before Roy came home. There had been trouble of some kind at the shop. Billy was still sleeping up at the Heights, but he was gone every night until late, and by day wasn't working for Roy Murphy anymore.

The eyes of Crazy Jane were on her, too, watching through

one of the windows, and Izzy would yell at her, from time to time, to go away. It made her skin crawl. But she counted the hours and stopped when she got to seven. That was close enough.

Some days, she was proud of what she had accomplished— that she had spread the tarp on his precious azalea bushes and not spilled the paint chips, that she had smoothed an old oak post almost to the bare wood. She would wait anxiously for him to notice, to say something, and ache when he trotted up the steps at night without a word.

She drank vodka or gin, whatever she could find in the house or Billy would bring her. She drank it while she was working because it was easier to endure the hours numb. But she took it from the water glass, careful not to have bottles out there when Roy Murphy came home from work.

A week passed, and then two, and then one morning she discovered that in the night he had put two hundred dollars into her purse. That afternoon she went down to Stewart's and gassed up the car and got cigarettes and a few odds and ends and a bottle of gin from the liquor store. She thought she would leave. She called Billy on his cell, and they met at a restaurant in Williamstown called Mr. Chips, where a farewell drink became drinks, drinks became burgers and fries, and when Billy had eaten the last of the fries from her plate, they sat at the bar and ordered rounds of Ketel One and he told her stories about Afghanistan.

"Captain Dickinson used to walk around at night, in the dark, reciting poetry," he was saying.

"The guy who was Roy's hero?"

"Our CO. Specialist Roy Murphy, Two Hundred Fortieth Army Airborne, known to all and sundry hereabouts as Bossman Hard-ass, used to follow him around like a little puppy dog." Billy began to bark, little falsetto yips and barks, and she laughed.

"When Bossman come up to the firebase, he was scareder 'n shit. First time he was supposed to go out on patrol, fuckin peed his pants, almost."

"Really?"

"'Billy, I cain't going out there alone, not with no Shakespeare!'" Billy started singing a corruption of a Beach Boys standard, "Hep me, Billy, hep, hep me, Billy! Hep me, Billy, hep hep me, Billy!" He finished with a volley of barks and yips.

"The guy really walked around at night, reading poetry?" she repeated, when she'd stopped laughing.

"He was one a you Yankees. Y'all a little strange in the head up here. A fucking soldier, though, give him credit for that. Afraid of nothing, that guy."

"No wonder Roy had a crush on him."

Billy Hall Jr.'s eyes glistened with drink. His voice fell quiet, and he said, "After he got killed is when Bossman got all bitter 'n' twisted, when he got up to things."

"What's that mean, 'got up to things'?"

Billy Hall Jr. leaned in close. His fetid breath washed across her, and the clownish grin left her uncertain whether he was serious. "I mean certain highly classified shit, which it would not be wise to discuss, no, ma'am."

"What—*what?*"

"Shit duly classified at the highest echelons. In consequence whereof Bossman had to hurry his hard ass home a little early, if you catch my drift."

"I don't catch your drift at all, Billy."

"Let's just say that measures were taken into hand, and when Bossman was called upon to testify, he declined to volunteer the details regarding a certain evening of dark deeds."

She laughed again. "You are too much, man! They, like, broke the mold with you!"

He drained his glass, and licked his lips, and then wagged a finger. "Very dark and mysterious deeds, concerning certain Afghans who are no more. Some would say civilians, but these matters have heretofore been classified and should not be discussed."

He winked and had another go at the glass, discovering to his evident surprise that it was empty. The bartender interrupted just then, asking if they wanted him to call a cab, and Billy said no, they were fine, and to prove it barked at him. And between the barking, and the check, and Billy searching his wallet and his pockets for money, and not finding any, she couldn't get him back on the topic.

The night had set her back to thirty-four dollars in the wallet, and nowhere else to go. And so, one a.m. found her weaving northward on Route 7 behind Billy's Mustang, trying to keep the taillights in focus and the road beneath her. Retreating again.

The Heights was dark when they parked, except for a single light, faintly glowing in the tower.

Izzy had shut the bedroom door behind her and was sitting on the bed, pulling her boots off, her head aching. She wondered what Billy had been getting at—what Roy had done in Afghanistan. He was so damned methodical, and brooding, and dark, and yet capable, she had no doubt, of whatever insanity Billy was hinting at. But it had been insanity in Afghanistan, as far as she could tell, and even after Afghanistan, it owned these men, each in a different way. Still her head pounded.

It was then she heard the footsteps on the stairs. She felt, as she always felt in those moments, a wave of shame and anger and at the same time anticipation and even relief, because finally he was coming for her.

He spoke not a word, but stood in the bedroom doorway offering her that slight nod of his head that said, "I'm asking." In the faint light from the hall, the cloth hung limply from his left hand. She was still whirling a little, even as she sat on the bed; she was swaying, and she wanted so much to say no—and to say it with venom, to spit at him and it, to kick him out, to leave him to his soused comrade-in-arms and all their self-pitying memories of whatever they had done, or had been done to them in Afghanistan. But when she met his eye, the words would not come, and all her façade fell away, so desperate was she to be wanted by him. She would do anything to try to please him.

He watched as her clothes dropped to the floor, until, in the lamplight, she was pale and vulnerable, a doll-like creature, a small, naked girl with a mass of hair, with a tattooed butterfly below her right collarbone, and eyes glistening with tears of humiliation.

She asked then, "Do I have to?"

But he handed it to her, and dutifully she put the dress on for him. As he watched, his breathing quickened. He was muscled, hard, dark—hot with desire but cold in his eyes. She trembled when he touched her, as his fingers plied the dress, shimmied up all that gown material, his rough hands on her smooth hips. The charade took only a few minutes. Soon he had removed the dress again, laying it carefully on the chair.

He lay down with her on the bed, but it was not love, it was release, and when it was over she begged him.

"Don't just leave! Please, Roy."

He sat up on the side of the bed, rubbing his temple, his back to her, as he mumbled, "I have to go."

"Please?"

He sat silently for a long time, motionless, and she began to think he might stay. But he stood at last and said, "Sorry—been a little confused. But I won't be able to sleep here." He dressed silently and then picked up Emma's prom dress. He stopped at the door, turning to face her. "You're doing good, Izzy," he said, softly.

"What?"

"On the porch. You're doing good."

And then he was gone, and the door shut behind him. She listened to his footsteps as he climbed the stairs to the tower. She rolled over and wrapped her arms around her pillow, fashioning in the darkness something like joy from those few words, the first gentle words she could remember from him. *I'm doing good.*

Those words, that hope—they were ever so much better even than him staying.

Roy Murphy called Emma Herrick's cell phone only once. The message itself was hardly unexpected, but the sound of his voice on that phone was a second shock to her. For a moment the message didn't register. She had to hurry into the bathroom, close the door, and ask him to repeat it.

Jane had left the kettle on. It wasn't safe anymore.

That's what Emma claimed he'd said, when she emerged. Or did she report in that first minute only that Roy Murphy had delivered an ultimatum, that she had to go up there at last and get her mother—was the kettle an ornament she added later? George could never remember exactly. The phone call itself had so shaken him that he couldn't focus on anything beyond the name, Roy Murphy. That name was the detail that mattered—and the fact that she'd retreated behind the bathroom door to take the call. Who knows what old lovers really say to each other, beneath and around and between the words spoken—who knows what semaphore they send through silences? Not George, who felt himself listing, slipping beneath the surface, as he watched that door shut between them, feeling again the sensation he'd had in law school, when he'd first asked her out—the disbelief that she was with him at all.

"I should have done this a year ago," Emma said. She stood firm and unwavering by the kitchen table. He caught her eye only for a moment. Each waited for the other to ask, but neither did, and so he turned away, pretended to busy himself in work.

She made other phone calls that night—to Charlie, to her aunt Patty. And to Anne? It was never clear to George whether Emma *had* called Anne, who after all lived closer to Jane and, more to the point, had no history with Roy Murphy. In George's mind she was the logical sister for this task. He never learned whether his wife had even tried to call her with the news, or why it had to be that Emma, not Anne, went north to try to remove her mother from the Heights. And he never asked her, later, what precisely had happened that night. Through all the proceedings and testimony, the stern look on her face ordered George not to ask for details, and he obeyed. He knew only that the night before she drove to Vermont, Emma had been up late, and had left spread out on their small kitchen table the file of brochures, phone numbers—"assisted living facilities" was the euphemism—research she'd been compiling for two years. And that the next night, she'd called George from Vermont twice: once, briefly, in the evening, and a second time, when she woke him from a restless sleep, after it was all over. She shut George out of both the before and the after.

And Roy Murphy? Maybe he just said, "Come home to me," this time out loud. No one knows for sure. Roy called, and she came back to the Heights that one last time. His ask and her answer: it had always been the way with them before.

# NINETEEN

*I*n effect there were two inquests. The formal proceeding
convened in Courtroom Two of the Bennington County
Courthouse, before Superior Court Judge Bennett C. Hirshman,
a tall, laconic judge who listened intently from behind the bench,
concentration throwing his face into an involuntary frown. The
evidence in that case was forensic. Mr. Harlan, the state's attorney
down from Montpelier, called the witnesses, and probed the details
of the night of the fire, searching for its cause. That proceeding
was conducted in secret—nominally—although the town's fascination sucked transcript-length rumors from beneath the locked
door, and whether their source was the witnesses, or Bill O'Toole,
the talkative session clerk, or the court officers, or the jurors, or
just the suction itself was beside the point.

For these rumors helped inform the parallel, public inquest
convening before dawn each morning in Toni's Lunch, and thereafter proceeding at Stewart's and in Garibaldi's Coffee Shop and
the town offices and the post office. This second proceeding suffered from no restrictions of secrecy or artificial lawyers' rules.
Its evidence was historical, psychological, anecdotal, moral; all in
town were witnesses, and all were judges. And under their very

different procedures, each of the inquests posed the same question.

That boy from the Park with a criminal past, who disappeared, went off to war, returned, carried out his astonishing coup, who was rejected by the daughter and despised by her family, did he set off the destruction himself? Whether directly, or indirectly, by assembling combustible human fuel in that ancient and sulky mansion? Was his arrogance, or vengeance, or hubris accountable in some larger sense? Or, as phrased in Toni's Lunch by Professor Emmanuel himself, was Roy Murphy hoist with his own petard?

As for the identity of the actual arsonist, the early suspicion fell hardest on the one they knew least well. "It stands to reason," said Ernest Gillfoyle, raising a fork like a baton over a plate of eggs and sausage in Toni's Lunch. "It's the obvious thing." That big, blubbery kid from the south, Roy Murphy's Afghanistan buddy, was "a PTSD case if I ever saw one."

Bill Dowling sat next to Ernest, helping him open for the prosecution of William Hall Jr. "Going through what those guys went through over there, that kind of killing and death, the regularity of it—"

"Exactly," Ernest agreed, "the *regularity* of it . . ."

"—when they were all in Afghanistan, some guys just don't get over that. It's not their fault. And look what happened to him—that same day."

"At the shop that same afternoon, in front of the whole crew," Ernest agreed. By common consent, this was the overwhelming point: Roy Murphy's public humiliation of this besotted and pathetic creature in the lot of Murphy's Landscaping at 4:15 on the afternoon of the fire.

"And," Bill added, "where is he when the fire trucks get up there? Not in the house."

"Hell, where is he *now*?"

Around the diner there were nods of agreement. It was obvious—post-traumatic stress disorder. You get these guys in the service, God knows what they've been through, what they've seen over there. They come back to a little stress at home and can't deal with it.

Someone at the counter asked: "What about Emma?"

"Emma Herrick? She loved that place!"

"I'm just saying," the speaker said. "Never was no trouble, then the one night she come up there, there's a fire."

"Emma Herrick set fire to a place that was in that family all those years, with her own mother in it?"

"I'm just *saying*."

And after the talk died down a little, another voice was heard, from a booth in the back. "You say the Hall boy got PTSD in Afghanistan. That Murphy—he was in Afghanistan, too, you know."

So a verdict had not yet been reached in Toni's Lunch when the cold November morning arrived, and the court officers locked the door to Courtroom Two and the odd, solitary lawyer from the State's Attorney's Office convened the formal inquest before Judge Hirshman. Mr. Harlan was short and stout, closer to sixty than fifty, bald, with tufts of gray hair above the ears, and a gray mustache neatly trimmed. He moved in an unhurried way, was precise in his mannerisms, monotonous in the tone of his questions. Each morning he wore a blue blazer, gray slacks, a white shirt, a different tie of red or blue, and in the blazer pocket, a pressed handkerchief. As the week went on, the jurors noticed that the handkerchief, pressed and folded and extending from his blazer pocket, would be different, each day, than the handkerchief he had worn the day before. They began to speculate before court each morning about the day's new handkerchief: whether it would have blue piping, or red, or none. They imagined him in the Holiday Inn, standing at an ironing board in his socks.

The courtroom was on the second floor of the County building, a handsome edifice built of creamy marble blocks cut from the Pownal quarries a century before. Downstairs, as they trooped in each morning, the jurors would pass by the door for juvenile court, and the slatted bench in the hallway outside where Eliza Murphy had so often sat, waiting. Past that bench, a broad staircase led upstairs, to the two courtrooms. Courtroom Two was at the end of the hall. It was a swell old space, rich with honey-colored wood, its high, narrow windows looking out at Main Street. The judge's bench sat above the far end of the room, and the jurors, from behind their rail, could look out the windows across, as the light slanted in from the west.

The proceedings ushered in the winter, for it felt to them as though the last of the warmth slipped away during that week—as though it were still fall when they went into Courtroom Two, but winter when they emerged. The sun hurried away without bidding good evening on those November afternoons. Sometimes they found Mr. Harlan's inquiries so engaged them that of a sudden the windows across the room had gone dark, and night had fallen without anyone's noticing.

Of all those interested in these proceedings, the public and the private one, all the firefighters and police officers, the six jurors, the coroner and assistant coroner, Professor Emmanuel, and the reporters from the *Hoosick Bridge Tribune*, the *Bennington Banner*, and the *Berkshire Eagle* and the public radio who all tried in vain to get a public comment from him—Mr. Harlan alone seemed to have no emotional investment. He showed neither determination to see the proud family finally brought low nor sympathy for the beautiful star witness, nor zeal of the avenger, nor the Solomonic view of some in town that there had been enough suffering, that everyone should let it alone and allow all those questions to go to the grave with them. Indifferent as he appeared to the emotional resonance of the case, Mr. Harlan would yet prove insatiable for its physics—and at that, the nanophysics, the smallest facts. Time and again his questioning would return to a matter settled, a small part of the narrative they thought they had understood. The first few times, one could feel the exasperation in the jury box, and even on the bench—we covered that!—until his questioning yielded a new fact, a question, a problem, and they realized, We haven't *quite* covered that. The way he would return his plow to plowed ground was tedious at first, but after a few times, they watched the furrow more closely. Chances were it would turn up some new stone not seen before, though they had passed two, three, six times down that row—passed through that corridor or by that window or into that conversation. On the third day, before court, one of the jurors said, "Wouldn't want to be one of his handkerchiefs. I'll bet he irons it, then irons it again, then irons it again, then says, 'About that crease, let's just go back and iron that crease again.'" And they all laughed.

The star witness was the only one to escape that fire; or more accurately, the only known survivor who had not disappeared. She was the only witness who had been inside the Heights on that dreadful night. Her presence there seemed a coincidence passing strange. For the speaker in Toni's Lunch was right: after the day Roy Murphy closed on the Heights, the only night she had ever set foot in it was the night it was destroyed.

For the jury, that was the gripping confrontation: the questioning of Emma Herrick by Mr. Harlan. Despite what her father had done, Emma was still a kind of royalty in Hoosick Bridge. She had a celebrity aura about her, the most beautiful young woman to come out of that town in memory, and perhaps the most gifted, too, who had gone on to success of some kind on Wall Street (so people said), and now was come back to play a match of tennis with Mr. Harlan. But without her husband. (What was his name? They could not remember.) The proceedings were secret, of course—it was not as though the husband might have sat in Courtroom Two to lend moral support. But he had not come up with her to Hoosick Bridge, to wait on the bench outside, as a good husband would do in supporting his wife through her ordeal. They noticed this.

They did not know that George had urged—urged, begged, *instructed* even—that she not testify. She had a privilege under the Fifth Amendment, and the proceedings were secret, there was no reason not to claim the privilege. "There is no reason to testify, Emma. Nothing good can come of it."

She had merely shushed him. Of course she would testify. There was nothing to hide.

But that was not true. *Protecting*, as she preferred to think of it, was the very reason for testifying. There were victims to protect, reputations to protect, and not to put too fine a point on it, facts to protect. Only she was left to protect them. And something more. In this confrontation she would complete a vow that she had made to herself nine years before. She would erase Tom Herrick's great sin, which was not criminality so much as failure to be the father of her expectation. She would do so not by perfect probity and rectitude, but rather, by facing down her crisis eye to eye—by defeating it.

She wore a wool skirt of dark gray and a pale, cream-colored silk blouse. Around her neck she hung the pearls that George had given her on their first anniversary. She had brushed her hair back and clipped it behind her head, and would be calm and lovely, gracious, erect through that endless questioning. Unconsciously, the jurors sat straighter when she was on the stand. And though Mr. Harlan volleyed shot after methodical shot to her backhand, she was the opponent who never seemed to hurry, or even to perspire, who might give up three points and then return three to come back to deuce, and never change expression. Who played without flourish, but tirelessly. It seemed they might play the match to its crack of doom, with the advantage passing back and forth over the net until the jury wearied.

But at deuce it seemed to hold.

"Now Ms. Herrick, I think you wrote in your statement that Mr. Murphy called you?"

"Yes, he called me at home the night before I drove up."

"Did he call you often?"

"No. It was . . . the only telephone call that . . . we ever got from him."

"I see. And what did he say?"

"He said he couldn't have my mother in the house anymore,

that she was no longer safe being left alone. And he described the incident, what had happened the night before."

She left the kettle on, Emma explained. Jane Herrick came down to the kitchen at some time during the day. She put a tea bag in her favorite mug and started the kettle on the stove. The kettle boiled, and she poured her tea. But then she put the hot kettle down on the kitchen table, where a brown ring like a brand burned into the surface. And after that she left the room, with the burner still on, and a tea towel lying on the stove. The towel didn't catch fire, but that was a matter of a few inches.

"He said he'd come home and found that burner on, he didn't know for how many hours. And he said he was sorry, but he couldn't leave her alone in the house anymore. He had housemates now, but they . . . they weren't able to watch my mother, was how he put it."

Mr. Harlan nodded. "What did you do?"

"I called my sisters. But Anne was—traveling, I think, and my sister Charlie was—it really was something for me to do. I am the oldest daughter."

"You drove up on October fifteenth?"

"Yes."

The witness stand was next to the bench, to the jurors' left. Mr. Harlan stood mainly at a table to their right, where he had manila files in a stack. He would pull one out for each witness, and spread papers before him, and then proceed. With the later witnesses, the jurors found their eyes drawn back and forth, from the witness on the left to Mr. Harlan on the right, wondering when he would pull out another file. But when Emma testified, their gaze barely strayed from her. Mr. Harlan became simply a recurring sound, a steady, rhythmic bass line of questions.

She had checked in to the Taconic Motel, with no intention to stay at the Heights. It was only her mother's agitation that led her to remain there with her that night.

In Mr. Harlan's manner there was no prurience, no hint of salacious suggestion. His tone was that of the methodical physician who requires all the small details to complete a diagnosis. Emma's voice was a subtler instrument. Dignified, confident, but never familiar with him.

"Who else was present in the house when you arrived, Ms. Herrick?"

"Roy and Izzy."

"Was Mr. Hall there?"

"I don't think so. I didn't see him. I suppose it's possible. I have never met him, as far as I know."

She had arrived at about eight. She went quickly upstairs to find her mother pacing in her room, frantic about the "savages" downstairs. Emma explained that later, after they had spoken and her mother appeared to have calmed, she went back down to the kitchen, where she found Roy and Izzy.

"Did you notice anything on the stove—any dirty pans, or tin of grease, anything like that?"

"I don't remember."

"You don't recall about any food cooking there, or left there?"

"No, I'm sorry, I don't remember the stove, or food at all. The kitchen was . . . untidy . . . but I was just . . . I just wanted to talk to Mr. Murphy, and we . . . he . . . asked Izzy if she could leave us alone for a bit."

"Why did you want to talk to him alone?"

Again the doctor's manner. He had a way of burrowing in on these personal details that suggested the medical, not the forensic. The metronomic voice did not appear to be prying so much as gathering the small but important details of the case history.

"To explain that my mother wanted me to stay the night, and that I would try to get her to come with me in the morning. But there was something else, too."

At this the courtroom grew still. But she was calm—she was not defensive when Mr. Harlan gave voice to the question that was in every mind, and she explained.

"I had been upset with him about my sister-in-law. Izzy was an unhappy person. She had no confidence other than in her physical self, and she covered it with a show of—if I may, Mr. Harlan—of immature sexual bravado. She was vulnerable. She had an addictive personality. After she was expelled from Skidmore, she had connected with him somehow, and later, when she came over to Vermont and moved in with him, I thought he was taking advantage of her—that he was exploiting her. Whether to get back at my husband's family, or at me, or for some other reason, he was living up there and she was not an equal actor in the matter, I thought. I was a little angry with him, for taking advantage of her."

At this point the eyes of the jury were like eyes of fans at center court, going back and forth between them. Mr. Harlan asked, "Ms. Herrick, Roy Murphy had been your lover, had he not?"

"Yes, for one summer, when I was seventeen. But that was a long time ago, Mr. Harlan. It was long before I met my husband."

"I'm sorry to have to bring up these personal matters. But to understand the cause of this fire, I'm afraid we have to establish the motives of the persons in the house. That is the only purpose of this questioning."

It was the way she answered questions like this that made her so formidable, Harlan later thought. She did not even frown. It was almost as though she were gently chastising him. She said, "Mr. Harlan, I understand perfectly. It is your job to do so. You needn't apologize. Please ask everything that you feel you need to ask. There is nothing to conceal here."

"Then I have to ask—were you jealous of Miss Forrester?"

Their eyes flew to Emma, searching for some trace, some betrayal of that old passion. But they saw none.

"*No.* Izzy was my sister-in-law and I cared for her. But he was a powerful man, and I worried about her with him."

She did not sound haughty or defensive, and the jury nodded with this answer. And it was oddly true—what existed between Roy and Izzy was never sufficient to warrant anything like jealousy.

"You say you asked Miss Forrester to leave the two of you alone. Did she?"

"Yes, although not happily. She said something and left the room."

"What did she say?"

"I don't remember exactly. Something ugly. I think it was to the effect that I . . . needed to stop interfering in other people's lives."

"In other words, suggesting that she might have been jealous of you?"

This was where Emma was so very effective, Mr. Harlan again reflected—the way she would defuse a point by agreeing with it.

"Yes, I think she was. I think she was in love with Mr. Murphy, and he was, unfortunately, not in love with her, in my opinion."

Mr. Harlan asked: "Where did she go?"

"I don't know." Softly, she added, "I never saw her again."

"Did you then speak with Mr. Murphy?"

"I did."

"Tell us what was said, Ms. Herrick."

She took a breath to compose herself. Mr. Harlan would often return, in his mind, to her answer to this question. He was certain that she had not given him a complete account. There was steel in her manner, but a protective steel. Whether she had been protecting him, or herself, or someone else, he couldn't say.

"I told him he was abusing a girl and should be ashamed of himself, and he basically told me to mind my own business, in rather stronger terms than that."

"Ms. Herrick, it is important to know the terms."

"The exact terms were, to fuck off and leave him alone. That was his phrase. He told me to stop trying to control him when I had run from him years ago, that it was his life, and he had never tried to control mine."

"I see. Please proceed."

"It went like that for fifteen minutes or so, and then . . . it ended. I hadn't expected to accomplish much, frankly; it was not his way to apologize for anything. But I felt he needed to hear it, and maybe, with time, he would come around to a more responsible view. Anyway, I then went upstairs . . ."

"Where was Mr. Murphy when you went upstairs?"

"He had been in the kitchen," she said.

It seemed to Mr. Harlan as though there was just the slightest hesitation in her response. Or perhaps she was only being careful to respond accurately.

"Had been? I don't understand 'had been.' *Was* he in the kitchen?"

"Yes."

At this point Judge Hirshman called a halt and sent them all off into that gray midday to find lunch in Bennington, reminding the jurors, as he had when they had begun, that the proceedings were confidential. They hurried over their lunch in neighboring restaurants, anxious to return, wondering, Was he in the kitchen? They wondered, too, some of them, whether they might see Emma herself on the streets of Bennington during the break, although they did not.

When they returned to Courtroom Two after lunch, it seemed as though the light had already begun to fade. It was that time in November when the days are halfhearted, scarcely days at all, when the year has wearied and speeds toward its end. Inside, Mr. Harlan soon resumed, and Emma returned to her mother's agitation in the upstairs bedroom. Emma had again tried to persuade her to leave the Heights, and indeed Jane had said she couldn't endure to be left alone with the savages in the house. Emma sat with her on her bed.

"I was thinking that in a while she would calm down, and maybe I could get her to come with me to the motel. She kept saying she could never leave the Heights defenseless, that it needed her—the house, she meant. I dropped off. And when I woke again, I smelled smoke, and she was gone."

"You awoke in your mother's bedroom?"

No pause at all here—"Yes."

"On the second floor of the house?"

"Yes."

"After you entered that bedroom, and before you fell asleep, did you see Roy again that night?"

A beat, another slight pause. But she said very calmly, "No." Mr. Harlan held her gaze for a moment. She did not shrink from him. It would be "No."

"What happened next?"

"I woke up. There was smoke in the room and my mother was gone. I called out for her. I went to the corridor, and it was heavy with smoke, black smoke, and fire was burning over on the foyer side. I screamed for her and ran down the back stairs."

Mr. Harlan took a moment. He had removed one of his files and was frowning at a document. "Now, Ms. Herrick, in your statement, you said you carried your mother up the stairs. That would be the back stairs behind the kitchen, the same stairs that you ran down?"

"Yes."

"So you first ran down the back staircase, then carried your mother up the same staircase?"

"Yes."

He wanted to know how, exactly, she had carried Jane Herrick upstairs. He wanted her to describe it physically. "Over your shoulder? Did you lift her off the ground?"

"No. I put her arm over my shoulder and my arm was around her waist and we went step by step."

"So she was on her feet—she was walking?"

"Well, not really."

"But she was upright?"

"I suppose."

"The stairs were steep?"

"Yes."

"And she was walking—she was upright, and walking with difficulty?"

"I . . . I don't remember. I think I was mainly pulling her upstairs."

"*Pulling,* Ms. Herrick?"

"I just remember choking on smoke and being scared to death."

"And yet you went up, is that right?"

"Oh, yes, definitely," she said. The jury was thinking, Just when Harlan makes a point, she agrees with him. It was confusing. He continued:

"You found her lying on the floor?"

"Yes."

"Outside the kitchen?"

"Closer to the back stairs."

"The back stairs. The position where you found her, that is, where she lay, was in the corridor, near the door to the dining room?"

"Yes. Outside the kitchen, not far from the dining room door."

"And in the dining room, the windows opened to the porch?"

She considered it for a moment. "That's true."

"Why didn't you go out through the dining room?"

"I should have," she said, quietly.

"But you didn't."

She shook her head, took a moment. "The smoke and fire was coming from the kitchen, and the dining room door was toward the kitchen."

"But only a few feet?"

"Mr. Harlan," she said, "I was panicked. It was so hot and the smoke was black down there, I thought I would choke to death, I had to get up the stairs and away from it."

"But you said before there was smoke upstairs?"

"Less."

He nodded, frowned. "The fire was more intense in the kitchen?"

"Yes."

"And your mother was outside the kitchen?"

"Toward the stairs. As though she'd come from the kitchen."

On it went like that. Where precisely were the doors? How

exactly had she found her mother lying? What had she said to her, if anything? Volley after volley she calmly returned, on and on as, outside the windows of Courtroom Two, the afternoon waned. It was then that Emma testified that Jane Herrick had said something odd:

"I just wanted to make you a nice breakfast, I'm so sorry."

The jury watched Mr. Harlan write down the words. He looked at his notes for a moment.

"To make breakfast—it was midnight, or after, wasn't it?"

"I don't know what time it was. It was the middle of the night. It wasn't breakfast time, certainly."

"I'm just trying to understand your mother's reference to breakfast," he said.

But the jury understood. Everyone from Hoosick Bridge would understand that—as Emma would have known. She said, "Mr. Harlan, my mother had been behaving in a disoriented way for quite some time. She was a brilliant woman, she led a wonderful life for so many years, she had a tremendous mind, as everyone in town knew, but in the last years, after my father died, I'm afraid she was not herself. It was the onset of dementia. And when Roy, when Mr. Murphy, bought the Heights, it seemed to accelerate out of control. The fact that she was still living there at all was— Well, as you might imagine, my sisters and I had been trying to persuade her to move out, and she refused. She was miserable, but she refused. You could no longer really talk to her in a rational way, she had become so erratic."

"I want to be clear—she said, 'I just wanted to make you a nice breakfast, I'm so sorry'?"

"Yes."

"Now, Ms. Herrick, it was very smoky down there?"

"Yes."

"You were coughing?"

"Yes, I suppose we both were."

"And in that smoke, with that coughing, she was able to say all that about breakfast, and being sorry?"

"It was only a sentence."

For the first time, the witness sounded defensive. Mr. Harlan paused, affecting to look at his notes.

"That's what I remember," Emma went on.

"Was she coherent, Ms. Herrick?"

Emma frowned, recalling it. "No, I would not say she was."

"Sorry about what, exactly?" he asked.

"She didn't say. She just said, 'I'm so sorry, Emma, I just wanted to make you a nice breakfast.'"

"But you suppose she meant, sorry about the fire—that she'd been in the kitchen? Cooking something? Is that right, Ms. Herrick?"

"I would think, Mr. Harlan, that my mother could be forgiven."

It was a declaration. Judge Hirshman, the jurors, even Mr. Harlan felt its force. Only later did Harlan fully comprehend the resonance of her answer. In days and days of testimony, a few lines will resonate, and the ones that do become the melody the jury remembers. All the detail of chords and harmonies can be hung upon the right melodic line. *Jane Herrick could be forgiven.*

"In any event you carried her—or helped her—up the stairs. And then what?"

"I was trying to get away from that fire—it was intense down there near where I found her, and I was thinking of the window over the porch roof."

"Where was that window?"

"Off of the upstairs corridor, past the room where Mom was sleeping, where I had been sleeping that night."

"And through the main hall, on the other side?"

"Yes."

"But the fire was in the main hall, I thought you said?"

"Yes, it was."

"Burning up through that main hall?"

"Yes, but not so bad yet on the second floor, at least that is what I was thinking. I thought, That is our only way out."

"You were thinking more clearly now?"

Mr. Harlan had again the impression not that this woman was reliving a terrible event but rather that she was steel and would cut through him, this hearing, this episode. That she would do whatever was necessary to leave it all behind her. She was composed, she never lost her smile. Her beauty, Mr. Harlan thought, was formidable with these people. It was formidable even with him.

"I wasn't ever thinking clearly that night," she answered.

It was one of those statements that sounded like the truth, a truth that might explain any number of troubling details.

"But more clearly, a little more clearly, maybe?"

"I don't know, Mr. Harlan. It was all happening so fast. We were coughing and choking and it was dark and she was saying, 'I'm so sorry.' I thought, Porch roof window, get to the porch roof window."

"So you led your mother down the corridor?"

"Yes."

"Through the heat of the flames coming up the staircase from the main hall."

"Yes."

"What was that like?"

She answered patiently. "It was like—flames. It was like Hell, Mr. Harlan."

"And you went through anyway."

"Yes."

The state's attorney felt the restlessness in the room. As though the jury was thinking, Of course she went through whatever it took to get out—wouldn't you? She almost lost her life, why is he putting her through this? And yet it was at this point that he landed his first real blow, with the business about the toggles.

"You know," one of the jurors said to another, as they left that day, "I've had windows like that—he's *right*."

It had seemed interminable at first, all that close questioning about the window: where it was on the corridor and how high the bottom was from the floor, how tall it was and how wide, how big a step it was from that window to the porch roof—on and on with it, as though he were trying to get an architect's drawing from her. And that microscopic vision he seemed to have: Had she opened *one* window? Or two? Was there a storm window? Was it in the up position? And so on, as the jury, and even Judge Hirshman, were all thinking, Of course there was a storm window. But this was simply Mr. Harlan's methodical path to the toggles, and Emma Herrick's uncertain pause, when she had no answer for what seemed a long moment, before she quietly said yes, it was that kind of window— you did have to push both toggles in simultaneously to lift it.

"*Metal* toggles?"

"Yes."

Mr. Harlan had been standing in front of the table where his notes were spread out. Now he walked back behind the table, as the jury watched.

"Ms. Herrick, the fire was raging. Weren't the toggles hot to the touch?"

The eyes flew to the witness.

"Didn't they burn your fingers when you tried to move them?"

In the jury box, one could see the involuntary muscle memory working in their thumbs and forefingers, remembering how balky such windows are on the best of days. One could see them puzzling this out. And one could hear, for the first time, the slightest defensiveness in her voice.

"Mr. Harlan, I honestly don't remember. I was in a panic. I was choking. We went through that window. Whether I broke it, or pushed it out, or slid the toggles, whether they were hot toggles or cold toggles or no toggles, Mr. Harlan, I don't remember. I was going to get through that window, onto the porch roof, with my mother, and I did. That's what I remember."

He had been shuffling through the papers before finding the one from the EMTs—the one that said there were no scratches on the victims. And after that painful moment he was back to the window, where now, to the jury, the heavyset lawyer's fascination no longer seemed vexing.

"No one *helped* you with this window? Not your mother—not Mr. Murphy?"

"No."

"Where was Mr. Murphy?"

"I don't know—in the house—somewhere," she said.

"And Izzy—where was she?"

"I didn't see her. I guess we all know that my sister-in-law and Mr. Murphy died together in that horrible fire, Mr. Harlan, in the basement. But where they were then—I don't know."

"So you don't know when they went to the basement, or why?"

"I never went to the basement. I never saw them there."

The testimony returned to the two women on the roof. Nothing seemed to slake his thirst for details about that window. Who had gone out first, and who second. And whether she was standing, or sitting, whether Jane was then conscious, or unconscious. And how steep or shallow the pitch of the roof was.

"My sisters and I, when we were children, used to sit on that roof on summer nights, looking out at the town."

"Ms. Herrick, through all of this, where was Roy Murphy?"

She looked straight at him, and never changed her expression. "I already told you, Mr. Harlan. Somewhere in the house. I can't say where."

*Steel*, he thought.

The jurors were beginning to feel stiff in the joints now, with this long day of questioning, stirring in their seats, frowning as they thought ahead about the errands that would need running after court, on their way home. Meanwhile Mr. Harlan had found a manila envelope. He pulled from it a photograph and resumed. "Ms. Herrick, when you reached the roof, what were you wearing?"

This caught their interest. They could see the back of that photograph.

"Blue jeans and a blouse, I think, and a cardigan."

"But you were not wearing a sweater on the roof, were you?"

"I honestly can't remember."

He came slowly forward. "Here is a photograph taken a few

minutes later, when you were down on the lawn, next to the ladder truck." He was by the stand now and handed her the photograph. "That's you, isn't it?"

"Yes."

"That is some sort of man's coat that you are wearing?"

"It's dark, I really don't . . ."

"A Carhartt? It looks big for you. Do you see that?"

She looked at the photograph. "Yes."

"Is that your jacket?"

"No."

"Was it Roy Murphy's?"

"I don't know."

"How did you get it?"

"I can't remember."

"It wasn't in your mother's room?"

"I wouldn't think so."

"So how did you come by it?"

"I must have grabbed it after I'd gone downstairs for Mom. There was a coatrack down there, by the back door."

He was peering at the photograph. "Is that some sort of necklace?" he asked. "Did you have some sort of necklace on?"

To the men, she sounded defensive again when she answered, "I really can't remember, Mr. Harlan." The three women on the jury were wondering if he would ever leave her alone.

Perhaps sensing this, Mr. Harlan backed away and returned to the table. "So let's review. You rushed downstairs to find your mother collapsed in the back corridor, but conscious, so that she could tell you she was sorry, she just wanted to make breakfast for you. The fire was roaring and the smoke was intense. You found a man's coat somewhere down there, and put it on. A moment later, your mother was on her feet, as you climbed the stairs together. And then a few seconds after that, after you ran down the hall and pushed her outside, she had collapsed, and was unconscious."

"Yes," she said. More steel.

Emma wished at that moment that Anne was with her. Since

her father's death she had felt the comfort of her sister's fidelity, taken quick nourishment from her smile. She loved both her sisters, but Charlie had responded to Tom Herrick's death by pulling away from the family, and though Emma loved Charlie, she had never felt the link to her that she had to Anne. Anne knew Emma's light and knew her darkness, knew her to the core and loved that core. Emma wanted only a glance, like a marathoner's snatch of a Dixie cup at a water station. A fleeting gulp and then she would be refreshed for the next mile. But she was alone. The gallery was empty in this secret proceeding.

Mr. Harlan saw it. He saw almost everything.

"What happened then, Ms. Herrick?"

"I heard the sirens. I saw the trucks coming. And I was screaming for Roy and Izzy."

"How long did it take for the firefighters to reach you on the roof?"

"It took forever, Mr. Harlan."

And there it ended. The lawyer walked slowly back to his table and began to hunt for the next file.

"You may step down, Ms. Herrick," said Judge Hirshman.

"Thank you, but . . . There is something further, something I thought . . ."

Mr. Harlan glanced up from his table. "There is no question pending," he said.

She looked helplessly, from the judge to the lawyer, and back. "But . . ."

"Ms. Herrick, you may step down," the judge repeated.

She left the courtroom as she had come to it: alone. The door swung shut behind her and the inquest moved on to the next witness. Outside, she found the hall empty. She put on her overcoat and then listened to her footsteps echo as she walked along the corridor toward the staircase. On the ground floor she began to hurry for the door, but a thought came to her and she stopped.

In the clerk's office she asked for a piece of paper and an

envelope. She stood at the counter for a few minutes, writing out a note in longhand. She signed the letter, folded it, and sealed it in the envelope.

"Could you give this to the judge?" she asked. "Judge Hirshman. In the—"

"The inquest, I know," the clerk said. "You're Ms. Herrick." He smiled, as if by way of apologizing for knowing all about her. He took the envelope from her. "It's a little . . . irregular."

"But important. You should give it to him," Emma said.

A few minutes later she was gone, driving south again for New York.

# TWENTY

"*I*t's so sad," Toni was saying.

"What?" Ernest rattled his spoon against the side of the mug.

Toni stood at the coffeemaker, refilling the machine with fresh coffee, remembering the matriarch who for so long had, in one way or another, presided over the town.

"After all she'd been through, that it had to be her."

"Jane, you mean."

"Setting fire to that house, poor thing. She was so proud of it," Toni said. "After everything else that's happened to her. It's just as well she didn't make it. It would have killed her to know. It would have been the last straw."

"You think it was her?"

It was still dark, and quiet in Toni's Lunch that morning: just a low burble from a few of them out at the tables, and Ernest at the counter. There would be more of them later, recounting and urging and arguing about all the secret testimony.

"That's what Emma testified—I mean, that's just what I heard," she said.

"Emma's testimony."

"That state's attorney from Montpelier had her in there for two days, you know," Toni said.

"You think Emma was telling the truth?"

The word from Bennington was that the state's attorney had now moved on to the volunteer firefighters, calling first to the stand George Brassard, who worked maintenance down at the college in Williamstown. He'd been the first up Washington Street that night, at the wheel of Ladder One. Short, broad chested, quick with a smile, eager to help, Brassard was popular in Hoosick Bridge. He had a lot he might have said about that fire, about how they fought it, and how astonishingly powerful it was, but Mr. Harlan didn't seem interested in that. His concern had nothing to do with firefighting at all, actually—mainly it was about Brassard's first glimpse of the Heights, as the fire truck reached the corner of Washington and Spring, and Al Palovic, riding in the cab, saw someone on the roof.

"Some one? One person?" Mr. Harlan asked.

"There was someone up there, someone at the window."

"Someone inside the house at the window looking out, or outside, on the porch roof at the window, looking in?"

"Outside, looking in. And maybe both. I was pretty sure I seen a person on the roof, at the window."

He couldn't say whether it was Emma Herrick, or someone else. What he remembered was a dark shape in the night, a silhouette moving before smoke and flames, a shape busy with activity somehow, doing something. "It seemed like that they were taking someone through the window."

"I don't understand."

"Helping as someone came out, or was eased out. With her arms, you know, at the window? Like she was helping on the outside and somebody was inside."

But he had not made out any other person inside the house. They were in a hurry, they had to get the ladder up and the lines hooked up. This was a brief observation, having little to do with what they'd had to do, or try to do to fight that fire, and he left the stand with a look of frustration. He'd had to miss half a day of work to come up there, and give the lawyers all that formal testimony, and they never asked him about the fire.

Two days they had her in there, and then George Brassard after, and the word was, there were things that didn't add up. Afterward, all around town, the talk was to the effect that maybe Emma herself had had something to do with this, because there were things that didn't square up clean. That lawyer kept going back through her story, and there were said to be little points you wouldn't hardly notice at first. Oh, he was a sharp one, that lawyer from Montpelier! And they would quickly add, "At least, that's what I heard." Because they all knew the inquest was supposed to be a secret.

Emma Herrick—how did the professor say it—that the Heights was the burden of her past? She had to set her mother free from it, and herself? He had a way with words, the professor.

It was reported that she'd been upstairs, gone downstairs, then claimed to have gone upstairs again, when she could easily have gotten out through the dining room windows.

It was reported she'd gotten into an argument with Roy Murphy.

It was reported that she'd been wearing Roy's coat. After.

Why?

Over morning coffee the men in Toni's Lunch were spinning a theory. It was jealous rage, they said. Emma could not forgive him for having that other girl in her house, in Emma's very bedroom. She could close herself to her childhood lover, but not to his taking up with another girl, particularly one she was related to by marriage. Many of those who still smarted from the Ponzi scheme drew this conclusion.

For Toni, this was absurd. She could locate nothing like a murderous intent in Emma's personality. She remembered the night of the fire, when Emma was hysterical, up on that roof.

Hadn't the Gilsons from next door heard her scream for Roy Murphy? No one who stood outside the yellow police tape that night, spellbound by the awful sight of the Heights going up in flames, could forget that. Could Emma really have set a fire that killed three people?

That was the very point made by still other doubters. Maybe neither Emma nor Jane set it—wasn't it just a little convenient, they asked, that the fire should be determined an accident, caused poignantly and without malice by the matriarch who had loved the place so fiercely, who had slipped into dementia, and then tragically been claimed by the conflagration that, without wit or intent, she had set off?

A steady wind blew all day from the west, stirring up the last leaves that still lay by the roadsides and along the sidewalks in town, stuffing them into garden beds and rock walls, where they would remain until spring. Overhead the sky never emerged from its morning shroud. All day the wind rattled the tall windows of Courtroom Two, as though trying to get away from that pallor. But the sun seemed to want no part of the proceedings. Pale at midday, dipping in and out as the clouds raced before it, the sun hurried down to the horizon in the afternoon. Outside the passersby hurried, too, pulling collars close, acquiring again for the long months ahead a shortened stride and hunched shoulders. It seemed to the jurors that they had scarcely returned from lunch when, outside the tall windows, it was dark again.

Mr. Harlan had begun that third day of the inquest by returning yet again to the porch roof, this time with Albert Palovic, who rode in the cab with George Brassard and was the first up the ladder. And again he wanted to know what he'd seen first—just as the fire truck reached the crest of Washington Street—one person?

"I can't say. Shapes, movement. A person on the roof, at the window, maybe two people, I knew someone was up there."

"Did you see someone inside the house at that window?"

"No, I couldn't see that."

"How long did it take you to get the ladder to the roof?"

"Not long after we got the truck up there. I don't know, a minute?"

The attorney seemed to want to follow Al up that ladder, to relive each small observation. Al explained that as he clambered off the ladder he had found Emma up there, crouching next to her mother, who lay unconscious on the roof.

"And Emma Herrick, what was her condition?"

"She was hysterical. She was screaming, 'He's in there, he's in there, you've got to go get him.'"

"And get him?"

"Yes, sir."

"Get *them*, or get *him*?"

"Get *him*. 'You got to go in there and get him.'"

"Did she give a name, at all, of who was in there?"

Al nodded. "Roy."

"Roy's in there?"

"Yes, sir. 'Roy's in there, he's in there, you've got to get him out of there.'"

"Mr. Palovic, it was not, '*They're* in there'?"

"I don't think so."

"And not 'Izzy'?"

"I don't remember hearing that name."

"What did you do?"

Mr. Harlan took him then through the confrontation, argument, call it what you will—Al Palovic's standoff with Emma Herrick there on the roof. The fire behind was roaring, loud, the heat intense, and the roar of trucks and sirens came up the hill behind them. In that din the two of them yelled at each other: she for him to get in there, to help Roy, and he for her to get down. He lifted Mrs. Herrick up and carried her to the ladder and then down. And then he climbed back up.

"And she's still screaming I got to go in there, and I says, 'Ma'am, get down.' The porch was involved in flame then, it was going to go. And she says, 'You got to go in there after him,' and

I says, 'Ma'am, first get down this ladder.' And finally she did go down the ladder. I says, 'Can you make it down there all right?' and she says, 'Yes, yes, just get in there and get him!'"

A blast of wind shook the windows in Courtroom Two, and Al stopped. Mr. Harlan turned, and they all looked over to make sure the wind hadn't actually broken glass. Outside the sky was gray and raw. It would be a gloomy respite from this testimony when lunch came. A moment went by before Mr. Harlan put another question, and Palovic resumed. He had not gone in, of course. He could not do so. No one could have gone in at that point. As he explained it: "I tried, Mr. Harlan. I wanted to. Brendan, he was up there with me by that point, too; he got up there and we went back toward the window, but it was just totally involved."

"Brendan Stern—another firefighter in the department?"

"Yes. He came up after me. But we couldn't get right up to the window, nor the one next to it, it was too hot and the flames were pouring out of there. We couldn't get near it. I wish we could of. I think about that a lot, and I wish we could of, but we just couldn't. I'm sorry."

At this point Judge Hirshman made a rare interruption, leaning over the bench to reassure the witness. "Mr. Palovic, you have nothing to apologize for. You did your duty heroically and helped save one life that night, and tried to save another. You have the admiration of everyone in the room. I think we'll break for lunch now."

Al was grateful for that break. He hung his head to compose himself for a moment, then rose and nodded politely as the jurors filed out.

After lunch, Mr. Harlan changed the subject, back to Emma Herrick.

"Mr. Palovic, when you found Ms. Herrick on the roof, what was she wearing?"

He didn't remember, but the attorney pressed him. "A nightgown? Pajamas? A ball gown with a diamond necklace? Try."

"Well, it wasn't none of those, I don't think. It was clothes, I mean, not bed clothes, not a bathrobe or nightgown or anything, and not dressed up, it was . . ." He frowned.

"A coat?"

He closed his eyes, tried to summon it. "Pants, and some kind of coat. A baggy coat, I think."

"A Carhartt coat?"

"Could have been. Big, baggy."

"Like a man's coat?"

"Could have been."

Mr. Harlan saved him with a merciful detail. "Mr. Palovic," he said, "I do have one question more. Do you remember, was the storm window open, in the up position?"

Al rubbed his chin for a moment and took a breath. Then he answered, quietly, "I stepped on it."

"What do you mean, you stepped on it?"

"It was lying on the roof, and I stepped on it by accident and broke it."

"The storm window—lying on the porch roof?"

"Yeah, it was lying on the porch roof, the whole window, a metal-framed storm window. I don't think it was broken, the glass I mean, until I stepped on it, because I remember breaking it."

"In your experience, would the force of the fire throw the window out of the frame?"

"Well, sir, a fire will pop the glass sometimes, but not throw the whole window, metal, glass, and all, out of the frame. Not that I've seen."

"It was large?"

"Yes, sir. That was a beautiful old house, the Heights. It had big windows on it like you don't hardly see anymore."

"And the whole metal window had been torn, or pushed straight out from the frame. Would that have been easy?"

"You'd of had to be pretty strong. Or pretty desperate. Or both."

Harlan paused, checking his notes. He thumbed back a page or two. "Were you able to revive Jane Herrick?"

"When I brought her down the ladder, the EMTs were right there with a stretcher, and we laid her down and they put the mask on her. I seen them get a mask on her, and I never saw any more than that. They was running her back to the ambulance, and I guess they took her up to Southern Vermont Medical, is what I heard."

"You never spoke to Jane Herrick?"

"No."

"She never said anything to you on the ladder, for example?"

"No. She was unconscious."

It was then, he explained, that Billy Hall Jr. had made his brief appearance. "Well, sir, I needed to get back up that ladder to get Emma Herrick, she was still up there, and that's when a red car pulled up right on the grass and a guy jumped out of it and come running over."

"William Hall Jr.?"

"I believe that was his name, sir. That's what I heard later. I didn't know him. He come running up to me as I was heading back up on the truck and he grabs my arm and says, 'Is he all right? Is he in there?'"

"Who?"

"Well, I guess he meant Roy Murphy. He goes, 'Is he in there?'"

"Could it have been, 'Is *she* in there?'"

Al considered it. "I thought it was 'he.' But now that you mention it, it happened pretty quick and in all that noise and confusion it might have been 'she.' I wasn't really listening, I was just trying to get him off me and get up there."

"What happened then?"

"It was all quick, like a second or two. Brian Stargell I think it was, Officer Stargell I should say, from Hoosick Bridge PD, he was right there and he pulled the man off me. I says, 'Get back!' or something. I yelled at him, I can't remember what I said. I never really spoke to him, and Brian come and pulled him back."

"And that's when you went up the ladder and got Ms. Herrick, as you said before?"

"Yes."

The sun had set when the jurors hurried from the building to their cars. They were trying to picture Emma Herrick on the roof that night, a hysterical version of the young woman who had so calmly taken questions. But she had left town as soon as her own questioning was done.

Roy Murphy had been absent from the accounts of the firefighters, scarcely visible even in Emma's testimony. To the jury he was a silhouette, and his absence made the proceedings incomplete. The jurors tried to picture him in that house, but when they strove to re-create his motive that night, it came up a blank to them—as his motives had always seemed, years before, to the adults who had tried to fathom the inscrutable boy. And that is why, although Emma held them spellbound, they were hungry for Joe Rouleau's account. The crew chief provided them with the only real glimpse of Roy Murphy himself.

He was lean, tall, with dark hair in a ponytail. And it was obvious from the moment he rose, uneasily, and walked to the stand that Joe didn't like being there. He wouldn't touch the rail with his hands. He didn't like strangers, lawyers from out of town—from as far away as Montpelier, he'd heard—coming down here with their poking and prying. When the lawyer started by nosing into what sort of man Roy Murphy was, asking him to talk about his personality and such, he arched an eyebrow, and his lips tightened. And then shook his head, as though a gesture would better express it.

The gesture did not satisfy Mr. Harlan. "Sir?" he asked.

"Boss was toughest on himself. He worked all the time, expected everyone else to."

"He was what, five, ten years younger than you?"

"Eight years younger, yes."

"And yet you called him Boss?"

"That's what he was," Joe said.

"Was he a difficult man to work for?"

Rouleau shifted in the witness chair. He cast an uneasy glance at the jurors, then back at the heavyset lawyer standing by the table with all those files of papers. "Depends what you mean by that," he said quietly.

"I mean, temperamental. Prone to anger."

"Then no, not at all that way," said Joe.

"Tell me how it depends, then," Mr. Harlan said.

Joe looked around again, but there was no escape. The judge nodded slowly, as though nudging him forward.

"He was a hard man," he said. "Demanding. There was no BS about him. So you could say difficult. But he wasn't the kind to yell and scream and hold grudges and such. He'd just say do it, and you'd better do it. He said to me, 'I'll pay you more, and I'll work you harder. And if that's what you want, you're in, and if you don't want that, you're out.' I was fine with it."

Rouleau glanced back at the judge, as though to say, There, I've done what I had to. Let's move on.

Mr. Harlan had a new file in his hand now. He removed some papers and asked, "Did you know Billy Hall Jr., Mr. Rouleau?"

"You could say."

Harlan then took Joe through Billy Hall Jr.'s arrival at Murphy's Landscaping the previous summer. It had been the first time Roy Murphy had been away since he started the business. At the shop they'd wondered whether he finally was taking a vacation, only later learning that he'd gone south to get his buddy. The word around the shop was that Hall, who was from Mississippi, had had a tough time after he got out of the service. He was drinking too much and couldn't find work. And so Boss had brought him up north, up to his house at the Heights, taken him in there, and then up to the shop for a job.

"Where he was assigned to your crew," Mr. Harlan said. "How did that work out?"

"Not so good." Joe frowned again. But he had known they were going to ask about this part. "Hall, he didn't have the same attitude about work. He just never had the same attitude. The guy could make you laugh, he loved to talk, and he was funny the way he talked and all. But on our crews, we work and expect each other to work. And he was just, slow. Like, if he went for a part or something, he'd be gone half the day. Now you're down a man plus your machine's down because you don't have the part. It was frustrating. It just didn't work out."

"Did this create problems at the shop?"

"Guys felt funny about it, like, Boss works our butts off, and why is this guy special, that type of thing. I went in to see him about it after work one night. Tried to explain to him."

"What happened?"

"Boss, he got an angry look. And says, 'Billy Hall Jr. is my brother. We were in Afghanistan, Joe, you understand that?' And I says, 'Yes, I understand.' I didn't really. I knew that they'd been together through something bad, that's all."

"Did he say anything else, Mr. Rouleau?"

"He says, 'You need to manage this, Joe. This is the way it's going to be.' And I says, 'All right, boss, I will.' But it just didn't work out on account of the drinking."

"The drinking?"

The jurors could tell Joe hadn't liked Hall. Still, he seemed to dislike even more the whole business of having to go over these things in a courtroom, as though they held him responsible, somehow. After a moment's pause, Joe continued.

"Hall would turn up hungover, or not turn up at all. On jobs he'd start sneaking off. So we were at a customer's this one time, she's an elderly lady, Mrs. Dana over on Royalton Street, she come out on the front steps and starts yelling at me, we got a drunk working on her backyard, he's back behind her barn with a flask. And she don't appreciate it one bit. Well, that was kind of the last straw, you know? I had to tell Boss, and Boss, he was pis— he was mad, with me, with Hall, with the whole thing. So he fired him."

"He fired Hall?"

"In the shop next morning. He says, 'Billy, you got a home

with me, but you can't work here no more. My business is my business, and if you can't respect it, you can't be here.'"

"When did this happen?"

"It was before the fire. A while, I'd say."

"A while," Mr. Harlan repeated. "Did Hall answer?"

"He was yelling at him. F this and f that. Who the f did Boss think he was, a general or something, he was f'ing this and that and Hall didn't need none of his f'ing charity and f him. That type thing. He went yelling out of there and drove off. And we didn't see him no more."

"Until the day of the fire?"

Joe nodded grudgingly. "Yeah, he come back to the shop that afternoon, around four. He was drunk. Gets out of his car in the lot, starts screaming over at the shop, like at Boss, like calling him out. I was in one of the bays unloading my truck. Screaming at Boss to come out and he would f him up, he was tired of his, you know, whatever. Just yelling and cursing him to come out."

"What did Mr. Murphy do?"

"Boss wasn't there when he come in. Couple of minutes later, Boss drives into the lot and climbs down from his truck and Hall is still standing there in the lot, cursing at him—f you, Bossman Murphy, who the f do you think you are, and such. He called him Bossman as a kind of insult," he explained.

"Go on."

"Boss was saying something, we couldn't hear it. Trying to calm him down. Hall keeps yelling and screaming and he starts kicking Boss's truck."

"Kicking his truck?"

"Front quarter panel. Kicking at it."

"What did Mr. Murphy do then?"

"At first, nothing. Just stands there. And then, Hall gets done with kicking and turns around and takes a swing at Boss, misses. He's stumbling around. Boss still trying to talk to him. And Hall swung again and then Boss dropped him."

"What do you mean, dropped him?"

"I mean one punch. Flicked out so fast you didn't hardly see it. And Hall's down."

"What happened next?"

"I was standing by the bay door watching, and Boss come running over to me and says, 'Joe, we need to get him home. Help me get him in my truck.' He was a big, heavy guy, he was moaning, kind of, but we got him up and in the truck. And then Boss drove him home. I drove Hall's car."

"Up to the Heights?"

"Yes. I helped Boss carry him upstairs."

"Was he awake at that point?"

"Yeah, he was."

"What passed between him and Mr. Murphy?"

"Well, it was kind of weird. They didn't hardly talk none. But Hall must of woke up in the truck, because when we got to the house he was weepy, and Boss was like, 'Gonna be all right, Billy, you sleep this off, you'll be fine.'"

"Weepy," Mr. Harlan repeated.

"Yes, sir."

"Was anybody else there?"

"Mrs. Herrick. She seen us coming and run upstairs and I heard a door slam. I didn't talk to her or anything. We carried Hall upstairs and put him down on the bed and Boss says, 'Thanks, Joe,' and I left."

"Was Emma Herrick there?"

He shook his head. "I didn't see her."

Mr. Harlan returned to his table to retrieve the photograph again, and then came up to the stand, alongside Joe. Rouleau's eyes narrowed, focused on the back of the photo in the lawyer's hand, as Mr. Harlan approached. "I want to show you a photograph, taken at the scene, that night, during the fire."

He passed it over the rail. At first, Joe wouldn't take it from him. Mr. Harlan waited patiently until he leaned over to look at it.

"Do you see Emma Herrick, there by the ladder truck?"

"Looks like."

"She appears to be wearing a large coat of some kind, do you see that?"

"Looks like."

"And a necklace. Or something around her neck. Do you recognize the necklace?"

"No."

"Mr. Rouleau, did Roy Murphy have a coat like that—I mean that he would wear to work, that you would see at the shop?"

Joe stared at the photograph for quite a while before looking up, and then his face seemed to do most of the testifying. It said that he didn't like where this was going. Of course that was Boss's coat, but these people were all dead now, and what was the point of snooping? Some things were nobody's damned business.

"Can't really tell from the picture," he said at last.

"And the necklace again—no idea what that is?"

"Can't really tell," he said.

Mr. Harlan stood by the witness stand awhile longer, but he knew that Joe Rouleau was not going to help him along with this.

"One more thing. Since the fire, have you seen Mr. Hall?"

"No, sir, I don't know where he is."

"We haven't been able to find him. Any idea where he might be, or who might help us locate him?"

"No, sir, he never really made too many friends up here. I really don't know."

Down in Hoosick Bridge the second inquest continued early the following morning. There were four of them in the booth at Toni's, each with coffee in a little white mug with black piping, three with their grilled corn and blueberry muffins slathered in butter, and the question before the panel was Ernest Gillfoyle's obvious thing. That was what it had circled back to. What about *Hall*? Wasn't he the obvious explanation?

Except it was a harder case now. Rouleau had described ("At least, that's what I heard!") what they already knew, dressed up with facts they hadn't known before. The detail didn't change the central point of Hall's humiliation that afternoon. Well, maybe a little: Toni said she heard that Roy Murphy himself drove the drunken Hall back up to the Heights, and helped him upstairs to sleep it off, and Hall apparently sobbed as he did so. It didn't seem to fit "humiliation" exactly.

Mel pointed out another thing, too, which was, if Hall set the fire, why did he come back to the scene? Why did he all but storm the ladder, wide eyed, as urgent on the ground as Emma was up on that simmering porch roof, both of them frantic for Roy Murphy's safety?

Ernest held court at the booth. He had the explanation. This is the way the disease goes, he said, his voice rising. The guy would bounce between extremes: one minute it would be violence, the next, blubbering contrition. "That's how they are," he repeated. "That's just the way it is with PTSD."

The men in Toni's nodded politely and in choral unison stirred coffee and were silent, pondering it. Maybe, they thought, that is the way it is with PTSD. Still . . .

# TWENTY-ONE

*H*aving buttoned the last clean shirt, and pressed the last of the handkerchiefs that he'd brought down from Montpelier, having checked out of the Holiday Inn on a cold morning and put his suitcase in the trunk of the old Saab sedan, Mr. Harlan drove over to the courthouse for the last time, and reconvened the formal inquest. He called to the stand his final witness, Fire Department Chief Steven Albert. With his report in hand, Chief Albert stepped up, was sworn, and began to describe the forensic evidence.

Like Mr. Harlan himself, the chief was a student of fires: their chemical births, their volume, their destructive power, the clues they leave behind; a lover of V-shaped burn patterns, of chemical assays of unlikely relics: stone, linoleum, concrete. His testimony went less like question-and-answer and more like a seminar between old friends, to which the jury had been invited. This was the area where Harlan expected no surprise, and yet it was the chief's examination that produced the biggest surprise of the proceeding—the theory that even patient Mr. Harlan had not anticipated.

The Heights had burned to the ground in a fire of profound power and heat. The miracle was that it hadn't leapt the gap to the nearest neighbor's, for at its height the fire generated flames that the chief estimated reached seventy feet in the air. The Heights collapsed, was consumed in that inferno, and the heat of that fire left behind three blackened streaks against the sky, chimneys rising implausibly from the hole, a rickety frame of charred timbers, and a mountain of ash. An acrid miasma hung over the town—people said the smell of char had gotten into their clothes. So hot was the fire that it was not until the next night that the chief and his men could do their thorough search for the bodies. They had illuminated the smoky site with floodlights, and a watchful crowd stood outside the barrier of yellow tape put up by the police department. They stood watching because, even that night, no one knew for sure who had been inside.

But Mr. Harlan would come to each thing in its proper order.

Chief Albert introduced the jury, which now was growing weary, to the mysteries of accelerant and burn patterns, to the different clues left by a fire set in paper and one ignited by gasoline. At the Heights, he said, the destruction was so complete that there was little to go on. The evidence appeared to show that the first concentration of the fire was in the kitchen area, either in the kitchen itself or in the basement below it, and that there was at least some gasoline involved in that fire. But Mr. Harlan was most interested in the bar, chain, and metal hardware pieces of Roy Murphy's chain saw, disassembled and scattered on the basement floor, beneath the ash.

"How did you know it was disassembled?"

"Because of the bar and the bolts. All the plastic and rubber components had been consumed, but the bar and the bolts that hold it, along with the cylinder, piston, and other metal parts, had been taken apart."

"Did you draw any conclusion?"

"A chain saw torn down might have been a source of gasoline and ignition. If a person were smoking while working on the motor, for example. On the other hand, that saw might have been torn down in the basement a month before. It could be irrelevant. No way of knowing."

"Did your chemical assay show signs of gasoline?"

"Yes, although limited." The chief walked them through the test results. "We couldn't draw a firm conclusion," he said. "We may have been seeing evidence of a gasoline combustion in the basement, or as Ms. Herrick described, some kind of stove fire, a grease fire that might have been inadvertently set by Jane Herrick, and later consumed gasoline tools in the basement below."

"Now, Chief Albert, in your inspection you observed the bulkhead steps in the basement?"

"Yes, on the north side, roughly beneath the kitchen."

"The bulkhead opened onto the back lawn, is that right?"

"Yes."

"A person exiting that bulkhead would not be seen by neighbors?"

"No."

"He—or she—could then cross the rear lawn, go through a stand of fir trees on the property line, and emerge on Francis Lane?"

"That is correct, Mr. Harlan."

"Whereas other escape routes from the house, like the front door, and the back door, all are positioned where neighbors might see a person leaving?"

"Yes, that's right."

Mr. Harlan made a note, pausing so that the point would sink in before he underlined it with a question. "And so, Chief, is there still another possibility? Could a fire have been set in the kitchen, and the arsonist—or arsonists—fled to the basement, planning to escape through the bulkhead?"

"It's possible, Mr. Harlan, although that theory leaves questions as well."

"Such as?"

"From the position of the skeletal remains, Mr. Murphy and Miss Forrester were overcome before they could escape the basement. And if the fire had started on the floor above, in the kitchen, it seems unlikely that an arsonist, fleeing to the basement, would have been so quickly overcome."

"Because?"

"Because fire burns upward."

Mr. Harlan nodded. "I see. What if the fire had been set in the basement, beneath the kitchen, by arsonists planning to escape through the bulkhead?"

"The arsonist might have been overcome, by a gasoline explosion, for example. An old basement will often have other combustible materials, and it may have gone up quickly. Maybe there was gas oil, for the saw, in a plastic jerrican. The can would have been consumed in the fire, but the chemical assay showed some residue of plastics."

"Was that conclusive?"

"No, it could have been unrelated. In any event, if a fire started there, fuel might have generated fumes and smoke that would quickly asphyxiate the victims."

"Thank you, Chief. Let's turn then to the two . . . victims. Was it you who found the bodies?"

At this, even Judge Hirshman leaned forward. It was indeed the chief himself, and Brendan Stern, who had found them in the basement on the next night, buried in ash. In deference to the Forrester family, and to Eliza Murphy, the chief adopted respectful terms to describe the grisly discovery within that thick bed of coals, white-hot that night, and later soaked to mud by the fire hoses. Chief Albert answered Harlan's methodical questions with the phrase "skeletal remains."

"Can you describe for us the position of those . . . remains, Chief Albert?"

"About eighteen inches from the bulkhead step."

"And their position relative to each other?"

"They were . . . they were one atop the other," he said. Here he paused, searching for a word. The jury could swear he blushed. "The remains were . . . intermingled."

\* \* \* \*

Before the inquest, it was widely known in town that the remains of Roy Murphy and Izzy Forrester had been found in the basement. That much Brendan Stern had leaked, and it had been in the newspaper. But the details had not been disclosed—certainly not that the bodies were physically entwined! Rumors of this testimony electrified Hoosick Bridge, where people conjured from Chief Albert's embarrassment, and that awkward word, *intermingled*, a kind of last, insane coitus between the two half-mad people, the soldier bent on vengeance, and the self-hating girl whom he had drawn into that unhappy mansion. *Intermingled*—wrapped together in white-hot passion!

And now there were at least two contrapuntal lyrics lodged in the jury's emotional songbook. *Jane Herrick could be forgiven.* And: *The remains were intermingled.* The new rumor pointed to a new resolution to the confusing point and counterpoint of the evidence: as Professor Emmanuel put it, that Roy Murphy had been hoist with his own petard. This was the conclusion that satisfied them— until Emma's question was asked.

They were weary of it now, Chief Albert's catalog of forensic evidence, the fragments of soapstone, of floor joist, of stove metal, the limited surviving evidence of burn patterns, the positioning. It had been a long week, and they frowned at his chart, up on an easel, nodded quickly at each point of testimony, as though to hurry to conclusion his explanations of where the items and the skeletal remains were found. In the afternoon, the chief summed up precisely where he had begun. The fire might have started in the kitchen. There were signs of gasoline accelerant on scraps of recovered soapstone. It appeared there had also been a grease fire in the area of the stove, evident from streaking and residue on the metal and stone surfaces that had been recovered from the scene. But he could not be certain. "In light of the evidence suggesting chain saw repairs," he said, "it is also possible that the gasoline residue derived from a fire that started in the basement."

At that uncertain moment, the hearing was on the point of ending. To the town, and maybe the jury, too, the forensics now seemed beside the essential point. The bodies had been intertwined, skeletons coupling in macabre fashion. That testimony, which had somehow leaked earlier in the day, gathered people into little knots in Stewart's and on Main Street, to spread that word—*intermingled.*

"Rodin's *Kiss*," murmured the professor, recounting the news to Ernest Gillfoyle.

In Courtroom Two, the chief had finished and was gathering up his report. But before he could leave the stand, Judge Hirshman interrupted. "Chief Albert, wait a moment there, if you would. Mr. Harlan, would you come forward?"

The jurors strained to hear the whispered conference at the sidebar.

"Mr. Harlan, the other day my chambers received a letter from Ms. Emma Herrick. I confess I wasn't sure what to do about it. It is quite irregular, of course. But the letter claimed there was a question that needed to be asked of Chief Albert, and having now heard the testimony, I wonder whether she's right. But that's for you to say. Here." He handed Mr. Harlan the handwritten letter.

"A question?" Mr. Harlan was taken aback. For a moment he didn't know what to say. "I . . . This *is* irregular."

"I agree, Mr. Harlan. It is your inquest. It is not for me to say how this should be conducted. But it strikes me that you may want to ask Chief Albert."

What was that whispering? the jurors wondered. What was that paper the judge had given to Mr. Harlan? The lawyer seemed to redden, as he stood by the bench reading the paper, embarrassed that he had not thought to ask this himself. And with Mr. Harlan, forensic curiosity for the last detail was a higher urgency. At the end of this long week, contemplating a long and solitary drive north in his aging Saab, he realized that he could not end the proceeding without putting this question.

"May I make this part of the record?" he asked.

"State's exhibit . . . forty-three," the judge said.

Mr. Harlan returned to his table with the letter in his hand. The room fell silent again.

He cleared his throat, appearing, for the first and last time during that hearing, to be flustered, to have lost a sense of timing, or control. He put the question.

Chief Albert's eyes went wide with recognition, and a kind of embarrassment, that he, too, had not considered it before. And then he had to admit, yes, it was possible Roy Murphy had been overcome by smoke on an *upper* floor, and when the house had collapsed and been consumed with fire, his body fell through, coming to rest, at last, in the basement, atop the body of Izzy Forrester.

That was possible. But it was also possible—indeed, the chief had to concede, it was more than possible, it was *plausible*—that *both* Roy and Izzy had been on an upper floor, and fallen through together.

"Chief," Mr. Harlan summed up, "suppose for a moment she had been overcome, and he had been carrying her—somewhere above the basement, on the first floor, or an upper floor, trying to carry her out, when he was overcome by smoke himself, and collapsed. Later, the floor burned beneath them, and the bodies fell through. How would they have ended up?"

"We're guessing," the chief said quietly. "I can't say for sure. But they might have ended up just as we found them."

That afternoon, Mr. Harlan began explaining to the jury the final step of the proceeding, that they would retire to deliberate whether there was probable cause to pursue any of the survivors on a charge of arson and murder. He seemed distracted to them, and he was: he wanted to speak to Emma again, for at least some acknowledgment to pass between them.

All fires have a cause, and if he could not find the cause in an inquest, Mr. Harlan felt he had lost. He reviewed the evidence in his head all through the long drive north that Friday night, realizing, somewhere near Rutland, that Emma Herrick had outplayed him. At the last moment she had put the last ace across the net from off the court. The truth was knowable, but it had remained just out of reach.

As to the jurors in the public proceeding, they were busy revising their verdict. And waffling, some of them—most notably Professor Emmanuel. Having hinted darkly for months about trouble brewing at the Heights, about the time having come round for eruption of another epic scandal, the professor began lecturing the diners in Toni's Lunch on something called Occam's razor, which meant, as Toni later explained to Dale the carpenter, "the simplest thing is probably right." (Leading Dale to wonder what that had to do with razors, but the professor hadn't explained.) The fire had been an accident. No one could deny that Jane Herrick had been slipping for years, and that, following the bankruptcy and the sale, she had lost her grasp on reality. The signs of dementia were obvious—take that childlike repainting of her porch. There was the business with the kettle. And weren't Jane's last words on this earth a confession?

Saving his earlier argument by a neat logician's trick, the professor identified Jane's dementia as the instrument of the ancient and volatile heritage of the Heights itself. And it was Roy Murphy who, by assembling the objects of his envy and resentment in the dark palace of his triumph, had set off these events. So it all hung together, sort of.

Others in town scoffed. That kettle story seemed a little too convenient. Jane Herrick never would have set the place afire, and if she had, she would have escaped through the dining room, just like the state's attorney said. Had not the dark and vengeful pair been found together in the basement, their actual skeletons enmeshed—fleeing, it was said, the destruction their rage had led them to (and as some gratuitously added, coupling there in fiery coitus)? He had come back for vengeance, she was mad with spite and self-loathing. Theirs was the emotional match that set the Heights ablaze, and this was its apotheosis.

But that explanation suited none of the guys from the shop,

who felt they knew Roy Murphy best. They said it must have happened just like Steve Albert admitted—those bodies could have fallen through later. Boss might have been a dark and brooding man, but his every step since returning to Hoosick Bridge had been rational. Maybe he had taken that Forrester girl for spite, maybe for simple physical need, but that, too, was a calculated thing—cold, maybe, but rational. Vengeance? He was a good guy, they said, he'd been through a lot, and he'd built a business that paid good money, hell, he'd sponsored a baseball team. Why didn't they all just leave him alone? Had pure vengeance been his motive, why buy the Heights first? Why service a monstrous mortgage, and pay insurance premiums that in the end did nothing but enrich the businessman Torruella? Why not just destroy it? Bullshit, they . said—Jane started the fire, he tried to get his girl out, and died trying.

Others thought that Roy Murphy had been rational as only mad men can be—rational as to means but not ends. He used rational means in business, to pursue the irrational end of buying the Heights. And he was fed by the insanity of its environment: the aging and demented woman, the self-hating girl, the alcoholic veteran, and his own silent, battle-scarred soul. It was a poisonous stew, and he had cooked it.

There were minority views to the effect that it must have been Emma, that it must have been Hall, that it must have been Hall and Izzy—hadn't they been seen a week or so before, down at Mr. Chips in Williamstown, plotting together? Some thought that maybe Roy Murphy had worked *with* Hall, and maybe with the girl, too. He, or perhaps they, had meant to flee the bulkhead and find an accomplice parked on a side street, with whom they would escape, start over somewhere far to the south, or west. According to some of these accounts, Hall, discovering that his accomplice had been caught in the fire, fled alone.

In the end the uncertainties led them all away from the search for a literal truth, with its inevitable disappointments, to the refuge of an emotional one. Whatever the details may have been, Roy

Murphy was the first cause in a larger sense. He assembled the human combustibles there. Surely his own presumption, his own ambition had led to this crisis. The professor had it right the first time, they said. Roy Murphy had been hoist with his own petard.

Legally speaking, Mr. Harlan's view was the one that mattered. With the jury's guidance, he would later write the final report, which explained that the evidence was too ambiguous to warrant a criminal charge. He was perhaps the only one who formed his views solely on the basis of the evidence; or more accurately, the only one who expressed them solely on that basis. And this rather proved that evidence, in the narrow, legal sense, was unequal to the task.

Mr. Harlan in his spare time was a lover of Shakespeare. In the small den in his farmhouse he owned two collections of the plays, and a shelf full of criticism. He never met the professor, or heard him go on about petard hoisting, but the suggestion that Roy Murphy was hoist with his own petard might have coaxed from him a tinge of wry amusement, a brief respite from the acute frustration that he brought back home. He might have pointed out to Professor Emmanuel that in *Hamlet*, the prince uses the phrase to describe one destroyed not by his own treachery but by the treachery of others.

But there was not even that consolation for Mr. Harlan, who drove north on Route 7 through that long night, certain that he had failed. Emotional equilibrium was not what he had been after. There was a knowable, literal truth, and he had failed to know it. He'd come close to it, he'd reached for it, almost touched it, but Emma Herrick had kept it from him. She kept the truth from all of them.

Emma had left Hoosick Bridge the afternoon she finished testifying. She left the letter with the clerk and returned to New York City, having done what she set out to do. There were people who had been hurt enough, families that had suffered enough. The Forresters had endured sorrow enough, and the dead ought at least to have the comfort of their reputations. There was her own husband to think of as well. Racked with uncertainty following that terrible night, he had been through enough. And so she decided there were points unnecessary to volunteer to Mr. Harlan. There were questions better left as questions. The answers belonged to the dead—and to her.

He was up late, listening to the night sounds outside—the roar of buses and the horns of the taxicabs—when George at last heard her soft tread on the steps. He rushed to open the door, and they embraced on the landing. "You okay?"

"Yeah," she said.

"It went all right?"

"It's behind us now," she said, and they went inside. "Let's open a bottle of wine. Let's have two bottles and watch a bad movie."

She would say no more about it. In years to come she would return to town occasionally to visit the graves of her parents, but she did not like to linger there. She had met her crisis, and defeated it face-to-face. She felt that she had done only what was necessary, that no one's memory was harmed by it. When on that dramatic afternoon she declared that her mother could be forgiven, and stamped forever on the jury's minds the resonant image of an accident in the kitchen, she was declaring to herself that she had done no injury to her mother, last of the Morses. The real Jane Morse Herrick had slipped away, hostage to a wasting disease. The community could indict the wraith left behind and yet forgive Jane herself for the tragedy, for they knew that Jane Herrick—the real Jane—had already died.

It was a tolerable resolution, a kind of emotional justice. But it was not the literal truth that Mr. Harlan had come south looking for. It was not the physics of the thing. He had been after facts—among them, for example, the curious fact that, on the night of the fire, Jane Herrick was the only person at the Heights who was never in the kitchen.

# TWENTY-TWO

Roy Murphy had telephoned her to say that Jane couldn't go on living there. Certainly that much was true. But there were other points about the call upon which Emma felt it unnecessary to dwell.

She'd rented a car and driven north to Vermont—alone. George was already distancing himself from forces that felt too powerful for him, and her silence—her failure to ask that he come with her—told him not to ask himself. Heading north, she began to feel the pull of Roy's beacon, the sense not of going to a place but of being drawn to it. She hunted through the radio stations, only half listening, distracted. Emotions flitted in and out of her mind like house sparrows at a feeder, alighting, squabbling with each other, flying off again. There was guilt—that she had not properly dealt with her mother's illness before; there was anger—at Roy Murphy, for exploiting Izzy; and there was fear—of the pull of the Heights itself, and of him. Most confusing were the many thoughts about George. Fondness, resolve to love him better, resentment that he had not insisted on coming with her, relief that he had not insisted—they all fluttered about her mind. And yet she was conscious, too, that loving him was a contrivance, as it always had been, as not loving Roy Murphy always had been. It was an act of will.

She reached Hoosick Bridge after dark. After checking in to the Taconic Motel, she drove across the little town and up to the Heights, thinking that she would speak to her mother. She would put her shoulder to the wheel and the next morning somehow uproot her from the Heights. And since no one else had, she would confront Roy Murphy about his exploitation of her sister-in-law. (The thought flitted in and then out again. *Her brother, my husband, should be doing this and is not.*) She would take on this duty out of loyalty to that vulnerable relative, and for no other reason—as she had assured herself through that drive.

It was a chilly night in October. As the car rounded the corner coming up from town, the shape of the old house appeared on the hill, massive and implacable, glowering like a stern father at the approach of a wayward child. It was as though the darkened house demanded that she give an account of herself. She drove slowly up Washington Street, and parked in the drive behind his truck.

It felt odd to rap on the front doors of the Heights as a visitor, and then to wait, listening for footsteps. She could just make out the dark letters above the door: "Come Home to Me." Emma had worn only a cardigan over her blouse, and she shivered and rubbed her arms until the doors opened. There he stood at her old threshold: unshaven, dark, wearing his work jeans, a brown and yellow flannel shirt unbuttoned over a white T-shirt. He wore steel-toed work boots, and a ring of keys was clipped to a carabiner on his belt loop. His eyes looked weary.

"Emma . . ."

"Hi. How's it going?"

"All right, I guess. Had . . . kind of a busy day around here."

His voice was soft, tired. He looked uneasy. Absently, he rubbed the back of his neck with his right hand. And then, embarrassed, he said, "You're cold. Sorry. Come in."

Inside, as the doors closed behind her, she asked, "Busy day— you mean with Mom?"

"No, no, she's . . . the same. I meant at the shop. Been having some . . . things with . . . one of the guys. Your mom's upstairs."

"I'll go on up alone, if that's all right. Roy, I need to talk to you, too—later?"

He nodded. "Get you anything?"

"I'm fine."

They were still just inside the door. His dark eyes searched her for a moment, and then he nodded toward the staircase. "I'll be in the kitchen." He turned and went down the corridor.

That imbalance she'd felt on the porch stairs came upon her again as she looked around the foyer. It was uncanny to see and smell and feel the presence of others in this place, to hear the low murmur of voices in the kitchen that were not the voices of Herricks. Unfamiliar objects littered the foyer. A toolbox sat on the floor by the doors, a pair of small Hunter boots lay in the corner. Coats were piled on the banister rail, and a yellow baseball cap with a black *P* hung on a hook. There was also a powerful smell of solvent, or gasoline. *Did I live here?* Strange to see a place that was your home taken over by others, who regarded it as their own. She stood for a moment longer, sure that something was missing but unable to identify it, until she realized that she couldn't hear the mantel clock in the parlor. No one winds it anymore, she thought. Not even Mom.

Upstairs, she found her mother pacing the small guest room where she lived now. Jane offered no greeting—she was no longer conscious of arrivals and departures, but only of immediate presence. "These savages, Emma!" Jane said, as though picking up a conversation from ten minutes ago. "They want to asphyxiate me!"

It did smell of fumes up there, too. Emma struggled to open Jane's window to get some air. The storm window was stuck, but she forced it up a few inches.

Her mother looked so gaunt. She didn't hold a gaze when Emma looked at her.

"Have you been eating?"

"Hmmph."

"Mom, you need to come away from here. It's time."

"Someone has to protect the Heights from these dreadful people," she said. "That girl, she steals things! And the other one— always drunk!"

"Let's get away from all of that, Mom. Come with me to the motel for tonight at least?"

She stopped pacing and held herself erect. "We will stay here, and I will make you a nice breakfast."

A nice breakfast, Emma thought. She excused herself for a moment to call George, but their conversation was perfunctory, neither of them saying anything important, each wanting the other to. She rang off and tried again to reason with her mother, but she could not seem to engage her eyes. When she spoke, Jane stared past her at the wall, as though reciting a speech. So Emma gave up trying to persuade her to come away, and at length said she would go back downstairs—to see what they were up to.

"That's a very good idea," said Jane, conspiratorially.

The fumes were stronger as Emma descended the back stairs. She came along the back corridor and into the kitchen.

Her first thought was that she could begin to see her mother's point of view. On the stove was a greasy cast-iron frying pan, and two dirty pots left over from meals unspecified. A blue coffee can at the rear was half filled with congealed bacon grease. But these were not the source of the fumes. Spread out on the kitchen table were parts of the chain saw. Roy Murphy had taken apart the two-stroke motor and was cleaning gunk from the parts, passing gasoline through a piece of wire mesh into a metal can, there on the kitchen table.

Across the table sat Isabella Forrester.

Emma stood in the doorway. "Hi, Izzy. Roy."

Izzy had been saying something, but when Emma came in, Roy put down the saw part and turned away from her, toward Emma. Watching this, Izzy's eyes began to widen, with that first look of helplessness a climber has when a foothold gives way and he begins to slide.

Roy said, "Izzy, let us talk."

Izzy felt herself slipping and sliding, tumbling back down into darkness. For she had seen it on both of their faces, heard it in his voice.

"What does that mean, Roy—let you talk?"

"She's been drinking," he explained.

"Oh, yeah, she drinks a lot, that Izzy. She's a *bad* girl. Not like Emma. Not like the good *Herricks*," Izzy said.

Emma expelled a breath. She said, "Maybe we can all—"

"You know what he makes me wear?" Izzy interrupted. "Roy, tell her what you make me wear."

"Get out."

Emma shuddered with the force of it, the sudden cold that came over the room when he spoke. Once this place had been her kitchen. To this room she had come as a child, for warmth, for food, for laughter. It was impossible now to place those memories here.

Izzy reached across the table, tried to take Roy's arm. "How could you bring her up here *now*? Roy? Why now, when everything—"

"I'll go," Emma said.

"No," Izzy said. "You won't." She turned to face her, and in Izzy's eyes Emma saw the dark ferocity of an animal cornered in its den. To be so loved by the brother, and so loathed by the sister, and to feel that she deserved neither.

"You'll never go, Emma," Izzy repeated. "You'll always be here."

"Look, this is too much . . . I'm sorry, I can't even breathe in here with these fumes. I'll go back to my mother's room, and in the morning, I'll try to . . . to arrange something. Try to leave in the morning. I'm sorry I've caused all this . . ."

"You haunt this place more than she does," Izzy's brittle voice continued. "You'll never leave. Are you going to tell her, Roy?"

He did not answer, and the anger rose in her. She had seen him react to Emma's mere presence—seen how it commanded him. Just when she begged for some sign, some hint that he was with her now, his eyes had fallen away. The hope she had for some human kindness from him now mocked her.

"That yellow dress—was it your prom dress, Emma? Is that why he brings it to my room, when he comes? Why he makes me put it on?"

Emma was speechless, and still Roy said nothing.

Izzy lashed out again, sobbing. "Maybe you could fuck *her* in the dress, Roy, instead of pretending. That's what you do to people, isn't it, Roy? Fuck them? And then when you don't feel like it, you don't even say hello. For days."

"Leave," he said.

"You know you want to! I'll go get the dress—let's bring crazy Jane downstairs to watch! Hey!" she called, getting roughly to her feet. "Crazy Jane!"

"That's enough. Leave, or I throw you out."

"*Please*, Izzy . . ." Emma said.

She sobbed. "You're *lifeless*, Roy Murphy, wandering around this dead house with *ghosts*, your precious Emma, your precious captain, and—"

He flew across the table at her then, shouting "Out!" He had her by the shoulders, such a small creature, but yet so fierce—and even he could not stop the torrent of angry words. She beat her fists against his arms, crying, "You love *ghosts*! And you drag everyone else down to your ghost world with you . . ." Shaking herself from his grasp, sobbing, Izzy ran from the room. Her footsteps crashed down the hall and then echoed away up the main stairs. Far away a door slammed, and in the kitchen it fell quiet.

"My *God*," Emma said.

His back was to her. He leaned now against the stove, panting.

"Roy—what have you done to her?"

"Fed her. Given her a roof over her head, when her family hasn't."

"Maybe that wasn't such a good idea."

He turned, his eyes dark with a sullen anger, his whole body tensed. "You coming up here tonight, was that a good idea, Emma?"

"Someone had to come and deal with Mom. You said so."

"Someone. But not you."

"Then why did you call me, Roy?"

"Why did *you* come alone?"

In this way they squared off as before, and each began to feed off the other's anger and frustration. For a while they circled that kitchen table like fighters, flicking out these pointless recriminations, working into flurries and counterpunches of accusations, dancing as they had danced the last time they were in that room— the day he bought the Heights.

*Why was she coming up here to lecture him about his life?*

*What had he done to that girl?*

It built to a crescendo, until the angry voices rang off the old walls, and at last he shouted, "Take them! Your mother, Izzy, both of them. You want her? Take her with you. Just go!"

"You don't just *take* people!"

"Do it, Emma! Take her and yourself and your mother, all of you, and fuck off out of my life!"

"Stop feeling so sorry for yourself, Roy Murphy! You're better than that!"

And then they both stopped, winded by it, and something in him changed. The look in his eyes, the cast of his face: he was like an actor coming into the wings, dropping role. He stood in the far corner of the kitchen, by the back door, his back against the wall, and he slid slowly to the floor.

"Emma," he answered quietly, "I'm not better than that."

It was a plea, and it did not register at first, as she sat wearily at the table and ran her fingers through her hair, and said, "All this misery just to keep reliving a single summer, from years before."

"What I love ends, Emma. Why can't I relive it?"

And then it did register. Something had turned. This was no cry of anger, but a sound she had never heard before from him: the sound of defeat, of supplication. He crouched on the floor, his arms around his knees, his head low.

"Let me have that, at least," he said.

In the summer of her seventeenth year she had loved him intensely, desired him constantly. But never once had he needed her comfort. She did not know what to do. The fumes, she thought—maybe it was the fumes. She rose and opened all of the kitchen windows as wide as they would go. Then, tentatively, she circled the table.

His head between his knees, his confession continued. "I bought this house because it was yours. I let your mother stay because . . . she's yours. I dress Izzy up as you . . . it's what you think. I'm twisted up, Emma." He raised his head, and his eyes were red now. "But can't you just leave me to it? Take her. Just leave me."

Of its own accord, her hand reached down to touch his hair, to stroke it softly. She did not understand what was happening to her, only that she felt his ache like a cramp in her own side. She crouched on the floor beside him, and leaned against his arm. The kitchen wall clock was an old one, with a second hand. They watched it circle round and round.

"Remember Bungalow Rock?" she asked him gently. "That was the first time you—"

"Held your hand. Long time ago," he whispered.

"You said you'd buy this house."

"Emerson would be the doorman," he said.

"Long time ago," she answered.

They sat in silence on the floor, leaning against the kitchen wall, until she asked him to tell her about the captain, the one who used to say the poem. It came pouring from him. It was confused, she could not follow a narrative, it was like a heap of photographs spread across a table, when you know only one face among them, and look at the other faces, trying to re-create a history from the one you know. Days and nights at a place called Firebase Montana; inside the wire and outside, patrols to the village, lying on a mountainside in the darkness with the mad captain, how he recited poetry and had read everything and taught Roy Murphy to read. How he believed in him. She closed her eyes, trying to conjure that far-off outpost, the face of the dead military officer, the bearing, the way he must have looked at Roy; the way Roy must have looked at him.

"He said we were the same—him and me. Me from the Park, the same as him. The only thing he ever said that wasn't true."

"Maybe he never said a truer thing."

When Emma ventured to the end of the story, asking for the last chapter, he shook his head. He had to stop at that brink; he could go no further. Then his broad shoulders began to quake. She reached and pulled him close, and his head tumbled to her lap while his shoulders shook, and he was like a child who has never known a lap finding one for the first time. She stroked his hair, his temples, she drew her finger along the stubble of his cheek. He lay tumbled over in her lap as the minutes passed.

At last Emma shifted and got to her feet. She reached down for his hands, and then eased him upright. She switched off the light and led him toward the hall.

It had always been Roy who asked, and Emma who answered. This would reverse just once, when she would ask—would plead, would beg—and it would be for him to respond. But that reversal would come only at the end, and they were not yet at the end. It was still Emma who answered, still she who controlled.

The great central entranceway of the Heights was dark now. Behind them were the front doors and before them, the sweeping oaken staircase. The question was in his eyes. "Emma . . . ?"

"Shhh," she answered, taking his hand, and leading him upstairs.

The lights were all off now. It was dark in the house, dark in the kitchen. A moonbeam faintly illuminated one side of the kitchen table, but around that pale light was darkness, and in the darkness the cigarette end glowed red. She was wreathed in the fumes of tobacco and gasoline and alcohol, and the deepest loneliness of her life.

Izzy may have been drunk, but her ears were sharp. She'd

listened to their footsteps up the one staircase, and then the next, and then, not stopping, up to the tower itself. She'd heard the door to his special room shut, heard even the latch click. It was the room where he slept alone, where he never let anyone else come, not even Billy. Once she had gone up there, bringing him a drink to be nice to him. How he'd raged—how he'd dragged her down three flights of stairs by the hair, pushing her, bodily, through the front doorway. She remembered the loathing in his voice.

It had been so cold that night. She'd had to beg, crying at the front doors, until Billy let her in.

She sat in the darkness, remembering, and the cigarette end glowed red.

How he made her sleep in Emma's old room, in that bed, alone for days and weeks.

How sometimes he came to her room and made her put on the dress. How he would touch her only if she wore that dress.

How he never kissed her when he was inside of her.

She remembered the scorn in his eyes, the way his brow hardened when he looked at her in the morning. How sometimes he refused to look at her at all for days—for weeks.

How her parents had never spoken to her since she'd moved in here, except the one time that her mother called, and said she was terribly sorry, Izzy, but she had to ask that she please not come at Thanksgiving.

How her former friends did not return calls or texts.

How she used to know everybody, how everybody used to think she was funny, and laugh when she told stories, and now there was no one.

How she had no job and no money, how she had nothing in her wallet except what he gave her.

How most of the faces turned away from her in that shitty little town; how the faces wound up with contempt for the slattern, the slut, Roy Murphy's kept girl.

How crazy Jane was always lurking somewhere in the house, behind doors, around corners, her mad footsteps clipping off along drafty corridors.

How she had to get out of there, and how she had nowhere to go.

How he looked away when she was talking, never at her.

How she'd even fucked Billy once, when he was drunk and she was, too, just to see if Roy cared.

How he wasn't even handsome—he had that ridge on this brow above his eyes, that scowl on his face, and little to say—and yet she loved him.

How he'd never given her the smallest trinket, never said anything sweet, never so much as held a door or taken her coat, until three weeks ago, when he spoke to her in a voice gentle and almost unrecognizable.

How he'd said, "You're doing good," and then repeated it.

How he'd said her name, *Izzy.*

How many times those words had replayed in her mind, how she'd bathed herself in them.

How, in the past weeks, there had been other moments: moments when he had looked at her kindly, and she'd hoped.

How she'd sprung from bed in the morning, almost as early as there were footsteps from above. Hoping.

How tonight Emma had come back, and instantly, hope had flown, because he had always loved Emma, and always would love Emma.

How he hated her for not being Emma.

How no one would notice—no one at all—if she were gone.

Izzy sat in the darkness. She took a drag from the cigarette, and the end glowed red.

The pale moonbeam came like a suggestion through the kitchen window. There were dark shapes on the table, among them an old soup can amid the saw parts, still holding the wire-mesh piece he'd been cleaning.

Still sitting in its bath of gasoline or solvent or whatever it was.

She held the cigarette between thumb and forefinger, looking at the faint glow. Her age was twenty-two years, four months, and seventeen days.

Hope is a liar, thought Izzy Forrester, as she flicked the ash.

That smell was again in Roy Murphy's nostrils. It yanked him into consciousness in the moonlit tower, and in that light he saw deadly fingers creeping through the cracks beneath the door.

"Emma!"

He leapt from the cot and pressed his palm to the door. The wood was warm, the glass of the doorknob hot to the touch. Through the door, he could hear the roar below.

He flew to the opposite window, but there was no way down from the tower—it rose high above a steeply pitched mansard roof. If, after jumping, you managed not to slide and fall off the slates, you would have to jump anyway—two stories to the porch roof.

He glanced quickly round the room, but there was no rope ladder or other escape device, no fire extinguisher. *Stupid!*

The fingers had grasped the door, they came over, under, and around, and the room was thick with smoke. He coughed, then shook her again. "Emma—fire!"

"My God, Roy!"

The roar from below grew louder.

"Emma, get pants, shoes on. Hurry!" He grabbed a jacket from behind a chair and tossed it to her. "Put this on!"

Her eyes were wide, terrified.

"You ready?"

She nodded.

But he stopped himself. Or perhaps the talisman stopped him, hanging on its chain from the brass hook on the back of the tower door. In 1861, in a mill in Winooski, Vermont, it had been worked from brass with the head of a stag, die-pressed with the emblem, stamped, cut, buffed, and then sewn onto a woolen coat.

A young soldier wore the coat on drafty troop trains to New York and Baltimore, and tramping south along dusty roads to Virginia with the Sixth Vermont Infantry. On December 13, 1862, in a stinging cold fog on Marye's Heights, just above where the frozen Rappahannock curled by Fredericksburg, Virginia, on a dreadful day that staggered the Army of the Potomac, the soldier was staggered, too—by what felt like a vicious punch to the sternum. He fell to the cold ground, panting. His chest would be black and blue for weeks, but the leather ammunition strap, and the smashed button beneath, had barred the ball from killing him. For decades afterward, the smashed button rode in the vest pocket of that soldier—as he grew old and his belly filled and as, at the end, he went dotty. It was in his suit pocket the day he died. His grandson had it framed behind glass, and it hung upon the wall of his beloved tower for almost a century. The lover Emma Herrick removed it from that frame on July 16, 2004, and carried it to Franck's Jewelers on High Street in Hoosick Bridge, where it was fitted with a chain. She gave it to Roy Murphy early in the morning of August 11, 2004. As a soldier in the 240th Army Airborne, he wore it about his neck: in Kabul, Afghanistan, in 2006, when an IED shattered a Humvee in the patrol ahead and left him unscathed; in the Korengal Valley in 2008, when he and Lima attacked the enemy and escaped unharmed; and again in 2009, when not five yards away, his captain fell. Ezra's button was hanging now from the chain around the hook behind the door, the last barrier between them and the fire, as smoke poured through the cracks.

He took it from the hook and put it quickly round her neck. Then he went to the window.

"When I open this, we breathe, then we run. Okay? Breathe deep, Emma—soon as we open that door the fire's coming in here. It will be hard to see, the smoke will be terrible. But you keep running after me. Okay? *You don't stop running!*"

"My mother, Roy!"

He barked, "You keep running, Emma! You don't stop!"

She nodded, her eyes wide with terror.

He flung the window open, and they felt suction. The smoke now poured around the door, mad for oxygen. He slammed the window shut, and then, with her face buried in the canvas of the Carhartt jacket, she followed him through that doorway into a dark wall of hot smoke. They leapt down the tower steps to the third-floor landing. He disappeared toward Emma's old bedroom, raced back, shaking his head. "Not there!" She realized that he meant Izzy.

Below them in the foyer, the fire was raging now, rumbling and racking and hissing. The foyer was engulfed, and flames were racing up the walls to the third floor. On the landing the heat was unbearable. The smoke was suffocating and terrifying. She would have stopped there and retreated upstairs, but he had her by the wrist and his grip pulled her roughly down the staircase to the second floor. The face of Ezra Morse emerged from the smoke, and then disappeared. Flames licked up the walls, and she was choking as they made for the hall window that opened over the porch.

He had forced her to the window off the corridor. He threw it open, and with a blow the storm went flying onto the roof. He pushed her out bodily, so that she fell to the slates. "Jump, Emma!"

"My mother!"

The smoke billowed around him. He sucked on the outside air for a quick second, and then he balled his shirt in front of his mouth and plunged back inside.

"Roy!"

But she couldn't see him. The smoke poured from the open window now, and he had disappeared into the blackness. The slates of the roof were hot to the touch. The porch, too, was on fire beneath her. He had said to jump, but she could not bring herself to do it.

From down Washington Street she could hear sirens.

Then there was a shape—movement—and she rushed back to the window.

"Roy!"

He had crashed through the smoke again to the window with Jane over his shoulder. And she thought, *Thank God, thank God.* He was a black figure inside that house, pushing that limp, slim parcel through the opening, shouting something that she could not hear. He pushed Jane like a rolled carpet, out to Emma on the roof, and she eased her mother down to the slates.

It was too much now, the smoke billowing from that window. "Billy's car!" he was shouting.

"What?"

"You see his Mustang in the drive? A red Mustang?"

She glanced quickly. "It's gone—Roy, get out of there!"

But he shouted back, "Izzy!"

She lunged at him through the open window and grabbed his forearm. Clinging to him, she became at last the one who asked.

"You can't! It's too late! Roy—I let you go once! I'm sorry! It was the mistake of my life!"

Here at last it was for him to answer, as it had never been for him before. But it was an easy answer, because it was the rule, and the rule simplified things. You never leave one of the squad behind. Whatever your feelings for them, you don't leave them behind. Not ever.

Their eyes met. Backlit by the lurid flames climbing the walls, deafened by that roar behind him, it seemed somehow that he smiled at her tenderly. "One more, Emma," he said. "One more's all." He slipped from her grasp and disappeared again into that maelstrom. She cried out, but he was gone.

The sirens were out front now, the lights whirling. The first of the fire trucks had reached the house. Below her the parlor and foyer windows exploded—rat, tat, tat, tat!—and the roar of the fire grew. She screamed for him again, but her voice was inaudible in that noise. The ladder truck was there, and the firemen were trying to extend the ladder from the truck. It moved with aching slowness. A fireman was yelling, and she could not hear him. Why did it take so long to get the ladder there?

*He was not coming out. He was not coming out!* She crouched by her mother's face and could not be sure she was breathing.

*Hurry!*

At last the firemen clambered up to the porch roof, first one, then another. One of them carried Jane down the ladder to the lawn, and by this time Emma was hysterical. The fireman came back up, and she begged him to go in after Roy. He promised. He said he would go in after Roy but only if she first descended the ladder. And so she went down.

Now an awful groan sounded from deep within the Heights. From the lawn she looked up on that porch roof, and the firemen were not going in. They had moved to the window and then turned back.

They were not going in!

She screamed his name. Fire trucks and ambulances and police cars were there now, and beyond the lights she could see the shapes of townspeople. A fireman was pulling her away from the ladder truck and she was screaming, he was in there, and they had to go in and get him. More fire trucks and ambulances and police cars arrived. A fire hose began working, and then another.

Then the Heights seem to keen its own death. They had never heard such a noise. On the sidewalk and in the street the crowd of neighbors fell silent, solemn before the pyre. Explosions and crashes sounded from deep within, and a rolling groan was swallowed by the predatory roar of that fire. Arcs of hose water fell like tears. And her own tears of rage flowed, too, as she begged for the firemen to do their job and go in after him. She tried to climb back up on the ladder truck herself and was dragged away from it.

From up above came another tat—tat—tat as the windows of the tower room exploded. The fire gorged itself on Ezra's keep, on Roy Murphy's keep, on all the old books that one day he was going to read. She looked back to the second-floor window. It was hardly a window at all anymore. Flames were raging up through the old white post and lattice of Ezra Morse's porch, and flames were pouring through the gap that had been a window.

And yet she stood on the grass, safe. Around her neck hung the chain, and she fingered the button unconsciously, as tears of anger and frustration fell.

Above, on the porch roof, the firemen retreated to the ladder, and it was finished.

# TWENTY-THREE

Murphy's Landscaping was tied up in the probate court for a while, for Roy Murphy had died intestate. There was trouble from Torruella, who demanded the equipment be sold to pay toward his debt, even before the insurance came in. So that shut the business down, although it would have dwindled away anyhow, as the fall slowdown came on just at the time of the fire. Murphy's Landscaping would never reopen.

Pastor John officiated at the memorial service for Jane Herrick, who was buried in the Morse plot. The Forresters took Isabella home. But Roy Murphy's remains were still up at the county facility a month later. Eliza Murphy had not claimed them. Just before Thanksgiving, Joe and a few other guys at the shop got up the money for a simple stone and a burial plot at Methodist Hill Cemetery in Hoosick Bridge.

And there things might have ended, with a simple grave rarely visited, and a shake of the head in Toni's Lunch about how inexplicably sad it all had been. There matters might have stood, had not that Army officer come up to the town offices the next winter, one bright morning toward the end of February. He spoke to Francine, the town manager, giving his name as Army Lieutenant

John Callahan. Francine had never really come to terms with Roy Murphy. She still had doubts about that fire. In her view it could not have been Jane, distracted, even demented as she might have become. The two bodies in the basement had always pointed Francine's way to the explanation. But for all that, Roy Murphy was a boy from Hoosick Bridge, who had been a soldier, who had served his country and come back to his hometown. After all he had been through, who could deny him that?

Francine told the officer it would be up to his mother. "She's the official next of kin, so far as that goes," she said.

That night, Lieutenant Callahan drove over to the Park. He stood on the stoop outside her trailer, and Eliza Murphy answered the door and ushered him inside.

"I never heard that," she said a few minutes later, after he had explained. She passed over the fact that she had never heard much of anything. Roy Murphy had spoken to her exactly twice after returning to Hoosick Bridge, once by telephone to tell her he'd bought the new trailer, and once by accident, when she turned a corner in Bennington and came face-to-face with him. The only real contact was the monthly check she'd received from him before he died.

"The Army will pay all the expenses. And, ma'am, we would be honored to have you as our guest at the committal."

And so the word went around town. When the ground thawed they would disinter Roy Murphy, and take the coffin down to Washington, because a veteran decorated with the Silver Star is entitled to burial at Arlington National Cemetery.

Two months later, on a morning in April, Eliza Murphy and Toni Reese boarded the bus for New York. At Penn Station they changed to a second bus to Washington, arriving in the capital late in the evening, during a warm spring rain, and accompanying each other to the motel across the river.

But there was another who came down by train from New York. She was the first to arrive at the cemetery the next morning, walking in alone to find it alive with birdsong and the chatter of squirrels. The sky was a robin's egg, the morning breeze warm, almost summery. The rain had cleared. With a guide's help she found the grave and knelt beside it: one white stone, in a long white file.

**IAN DAVID DICKINSON**

**CAPT.**

**U.S. ARMY**

**NOV. 1, 1974**

**JUNE 7, 2009**

**AFGHANISTAN**

Roy's will look no different, she thought, and then remembered: *He said we were the same, him and me.*

After a while she reoriented herself on the map, stood up awkwardly, and traversed the grassy hillside until she found a spot overlooking the fresh grave site. There she sat down again and closed her eyes and waited for them.

As the hour approached, the soldiers began to appear, walking up the road and then across the grass, some in uniform, the ones now out of the service wearing dark suits. She did not know them, but John Callahan, Billy Hall Jr., David Lima, DeSean Fowler, and Vincent Tatel were among them. At 10:00 a.m. the chaplain and the casket team arrived. Toni introduced Eliza Murphy to the chaplain as Roy's mother, and he welcomed her as a person of honor.

When the committal began, Emma stood, still up the hill and a little off from the grave site, for she wanted to be alone and yet be close enough to hear. The squad all noticed her immediately. Who could help but notice her? Billy Hall Jr. whispered, "That's the girl. I seen her the night he died." Toni spotted her, too, and waved, and Emma lifted a hand in return. Toni whispered to Eliza, "Wait—do you think . . . ?" And Eliza nodded.

But Eliza's eyes were mainly on the young men in uniform, folding the flag with their brilliant white gloves. She thought she'd never seen anything so beautiful, or heard anything that so rinsed the ear as the sound of that bugle. And then the triangle was in her arms.

In the days following the fire, George Forrester knew that Emma was not weeping alone for the horror of it, or for her mother, certainly not for Izzy. It was some more primal cry of separation. When she prepared for the inquest, George believed that she meant to keep vague what had happened up there with Roy Murphy that night. The rift that had opened between them on the night of Roy Murphy's phone call only widened. He would not speak the worry he felt, and she would not deny it. Later, after doctor visits, he retreated from the day of the child's arrival even as she sprinted toward it. She traced the days forward, but he traced them back to the Heights.

She stood alone on the hillside above the grave site. She thought, He left all those years ago, he came back, he's gone, and still it goes on, and when they are done with this funeral, that honor guard will march to the next one.

Her right hand strayed to her belly. Her left was in her pocket, fingering the chain, and Ezra's button. Roy's button. She stood on the hillside, remembering the last thing he'd shouted through the window. *One more's all.* One more, and each of them would be free from the burden of the past. But it was not so: she was not free.

The sound of the chaplain's voice called her back. He finished a prayer, and the mourners murmured "Amen," and then he said a short homily. She heard him say that a soldier had come home, and she remembered the inscription over the front doors at the Heights.

When it was over, and the last notes of taps faded, silence gave way once more to the chattering of birds and squirrels on that balmy morning. Emma took another moment before leaving; she wanted to impress the place upon her memory, for she might not be back for a long time.

Then one of the soldiers was hurrying up the hill toward her.

"Ma'am?"

Words tumbled from him: "Excuse me, ma'am, my name's Tatel, Specialist Vincent Tatel, and I just wanted to say . . . wanted to say how sorry I am . . . about Roy."

She took his hands in hers, and they embraced stiffly, as mourners do, and when they stood apart again, the young soldier said, "Can we help you or anything, ma'am? Get you a ride?"

"Oh, I can walk fine, thanks."

Tatel lingered, for there was something else. His face reddened and he looked down, and then away, and quietly he said, "Ma'am, I wanted to tell you that . . . he saved my life. In Afghanistan, I mean. Saved my life, and really, I never even knew him. I just wanted to tell you that." Then the soldier turned and hurried back down the hill.

He looked too young to have had a life at all, never mind a life saved. Watching him descend to his buddies who lingered at the grave site, she stroked her belly, thinking, *That makes three of us.*

Anne Herrick was not at the cemetery, but she might have predicted what was happening there, for she had seen the link between them in life—how the mood of one so often became the mood of the other. His body may have come home, as the chaplain said, but his restless spirit had to pass to her. Emma had always been confident of her path before—so certain of direction that in the summer of her eighteenth year she thought she could confine love to a calendar, and in the autumn of her twenty-sixth, rewrite history in a courtroom in Bennington, Vermont. But on that morning and in that place, you might say that his restlessness took hold of her. It was the special urgency of *nostos*—the longing to return that springs from a single place upon the earth, even from a home that is lost. She had always thought herself in control, but the traveler controls only the setting out. *Nostos* controls the return.

She thought she had better leave, find a taxicab outside the cemetery, go to Union Station, board a train. For some reason she felt she had better hurry. She had better come home. She was not thinking of the apartment in Brooklyn, or of George, but rather that she did not know where home was anymore, and she had to find it. She turned and picked her way down the hill, hurrying between the stones, not wanting to have to greet any more of the mourners.

They watched her from the grave site. Maybe she is crying, they thought—maybe that is why she rushes so. But Emma was not crying.

Only their eyes followed the solitary figure of the pregnant woman descending the hill. She receded from them, moving down through a copse of oaks, reappearing as a smaller figure in a more distant field, still hurrying, as she passed among the white files, row on row, that stand a silent post on the broad back of that quiet earth.

# ACKNOWLEDGMENTS

Roy Murphy was born at Guantánamo Bay, where I went for so
many years as a lawyer. At night I would look up at Cuba's astonishing bowl of night, thinking about some poor civilian in solitary,
or some young soldier who'd boasted to me of his imminent deployment to Iraq or Afghanistan. I'm less sure about Emma—but
maybe she, too, took shape on that surreal military base, in whose
camps I saw the failure of hatred as a policy and wondered, in idle
moments, whether love might have been a more potent weapon.

A writer is a magpie, and I thank all the persons and places
from whom I gathered bits of string. Old friend Stephanie Cabot
walked a long journey with me on this one. I'm grateful for her
guidance and perseverance. New friend Trish Todd edited the
book with care, insight, and persistence, and is responsible for
many improvements. I'm very grateful to her, too. I was fortu-
nate as well to have insightful readers join at points along the
way—Beth Gilson, Sue Bergen, and my mother, Carolyn Willett.
George Clarke was a big help, and not just with the book. Long
before it took shape, he showed us how a Marine fights for the
flag—in and out of the courtroom. Semper fi.

But my debt is deepest to my special listener. One has to

sound the words to know whether they do justice to their sense. During those long rides to Vermont, I'd read from the laptop while she drove the car. She listened patiently, signaling by subtle changes in her face that miles were yet to go. And then—once in a very long while—the glisten in her eye said that we had at last come home. Thanks, Matty.

SIMON & SCHUSTER PAPERBACKS
READING GROUP GUIDE

# Abide with Me

# INTRODUCTION

Neither the fires of the war in Afghanistan nor the ongoing tragedy of life at the Heights can extinguish the spark ignited between Roy Murphy and Emma Herrick. In spite of their vastly different worlds, they are inextricably connected and unavoidably drawn into a hurricane of fatal attraction that will forever change everyone in its path. Inspired by *Wuthering Heights*, *Abide with Me* is an epic love story that will not let you go.

## TOPICS & QUESTIONS FOR DISCUSSION

1. On page 38, the captain tells Roy Murphy: "Murphy, we're not different. Where it counts, I think we're the same, you and me." In what ways are they the same? What qualities do they share? In what ways is this statement a theme throughout the book?

2. Which character do you identify with the most or like the most? What are some of that character's strengths? How does that character change or grow throughout the story? Is there a fatal flaw?

3. On page 64, Emma Herrick says about Roy Murphy: "I followed him from Pine Cobble School in the fifth grade. I went down to the Hoosick in the seventh grade hoping he might be there. Why on my prom night am I still following him?" Describe why you think Emma keeps being drawn to Roy Murphy. In what ways are they similar? In what ways are they both orphans?

4. As a high school senior, Roy Murphy describes Juvie as one of the best things that happened to him so far in his life. What does Juvie give him that he never had? Has there ever been a

situation in your life that you assumed would be punishing or painful but that ended up being an unexpected gift?

5. Describe the contrast between Roy Murphy's brothers and his comrades at Firebase Montana. What at Firebase Montana creates a bond that becomes stronger than the one between blood relatives?

6. What role does poetry play in the life of Captain Dickinson? How is it both an appropriate and absurd part of life at Firebase Montana?

7. What does Roy lose when Captain Dickinson is shot? Describe the irony in the scene of the shooting.

8. There is much speculation about Roy's motives for returning to Hoosick Bridge after his time in Afghanistan. Why do you think he came back?

9. What do you think the author had in mind by bringing together Roy Murphy, Emerson Rodriguez, and Emma Herrick as seventh grade friends?

10. Tom Herrick's "personal vortex of avoidance" is something Emma is determined to change in her own life. Do you think she succeeds where her father failed? Have you ever vowed to forge a certain path after being disappointed or hurt? How did it work out?

11. What role does Izzy play? Given Roy's seemingly single-minded focus after he returns to Hoosick Bridge, why do you think he allows her into his life? In what ways are they caught in the same struggle?

12. Describe Roy's strategy of staying disconnected from people

in the United States while in Afghanistan so that he can be "all there." In what ways is this both beneficial and harmful? Did reading this story heighten your sensitivity to the trauma that soldiers undergo, both during their active duty as well as upon their return?

13. Describe the irony of the process by which Roy acquires the Heights.

14. How does Roy's decision to "never leave one of the squad behind" affect you? What does it reveal about his character? Do you think someone who grew up at the Heights (as opposed to the Park) would have made the same decision? What would you have done?

15. Do you identify more with the Heights or the Park? What are the unexpected challenges and virtues of each?

16. How do you feel about the way the story ended? How has Emma changed?


# ENHANCE YOUR BOOK CLUB

1. Invite a soldier who fought overseas to visit your book club to share his or her experience of serving in the military and of reentering civilian life.

2. Read *Wuthering Heights*. Compare and contrast its characters and plot with those of *Abide with Me*.

3. Watch the *Band of Brothers* miniseries and discuss the impact, both positive and negative, that fighting in a war together has on the soldiers.

# A CONVERSATION WITH SABIN WILLETT

**What was the inspiration for writing *Abide with Me*?**
There were many. I wanted to write a serious love story—I had not done that before. Meeting young soldiers in Guantánamo triggered something in me, and some of the nights there found their way into episodes. The bowl of night, for example. The stars in Cuba are astonishing on a clear night, and I remember on a lonely night there being reminded of the first quatrain in Omar Khayyam—that in turn led me to picture a night in a mountain firebase, where a lonely soldier studies the stars. Williamstown, Massachusetts, suggested to me a look and feel of the Heights itself. Emma I created, but where creations like her come from, I can't say.

**Have you been to Afghanistan?**
I have not.

**What character did you most enjoy developing as the story unfolded?**
It would be Emma, I suppose. I enjoyed them all, but it took time for Emma's personality to grow for me from remote and numinous to real, injured, and determined.

**Who are some of your favorite poets? Do you regularly read poetry?**
I do love poetry. I recommend Fitzgerald's translations of Omar to anyone—they are marvelous. I enjoy Wordsworth, Tennyson, Eliot. Recently I have come to know Derek Walcott. His *Omeros* is staggering.

**What compels you to advocate for the Uighur prisoners at Guantánamo Bay?**
I got into that case mainly because the idea of sanctioned torture was abhorrent to me, and the idea of a prison beyond law equally

so. Once I met the clients, the injustice riveted me, and it became very personal.

**If you could make one change to the process by which soldiers reenter civilian life after returning from war, what would it be?**
I don't have a good answer to this question. The transition to civilian life is too abrupt for most to manage, but I don't know what would improve that other than a national resolve never to go to war except where there is an existential crisis. I think what bewilders many soldiers is the idea that their return is unremarked, just as their experience in the war was unimportant to the people back home. That may be the intolerable thing.

**What was the most challenging part of writing this story?**
Trying to get Afghanistan right.

**What kind of books do you enjoy reading?**
All kinds. History, biography, a good novel.

**When do you find time to write novels in the midst of your career as a lawyer?**
Time is never found—it has to be made. I find a daily discipline of writing—but not too much—is helpful.

**It's been ten years since your last novel (*Present Value*) was published. Did you miss writing?**
Yes. From 2005 to 2010, I found that Guantánamo quite consumed my imagination. I believe I'm back now.

**When did you first read *Wuthering Heights* and how did it affect you?**
I read it in school. I found the characters compelling, and the idea that love could be a darker obsession stayed with me.

**Do you have plans to write another novel?**
Yes. At present writing I am just over halfway through *Cornerstone*, the novel that tells the story of how the Heights came to be built and follows the strange course of love between Ceda Garland, the brilliant, convention-breaking woman who would not come home, and Ezra Morse, who survived the Civil War, became rich in the age of railroads, and later built his mansion so that she might come home to him.